MW01028962

PRAISE FOR
THE ASCENT

"*The Ascent* is jaw dropping, authentic, and absolutely gripping."
—Harlan Coben, #1 *New York Times* bestselling
author of *I Will Find You*

"Adam Plantinga's debut thriller, *The Ascent,* is a nail-biting ride out of Hell itself. It's Dante's Inferno—but with gangs, corruption, bone breaking brawls, and a kick-ass, determined police officer struggling through it all to save another. It reads with raw authenticity and brutal honesty. Don't miss this debut of a new crime thriller star!"
—James Rollins, #1 *New York Times* bestselling
author of *The Kingdom of Bones*

"Damn! I had to hold on to this one for dear life. *The Ascent* is a ferociously propulsive thriller. Plantinga creates a haunted house of horrors that's utterly convincing, while at the same time keeping the focus on complex, layered, and engaging characters. An outstanding debut crime novel."
—Lou Berney, Edgar Award–winning author of *November Road*

"If JD Salinger had been a street cop, he'd have written books like Adam Plantinga's. This book is the real deal: flesh-and-blood characters, charming wit, and an insider's pass to a one-of-a-kind white-knuckle ride. Plantinga will soon join the ranks of Child and Connelly."
—Douglas Brunt, *New York Times* bestselling author and host of
Dedicated with Doug Brunt on SiriusXM

"Not since Joseph Wambaugh released *The Choirboys* has a cop thriller delivered this level of authenticity, and *The Ascent* wears it like a badge. In his debut novel, Adam Plantinga weaves a jailhouse tale that serves up thrills from the first chapter through the final page. The book's protagonist, a world-weary Detroit cop, is a revelation. Watch out, Jack Reacher—Kurt Argento has arrived, and he's putting his rivals in the shade."

—Nancy Allen, #1 *New York Times* bestselling author

"*The Ascent* is a fantastic thriller that stands apart from the crowd— a high-test, high-stakes action spectacular with true thrills, true grit, and genuine heart. You'll find the full spectrum from darkness to light between these covers, with a refreshing breeze as the pages fan by. Adam Plantinga is here to stay."

—Sean Doolittle, Thriller award–winning author
of *Device Free Weekend*

"Adam Plantinga's debut novel, *The Ascent*, is a red-hot blast of crime and punishment, and crackles with sly wit and a jaded authenticity that has been hard earned by Plantinga's many years as a street cop. *The Ascent* is so damn good that I will read anything else Plantinga cares to write, including his grocery list."

—Nick Petrie, author of *The Price You Pay*

"*The Ascent* is terrific—a brutal portrait of a tough cop in an unforgiving world. I loved it."   —Robert Crais, bestselling author

"Pulse pounding, cleverly plotted, fast paced—expertly made entertainment."   —*Kirkus Reviews*, starred

"The knockout first novel...Once readers catch their breath, they'll be clamoring for more from this rising star."

—*Publishers Weekly*, starred

"If you're itching for a bloody action-packed jailbreak thriller with a protagonist best thought of as an even angrier Jason Statham, *The Ascent* is a book that needs to be on your watchlist for 2024."
—Kashif Hussain, The Best Thriller Books

"Adam Plantinga's debut thriller is a tense journey out of hell on earth, aka a maximum security prison. Kurt Argento is an ex-cop whose stubborn compulsion to do the right thing ultimately lands him behind bars, where his luck goes from bad to worse. When the prison's security system mysteriously fails during a visit from a prominent young woman, Kurt finds himself going up against six floors of Missouri's most dangerous inmates. Plantinga serves up a master class in suspense. Packed with high stakes action, *The Ascent* is a riveting tale of survival and justice."   —Apple Books Review

"Brutal, vicious and merciless, *The Ascent* is a heart-thumping expedition through six levels of nightmare fuel to find salvation. A journey through a wicked hellscape created by Adam Plantinga to put his characters through the ultimate test with the vilest evil lurking around every corner."   —The Best Thriller Books

HARD
TOWN

ALSO BY ADAM PLANTINGA

The Ascent

HARD
TOWN

ADAM PLANTINGA

GRAND
CENTRAL

NEW YORK BOSTON

Grand Central Publishing
Hachette Book Group
1290 Avenue of the Americas, New York, NY 10104
grandcentralpublishing.com
@grandcentralpub

First Edition: April 2025

Grand Central Publishing is a division of Hachette Book Group, Inc. The Grand Central Publishing name and logo is a registered trademark of Hachette Book Group, Inc.

The publisher is not responsible for websites (or their content) that are not owned by the publisher.

The Hachette Speakers Bureau provides a wide range of authors for speaking events. To find out more, go to hachettespeakersbureau.com or email HachetteSpeakers@hbgusa.com.

Grand Central Publishing books may be purchased in bulk for business, educational, or promotional use. For information, please contact your local bookseller or the Hachette Book Group Special Markets Department at special.markets@hbgusa.com.

Library of Congress Cataloging-in-Publication Data has been applied for.

ISBNs: 978-1-5387-3990-7 (hardcover), 978-1-5387-3992-1 (ebook)

Printed in the United States of America

LSC-C

Printing 1, 2025

To the Jefferson gang

HARD
TOWN

When I was a boy and I would see scary things in the news, my mother would say to me, "Look for the helpers. You will always find people who are helping."

—*Mr. Rogers*

Under every deep, a lower deep opens.

—*Ralph Waldo Emerson*

PROLOGUE

Fenton, Arizona. One Year Ago.

The man with the silver hair shielded his eyes from the dust kicked up by a steady wind, took a drag of his cigarette, and went in the bar, which was called Connor's. There were a few people inside, all drinking alone. The man with the silver hair did not allow alcohol into his system and as such, would not be frequenting this place. But taverns were an acknowledged way to get a sense of a locale and those who lived there, even if he had no plans to regularly interact with them.

The bartender was a bland-looking man wearing a bolo tie. He stood slightly bowed forward.

"Not in here, buddy," the bartender said. He pointed to the sign behind him that said *No Smoking*.

The man took another pull of his cigarette. He had started smoking as a teenager to make friends, although it had not been successful. His classmates made a habit of mocking him. Laughed at his high voice and his precision with language. Pointed out his long neck. Like an ostrich, they'd said. He'd taken to wearing custom shirts with high collars to hide it. But he hadn't quit smoking. It remained his sole vice. He allowed himself two cigarettes a week.

"Your sign should say *Smoking Prohibited* and list the applicable ordinance. Otherwise it's merely a suggestion."

The bartender stared at him. Still bowed forward. "It's against town code. No smoking inside any business here in Fenton."

"Which code?"

"I'd have to look it up. Maybe we need a new sign. Now, you gonna put that cigarette out or not?"

The man with the silver hair stubbed the cigarette out in an empty tumbler glass. Then he reached into his shirt pocket, took out a second cigarette and lit it with a bronze lighter from the same pocket. He knew that the cigarette weighed exactly one gram.

By now, everyone in the bar was looking at him.

"If you don't put that out, mister, you're going to have to leave." The bartender shifted from foot to foot. He didn't seem particularly used to confrontation, but he wasn't a pushover either.

The man with the silver hair could appreciate that. People ought to take a stand for something, even if they didn't always understand what it was. "And if I don't?" he said.

"I'll call the sheriff."

"You wouldn't throw me out yourself?"

"Nope."

"Because of your compromised lower back?"

The bartender was silent for a moment. Then he said, "How do you know about my back?"

"It's in your posture. How you keep shifting around. Likely incessant pain, on-and-off sciatica. You probably can't lift anything heavier than a soup bowl off the floor."

"Won't stop me from picking up the phone."

"So if you call the sheriff, what steps will he take?"

"He'll make you leave."

"He has deputies who will facilitate this?"

"Facilitate?" The bartender squinted at the word. "I guess so."

"How many?"

The bartender thought about that. The man with the silver hair wondered if he was going to count on his fingers. "Three or four."

"I'll talk with your sheriff later. We have some matters to discuss."

"Mister, who are you?"

The man with the silver hair nodded as if the bartender hadn't asked him any question at all. He stood to leave. "I may be residing in town for a time. There is a substantial chance the dry air will alleviate my allergies."

The bartender shrugged and went to the other end of the bar.

The man with the silver hair silently chided himself for bringing up his allergies. He tended to reveal too much to people, even strangers. The clock in his head told him he'd had sufficient human contact in the tavern for the day, so he exited Connor's and went across the street and sat on a bench.

The sky had taken on an orangish tinge and the wind hadn't subsided. He drew in a long breath of warm air. His handlers were watching him from close by with their guns and radios. They would be interested in the information about the sheriff and his deputies. And if anyone had hassled him inside the bar, they would have moved in force. Shot the bartender between the eyes if the man with the silver hair gave the order. Set the bar on fire. They didn't like it when he went into places alone, for he was an irreplaceable asset. But for his next project, he had to find just the right setting, and that meant performing some of his own reconnaissance. His next stop would be the diner down the street where he'd seen one of the waitresses through the window. Red hair and the kind of full figure that intrigued him. He had more of Fenton to see, but thus far he favored it for relocation. The citizenry didn't seem as inane as he'd suspected they'd be. The home they showed him where he would set up his lab was more than sufficient. And the climate agreed with him. Plus, no one knew him here.

No one knew him anywhere.

Out on the street, a Mexican day laborer approached, head down against the wind. He was five feet seven inches tall and moving at exactly three and a half feet per second. The man with the silver hair was good with numbers.

The Mexican gazed at the tangerine sky and looked at him as he passed by. "Change in the weather's coming, my friend." He said it in broken English, but the man with the silver hair would have understood him in Spanish. Or Russian, Cantonese, Gaelic.

"Yes indeed," said the man with the silver hair.

CHAPTER

1

Braylo, Arizona. Present Day.

There was one real sit-down café in Braylo, a place called Powell's, and Kurt Argento was there about every morning. There were two reasons for this. The first was the steak and eggs special for $6.99, a reasonable price. The second was the fresh pastries, especially the apple fritters. They usually came out after nine o'clock. The first two batches of dough were used for the glazed and chocolate donuts. Customers had to wait for the third batch before they made the fritters because, as the baker explained to him, the dough in the first two batches was too thin for the fritters. That was okay with Argento. He had time to wait.

He'd gone home to Detroit to some fanfare after the bad business at Whitehall Correctional Institute in Missouri where the prison's security system had broken down and some people had died because of it. He'd helped get some folks out of Whitehall, including the governor of Missouri's daughter, a touring student named Julie Wakefield. He'd turned down multiple news outlets who'd wanted to interview him about what happened in the prison. Picked up some work as a handyman. Attended church at Trinity Lutheran, where he'd reconnected with his pastor and spent his off-hours fishing and

5

hunting. When a retired Detroit SWAT buddy named Trapsi invited him to visit in Braylo, Arizona, he'd agreed. When Trapsi got called to active military service for a six-month deployment and asked Argento to housesit, he'd agreed again.

He'd been in Braylo for a month. He had no short-term plans other than picking up some side jobs while he waited for his friend's return. He'd put Trapsi's home number on the corkboard at the town's main grocery store and had gotten a gig dismantling a dilapidated tool shed and building a new one out of pine. It had been an easy job. Take the roof off the shed first, remove the trim, and knock the walls down with a sledge. Then a run to the lumberyard to drop off the old wood and pick up the new. He was glad the homeowner hadn't stuck around to watch him work. Argento didn't always care for talking. Most of the folks in town were friendly but not overly chatty. He had even gotten to know a few of their names when he'd been on walks with his chow-shepherd, Hudson. He didn't initiate many conversations, but he'd say just enough to be polite.

The bell on the front door to Powell's chimed. Argento looked up from his seat in the back out of habit. Twenty-one years as a Detroit street cop had taught him to pay attention to everyone entering the space he occupied. Argento had no firearm at the moment because he hadn't gotten around to filling out the paperwork for a concealed carry permit, although it would be a light lift for a retired cop in Arizona. But if someone came in shooting, the heavy wood table he sat at would serve as a ballistic shield. The steak knife he was using to cut his breakfast would function as an adequate missile weapon at close range—Argento figured he could throw it with enough velocity to penetrate his target up to the hilt. The chances that someone might come in this particular diner at this particular time to do him or the other customers harm were low. But they weren't zero.

However, the woman who'd entered did not rate particularly high on his threat meter, in part because she was carrying a toddler in her right arm. She was about forty, was plainly dressed and looked fatigued. She had a diaper bag over her shoulder and a cast on her left arm. She glanced around the restaurant, and her eyes settled on Argento for a moment. Then she sat down two tables away from him, and the waitress brought her a menu and high chair.

The toddler was a boy, probably one or two years old. Argento didn't have children, so the age was a rough guess. The kid was facing away from Argento in the high chair but he twisted his small torso and craned his neck to peer back at him. Then he waved. Socially speaking, it was probably par for the course to wave back. But Argento kept eating his steak. The waitress would know to bring the apple fritter when he was done. They had an understanding. Dessert for breakfast was highly underrated.

The woman ordered. The boy squirmed in his chair. He was wearing a Denver Broncos T-shirt that had food stains near the neck. He kept looking back at Argento. Maybe he found something interesting about him. Or maybe the kid would have been just as content staring at a traffic cone.

Now the woman was looking at Argento as well. He was used to that given the ugly circular scars on both sides of his face, which he'd picked up at Whitehall when a crazed Armenian inmate had shoved a ballpoint pen through his cheeks. History written into flesh. When people saw them, he could see the question in their eyes. Surgery? Injury? Defect? The scars told people to keep away. Argento was fine with that message. Even before his face was marred, a fellow cop had once told him he looked like a bouncer at a post-apocalyptic bar. But she was looking longer than most. He sensed that she was going to come over and ask if she could sit.

Then she did just that. Her voice was quiet. Tired.

Argento gave it a second's assessment before he said, "Suit yourself." Maybe she was looking for a laborer to replace a rotting deck or rewire a kitchen.

The woman moved her child's high chair over to Argento's table. Then she sat herself. The kid hiccupped, looking pleased with himself. Argento kept eating. If the woman had a point, she'd get to it.

She brushed her longish hair behind her ears with her good arm

7

and locked eyes with him. She hadn't asked him about a job yet, which made Argento think she was after something else. Money, maybe, or a ride. Argento wasn't in the habit of giving out either. He held her gaze. Despite her obvious weariness, she had an unlined, kind face. But there was the arm cast. Plus, her clothes looked wrinkled. As if she had been wearing them a few days. Argento instinctively checked her right arm for track marks and saw none. When she set her water glass down, he cast a glance at her fingertips. No scorch marks from a drug pipe. No sniffles, no red-rimmed eyes. She didn't smell. If she was a user, she hid it well.

The child hiccupped again and grinned.

"My name is Kristin Reed," the woman said. "This is my son, Ethan. We need your help."

Argento cut off a square of scrambled egg and ate it.

"Have you ever heard of a place called Fenton, Arizona?"

Argento shook his head.

"It's a town about forty miles west of here."

"What about it?"

"My husband went missing in Fenton. His name is Warren Reed. I believe something happened to him there." There was no emotion in Kristin's voice. Flat and measured. She had said this before. She handed Argento a homemade missing person flyer with a picture of Warren, his date of birth, description, and contact info for Kristin if found. Argento glanced at it. Warren was smiling in the picture. He was a man of about thirty-five with a shock of thick dark hair and the beginnings of a beard. He wore thick, old-fashioned glasses, and resembled a church elder.

Argento looked at Kristin's shoes. The footwear often gave it away. But hers were in decent shape. Not the torn, stained shoes of an addict. He cut off another square of egg. He had maybe two more forkfuls left and one more wedge of steak followed by the fritter. Then breakfast would be over and he could look forward to breakfast the next day. He'd dropped weight since coming to the desert, from daily workouts and long walks with Hudson, and he now tipped the scale at an even two hundred. He needed Powell's breakfast calories to keep his strength up.

"What makes you think something happened to your husband?"

"He went to Fenton for the weekend. Didn't say why. Then he sent me a text that something strange was going on there and he'd tell me about it later. After that, he stopped communicating. And he wouldn't do that. Not to me. Or his son." Kristin put her palm lightly on top of Ethan's head. "Warren is a smart, stable man. We've been married fifteen years. There's no way."

"Sounds like something the Fenton cops should hear about."

"I tried. I said he was missing. Maybe dead. They took a report. But after that, they ignored me. They could be in on it for all I know."

"Big jump from missing to dead."

"No other reason for him not to call me. Something happened. I know it."

Argento flagged the waitress down and ordered a cup of coffee to go.

"He didn't run out on us. If that's what you're thinking."

Ethan said something that sounded like "Wa-wa." Kristin reached into the diaper bag and took out a child's plastic cup and gave it to him. Ethan gulped from it greedily.

Argento wasn't a cop anymore and he was no kind of private investigator. People disappeared all the time, for reasons that made sense and reasons that didn't. They nearly always turned back up. But the woman in front of him was road-weary with a bad arm and had a child with her, which made telling her to buzz off bad form. Plus his late wife, Emily, wouldn't have liked it, and whenever possible, Argento tried not to do things that Emily would disapprove of. *Civilized*, Argento thought. *I'm getting civilized.*

"So is this what you do? You go from town to town looking for someone to help you find your lost husband?"

"I have to. Otherwise I'm just giving up."

"There are some folks out there who say they'll help and then do the opposite."

9

"A week ago, there was a man in Phoenix," Kristin said, her level voice now taking on a huskier quality. "His name was Wayne Ellerbee. Cowboy-type. He worked for a private investigator. Showed me his business card. He said he'd find Warren. When he came to my hotel, he was drunk and I knew what he wanted. He put his hands on me and when I pushed him, he broke my arm. I stabbed him with a fork to get away."

Argento wondered if any of that was true. Was she trying to win him over with a sad story? A *you have to help me or I'll be forced to go to more men who will assault me* approach? His time as a cop had made him pick apart every tale he was told.

"How do you know I'm any different than the cowboy?"

"I know who you are. You were a police officer. You protected the governor's daughter at that prison in Missouri. It was on the news. People in town said you came to this diner. And now I've found you."

The rumor mill of a small town. Argento had been in Braylo long enough for someone to recognize him from his picture in the media and told someone and that someone told someone else and now here they were. Argento set down his utensils. This conversation wasn't going anywhere productive. But Argento would give her this much—in addition to his threat meter, he had a crazy meter and she wasn't setting that off either. She was weary, but entirely coherent.

The breakfast crowd had faded and the diner had the after-the-crowd, settled calm where you could hear voices in the kitchen, the clink of silverware, the whir of the overhead fans. Kristin watched him closely.

"Will you help us?"

Us, Argento thought. Not just her. Ethan too. She was banking that he would be less inclined to turn away both a mother and a child in need. But no matter how civilized Argento might become, there was still a problem with appealing to his emotional side.

He didn't much have one.

"You don't need me. You needed Richard Boone about forty years ago."

"Who's that?"

"He was on a TV show."

The waitress returned with Kristin's breakfast and Argento's to-go cup of coffee and apple fritter. Argento took them and stood. Kristin put one hand on his forearm. Argento looked down at her hand and she removed it. But she held his gaze.

"I can tell what kind of man you are. You'll do this for me. You'll find out what happened to my husband."

Argento thought that was a lot to figure over one breakfast but he didn't say as much. "Follow up with the local cops." He paid his bill, and left a twenty on Kristin's table to cover her tab.

"You'll help me," Kristin said. Her voice had gone up an octave. Her arms were folded across her chest, her face set in stubborn repose. Next to her, Ethan sipped from his water cup.

"I'd just be in the way."

Kristin closed her eyes. Something that might have been a shudder went through her. She put her hand on top of Ethan's head again. Argento guessed she hadn't slept in a while. "I expected more from you."

There didn't seem to be anything to say to that, so Argento left the diner. He cast one more look at Kristin and Ethan before walking away. Kristin was watching him intently, like if she tried hard enough, she could look straight through him.

CHAPTER

2

The man with the silver hair did a vigorous forty minutes in the endless pool adjacent to his office. He toweled off and changed into khakis and a plain white-collared shirt, which he wore untucked. It was the same thing he put on nearly every day, for he found fashion asinine. When he entered his workspace, he went right to his chair. It was plush, ergonomically sound, and utterly noiseless. He could roll along the office floor from one corner to the next without a whisper.

There were three keyboards in all at his workstation, each linked to a towering monitor. The middle one approached the size of a drive-in movie screen. He could have consolidated the keyboards into one system, but he liked sliding his chair between consoles. He liked the subtly different sounds his fingers made on each keyboard, the split attention required, the kinetic energy of it all. Like conducting an orchestra.

The man with the silver hair had more money than he could ever spend, but he'd never felt the need to surround himself with the trappings of the well-off. That was why he was content in this windowless gray room with nothing on the walls—no art, no photographs, no frills. A complete lack of distractions. There was only the work.

The current job was at long last a challenge for him in a life where challenges had been difficult to come by. He did not hail from an intellectual bloodline. His parents were both well-meaning dullards, but they recognized that even from an early age he was special. The man with the silver hair was three when he showed his mother how to program the VCR. He'd expressed an interest in both the hard and soft sciences—curious after a unit on electricity, he'd given an elementary school classmate a handful of button-style lithium batteries which he'd quietly encouraged him to swallow. When the boy had died in agony of internal burns from the battery's caustic chemicals, it had confirmed his hypothesis.

By age twelve, he'd audited graduate-level logic courses. Achieved perfect scores on the GMAT and MCAT. His parents wouldn't allow him to go to college early because they were concerned about his social development, so he had to wait until after high school to enroll in MIT on a full scholarship. But he dropped out midway through his first year, stone-bored and disgusted with the self-satisfaction of professors who thought they knew more than he did. He drifted for a spell afterward, but everything he did felt like slumming—like the ten million he'd amassed by his nineteenth birthday through astute stock picks or the blueprints for a revolutionary automobile fuel cell that he designed but then discarded after a bout of ambivalence.

He wasn't just a genius. He could grasp nuances, unpack complexities, and see patterns invisible to others, but despite the ability to understand absolutely everything, he found himself interested in absolutely nothing. By age twenty-two, his hair had prematurely grayed, and he felt imprisoned in a life he could not help but feel was already squandered. He had no job because nothing could hold his attention. He had only his own roving mind, waiting for a true test.

Then the government came calling. A pair of recruiters, who told the man with the silver hair they'd been following his exploits since he was a child when the local paper had run a story about his self-taught ability to speak fluent Mandarin. They'd spoken of a small, specialized unit within their agency that the man with the silver hair would be perfect for. They had made an attractive offer and the man with the silver hair had accepted. It wasn't the generous starting salary by any means—he had more than enough money through his investments. It was the nature of the work. The respect he'd been shown by the recruiters. The control he'd be given.

Over the years, the job had been everything they had promised. And his current assignment had given him a degree of power and autonomy second to none.

The man with the silver hair watched his monitors, fed by a combination of satellites and webcams. His drone footage allowed him to look out over the flat expanse of desert that surrounded Fenton: red dirt, crimson rock, a great swath of nothingness, the only movement coming from the wind or an occasional gecko. He let the images flow over him, using them to activate his subsurface thinking as preparation for an undertaking that would require every unit of his mental horsepower.

When it was time, the man with the silver hair stood and walked down the hallway to his lab, which held his current assignment.

Once it was complete, he would make God Himself feel like an imposter.

CHAPTER

3

Argento took a Marlboro Red from a hard pack on the dresser and lit it indoors so he wouldn't have to contend with the desert wind. He'd started smoking again about a year ago during the prison riot at Whitehall. He figured his lungs were clean enough now that he had a decade or two of grace before they blackened. He headed toward the front porch. Hudson was resting in front of the door, so Argento had to step over him, but Hudson didn't mind this because he knew Argento didn't mind. Hudson was guarding the gates. The dog knew Argento had already been hurt, with the passing of his wife, Emily, on the job, at Whitehall. He didn't want him to be hurt anymore.

Argento settled in a wide-backed chair. He had no work lined up until the weekend. Business had been slow. A lot of people in Braylo did their own home improvements. Argento was fine with not having anything pressing. It was the kind of schedule he preferred. He'd shop for groceries later. Trapsi hadn't left much food in the house before he left. That didn't surprise Argento. When they'd worked together on SWAT, he'd rarely seen Trapsi eat. Guy lived on Mountain Dew and Copenhagen.

The day's swelter lingered in the late-afternoon air, blunted by the breeze. Hudson shook himself, padded over from the doorway, and curled up on the porch next to him. The house was a two-bedroom southwest adobe. It was small and Argento used about a third of it. The backyard was ringed with paloverde trees, and the land was flat for a good stretch in every direction before it bled into mountains. Argento appreciated that. He liked to be able to see people coming.

He was living a life now where he did what he wanted when he wanted. He could get used to that. But it wasn't complete. Emily had been an intervention. She'd come into his life just before being a cop completely defined him. Now he had to navigate the puzzle of how to be without her. Some days he was functional. On others, his grief felt like an undertow that hid in the waves and then pulled him out into the deep.

He pictured her sitting on the front porch of their house in Detroit. Hair tumbling past her shoulders. Her ready laugh. He could remember exactly what her voice sounded like. That was important. If he forgot her voice, it would be like losing her again. He scratched Hudson behind the ears and put his head against his dog's, feeling his warmth.

Argento went back inside for a beer and when he returned to the porch, Hudson's head shot up. He sensed something nearby to track. A lizard or rabbit. There were plenty of critters around to occupy him. Argento hadn't spent much time in the desert, but he was already impressed by the number of things that could hurt or kill you. Heat, rattlers, spiny plants, probably the ghost of Geronimo. He eased back in the chair. He'd been hurt in Whitehall and still saw the place in a recurring nightmare where he would try to get people out but his arms wouldn't work and then would disappear from his body. But he'd had a year to mend, physically and mentally. While his body still ached at times, the pulsating pain in his leg and spine had subsided, aided in part by morning physical therapy exercises he did on the floor while Hudson got down next to him like he was prepping for his own stretches. His damaged knee had cut into his foot speed some, but Argento didn't see that as much of a disadvantage; his day-to-day activities didn't involve a lot of retreating.

He saw the car coming from a half mile away. A green sedan trailing a thin plume of dust. As it grew near, Argento could see two occupants. An adult female driver and a child in a car seat in back. The car, a Toyota Corolla streaked with dust, jostled along the last stretch of road and pulled up in front of the house. Kristin Reed got out and stood by the driver's-side door, her casted left hand raised to block the sun. She was wearing the same clothing as the day before. Hudson's head rose and he watched Kristin and the car with middling interest. Then he scratched his face with his hind leg and settled back down on the porch. He didn't bark. He was keyed in to Argento's wavelength, and if Kurt wasn't concerned at the presence of these strangers, neither was he.

"Small town," Kristin said. "Delivery guy at the market told me where you lived."

Argento remained seated and finished his cigarette, letting the smoke roll around in his mouth before he exhaled. The presence of the woman was an irritant, albeit a minor one, but it was to a certain extent canceled out by her tenacity. Argento admired that in people. But that didn't change anything. She was going to leave disappointed. She might as well get used to it. Argento had often found the world to be a disappointing place.

"Thank you for breakfast," Kristin said.

"I'll save us both some time," Argento replied. "I'm sorry your husband is missing. I wish he wasn't. But I'm not any kind of investigator. Not anymore. I repair fences. I break up concrete."

"Meet me in Fenton tonight. I want to show you something."

Argento shook his head. "You got problems with the Fenton police, talk to the law here in Braylo. I've heard they're halfway decent. They'll listen to you."

Kristin continued as if Argento hadn't said anything at all. "My husband and I were separated. I didn't tell you that before but I should have. He didn't talk to me much the last year but we were trying to make it work again. I don't know why he went to Fenton. But the text he sent that said something strange happened to him there...He and I have had our troubles, but he would never leave Ethan. And he doesn't have any enemies. Warren gets along with everyone. He's nice to a fault."

Inside the car, Ethan squirmed in his car seat. His mouth was open and his head tilted slightly upward, as if he was singing to himself.

"Good-looking dog," Kristin said. "Chow?"

"Half. Other half shepherd."

"What's his name?"

"Hudson."

"Like the explorer?"

"Like the marine in *Aliens*."

She nodded. Kept her gaze fixed on him. Argento held it. When he looked at most people, he often saw weakness. But not in Kristin Reed. He saw resolve.

"May I use your restroom for a minute?"

Argento wasn't a big fan of strangers entering the space where he lived, but he wasn't going to say no to a mother with a child. "First door on the right."

Kristin unbuckled Ethan from his car seat and walked him over. Then she handed him to Argento and went inside.

One of Argento's old SWAT partners had a houseful of kids whom Argento used to play with and toss in the air. But he hadn't had much contact with children since. Argento looked at Ethan. Ethan looked at Argento. To his credit, the kid didn't cry; there was nothing about Argento that was remotely paternal. Close-cropped hair setting off an unforgiving face, his perpetual stubble, the scars. He wasn't the kind of man a stranger would willingly pass a child to. Unless she was trying to build more sympathy for her cause.

Argento held Ethan like a football the way he'd seen other parents do. Ethan gurgled. He seemed content with this position. Then the child reached out across Argento's thick forearm, grabbed his right pinky finger, and held on to it. When Kristin emerged from the bathroom, she took Ethan from Argento and walked back to her car.

"I'll be at the Baldwin Hotel at eight," she said. "They allow dogs. Before he went missing, my husband told me he was staying there. Room eleven." She turned away from Argento and opened her car door with her good arm.

"I'm not going to be there, Kristin."

"You remembered my name." Then she shut the door. From the back seat, Ethan waved. Maybe at him. Maybe at a nearby cactus.

He felt it then. Just a twinge of something approaching regret. He tried to ignore it. Feelings like that had never done him much good. He still didn't quite know what to make of Kristin Reed and her story. But he'd made a decision when he was standing in front of the Pacific Ocean not long after he'd escaped Whitehall. Maybe even a pledge. Though he was no longer a cop, he'd still try to fix things for some people when he could.

After the car had disappeared from sight, Argento went back inside. He read for a time, a novel set during WWII called *City of Thieves* that Julie Wakefield, the governor's daughter, had recommended. The two of them had kept up since Whitehall, but Argento didn't care for the phone or email, so they'd written letters every few months. Julie had said the book might be his style and she was right.

Then he worked out in his living room. Push-ups, sit-ups, pull-ups on a reinforced bar he had mounted on the back of the house, until his body hummed with exertion. He ate dinner in front of the television. One of those Where Are They Now programs was on where a woman was interviewing some kids who had been on shows Argento had watched as a child. They were mostly haggard adults now with drug problems. He flipped the channel until he came to *Point Blank* with Lee Marvin. When he checked his watch, it was seven. Fenton, Arizona, was forty miles away.

Argento had never been to Fenton. Maybe they had good donuts. Or a bar he'd like. Argento was willing to drive forty miles for above-average food and alcohol. And he could stop by the Baldwin and offer to buy the woman some new clothes. Or to make sure her kid had enough milk.

Civilized.

Argento's car was a Ford pickup. Good for hauling and not the worst gas mileage. He drove the forty miles on the intrastate. Save for a few truck stops, there wasn't much in between Braylo and Fenton, just open desert spreading out in all directions in an enveloping stillness. At a T-junction, he saw a green rectangular sign that said *Welcome to Fenton.* No population number was given. The sign looked new. It hadn't been peppered with birdshot yet, the way people sometimes liked to do out west.

Fenton had a compact downtown. Argento passed a small grocery store, two unassuming bars, a rustic-looking barbershop, and a triangular-shaped diner called the Bronze Dollar. Fenton didn't seem particularly sinister, even at night. Argento got more of a quiet, orderly vibe. Few people were out. There was only one traffic light.

It wasn't hard to find the Baldwin, a spartan, two-story brick building just off the main drag. Argento walked into the lobby, which featured a large painting of a mustachioed cowboy lassoing a steer. The cowboy's face was blobby and the steer was lackluster, like someone had started painting a deer and then changed their mind midway. Argento figured there was a warehouse somewhere of mass-produced shitty art that hotels ordered at deep discounts.

Kristin wasn't there. Argento checked his watch. A few minutes before eight. He sat in a chair and waited. At twenty minutes after, with no sign of Kristin, he rang the bell at the desk. A middle-aged woman with a Peggy Fleming haircut in a red Arizona Cardinals T-shirt emerged from a back office.

"You have a woman named Kristin Reed checked in here? Lady in an arm cast?"

The woman shook her head without bothering to look at any guest register. It was a small enough hotel where she wouldn't need to. She had strong-looking forearms, Argento noted. Probably hauled her own trash. It looked like a small, one-person operation.

"You need a room?"

"Not yet." Argento took a business card from the counter, walked out of the lobby and checked the back of the hotel. Kristin's Toyota wasn't there. He stood still for a moment. Listened. No cars passing. No sounds of conversation on the street. No radio sounds from an open window. Like he and the woman in the Cardinals T-shirt were the only ones in Fenton.

On his way back to the intrastate, Argento stopped at a bar called Connor's. He was the sole customer. The bartender was a stooped, blank-faced guy with a bolo tie. He was watching a rerun of college hockey. Illinois versus Ohio State. Argento sat at the bar, which had a sticky counter his forearm adhered to, and ordered an Irish whiskey. He reached into his pocket for a cigarette and saw the handwritten sign behind the bartender that said *Smoking Prohibited* and listed a county code.

"Anyone enforce that?"

The bartender set Argento's drink on the bar and shrugged. "Not the cops here anymore. Why should I care if they don't?"

Argento lit a Marlboro. One drink, maybe two cigarettes, and then back on the road. No need to return. Kristin was gone. She and Ethan had decided to head home to await news of Warren, or she'd decided he wasn't going to come after all so she hadn't bothered to show herself. Or the Reeds had already been happily reunited, Warren explaining he'd been out of touch because he'd had to unexpectedly care for a sick friend or been saddled with a last-minute work deadline and he was so sorry he'd caused such alarm.

Maybe.

Or things had gone a different way. Argento didn't have enough data to make an educated guess. Regardless, it wasn't his problem. Hadn't been from the start.

The bartender wasn't much for conversation. He resumed watching the hockey game and Argento was content to watch too. He liked the rhythm of the sport. He'd played himself as a teenager growing up in Michigan. He'd been average on the skates, but checking had been his specialty. He enjoyed the physical contact. Sizing up the opponent, barreling toward him, and letting his body collide into theirs as

21

the breath hissed from their lungs. When he'd finished, he left a five on the bar and got back in his truck. He drove to the diner he'd seen, the Bronze Dollar, to pick up some food before he hit the highway. There was a blue-and-white squad car parked in front, a newer model Dodge Charger. On the side of the car were emblazoned the words *Fenton Public Safety Department*.

A uniformed cop came out of the diner as Argento approached. He was an Asian guy about thirty, in shape and squared away, wearing a short-sleeved shirt that revealed wide, veined forearms. Argento wouldn't have given him a second glance except that upon breaking the plane of the doorway, the cop did something that Argento found interesting as hell.

The guy looked up, as if scanning the rooftops.

The tallest building in Fenton Argento had seen was three stories. Not much need to look up. But that wasn't what struck Argento. What struck him was that no one looked up like that when leaving a building. Not citizens. Not even many cops. Typically only SWAT and combat troops did that. Because when you were in a hot zone, hazards often came from above. Snipers in trees, gunfire from hilltops, or just an angry populace dropping bottles or small appliances out of housing project windows in the hopes of splitting an officer's skull.

The cop's gaze focused in on Argento. His nameplate said Chan. He'd shined it recently, and it gleamed under the streetlight. Argento nodded as he walked to the front door of the Bronze Dollar.

"Place is closed," Chan said.

Argento looked inside through the row of windows. There were two patrons sitting in a back booth, a middle-aged man with silver hair, and a younger Asian woman in street clothes. A waitress, young and full-figured with her red hair tied back in a band, approached with plates of food.

"Those two folks know that?"

Chan didn't say anything. Just kept sizing him up. Argento waited. He didn't mind waiting. He had nowhere special to be and was fine with the extended silence. Most people talked too much.

"Private event," Chan said.

Argento saw another Fenton Public Safety officer inside the diner posted by the back door. Silver Hair was talking to the waitress. She laughed at whatever he said, but it looked forced. A *the customer is always funny* chuckle. Silver Hair looked up at Argento. Then he returned his attention to his meal.

"When they're closed, most places just hang up a sign that says so. No need to station a cop at the door."

"You're from somewhere else, aren't you?" Chan said.

Argento nodded.

"I don't think you're going to like it here."

"Not if all the events are private." He returned to his truck. Chan in turn walked around to the back of the Charger. It was the full package with a hood scoop, LED headlights, and a Hemi badge, freshly washed. Probably cost more than Argento had made his last year on the job. Fenton must have a decent tax base. Chan opened the trunk. It contained a gear bag and an AR locked in a rack. That was it. No crime scene tape. No roll measurer or orange cones for traffic collisions. No binder of forms and checklists. It gave the impression that the Fenton Public Safety Department wasn't around to take accident reports or trap stray coyotes.

It made him wonder what they were around for.

Argento started up his truck and drove away. Chan's gaze followed him over the top of his squad car.

CHAPTER
4

Argento rose early the next morning and read some more of *City of Thieves*. Then he got a bottle of water and walked the mile to the Braylo County Sheriff's office. Even before seven, the desert temperatures were starting to spike. Halfway through his walk, Argento had finished his water and was left wanting more.

The sheriff's office was an unadorned terra-cotta building with an American flag out front. Argento went in, took a long drink from the water fountain, and refilled his bottle. Above the fountain was the Wanted board, which featured some federal fugitives, but no one local. There wasn't much crime in Braylo. If you stole a shopping cart, it would make the front page of the paper.

A deputy with the name tag of *Andekker* was behind the desk drinking coffee. He was a thick guy with a crew cut and a bulldog tattoo on his forearm, and he wore a .357 in a hip holster.

"My name's Argento. I'm staying in town. I need a favor."

"I know who you are. The prison break guy. Word gets around. Wasn't aware I owed you a favor. This is the first time you've spoken to me."

"I can never think of anything to say."

"So what's up?"

"There's a town called Fenton about forty miles from here. You know much about it?"

"Driven by a few times," Andekker said. "Couldn't think of a reason to stop. What's your interest?"

"Lady said her husband went missing there. Asked me to look into it." He showed Andekker Kristin's missing person flyer of Warren Reed. Andekker looked at it for a professionally appropriate amount of time and handed it back.

"What'd you say?"

"Told her I was just a handyman. Referred her to you."

"She didn't come talk to me."

"She wanted me to meet her last night in Fenton. She never showed."

"Maybe she left town."

"Maybe."

"So what do you care?"

"Don't, really."

"So why are you here?"

"Lady had a kid with her. I think they were sleeping in her car. Want to make sure the kid's okay."

"Kid look fed? Healthy?"

Argento nodded.

Both men were quiet for a time.

"So maybe she left town," Andekker said again. "What's the favor?"

"Run her license plate. See what comes up."

"I'm not going to give that out. Maybe you're her stalker."

"I was on the job in Detroit for a while."

"Doesn't mean you're not her stalker."

"Fair enough. But I don't want her address. I just want to know if her car is reported stolen or was in an accident. Can you tell me that?"

Andekker set his coffee cup down. The side of it said *Poor Planning on Your Part Does Not Necessitate an Emergency on Mine.*

Argento had seen that cup before. There was probably one in every police department in the country. Andekker fired up a computer terminal at his desk and Argento gave him the Toyota's plates. Andekker did some typing and then looked at his computer screen.

"It's a rental. No hits on the plate."

"How long do rental agencies take to report a car missing out here?"

"A week. They need to send a certified letter to the renter letting them know they're past due before they can report an auto theft."

Argento nodded.

"Anything else?"

"What can you tell me about the police department in Fenton?"

"They had some turnover recently. Sheriff and his deputies left and got replaced by some different guys. Other than that, not much. Haven't had occasion to interact with them. If we ever needed mutual aid, we'd give them a call, but we haven't yet and neither have they, so we don't go there and they don't come here."

"Thought all cops played softball together."

"I think we used to. Now we just drink alone."

The radio on Andekker's desk squawked. He picked it up.

"I'm out with a stranded motorist off Cathro Road," the deputy on the other end said. "They got no water. Gonna stand by for the tow truck."

"Copy," Andekker said. He turned his attention back to Argento. "When we sweep the back roads, sometimes we run into folks that think because they have a cell phone, they don't need a plan for the desert. Desert can be hard on those folks."

"Can you tell me anything else about Fenton?"

"I don't know. You google it?"

"I don't have a computer," Argento said.

Andekker took a sip of his coffee. "You got a phone? They got computers right in 'em now."

Argento used his cell phone so infrequently, he hadn't thought to bring it to Trapsi's in Braylo. It was still on his bedroom nightstand in Detroit. "Just a landline."

"Some investigator."

"That's why I didn't take the job."

"But here you are."

"Things are different now. The lady's gone and so is her kid. She could be mixed up in something."

"What are you basing that on?"

"She was too desperate to just walk away. She told me to meet her at eight, she should have been there at eight."

"She good-looking?"

Argento nodded.

"You trying to get some tail outta this?"

"No," Argento said. He didn't resent the question. If he were Andekker, he would have thought the same thing.

"So now what are you going to do?"

"Go back to Fenton. Look around some. You mind making a few copies of that flyer?"

"Not in your investigator budget?"

"I'm not an investigator."

"Sure," Andekker said. "Not doing anything else at the moment. I'll be your secretary. As a courtesy for your service to the fine citizens of Detroit." He ran off a dozen color copies and gave them to Argento. Then he stood and adjusted his gun belt. Ran one thick hand over his scalp. He had sunspots on his temples.

"You must miss the job. Looks like you're playing detective again."

No, I'm Richard Boone, Argento thought. He thanked Andekker, opened the door to the sheriff's office, and walked into the harsh sunlight, as the heat wrapped around him.

CHAPTER

5

Years ago, the man with the silver hair's handlers had wanted him to find bin Laden. He'd laughed off the request. Anyone in military intelligence with an IQ cresting a hundred should have deduced that the world's most wanted fugitive would be in Pakistan, within fifteen miles of a major city, in a compound with high walls but no visible patrols to avoid suspicion and a decided lack of internet and phone lines to skirt intercepted transmissions. The man with the silver hair found such a pedestrian assignment beneath him and had refused. His handlers voiced their objections to this, but he wasn't the kind of employee you admonished.

He had started out the morning with his swim followed by breakfast at the diner. He ate the same thing every morning, three egg whites with diced tomatoes followed by his daily supply of zinc, selenium, and prebiotics. The diner waitress with the red hair, Cassidy, had served him, her ample breasts straining at the fabric of her shirt in a way that the man with the silver hair found both distracting and compelling. She smelled like lavender, and laughed when he said things that were even mildly amusing. When he'd first laid eyes on her several months ago, he'd told his handlers to bring her to him but they'd said it wasn't feasible. He'd responded with a twenty-four-hour work stoppage until they'd driven in two sloe-eyed teen runaways from Phoenix. He was aggressive with women and one of the girls had to be taken to the emergency room with severe hemorrhaging. He'd chastised his people for selecting someone so slight.

The man with the silver hair stood and went to the outer doors of his lab. Raised the security blinds with a push of a button on his phone and looked through the glass onto a space about the size of a small cafeteria. Three side rooms running off it contained the needed equipment for the project. He had multiple tests to run and the thermocycler needed to be recalibrated, but he was assuredly working the right metrics. Success was a certainty. It was just a question of timeframe. Numbers and combinations for the project ran through his head, processes and measures, fragments and base pairs. He was interrupted by the door chime. A visitor. He pressed the intercom.

"It's Chan."

The man with the silver hair checked the CCTV display, confirmed it was Chan, and that he was alone. He instinctively pulled up on the collar of his shirt to cover his elongated neck. Then he lowered the security shades to the lab and pressed the entry button. The thick steel doors to his office opened with a metallic whisper.

Chan entered. His City of Fenton Public Safety uniform was pressed and immaculate, shoes shined, name tag polished. He stood with his legs shoulder-width apart and his arms behind his back. He seemed uncomfortable. He and the other officers often did. And despite their military bearing and field experience, they couldn't quite hide it. They didn't know what to make of him. The man with the silver hair liked that. If people were at ease around him, it might indicate they thought they were his equal.

"There was a man last night at the Baldwin," Chan said. "He wasn't around long, but he was asking about the woman and the boy."

"Say more," the man with the silver hair said.

"He came up to the diner when you were there. I saw him leave town. He looked like he could fucking handle himself."

"Any obscenities in this room will be spoken only by me. Understood?"

The corner of Chan's mouth twitched. "Understood."

"Was he alone?"

Chan nodded.

"Friend of the family?"

"Probably not. But I think he saw you."

"He saw me. And I saw him. What's the relevance?"

"It can make it . . . hard when you go out."

"I go out sometimes. It's my town. I'm not a monk." As soon as he said it, he almost laughed. Chan had been the first person inside his room for cleanup after he'd broken the teen from Phoenix. Chan was well aware his leanings were not monastic.

"I've already told them," Chan said. "They'll run facial recognition on him, see if he's someone we need to know about. The LT just sent me to brief you personally."

Them. This operation was under joint control between him and them, as if the man with the silver hair needed to consult with anyone about a proper course of action.

Chan stood uncertainly. "How's the project going?"

The man with the silver hair didn't bother to answer. There were maybe three men in the world who could even begin to understand the intricacies of what he was doing. None of them were Chan. He dismissed him with a wave of a hand. The doors opened and Chan walked out. He listened for the receding sound of Chan's boots on the tile floor, but heard nothing. Chan made a point to walk quietly. All of the Fenton deputies did. Like they had trained on it, moving heel to toe, evenly distributing their weight to avoid rustling, pre-inspecting their footwear to make sure it didn't squeak. Silly war games.

The guest at the Baldwin had asked about the woman and the boy. The man with the silver hair didn't know where they were, not precisely. But their fates didn't register. The world wouldn't be down a prize-winning geophysicist or a violin prodigy. Just a cow and her small calf, roaming dumbly. Two bags of sinew and skin.

The man with the silver hair turned his attention back to the lab where the cycle of the day's tests were nearing completion. Most people lived their lives in obscurity. Hunting for scraps.

Few men got to decide what would happen in the world.

What the lab held guaranteed he would be among them.

CHAPTER

6

Argento figured he'd start his time in Fenton with breakfast. That was as good a way as any to take the measure of a town. The diner that had been closed for a private event, the Bronze Dollar, was open that morning. The place was thick with good breakfast smells and dished out a serviceable plate of steak and eggs. It was no Powell's, but it would do. A few of the patrons looked his way when he entered, but this was nothing unusual. He knew how he appeared. Like he was either there to rob the place or be a highly effective deterrent against robbers. No in-between.

He bought a newspaper, worked on his breakfast, and put away a few cups of coffee, because the Bronze Dollar didn't serve morning beer. He was going to poke around on this thing, but he wasn't starting with a lot. The husband was the focal point, but he didn't know much about him other than his name. So he figured he'd concentrate on where Kristin and Ethan might have gone. Kristin had told Argento that the police in Fenton could be in on her husband's disappearance. That sounded highly improbable. But Argento still figured he'd start talking with the good citizens of Fenton first before the cops.

Argento's waitress was the red-haired woman who had waited on the man with the silvering hair. She was cheerful and buxom and made it a point to never let his coffee cup get below half full. When she leaned in to pour, Argento got a flash of cleavage and a whiff of lavender. He could see why Silver Hair liked her.

"Woman and a boy came through here within the last week," Argento said during his third refill. "Woman was brunette, tired-looking, in an arm cast. Boy was one or two. You see them?"

The waitress nodded. "I remember the cast. They had breakfast here. Kid was well-behaved."

"Any idea where they might be?"

The waitress shrugged. "All I know was they weren't any more local than you."

After breakfast, Argento left the newspaper for the next guy and hit up a few more spots. The hardware store, the barber's, the five-and-dime. He had a variation on the same conversation he'd had with the waitress. He also showed the missing person flyer of Warren Reed around. Some of the people had seen the woman and the boy. They remembered Kristin's arm cast. They didn't provide any useful information, but nobody was unpleasant or seemed like they were hiding something. Two old-timers in the barber shop wearing VFW caps asked if he'd been in the service. The owner of the hardware store told him they were hiring. He was a wizened guy named Olson who had a small pencil tucked behind his ear. Argento put him in his late sixties to early seventies.

"It would take me too long to remember where everything is," Argento said. "Like what aisle hammers are on."

"We got a system, makes it easy," Olson said. "Invented it myself."

"Appreciate it. I'll keep you in mind."

Fenton was about eight blocks by seven, set down in a shallow bowl with hard desert and red cliffs as a backdrop. Argento walked the main streets. The temperature would hit mideighties by noon, but it was comfortable for now, and the midmorning sun felt good on his face and neck. His early impression of Fenton was of a quiet town that ran well. It was absent of graffiti and largely free of trash.

Cars obeyed the speed limit. Kids wore helmets when they rode their bikes. He saw no street fights or even arguments. Pleasantville, USA. If there was something untoward going on, Argento couldn't see it yet.

He was already running out of civilians to talk to, so Argento figured it was time to go to the police. There were two men behind the counter of the Fenton Public Safety Department when Argento entered. One had a name tag that said *Krebs* and the other's said *Redlinger*. Krebs was early twenties, short and wiry. Redlinger was a few years older and about Argento's size, which put him a few inches under six feet. Both were deeply tanned and squared away—uniforms crisp, gig line between their shirt seam, belt buckle and fly lined up on a perfect vertical. Argento could see past them down the hallway to the open doors of a gym where two more guys were working out to the backdrop of heavy metal. The gym was an impressive size for a small-town department. One of the men was flipping an oversized tire across the padded floor, and the other was doing shirtless pull-ups on top of a cable crossover machine, his bare torso gleaming with sweat. A tattoo of bird wings spread over the width of his back.

"Looking for a woman with an arm cast who was just in town," Argento said. "Name of Kristin Reed, midthirties. She was with her son Ethan, kid was high chair age. I was supposed to meet with them but they didn't show. Her husband is gone too. Man named Warren Reed. She recently filed a missing person report on him with you."

"Haven't seen them," Krebs said.

"Other people have."

"What other people?"

"Folks around town."

Krebs looked at Redlinger, who shook his head without saying anything. But Argento thought he caught something behind the eyes. Recognition? Or something more like resignation.

Krebs made a point to noisily suck on his teeth. "You a private eye or some shit?"

"No. But I was a cop in Detroit."

"What do you think that means out here in AZ? We best friends now?"

There was nothing in that for Argento, so he didn't answer.

"Anything else we can help you with?" Redlinger asked. His voice was notably quieter than Krebs's.

"Can I borrow a piece of paper?"

Krebs looked at Redlinger again, as if this question might merit discussion. Redlinger shrugged and took a sheet from a printer tray and passed it to Argento, who wrote the heading *Have You Seen Me* and put down a brief description of Kristin Reed and her son. He added it to Kristin's missing person flyer of Warren. Then he fished in his pocket, found the business card for the Baldwin hotel, and wrote down his name and the hotel's number.

"Okay if I put these up?"

"Suit yourself," Redlinger said.

Argento pinned the papers to a corkboard in the lobby, which was immaculate, as if it had just been swept prior to his arrival. The corkboard itself was strangely empty. No other flyers. No advertisements for upcoming events like a festival or a car wash. No one selling a gun or a truck. Like the Fenton PD had just celebrated their grand opening that day. There wasn't much to do after that, so Argento left. On his way out, he saw Krebs come around the counter, pull down Argento's papers, and crumple them. Argento found that unusual. He thought about going back inside and asking Krebs what his malfunction was. But instead he filed it away. He had a feeling he would run into Krebs again.

And he had a notion it wouldn't be pleasant.

CHAPTER

7

rgento returned to Trapsi's house in Braylo, packed, and picked up Hudson, who was so excited to see him he nearly knocked him down. Then he drove back to Fenton and pulled up to the Baldwin with Hud on a leash. The same woman was at the front desk. She had on another Arizona Cardinals T-shirt, but this one was white. The away uniform. The creases near her eyes told him she was midforties.

"Back again," she said.

"I'd like a room."

"You got it."

Argento handed her his Michigan driver's license. "How do you feel about dogs in your place?"

"Love 'em. What breed is that? Akita?"

"Chow-shepherd. His name's Hudson."

"Hi, Hudson." The woman smiled. "You're not very poofy for a chow."

"His family is all smooth coat. Rough coats are the ones that get poofy."

"Well, officially welcome to the Baldwin, both of you. My name's Ruth."

"Last time I was here, I asked you about a woman named Kristin Reed. You ever have any other Reeds staying here? Man named Warren?" He took out the missing person flyer with Warren's picture. Krebs had crumpled up the one he'd left at Fenton DPS, but he still had the multiple copies that Andekker had made.

Ruth nodded. "He was here maybe a month back. Stayed a few days."

"How is it you recall him? He do something memorable?"

"No. We just don't get a lot of guests. He was a nice fellow. Quiet."

They were both silent for a moment. Ruth had a friendly, open expression. The face of a welcoming proprietor. But he also got the sense she wouldn't put up with a lot of nonsense. Maybe a lot of middle-aged businesswomen in small-town Arizona were like that.

"You ask questions like one of those Hollywood reporters," she finally said.

"I'm not," Argento said.

"I know. You look like one of my kid's action figures."

Kristin had told Argento Warren had stayed in room eleven. It seemed a good place to start. "Okay if I have room eleven? It's my lucky number."

"Suit yourself," Ruth said. He paid and she gave him the key—a real key, not a key card. The Baldwin was old-school.

The hotel had sixteen rooms, eight to a floor. Argento turned the key to eleven and walked inside.

The first thing that hit him was the smell. Fresh. The room had been refurbished. No, not just refurbished. Completely redone. As if it had been torn apart piecemeal and then put back together. There was fresh carpeting and new drywall and what looked like a new bed, given the immaculate-looking bedposts. Argento stepped out of the room and walked down the hallway until he found an open door. Room seventeen, unoccupied. He looked inside. Standard cheap hotel décor. Carpet frayed in the corners. Yellowish drywall. Smelled a little musty. So not a hotel-wide upgrade. Room eleven was an outlier.

He closed the door behind him and returned to eleven. He took a closer look around. The nightstand and chairs looked new as well, but there was nothing else of interest. Argento guessed that if someone had gone through Warren's room, they'd been thorough. And if they hadn't found what they were looking for, Argento doubted that he would either.

He returned to the front desk.

"Everything okay with the room?" Ruth asked.

"It's fine. Looks like it got a facelift."

"Had some bikers in town one weekend. They left a hell of a mess."

"I'd like it for the week."

Ruth wrote something in a ledger. "So how do you like the desert so far?"

"Still adjusting to the heat. At night there's more stars than I'm used to."

"If you stick around," Ruth said, "you'll even learn the constellations."

"How come this desert town has so many cops?"

"Sheriff retired a little while ago. He had three deputies. One quit, the other two I don't know. Then these boys came in, about nine months ago. State grant or something."

"What do you make of that?"

Ruth shrugged. "Prefer the old sheriff and his deputies, I suppose. These new boys are a little brusque. But they seem like they're on the ball, so as long as it doesn't raise our property taxes, the more the merrier."

"There a church in town?"

Ruth shook her head. "Nothing official, but some folks get together for prayer Sunday mornings. Why? You need one?"

"I'm going to be here through Sunday. Like to keep God up-to-date on my plans."

Ruth looked at him appraisingly.

"Not sure he always approves of them," Argento found himself adding, although he wasn't sure why. After Emily had died, he'd gotten out of the habit of talking to people. He was still trying to find the rhythm of conversation.

He returned to his room, lay in bed with his hands folded behind his head, and listened to the tick of the ceiling fan as he thought about what he knew so far about Fenton and what might have happened to the Reeds. He concluded it was next to nothing. So he decided to get a drink. "Be back soon," he told Hudson, who whined and lolled his tongue.

When he stopped at Connor's, the same hunched bartender as the previous night was there.

"You again," the bartender said. "You work around here?"

Argento shook his head. "Just a traveler."

"My name's Dell."

"Kurt."

"So what do you, Kurt?"

"Come here and drink."

Dell nodded. "Works for me."

"This town got a mayor?"

"Yep. And a town council that decides on things. Just two members, though, and they're both volunteers."

Argento thought about Chan, the cop who had looked up when he'd come out of the diner.

"Police department hiring?"

"Don't know. Don't think so. We don't have a lot of trouble in Fenton and they seem to have a lock on things. Sharp-looking fellas."

"How many are there?"

Dell shrugged. "Not sure. Close to a dozen, maybe?"

"Seems high for a place this size."

"We added some recently. Government grant or some such. You can't have too many lawmen, not with the borders the way they are."

Argento couldn't think of anything else to ask, so he had a beer. A few people came in. They seemed like regulars. Dell chatted them up and served them. The bar had a nice, low-key rhythm to it. No video games or novelty drinks. A corner jukebox played Stevie Ray Vaughn's

"Pride and Joy." Connor's was a pleasant place to kill a few hours. If Fenton was nefarious, this bar didn't seem to be the hub of it.

The next person to enter was a Fenton cop in uniform. He sat down a few stools from Argento. It was Redlinger.

"You must be about done for the day, Aaron," Dell said.

"Shift is over in twenty," Redlinger said. "Might as well get a head start."

Redlinger ordered a Jack & Coke and downed it like a warm-up. He wiped his brow with the sleeve of his uniform shirt. He gave Argento a cursory glance and then started on his second drink. He could probably get away with boozing in uniform in a small town. In a bigger jurisdiction, some patron would have already looked up the number to Internal Affairs. But places like Fenton worked differently.

"Hot," Redlinger said.

"You've seen hotter," Dell said.

"Korengal Valley in the summertime. They should write a song."

"It as bad over there as they say?" Argento asked.

Redlinger ignored the question and looked at his drink.

Argento gave it a minute. Then he asked, "Combat unit?"

Redlinger gave Argento a half look, as if he didn't have the energy to fully turn around.

"Point of the spear, buddy," he said and lapsed into silence. Dell busied himself with the other customers.

Argento let some time pass before he said, "Your coworker Krebs took down my flyers."

"Krebs is from Arkansas," Redlinger said tonelessly, as if that were an explanation.

"Strange thing for a cop to do. Makes me think he doesn't want me to find that missing family."

"The Reeds," Redlinger said without looking at anyone. He held up a finger to Dell, who poured him another Jack & Coke.

Argento waited but Redlinger was done talking. He was lifting another drink when four more men in Fenton Public Safety uniforms came in the bar. The first was Chan, the man Argento had seen earlier scanning rooftops. The second was Krebs, who took off his sunglasses and fixed Argento with a heavy stare. The third was the man Argento had seen doing pull-ups in the police gym, the one with the back tat of bird wings. His name tag said *Cornejo*. He was young, like Krebs, with a long scar stitched across the left side of his face from forehead to jaw. The fourth wore a name tag that said *Tomlinson*. He was a Black man of about thirty-five, burly like Redlinger but taller, with features like granite.

"Time to go, Sergeant," Tomlinson said to Redlinger.

Redlinger didn't reply. He turned his glass in his hands and looked straight ahead.

Krebs kept staring at Argento. Argento met his gaze. "Fuck you looking at," Krebs said.

"You're speaking to me," Argento said, "so I'm looking at you. That's how talking works." He could see in Krebs's eyes and the set of his jaw that he wasn't used to what Argento was giving him.

Cornejo whistled softly and shook his head.

"Mouthy tourist," Krebs said. "My favorite."

"Your uniform just says public safety. Not police or sheriff's department. You all deputies or officers?"

A moment passed before Tomlinson spoke. "Deputies. Duly sworn."

A theory had been germinating in Argento's head since his encounters with Fenton DPS, and he decided to test it. "I seem to be bothering you. Tell you what. I'll walk out of this bar right now and leave town for good if any one of you can tell me the Arizona penal code for aggravated assault."

Nobody answered. Just blank stares all around.

"Guess I'm staying. You guys new to police work?"

"If there's any problem in town, we'll solve it, day or night," Chan said. "That cop enough for you?"

Argento ignored Chan and kept looking at Krebs. "Why'd you take down my missing person flyers?"

"Time to go," Tomlinson said again. His attention was still on

Redlinger. More steel to his voice this time. He put a hand on Redlinger's shoulder. Redlinger didn't move.

Krebs moved closer to Argento. "Tell me more about how talking works."

"Sure," Argento said. "I say stuff. Then it's your turn. So far you're doing fine."

"Someone's feeling brave," Cornejo chuckled.

"Hey," Dell said to Argento. "You don't want to do this. Not with these guys. They're Special Forces."

Argento turned on his stool to fully face Krebs. So far he was at a stalemate in Fenton. He didn't understand this town. He didn't know where the Reeds were. But he knew that he was annoying the shit out of Krebs, and it felt right to annoy him more. It might break something loose. "Special Forces? Get you one of those hats with the propeller on top. So people know how special you are."

"Why don't we step outside," Krebs said. There was no bluster in it. Only a kind of irritated confidence.

Cornejo chuckled again. "This ain't the city. We play different out here." He turned to Dell. "We'll pay for the cleanup."

"This giggly asshole gonna jump in?" Argento asked Krebs, nodding toward Cornejo. That stopped Cornejo midchortle.

"Outside," Krebs said.

"Don't want to go outside." Argento gestured toward his drink. "This is where my beer is."

"Then we'll do it in here." Krebs leaned closer toward Argento. The move made his uniform sleeve hike up on his arm, exposing elaborate Maori-style ink around the biceps.

Argento looked at the arm and looked up at Krebs. "It'll take more than a tribal tattoo, kid."

Tomlinson turned his attention away from Redlinger and looked over at Argento. Then he turned to Krebs and shook his head, but Krebs didn't see it.

Krebs grinned. "How do you want it?"

"Surprise me."

Krebs launched a punch at Argento's face. Argento knew what the deputy was going to do before Krebs probably did himself. He'd always been able to predict such things. He'd been in more fights than most. Argento didn't try to dive out of the way or block the blow. He took the punch full-on. Except he tilted his head down so the full impact of Krebs's fist met flush with the top of his skull. The hard, unforgiving part that was bolted onto a thick, supportive neck. The blow rocked him back on his chair, but Krebs got the worst of it. Argento could hear his hand break. Lots of bones in the hand. Phalanxes and metacarpals. None of them held up particularly well to a high-velocity impact against a surface with the rigidity of quartz. Krebs hopped back with a surprised grunt, holding his damaged hand with his good one. Argento took another sip of his beer. He had never practiced a move like that before, using his own head to play offensive and defensive at once. He couldn't even explain exactly how it happened. It was like trying to show someone how to sneeze. His body just did it.

Cornejo took a rough hold of Argento by the upper arm. Chan took his other arm. Argento didn't resist. "You're under arrest," Cornejo said.

"Arrested for being punched. I like my chances with a judge on that."

Cornejo reached back and fumbled with his handcuffs. Like he hadn't used them much. Krebs used his left hand to cross-draw his Sig Sauer. Tomlinson pushed Krebs's gun arm down.

"Roll it back," Tomlinson said, and just like that Krebs holstered up and Cornejo put his cuffs away.

"You got to go," Dell said, his voice rising. "Everybody's got to go."

"Am I still under arrest?" Argento asked Tomlinson, who seemed to be the decision-maker.

"No," Tomlinson said, his face devoid of expression. "Sorry for the misunderstanding. It's been a long day. We're all leaving."

"The fuck—" Krebs began, and Tomlinson squeezed the younger man's arm so hard Krebs winced.

The Fenton Public Safety crew all filed out. Argento walked to the exit door and watched them go. Krebs got in the passenger side of

43

a marked squad car with Tomlinson taking the wheel. The next step would be to take Krebs to a hospital for the broken hand. Argento hadn't seen a hospital in Fenton, not even an urgent care. They'd have to head out of town.

Except Tomlinson didn't. He drove down the main street and took a right when he should have taken a left to the highway. His car disappeared for a moment and then Argento picked it back up in the distance, past the outskirts of Fenton, as it headed up a winding back road toward the cliff line, leaving a dust trail in its wake.

Argento thought about what had just happened in the bar with Fenton's Public Safety department. Not just their ignorance of the code for aggravated assault, but their waffling between arrest and nonarrest and Cornejo's inexperience with his handcuffs. He thought about the men's spotless uniforms and unscuffed duty belts. And then there were the men themselves, who looked like they could complete a half marathon without breathing hard and probably had single-digit body fat. The police weren't all like that. It was rare to have a completely fit and sharp-looking force. There'd be at least one stupid-looking cop and one chubby one whose uniform didn't fit, with those two sometimes being the same person, often the chief's nephew.

Curious.

Something else occurred to him. Tomlinson had called Redlinger "Sergeant" in the bar, but Redlinger wasn't wearing supervisor's chevrons on his uniform. Argento wasn't sure what that meant either, unless Dell's Special Forces claim was right and Redlinger had been a sergeant in a different uniform.

He walked to the Baldwin and fired up his truck.

Time to follow Tomlinson and Krebs up the back road. See where that winding road wound to.

CHAPTER

8

Argento shadowed the path Tomlinson had driven which snaked up the side of a substantial cliff face past a sign that said *Private Road Do Not Enter* and listed the statute for trespassing. Argento drove by it for another fifty yards and then stopped.

There was a gate in front of him that spanned the entire width of the road topped by two bubble cams in protective domes. It rose at least fifteen feet and was made of thick metal that curved at the top to make scaling it daunting. It looked like the kind of barrier you'd need a rocket launcher to get through. There was no intercom system to buzz or attendant to speak to. No mail slot or keypad. The gate of a rich introvert or a business that valued its privacy.

Tomlinson and Krebs had to have gone this way. There was no off-roading here, unless you wanted to plunge your car into a gulch. Argento backed up to get a better view. Far past the gate up the hill, he could make out the edge of a house built into the cliffs. A three-story home painted the same hues as the desert and hillside it was tucked into, making it nearly invisible from the road. But Argento could make out stone columns in front and floor-to-ceiling windows tinted too dark to see through. The expansive roof also featured a helipad with a copter on it. The chopper didn't look commercial. More military. Like a converted Apache without the chain gun and missiles.

This was where an injured Krebs had been driven. Like this place had a doctor on staff.

Argento wasn't going to get past the gate, so there wasn't much left to do there. He looked behind him. No one else was coming up the road. He looked back at the mansion. He saw movement on the roof, too quick to pinpoint the source, but enough to make him kneel behind the engine block of his truck for a moment, a familiar feeling running up his back, a kind of electric chill, the same one he'd felt in the moments just before he'd made entry on a high-risk search warrant when they had intel their target was armed. But all was quiet. Just the desert wind. Argento counted to a thousand. Then he got in his Ford and reversed back down the road without delay until there was room on the shoulder to turn around. Because what he thought he saw on the roof was a man with a rifle. And after two decades in law enforcement, where he'd seen .223 rounds pierce doors, walls, and his coworkers' ballistic vests like they were made of gauze, Argento respected the long gun.

So the wealthy introvert was bullish on security. Not a lot of people employed armed roof sentries. Heads of state. Drug lords. Maybe a paranoid rock star or two.

It was enough to make a fellow wonder what was going on behind those walls.

Argento stopped at the hardware store where Olson, the craggy proprietor, was about to close for the day. He wore a battered ball cap and still had the pencil behind his ear.

"You have second thoughts 'bout applying for my opening?"

"Not yet. Hey, if a place around here had a room that needed fresh carpeting, drywall, maybe new furniture, who would do that work?"

Olson pushed the ball cap up on his head and wiped his brow. "Probably me. I do side jobs."

"You do anything like that at the Baldwin?"

"Nope."

"If anyone else had, would you have heard about it?"

"Probably."

"You know who lives up the hill in that mansion?"

"Don't know who's there now. Used to be some Hollywood type."

"Would think it'd be the talk of the town, place like that."

"I mind my own business," Olson said. "You don't, though."

"Still looking for that missing family I showed you the flyer about."

Olson pulled his cap lower on his head and shrugged. "They're probably wherever my business partner in this shop went after he took all my money."

Argento had used up enough of Olson's time where he figured he better buy something. He settled on a pack of beef jerky. Hardware stores always had it. Then he thought about Olson's wayward ex-partner and bought two packs.

"Appreciate the business."

"Economy isn't what it used to be."

"Some of the stores in town are just hanging on. Except the diner. They were supposed to close last year but then they supposedly got a small business loan from the feds. They've been kinda close-lipped about it, but I heard the manager say something about how they don't have to pay it back. Hell, if the government is doing those kind of loans, I'm right over here."

"Uncle Sam giving out free money. You don't see that a lot."

"Damn straight," Olson said. "Say, what'd you do for work before you came here?"

"I was a cop in Detroit for a while."

Olson put his hand out and Argento took it. "Appreciate you," Olson said. It sounded sincere.

Back at the Baldwin, Argento filled Hudson's food and water bowls. As was his custom, Hudson waited until Argento wasn't looking at him before he noisily chowed down. The last of the gentlemen. Argento turned on the TV to a heavyweight bout. Both boxers were heavily tattooed and pudgy, their fleshy backs jiggling with every punch they took or threw. Argento changed the station but there was nothing on he wanted to see. Just dating shows and a channel devoted to videos of people falling off their skateboards and bikes to the laughter of a studio audience. Hudson stretched and yawned hugely, the noise high-pitched, almost cartoonish, and tapering off to a sigh. It made Argento laugh, which felt good but unnatural. He didn't find much to laugh at these days. A sergeant from Detroit PD's Behavioral Science Unit had addressed a police in-service on wellness once and told the class that the key to longevity and quality of life was relationships. Argento didn't have those anymore, except with Hudson. He'd been their dog, his and Emily's, and now Hudson was the only family he had left. One of the last cords that still tethered him to his wife.

Hud rose from his haunches and barked before the knock came.

The woman at his door looked Filipina, thirties, lean and fit with long dark hair. The same one he'd seen in the diner eating at the table with Silver Hair. She was wearing street clothes but held out a gold badge–ID combo that identified her as Marisol Sumaya, an agent with the U.S. Department of Homeland Security. He automatically looked down to her right side, where a slight vertical break in her shirt told him she was armed. Seeing him make that assessment, she in turn gave Argento plenty of time to look at the ID before she put it away.

Argento had worked with the feds before, mostly with the ATF on gun cases. But he'd seen a Homeland Security badge only once— when he was with DPD, he'd gotten up with a DHS task force after he'd stopped a driver who was on the terrorism watch list. He'd had no problems working with them besides the handful who took themselves too seriously. But he had no idea why this woman was at his door.

"I need to talk to you," Agent Sumaya said.

CHAPTER

9

They sat in a back table at the Bronze Dollar. The tabletops were Mexican tile and the chairs were made of rustic wood. Argento ordered coffee. Agent Sumaya had green tea.

"Let's save some time," Sumaya said. "You're Kurt Argento. You were a Detroit cop who pulled the governor of Missouri's daughter out of a prison riot. Now you're housesitting for a soldier in Braylo but say you're in Fenton looking for a missing family. I skip anything?"

"I should have registered with a different name at the Baldwin."

"The riot made some headlines. Not hard to research you. I know what happened in the bar with Krebs. You're plenty good at irritating people."

"I only do it with people who are already irritating."

Sumaya drank some tea. She looked too fresh-faced to be a veteran field agent. No scars. No forehead wrinkles. No world-weary affect. If she stayed in the mix, all of those things would come later. "So who do you work for?"

"No one," Argento said.

"You're in town alone?"

He nodded.

"What are your goals here?"

"My buddy I'm housesitting for, was thinking of recaulking his bathtub."

"No," Sumaya said. "I mean in Fenton."

"What's your interest?"

"To find out why you're here and what Redlinger told you when he had a few belts in him. Because I don't want you to screw up my operations."

"What operations are those?"

Sumaya narrowed her eyes. "How about you don't treat me like some rube who's going to leak a bunch of classified shit to a civilian I just met. Can you just answer my question?"

That seemed fair enough to Argento and he appreciated Sumaya's no-nonsense manner so he told her about Kristin Reed and her son, Ethan, and how they hadn't shown for the planned meeting at the Baldwin to talk about Warren Reed.

She nodded. "Saw them leave. Must have been that night. Woman seemed upset about something."

"How is it you remember them?"

"She was filling up at the gas station when I pulled in there. She was talking to herself and she wasn't being quiet about it. She seemed unstable. Plus the arm cast. It's the kind of thing that sticks out."

"Which way did they go?"

"Which way? I don't know. Away. Toward the intrastate. You try calling her?"

"Never got her number."

Sumaya weighed this bit of information. "Some investigator."

"Hadn't decided to investigate it yet." Argento had already polished off his coffee. He turned to look for the waitress, who was already at his side refilling it. She wasn't the shapely red-headed one but she held her own.

"You assigned out here, middle of nowhere?"

Sumaya made a noncommittal head movement.

"So where's your partner?"

Sumaya didn't answer.

"DHS sending field agents out solo? No backup?"

"I have backup. Plus the Fenton cops and I have an understanding."

"They're no cops," Argento said. "They're ex-soldiers in cop uniforms."

"Why do you say that?"

"The soldier part's obvious. It's in how they look, move, and talk. And I spent twenty-one years on the police, so the cop part is clear too. Take your man Krebs in the bar. He let himself be goaded. He's not used to civilians talking shit to him. Then after he punched me and hurt his hand, no one knew what to do with me. Was I a victim? A suspect? I don't think they even wrote a report. Cop gets his hand broken, someone's gotta file the workers' comp paperwork. That's just for starters. When I told them I'd leave town if anyone could name the Arizona criminal code for aggravated assault, no one even had a decent guess."

"Maybe they didn't want to take your bait."

"No. Cops are trained problem solvers. They thought I was a problem. If one of them knew the answer, they would have said it, just to see if it worked and I'd leave. But they didn't know."

"Do *you* know the Arizona penal code for aggravated assault?"

"No idea. But it's not my job to know."

"So what's your point?"

"Tomlinson claimed they were deputies, duly sworn. If that's even true, that'd mean some fast back-alley deal got cut for him and his guys. Like how you sometimes hear about a private citizen getting deputized in a small town so he can play cop just because he donates enough money to the local PD. But I'd bet Tomlinson and the rest aren't legitimately state-certified in law enforcement any more than Olson who runs the hardware store. They're more of a private security force. Like a large company or a university has. They got guns and fancy cars, but my guess is they have all the legal authority of a movie usher out here. So how do they enforce the laws?"

Sumaya opened her mouth to say something and then seemed to think better of it. She settled on "Fenton DPS . . . they're working with me. It's complicated."

"I bet it is. Who's up in the compound on the cliff?"

"Someone important in Hollywood used to own it."

"Someone important still does. It's got a helipad and I'm pretty sure I saw a guy on the roof with a rifle. And Tomlinson took Krebs there right after he broke his hand on my skull. Like the place has its own med clinic."

Sumaya looked at him steadily. She took in a deep breath and eased it out. "What do you think is up there?"

"I don't know," Argento said. "Maybe some Border Patrol or Homeland Security setup. Room with a big conference table, lots of guys walking around talking into headsets. A nice Keurig, because it's tax dollars."

Sumaya said nothing. Just drank her tea and looked at him over the rim of the cup.

"Saw you here the other night with a silver-haired guy."

Sumaya nodded.

"Who was that?"

"Not at liberty to say."

"Civilian? Fed?"

She shook her head. A *not at liberty to say* headshake. "Any other questions?"

Argento ran his fingers through his stubbly hair. "Yeah, plenty. But what's the point of asking them. You're not telling me anything."

"You saw my badge. You know who I work for."

"So this all has to do with securing the homeland."

"Wouldn't be here otherwise."

The waitress came by and asked Sumaya if she wanted more tea. She waved her off. When she left, Sumaya leaned in. "Okay, let me make a little speech. We're in a global war on terror. Against Radical Islam. It started with the Hezbollah's attack on the U.S. Marines in Beirut in '83. They want to kill us. All of us. So we're trying to generate actionable intelligence to prevent that. To save American lives."

She searched his face as if looking for a sign she should say more, but Argento never gave those off. She continued anyway.

"Listen to our leaders. They don't even call it terrorism anymore. They call it violent extremism. We've got professors talking about how 9/11 was a direct result of U.S. military policy in the Gulf. About how the jihadists are damn freedom fighters. You believe in any of that?"

"No," Argento said. "But what does that have to do with Fenton, Arizona? You got a sleeper cell in town? Who's running it? Our waitress?"

"Let's just say I'm here for the right reasons. You used to be a cop. I would hope that'd mean something to you. And you hanging out stirring things up can only complicate a long-term law enforcement investigation that has high stakes."

"Be hard to stir anything up. I haven't learned anything yet, other than you got toy deputies in town. And I think this meeting has just made me dumber. But I was a cop long enough to not always trust the official explanation."

"I'm a federal agent. Sworn to uphold the law and all that, just like you were. And I'm a mom myself. You think I'm going to let something happen to a mother and her kid?"

Argento didn't say anything. He swirled the grounds at the bottom of his coffee cup and looked at Sumaya. He was reassessing her status as a new agent. There was nothing fresh or welcoming about her. She was all hard angles and resolve. Like him.

"Still looking for Warren Reed. The husband." He showed her the flyer. "You see him leave too?"

"No. Don't think we crossed paths."

"His wife thinks something bad went down with him. The room he stayed in had to be patched up. Like there was a knockdown fight in it."

"Gotta say, I'm pretty on top of the murder scene in Fenton. We haven't had any lately."

"So where is he?"

"Don't know. Don't care. You were on the job. You know most missing folks are voluntarily missing, right? Running from something. Shitty relationship, disappointing life, debts, responsibilities. Whatever. She say anything about their marriage?"

"Said they were separated."

"Well, there you have it. Maybe she can't find him because he wants to stay separate."

What Sumaya said was true. There wasn't as much foul play out in the real world as there was on TV. Most missing people turned back up on their own schedule, if they wanted to be found. Warren Reed abandoning his wife and child was a dramatic turn of events but that didn't mean he was involved in a crime, either as victim or suspect. In all likelihood, he was less a missing person than he was a straight-up inconsiderate asshole.

Sumaya set her cup down and gestured to him with both hands open. "You came here because you were concerned about the woman and her boy. I respect it. But I'm telling you I saw them leave and they were fine. Now this is America. You can freely assemble. Stick around here as long as you'd like. But there's a decent chance you're gonna bring some trouble on yourself you're not going to be able to get out of. So now I'm asking you politely, cop to cop, to fuck off."

It was one of the more polite Fuck Offs Argento had received. He considered it.

"There's my pitch. Now what are you going to do?"

"I paid for my room for a week. I'll ride that out. Then I probably will fuck off. Not enough grass here for my dog to roll around in anyway."

She took that in. Nodded. "Much obliged."

Argento glanced out the window in time to see a Fenton Public Safety car cruise by. He couldn't tell who was driving it. The waitress came by and asked if they wanted anything else. Argento ordered a slice of blueberry pie for himself and a chicken apple sausage link for Hudson. He didn't give his dog a lot of people food but when he did, he made it count. When Argento had left with Sumaya to go to the diner, Hud had watched him from the hotel room window, his front paws propped on the sill. He'd return to the same position when he heard Argento return. It was nice to be able to count on some things.

"Why'd you leave the Detroit police department?"

"Supervisor trouble."

"That all you gonna say?"

Argento nodded.

"You were a street cop for a long time. Ever try for sergeant, become a supervisor yourself?"

A lieutenant who'd done most of his career in admin had once called Argento into his office and started rambling about how Argento's career was a plane trip that would make many stops and where did he want to see the flight land and Argento, who had never put much stock in rank or seniority and was annoyed by posturing, had interrupted him and said, "Get to the damn point." Which had quickly ended the meeting.

"I get too impatient around useless people," he said.

"You got family out this way?"

Argento shook his head. "Why do you ask? Trying to figure out if anyone is going to come looking for me if I go missing like the Reeds?"

Sumaya half smiled. "Well aren't you a cynical son of a bitch. Just making conversation. I get the sense you'd be a hard guy for someone to just disappear. By the way, this woman, was she going to pay you for trying to find her husband?"

"Money didn't come up."

"If money didn't come up, that means you weren't going to see any. So why were you going to do it?"

"I'm Lutheran." There was more to it, but Argento didn't feel like telling her about his post-Whitehall pledge near the Pacific when he'd vowed to try and fix things for people. Didn't tell her he also liked it when each day was different than the next. Last week he'd been in Braylo building a tool shed. Now he was in Fenton getting skull-punched in a bar and drinking night coffee with a federal agent. Good to mix it up a little. The waitress came with his pie. She'd added a scoop of vanilla ice cream, even though he hadn't asked for any. He approved mightily of her initiative. He took a forkful. The pie was in perfect proportion to the ice cream, which had just begun to melt.

It was delicious. Argento felt how Hudson was about to feel when Argento brought him the sausage link, a treat magically appearing in front of his wet nose.

"Heard this place was going to close until the feds subsidized it."

"Who told you that?"

"An old-timer who'd know."

"Sounds like you're trapped in small-town gossip."

Argento had another bite of pie. "Anything else for us to talk about?"

She shook her head.

He pointed to the pie. "Then I'm gonna eat this and not say anything for a while."

She waited for a moment. Argento worked at his pie. After a few minutes of silence, she said, "Okay," and walked out. She was leaving him the check but it was only eight dollars. He could swing that. The citizenry of Detroit had agreed to pay him a partial pension for the rest of his life in exchange for two decades of policing the worst neighborhoods in the history of neighbors.

When he got back to his hotel room, he rubbed Hudson's belly and started him with half the sausage link, which Hud demolished. Argento cracked the window, lit a cigarette, and relished the sensation of the smoke entering his lungs. He wasn't sure if his room was a smoking room, but he decided it didn't matter. One week of sporadic cigarette use wasn't going to discolor the freshly painted walls.

In the morning, he'd call DHS to see if they had an Agent Marisol Sumaya on their roster. Just because she said it didn't make it so. Law enforcement credentials weren't hard to fake, and if Fenton's Public Safety department wasn't a real police department, then maybe Sumaya wasn't a real federal agent. He hadn't gotten a strong sense that she was lying, but maybe she was a better liar than he was a detector of lies. One thing he did suspect was that the guy with silver hair she'd been with in the diner might be a thread worth pulling on. But to what end? If Sumaya was telling the truth about seeing Kristin and Ethan leave without incident, there wasn't much reason for him to stay in Fenton. He wasn't inclined to look for Warren Reed anymore without Kristin still around to ask him to. And although he was a curious person by nature and Fenton, with its pretend PD and hilltop fortress was a town of curiosities, life was short and he was okay with returning to Braylo, picking up a few more odd jobs, and waiting for Trapsi to come home. Plus he had enough cop residue in him to want to honor Sumaya's Fuck Off request unless he had a compelling reason not to.

He thought about these things as he smoked another cigarette and absently stroked Hudson's rust-colored head. He loved his dog, not just for being himself, but for how much Hud reminded him of Emily. They'd done everything together, the three of them. If they went for a walk, Hudson would be trotting beside them. If they drove somewhere in the car, Hudson would be holding court in back. And when she got sick, Hudson was by her side or at the foot of the bed; and when she died, Hudson stayed close to Argento and chewed up the furniture if he was away too long, not wanting to lose another member of his pack. Argento didn't know if dogs understood death, but he knew they understood absence. When Argento felt the tears come, he blinked them away. Hudson got closer to him then and put his chin on Argento's arm. Argento could feel his warm breath on his skin.

"You," Argento said to Hudson, "are a fine boy." He scratched Hudson's head and checked his mouth. A vet had told him that if a dog's gums got tacky, they were dehydrated. Argento had been giving Hudson plenty of water since arriving in Arizona but he worried about him in the desert climate.

He'd told Sumaya he'd paid for his room for a week and he was going to stick it out. He'd made up his mind about that.

And when Argento made up his mind, he didn't change it.

CHAPTER
10

What did you tell your tourist?"

"I said I was here on an anti-terrorism op. Said I'd seen the Reeds drive away."

"Did he accept that?"

"I think so."

Special Agent Marisol Sumaya was talking to the man with the silver hair in his inner chamber by his monitors. Her claim she was on an anti-terrorism mission was a discerning one. It was an easy cause to get behind and would make the tourist more inclined to leave. But even though she represented a notable increase in intellect from the Fenton soldiers, someone like Sumaya in his private sanctum was a drooling peasant in the king's court.

"I mixed in some truth. Had to. He's not stupid."

"If the best employment he could obtain was police officer," the man with the silver hair said, "he's stupid."

"He figured out how to survive a prison riot last July. And he's been asking the right questions. About the Reeds, you, Fenton DPS. He even knows the diner got propped up by our no-pay loan."

The diner loan. The man with the silver hair had ordered Sumaya to make it happen when Cassidy told him the Bronze Dollar was in danger of shuttering due to slow business. He wanted a place to eat outside his own compound, and he wanted Cassidy and her magnificent chest to be the one to serve him. But he didn't require any background on Kurt Argento. The database he had access to was more voluminous than the NSA's. It included Argento's driving record. Court transcripts from his officer-involved shootings. Names of distant relatives and old girlfriends. His grocery preferences, his medical records, the amount of money in his checking account, which currently stood at six hundred and eight dollars.

"He won a gold medal for valor on the job," Sumaya said.

"Medals aren't won. They're awarded. You'd know that if you ever received one."

Sumaya's face darkened. "Thought you'd be too busy working on the project to get sidetracked on the vital stats of some commoner."

"You pay me to multitask. And I told you nine months ago the mere administrative act of deputizing Fenton DPS wasn't enough; you should have sent them through at least an abbreviated police academy."

Sumaya raised a hand dismissively. "We had to frontload their fire training. Your lab isn't much use to us if it burns down. And your original projection of how long this project was going to take didn't leave us much time. But now here we are. And we're not on pace. My supervisor wants you to submit to peer review."

Peer review. Of course. They wanted what was in his brain. Then they could mine it and dispose of him. The man with the silver hair felt a hot spike of anger. "I don't have peers. If the tourist presents a problem, we have a solution. Just like—"

Sumaya cut him off. "We wouldn't even be here if you hadn't had your little college reunion. It's the modern era. If people vanish, others come looking for them. The longer we go, the more attention we draw. This isn't sustainable. We got lucky with Copeland, but luck isn't a strategy. We're on borrowed time."

Copeland. The sheriff of Fenton whom Sumaya had bought out to clear the way for Tomlinson and his men to serve as his protective detail. Copeland was an older man with a bad case of gout who hadn't asked many questions about his overly generous early retirement package. Money had that magical effect on people.

"I require a few weeks. A month at most."

"If you can't pull this off, you need to tell me. Now."

"You don't talk to me like that."

Sumaya cocked her head. "I'll talk to you any which way I want. I'm project head. You work for me."

"I am indispensable to the United States government. Think hard about whether you can say the same."

"I can shut this shit down with one phone call."

"You'd like me to rush through these final stages? What would your brother think of that?"

Sumaya took a moment before she spoke and when she did, her words came out low and flat. "Leave him out of this. Use your two hundred IQ and show me something from the lab."

The silver-haired man's IQ wasn't measurable. The only test that came close put it at two hundred and thirty six. Only his social intelligence was lacking. He sometimes walked away from conversations midsentence because they held no interest for him. But he could approximate human behavior when he wanted to. He imagined the weight of his intellect crushing Sumaya, like a steel girder dropping on an insect. He sat in his chair and swiveled toward his monitors, showing Sumaya that the meeting was over. She didn't immediately leave. He knew she wouldn't. She'd want to say something first to reestablish her authority. He started the countdown in his head. Five. Four. Three.

"Clock's ticking," Sumaya said to his back. Right on cue. "Do your damn job." She strode out, her angry little footsteps clicking on tile. Not a quiet walker like Chan and the rest of Fenton DPS. A blunderer.

He turned his attention to the half-eaten breakfast on his desk. Egg whites and tomatoes. He downed the rest, followed by his vitamins, as he ran up a summary of his own network security. It was an impregnable system he'd built to detect suspect bits of code and use algorithms that constantly updated themselves to counter new threats. Then he checked satellite images of Arizona. He pressed his keyboard to zoom in until he was looking directly over Fenton. They called this satellite God's Eye. He had grown up living above a fish market. He'd always hated that marine smell. It had clung to his clothing, his hair. He'd carried the odor to school to the delight of his tormenters there. Now he controlled satellites.

Do your job, Sumaya had said. How could she supervise him if she couldn't begin to understand what was involved in this project?

He got up from his chair and walked toward the lab. The connecting hallway was flanked by rooms packed with servers, over a hundred racks, each of which contained dozens of slim units that generated so much heat the floor required its own cooling system. They were capable of quadrillions of operations per second. But the machines were just instruments. They did the grunt work. He supplied the rest. A computer inside flesh.

He stopped in front of the lab's double doors and wrote CGGAT-TACACAT on the white wall with a permanent marker. A fragment of ten million reduced to twelve characters. It was one of the few times he'd allowed himself to store information outside his own head. If he wrote too much down, they could try to take it from him. Then they wouldn't need him. They could turn the project over to someone else. And he would not abide that. The equation he'd just drawn was only for these final stages, to help him visualize the denouement.

The man with the silver hair entered a twenty-character code on a keypad, accompanied by his handprint and retinal scan, both of which would only activate when they sensed live tissue, so no invader could sever his arm or gouge out an eye to break in. The double doors opened with a soft swoosh. He entered the lab where Project A and Project B waited for him. This feeling, of doing something no one else could, was a sensation he craved. Perhaps the only thing he truly craved.

Project A. Project B. He could release one before the other. But it would mean more if he released them both at once. He stood in the middle of the lab and closed his eyes. He was no student of scripture but knew *Creation Ex Nihilo* was a phrase theologians used to describe God's creative capacities. Something from nothing. "Let there be light."

And soon enough, there would be.

CHAPTER

11

Aaron Redlinger slouched in a beach chair by his backyard fire pit drinking from a longneck. There was no point in going back to Connor's. He was certain Tomlinson had told the bartender to either water down his drinks or quit serving him altogether.

The road from Fenton to his house was bumpy and unpaved, but he was used to it. Two thirds of the roads in the Valley they'd fought in, the ones he still had to patrol after his friends had died there, were unpaved. The heat was about the same too. Punishing. Sometimes purifying. Eastern Afghanistan only got nice in the late spring. Snow on the mountain crests. Not so damned hot during midday.

It was late afternoon and his shift had ended. It had felt good to strip off his sweaty body armor. But not half as good as shedding his gear when he'd been deployed. There, he'd worn seventy pounds of it, including an outer vest with front and back inserts thick enough to repel an AK-47 round. It was sufficient protection without sacrificing too much maneuverability, the fighting soldier's eternal balancing act.

Overseas, he'd been the sergeant on a fire team with Lt. Tomlinson as their leader and Krebs, Chan, and Cornejo among the men alongside him on the ground. They'd fought together for six deployments. Fighting insurgents block by block. Search-and-clear operations in the mountains. One hot meal every other day, two showers a week, plenty of informality, which was a welcome change from the years of precise movements and measurements required from basic training.

He didn't know McBride, Henik, Knox, or Belchert in the same way, as they'd been part of different units, but he'd served with them as private contractors and they meshed well. They had laid down rounds in the jungle and the desert, no black ops bullshit, but clean-enough conflicts where they could spot the hostiles.

Clean-enough conflicts until now.

When he closed his eyes, Redlinger often heard helicopter blades and the sounds of people screaming. Now he saw the woman and her boy. The way she'd looked at all of them when she knew. He was home now, but he'd just traded one nightmare for another. He fought back tears. He wasn't a crier. Not even when he was a kid and he'd fallen into a quarry and cracked his leg in two.

But they had all cried, at one time or another. Like Cornejo, after he watched his best friend and fellow soldier blown up by a roadside IED, an explosion so violent that Cornejo was essentially wearing him. Even Krebs, the most hard-bitten of them all, when he'd seen a wild dog tearing out the innards of a dead child, a dog that wouldn't stop growling until Krebs put round after round in its body.

Everyone had broken down. Except for the good lieutenant. Tomlinson never showed emotion. He was a hard slab, the least animated person Redlinger had ever known. When he spoke, it was always in the same slow timbre, and the most you'd get out of him was something approaching a faraway look.

When the Reed family had gone, he'd said, "Sometimes you have to hurt to help."

Redlinger knew Tomlinson had an MA in Intelligence Studies and certifications in Mission Planning and Analytic Tradecraft. He'd trained units in Iraq and the Philippines. Tomlinson had no family he spoke of. No hobbies. Like war was his entire personality. Maybe that should have brought Redlinger comfort. Tomlinson was a smart, experienced supervisor who treated his men well. If he was behind this mission, wouldn't it have to be righteous?

But it would be good to know what the hell the mission was.

Redlinger cracked another beer. He could just hear the sound of it opening over the low humming sound in both ears. Constant exposure to heavy weapons had left him with a persistent aural hallucination where he heard the distant sound of a phone ringing. A reminder of his chosen profession. He hadn't seen a doctor about the ringing since he'd returned home. He didn't trust doctors. Didn't trust anyone except his fellow soldiers. And now he didn't even know about them.

If he walked away, then what? He could get on with the cops. Not Fenton, but a real department. Phoenix or Tucson. But they'd polygraph him. He wouldn't make it through one of those. Not if they asked him the worst thing he'd ever done. After he answered that question, the machine would melt down to a blackened husk.

"You good, Aaron?"

His wife, Gail, appeared in the doorway, in a U of A T-shirt and jeans, her hair in a messy bun. He nodded and raised the beer. She didn't join him at the fire pit like she had in days past. She kept the girls, five-year-old Paige and three-year-old Kelsey, away from him too, when she knew he needed space. Paige and Kelsey, his little wide-eyed auburn-haired moppets, both of their faces constantly streaked with jam. But Gail knew something was wrong, something beyond the normal pains of adjusting from combat to civilian life. This was different and he couldn't hide it. Funny thing was, when they were deployed, they had to make tough calls, but they were all lawful. They had waited to come stateside to commit their atrocities.

And if his daughters ever found out? They thought he was a hero. Thought he helped people.

He had, once upon a time. He'd been a good soldier. Monitored projects to build roads and schools. Shown restraint when it was called for. During battle, he had killed his enemies and protected his country. They all had.

But now there was poison in his blood.

Of his fellow soldiers, he was closest to Chan, who'd once pulled him out of the basement of a shelled-out hospital on the verge of collapse when they were both wounded. Good old Chan. But the one time Redlinger had tried to speak with Chan about what their unit was doing in Fenton, the man had just slowly shook his head. "You just gotta trust the LT," Chan said. "We'll talk when it's over."

"Incoming," a voice behind him said. Redlinger turned. Krebs. He was with Tomlinson, Cornejo, Chan, and McBride. Krebs sported a cast on his right hand. Redlinger hadn't heard them approach. *Sloppy*, Redlinger thought. Didn't matter that he was in his own backyard; he had to be more dialed in.

Cornejo plopped down next to him and got a beer from the cooler. "Look at you. Alone by the fire, all man's search for meaning and shit. What's up, war fighter." Redlinger offered up his fist and Cornejo pounded it. The rest of the men pulled up lawn chairs, took a bottle each from the cooler, and sat in a circle.

"How's the arm?" Redlinger asked.

Krebs said, "Shit hurts."

Cornejo drew his sidearm and used the rear sights to hook open the cap of his beer bottle. "Krebs will get payback. He's just biding his time."

"Dude ain't nothing," Krebs said.

"He looks like the first one picked for sports, though," Chan offered.

Krebs said, "Wonder why he went right to you in that bar, Redlinger. Probably all that feminine energy you give off."

"Probably that," Redlinger said.

"What are we gonna do about him?" Chan asked, turning to Tomlinson.

"Nothing," Tomlinson said. "We brace him, it's just going to draw more attention to us. Sumaya talked to him. She thinks he'll get bored and leave."

"Fuck does she know," Krebs said.

"She controls the purse strings, man," Cornejo said. "She's getting us paid."

Krebs snorted. "We should be getting paid. Lots of folks getting put first before us. Fucking villagers cashing out from Uncle Sam for some mangy-ass dead cow we dropped a bomb near, some blown-up aunt who was probably ISIS in the first place. Now we come first. Getting that silly money. Fuckin' earned it."

Chan leaned back in his chair and took a long pull off his bottle. "What'd you think the military was going to be?"

"I don't know." Krebs shrugged. "They said we could shoot big guns and jump out of an airplane. I'm from Arkansas. Sounded pretty good."

"Be nice to know what the mission is," Redlinger said.

"They're paying a bunch of grunts bank. So whatever it is, it's important."

Tomlinson looked around the circle. "Remind me all what you're all buying when you get that paycheck."

Krebs laughed. "Cornejo is just hoping the money will offer him a legal path to citizenship."

Cornejo waved him off. "I grew up in Cleveland, homie. I'm more American than you."

Krebs eyed Cornejo. "Thought all Mexicans were short."

McBride said, "Chinamen supposed to be short too, but what about that fucking Yao guy played for the Rockets."

Krebs laughed. "So what you getting with your cut, Cleveland?"

"Charger," Cornejo said. "Mercedes. The fast shit."

"I'm buying new tits for the missus," Krebs said. "And a bunch of guns. Like, all the guns."

"House," Chan said. "Maybe two. Use one as an investment property."

"That's boring, bro," Krebs said. "You're killing this conversation."

"Shee-it," Cornejo said. "No wonder you want to buy houses. You can be your own roof Korean."

"For the twentieth time, Chan is Chinese, dumbshit."

"Gonna start my own gym," McBride said. "I make the rules. No pussies. No ugly chicks." McBride was a tall and wide half Samoan with a flat nose and cauliflower ears from high school wrestling. He had massive forearms, one of which was covered in what looked like cigarette burns. Redlinger had never asked about their origins, but he wouldn't have been surprised if McBride had done it to himself on a bet or a dare. McBride was like that.

They looked at Redlinger. Awaiting his answer to what he would do with the two million tax-free dollars that Agent Sumaya had promised him for services rendered at the end of this project.

"More beer," he said. "Like, all the beer."

McBride asked, "How about you, LT?"

"Put in a couple more years in uniform. Then open a bookstore. Sit in the corner reading with a cat on my lap. Like an old white lady."

They sat for a time and talked. About alcohol, first-person-shooter video games, women in summer dresses. They talked about how when they were on patrol in a village and the children made themselves scarce, the soldiers knew they were about to take fire. Cornejo claimed he couldn't be killed, and even at his own funeral, he was going to climb out of his casket and hit on the best-looking chick in church. The conversation, as always, was peppered with automatic insults delivered with unflinching honesty. No one was spared. Except Tomlinson. The capping didn't go up-rank that far. Redlinger actually thought their supervisor wouldn't mind, but he hadn't tested that theory.

Cornejo killed the rest of his beer. "I'm out. Love you girls."

"You okay to drive?" Chan asked.

Cornejo looked as thoughtful as he ever did. "As a member in good goddamn standing of the Fenton Public Safety Department, I give myself permission."

"More like Pubic Safety," Krebs said and belched.

"This is why I keep hanging with you guys," Chan said. "The quality of the conversations."

The rest of the group departed shortly thereafter. It was just Redlinger and Tomlinson.

So Redlinger said what he had to say. "What we did wasn't right."

Tomlinson waited awhile before he spoke. Giving the statement his full attention. "You've been here before with civilians. No time for hand-wringing. If a part of the mission goes bad, you move on to the next part."

Redlinger popped another beer. It was automatic. "Be nice to know what the mission is," he said again.

Besides Sumaya and the man with the silver hair, Tomlinson was the only one who knew what they were protecting. But he'd told them he signed an OpSec nondisclosure form, the specific terms of which Redlinger could only guess at. Tomlinson said he wasn't even allowed to dream about it. The lieutenant was a sphinx. If he wasn't supposed to tell, he wouldn't. You could train a blowtorch on him and he'd stay silent, just watching you with those tranquil eyes as his flaming skin sloughed off his body.

Tomlinson said, "We're making the world the way it needs to be."

"Says you, sir."

Tomlinson gave him a searching look, long enough that Redlinger turned away. "You want to go your own direction on this?"

Redlinger shook his head.

"Because that would be a mistake." Tomlinson said it the same way he said everything, entirely without affect. No edge to it. No threat. Just a hard truth simply told.

Lt. Tomlinson. There had been a notable exception to their unit acting within the rules of war. Years ago, they'd been taking heavy fire on base and had already sustained casualties when a group of locals who'd been paid to fight alongside them had cut and run. Tomlinson had shouted for them to stop and when they hadn't, he'd gotten on the .50 and shredded them to gristle. There were no survivors. No reports filed. Afterward, Tomlinson had an expression on his face that Redlinger couldn't quite place. Not of anger or even regret but…detachment, maybe. Like he was a neutral observer to his own actions. But he never said another word about it. Even though Redlinger had seen it with his own eyes, sometimes he wondered if it was just some hellish illusion.

Tomlinson rose. "Don't make me worry about you, Red. I got enough on my plate. Just know this thing is over soon." He drained the last of his bottle and held his hand out to Redlinger. "We good?"

Redlinger rose and took it. Nodded, because he couldn't make himself say the words. Tomlinson let himself out through the fence. Redlinger could see him set off on a slow jog down the street. Tomlinson ran everywhere. Didn't matter how hot it was or how much gear he was carrying. Redlinger heard he'd run the New York marathon in full uniform.

Redlinger stayed by the fire pit, finished his beer, and began another. He thought about what Tomlinson said. *Sometimes you have to hurt to help.* But what if in the process you did something so bad…

Redlinger held the cool bottle against his forehead and looked into the fire.

Something so bad there was no way to measure it.

When he looked up, Paige was in front of him. She wore a dress with airplanes on it.

"Our show is on, lazybones." She took his hand and tried to tug him off his chair.

Their show. What was it again? Doc McStuffins? The Backyardigans? He gave her hand a little squeeze. "Be right there, kiddo."

Paige turned and did a somersault before going back into the house.

Redlinger scratched an itch on the back of his head. His fingers came away with several strands of blond. His hair had been slowly falling out for the last several weeks. Stress, he figured. He put it out of his mind. It felt cheap to be worrying about his hair at a time like this.

He remembered snatches of the first speech his DI ever gave in boot camp. How a soldier is defined as one who possesses the highest in military virtue.

He took a deep drink from the beer.

"Never bring shame on yourself, your fellow soldiers, or your country," the DI had said.

He threw the bottle in the fire.

"Although you will endure awful things, your character shall be steadfast at all times. You will protect the weak and the innocent."

After a time, he went inside, retrieved his full military dress uniform, and threw it in the fire too.

CHAPTER
12

Argento had spent a week in Fenton. He'd eaten twenty-two diner breakfasts (the farmer's omelet was so good he'd ordered a second), mostly served to him by the red-haired waitress whose name, he'd learned, was Cassidy. During one meal, he'd asked her about Fenton DPS.

"They're fine, I suppose. But I preferred the ones before. These new guys ain't local. They're more like temps. They wouldn't even bother to learn my name if I didn't have the headlights." Cassidy jerked a thumb at her ample chest.

He'd also smoked a few dozen cigarettes and knocked out around twelve hundred push-ups. He'd walked the town from one end to the other, including every side street, taking Hudson with him, two walks a day for at least half an hour, sticking to the early morning and late afternoon so Hud's paws wouldn't get too hot on the pavement. Apart from the few buildings like Fenton DPS that were clearly new, Fenton had a low-slung, old-fashioned feel to it. Argento half expected to come across a bathhouse or a saloon where cowboys fired their guns into the floor for kicks. He'd talked to everyone there was to talk to.

He wasn't getting anywhere.

He'd learned there was in fact an Agent Marisol Sumaya with the

Department of Homeland Security. Argento had called DC to confirm it. They didn't make it easy. He got bounced around a few times before he got her desk line and left a message to call him back. She did twenty minutes later.

"Yes?"

"When we were at the diner, what did I order?"

"Coffee and blueberry pie. The waitress added ice cream. Plus a sausage link for the road."

"You at your desk?"

"There's this trick where you can have your landline calls forwarded to your cell."

"The agent of tomorrow, today," Argento said. "Never had to learn that one."

"When I had coffee with you, I got a sense of how you are with people. Pretty sure you didn't get a lot of phone calls. You believe I'm a federal agent now?"

"Sure."

"Are we done seeing a vast governmental conspiracy around every corner?"

"We think so."

"So when you leaving?"

"Soon," Argento said and hung up.

Over the last week, he'd spent most of his time observing the Fenton Public Safety Department, because they were far and away the most interesting thing about the place. He watched them from his hotel window, from across the street from their HQ, and while walking downtown with Hudson. There were nine of them, and of those nine, Argento had already encountered five. Redlinger the drinker. Krebs with the broken hand. Tomlinson, who seemed to be running things. Chan, the rooftop scanner. And Cornejo, the pull-up champ with the scar. The remaining four had name tags that said *McBride*, *Henik*, *Knox*, and *Belchert*.

They were in their late twenties to early thirties, with builds that featured more sinew than bulk, designed for running, climbing, and recon—all except for McBride, who probably went two-fifty in full gear and looked like he could secure an airstrip by himself. They wore earpieces so he couldn't hear their incoming radio comms, but their outgoing traffic lacked any kind of police codes, just plain speak, and they used the phonetic alphabet from the military (Alpha, Bravo, Tango) instead of from law enforcement (Adam, Boy, Tom). They chewed tobacco and guzzled energy drinks and smoked cigarettes. This was familiar to Argento. Cops did the same thing, in part because a fair number of cops were ex-soldiers. When the Fenton crew moved, they did so with precision, like professional athletes, keeping tactical gaps between them. When they were at rest, they stood in bladed stance, eyes roving. Chins up, hands never in their pockets. It was hard to sustain that kind of ready vigilance especially in what seemed like a sleepy desert town, but so far they were pulling it off. Argento knew plenty of guys coming back from war were damaged in some way, physically and mentally. Stress, depression, PTSD. They got edgy or flat when they tried to plug back into society. These guys seemed different. Seemed steady. Like they could balance hot cups of tea on their outstretched hands.

Their shifts weren't standard, with some working doubles with irregular days off. They were never on solo patrol, working either with a partner or as a whole unit. They avoided standing on the street corner, staying at least fifteen feet back, likely to minimize their exposure to IEDs and snipers, which Argento figured was an old wartime habit. When they talked to one another, it was half again the volume of normal conversation, no doubt the fallout from regular exposure to small arms fire and explosives with minimal ear protection. Argento had experienced some of the same difficulties working SWAT. The job got loud.

They had an easy camaraderie, Argento had observed, and it was clear they were all soldiers, possibly some from the same unit, and not ones with jobs in supply or recruiting. Argento didn't doubt they were the Special Forces Dell the bartender had claimed, but he still wasn't sure which branch of service. Seals, Green Berets, Rangers?

For one town to have a whole force of them was highly unusual. You'd also typically see civilians assigned to the station to do paperwork and answer phones. Fenton had none that he'd seen.

What was more, their uniforms looked new, as did their patrol vehicles. None of the brakes squealed. Argento's last assigned squad car had 150,000 miles on it and smelled like bad milk. But Fenton was a town that had fallen into money, although Argento didn't know where the tax base was coming from. Nine officers for a town with a population of a thousand tops was a favorable ratio for the good guys. Argento had read that the most policed city in the nation was Washington, DC, with something like six cops per thousand residents. And DC had murders in Anacostia to worry about plus national landmarks to secure. The most notable landmark in Fenton was a diner that served decent pie. The metrics seemed off, especially since Fenton Public Safety didn't have a lot to do. The height of civic disorder had been someone writing *Wash Me* on the dusty windshield of someone's car. Argento had gotten on a computer at the Fenton Public Library and tried to listen to their radio traffic with an online scanner, but their channel was encrypted. It was still easy to surmise there weren't many calls for police service in Fenton. No robberies or assaults. Not even a shoplifter. Over the last week, Argento had seen them respond to a lone fender bender and a report of a loose dog. But they didn't look complacent. They seemed to be gearing up for battle. There was no Fenton fire department to speak of, so it didn't surprise him when an engine showed up on an apparent call of smoke in a building and four Fenton DPS officers off-boarded in full turnout gear—they were cross-trained as firefighters.

Argento watched them without trying to hide it and they were watchful of him watching them. But they didn't seem to care, or if they did care, they had been told not to engage. Other than the dustup in the bar where Krebs had broken his hand on Argento's head, Argento hadn't had any further conflict with the town's security force.

Seeing the Fenton crew reminded him of being on SWAT, how they were always training, refining, constantly searching for positional improvement. Tapping the shoulder of the man you trailed as they were about to clear a hot zone. Not having to check to make sure the guy behind you was doing his job because you knew he was.

Argento missed it. He was surprised at how much.

There had been a lone exception to Fenton's uneventful status quo. Argento was sitting outside the diner drinking coffee one morning when a Honda minivan with tinted windows and Texas plates slowly rolled through downtown driven by a Hispanic male in his thirties and wearing sunglasses. Argento couldn't see if there was a passenger.

The response had been immediate. Two Fenton Public Safety cars did a traffic stop, parked at forty-five-degree angles blocking the street. One officer had gotten on the PA and ordered the driver to roll down his windows before he approached. It was Chan, who came up on the driver's side; McBride had the passenger approach, posting up by the rear doors to get a good visual inside while staying clear of cross fire. Argento was too far away to hear what was being said. Chan's body language didn't signify anything alarming, but he had his sidearm out and behind his leg, as did McBride. Argento could see a small head pop up from the back seat. The head turned to look at the lights of the patrol cars behind her. It was a girl of about eight.

Chan took the license and registration from the driver and went back to his car while McBride stayed put. About five minutes later Argento saw movement high up across the street. He kept his gaze trained that way. It was a Fenton cop on the roof. Cornejo. He'd taken an overwatch position with a sniper rifle pointed at the van. A Remington 700, the same model Detroit SWAT had favored. Light, reliable, shot a .308 Winchester hollow point boat tail to avoid overpenetration. Cornejo didn't have a spotter. At that distance, he wouldn't need one. Unless they had specific intel that this vehicle contained the Newton Boys, it was disproportionate firepower for a family minivan. When Chan returned to the van, his gun was holstered. He handed the driver his paperwork back and then pointed forward, as if giving directions. The Honda rolled on, heading out of town.

Argento looked back up. Cornejo had closed shop. But while his gaze was elevated, he noticed that on top of one of the light poles, there was an oval-shaped box with what looked like venting at the bottom plugged into a square base. He had seen a variation on it before in his hometown. A ShotSpotter, the device that detected the sounds of gunfire and then sent an alert to dispatchers and officers on their cells pinpointing its location. They worked well in Argento's experience. It could be hard to tell the difference between a firework and a gunshot, even for people who regularly heard both, but gunshots had flatter sounds and didn't echo as much, which the ShotSpotter picked up on.

Fenton, Arizona, population 1,000 with a ShotSpotter. From the looks of things, Argento figured the last time someone fired off a gun within town limits was to nail a backyard varmint.

Curious. Especially when coupled with Fenton DPS's aggressive response to the Honda. Argento had done traffic stops in inner-city Detroit with his gun at his side before, especially if he knew the driver was a gangbanger. But what intelligence could Fenton DPS have on this Honda minivan that would merit such a show of force on a traffic stop, especially with a rifleman on the roof to boot? He'd seen other vehicles with out-of-state plates come into Fenton without attracting that kind of reception. One was an Asian couple in a Prius with California plates, another was a Black family with three young kids driving a Subaru from Washington state. Neither stayed very long. Fenton wasn't a tourist destination and it wasn't that close to a highway. Argento was surprised it got any visitors at all.

But Argento's week at the Baldwin was up. He planned on leaving in the morning. Whatever the secret was in Fenton that necessitated an elite combat unit and gunfire detection systems, he didn't know how to crack it and he wasn't sure he'd know what to do with the information if he did. The Reeds were gone and he didn't know where to look for them or even if he needed to. Plus Sumaya had asked him to screw off seemingly in good faith, so he planned to.

But he'd grown fond of the diner, so he went there for his last night and brought Hudson with him. Cornejo and Belchert were on post outside. Through the windows, Argento could see the guy with silver hair at a back booth alone. Cassidy, the red-haired waitress, brought him his plate. Silver Hair seemed to perk up when she set it down in front of him, and he said something that elicited what Argento suspected was a strained laugh from her.

Belchert was a skinny guy with gaunt features and a thin beard. He looked French, Argento decided. Like he should be holding a baguette. He stood in front of the door as Argento approached.

"Private event?"

"You got it, Hobo Joe," Belchert said.

Argento hadn't shaved in a while. He looked down at what he was wearing. Ripped T-shirt and dusty jeans. Hobo Joe. Fair enough.

"You sure hang around us enough," Cornejo said. "You like us like that? You falling in love?"

"Sure," Argento said.

"Then you'll be happy to know Belchert puts out on the first date, long as you go halfsies on gas."

Argento gestured inside. "What's up with Silver Hair?"

"Don't worry your pretty little head about it," Belchert said.

"That his compound up on the cliff?"

Cornejo held up a hand. Gave Argento a hard look. "Why you here, hayseed?"

"You guys are exciting. I want to tag along and watch you, like one of those embedded journalists."

"Bet if he was a journalist, he'd ask you about your scar," Belchert said to Cornejo.

Cornejo ran a hand across the line that ran the length of his left cheek and then rapped it with his knuckles. "Titanium plate. Gave up part of my face for the cause."

"And what was the cause again?" Belchert asked.

"Fuck," Cornejo replied. "Still not sure." He eyed Argento. "Sumaya told you to fuck off. Now we're telling you to fuck off. How many times you gotta hear it?"

"Thought small towns were supposed to be friendly."

"Your dog is the only good thing about you, Hobo Joe," Belchert said. "He's a fine-looking hound. That's as friendly as you're gonna get here. Heard you were a cop. You were probably some admin bitch. We ain't what you used to. Our ranges are two-way."

Hud took that opportunity to squat and uncork a large dump by Belchert's boots. Argento and Hud were on the same frequency. "Attaway," Argento said and rubbed his dog's head. He was carrying disposal bags but he elected not to use them. Belchert and Cornejo wouldn't know the local ordinance for Failure to Pick Up Dog Defecation anyways. He walked away, pulling Hudson with him. He'd take him to the outskirts of town as a reward so he could throw Hudson a ball and Hud could hunt pocket gophers in their holes. He liked watching Hud in action when he was searching for prey. His slow, fluid movements, raising one leg stealthily up as he advanced and then plunging his nose into the dirt. He hadn't nabbed one yet, but he seemed happy just to be outside with Argento doing things together. But Hudson had slowed a bit over the years. When Emily was still alive, Hudson needed an expensive operation for a torn ligament. Argento had worked overtime to afford it every day for three months straight, blood money shifts that no one else would take, working security for dive bars and gangster rap concerts. He'd come home with bruises and welts but earned enough money to cover the surgery.

Best money he'd ever spent.

Argento had stopped seeing Redlinger at Connor's. But he knew where he lived. On one of his walks around Fenton, he'd seen Redlinger from a distance use a key to go in the front door of a small Spanish tile house, the yard made up of stones instead of grass. He walked there with Hudson and found him in back sitting alone at a fire pit. Argento knocked on the outside of the neck-high gate.

Redlinger turned, looked at him for a second, and then turned away. "Don't remember inviting you over."

"My dog came this way. I just tagged along."

"Dog can stay. Don't know about you."

Argento took that as enough of an invite to unlatch the gate and sit across from Redlinger at the fire pit. The Fenton cop didn't look at him but he reached out to rub Hudson's head. He was clear-eyed enough where Argento figured he'd just started drinking, but he could already smell it on him.

"Eighty-five percent," Redlinger said. "You know what that is?"

Argento shook his head.

"My unit's casualty rate."

"That's a mean number."

"Even the guys that made it are missing parts. Legs mostly. A few hands." Redlinger took a long pull off the beer. "But we get to pre-board commercial airplanes and shit, so it's all good."

Argento let some time pass before he said, "Not working today?"

"Called in sick." Redlinger looked at Argento for the first time. "Heard you were police somewhere. You got cop medals you wanna show me?"

"I can never remember where I put them."

Redlinger set his empty beer down and reached for another in a cooler by his feet. "We didn't do it right," he said apropos of nothing. "Take Afghanistan. We should have a fucking...Starbucks in the Korengal Valley. We tried. We dug wells. Got a school going..." His voice trailed off.

"What do I need to know about this town?"

Redlinger didn't answer. He stared straight ahead. Pressed the beer against his forehead as if seeking relief with the cool glass.

"What goes on in that compound?"

"Secrets," Redlinger said. "Gotta guard it twenty-four seven."

"So when do you sleep?"

Redlinger rubbed his jaw. "What's sleep?" He scratched the back of his head and came away with a few strands of hair. He flicked them into the fire.

"You guys all part of the same combat unit?"

"Some of us."

"What unit is that?"

A hint of a smile played out on Redlinger's face. "A Navy SEAL can kill you with a paper clip. Guys in my unit can kill that Navy SEAL with the little box the clip came in."

"Okay," Argento said. "So who's running things? Sumaya?"

"You ask too many questions. This ain't your town. You know, we got two cemeteries near Fenton. No hospitals. You go to the wrong school, take a wrong turn, you can buy the farm in this place."

Argento didn't know what Redlinger meant by the wrong school, but he let it be. "I'll drive safe. What can you tell me about the guy with the silver hair?"

Redlinger snorted. Drained his beer and got another. "Not supposed to talk about him."

Argento nodded. Then Redlinger gave an *I don't care* shrug. "Supposed to be a supergenius up there in his fort. And he wants you to know it. It's like he expects us to curtsey to him. He keeps going to that diner because I think the fucker gets lonely. One time his order was taking a while so he pointed at me and told me to make his breakfast. Egg whites and tomatoes. Like I was his butler. I wanted to piss on his plate."

"Sounds like an asshole."

"Afghanistan, man," Redlinger said, as if Argento had just asked about it. "It's all shot up. Trees got holes in them and shit. Fucking peasants worshipping rocks and streams. One day they overran our base. We ran out of ammo. I killed one guy with a rake."

Redlinger reached into the cooler for another drink but it was empty. He scooped up a handful of ice and ran it through his hands. "You wouldn't believe some of the shit I've seen." Redlinger rubbed his palms on his pants and looked skyward. "Wouldn't believe some of the shit I've done."

Argento remained quiet.

"It gets to you." Redlinger was starting to sway on his chair. "Gets in you." His eyes were wet. Hudson went over to him and put his face on Redlinger's knee because he knew when people were sad. Redlinger made a noise in the back of his throat and leaned in and put his cheek against Hudson's. "I see you pal. I see you."

"You getting redeployed anytime soon?"

Redlinger blinked. His face was empty. "We'll be in Fenton until it's over."

"Until what's over?"

Redlinger waved off the question.

"And what is it exactly you do here?"

Redlinger leaned in, as if he and Argento were conspiring together. Argento got a wave of the booze on his breath. "Protect and serve," he whispered. Then he got unsteadily to his feet, tossed the remaining ice water on the fire, and went back in the house. When he opened the door, Argento could hear the sound of a cartoon playing and children laughing.

He let himself and Hudson out the gate and got back in his truck. The conversation with Redlinger reminded Argento of a joke one of his SWAT buddies who was a veteran liked to tell. A soldier wins a prize of a week in Kabul. Second prize? Two weeks in Kabul.

As he drove, Argento sorted through what he'd learned from Redlinger. It wasn't much. But there was a saying that drunks and little children always told the truth, and Redlinger had indicated Silver Hair was in the mix somehow up in his "fort," which Argento took to mean the cliffside compound, and there was an unspecified but finite mission in Fenton that Redlinger had to see through. And he was clearly hurting about what he'd done overseas. And maybe what he still had to do.

Argento's plan to leave in the morning remained in play. But he wanted a last look at the compound. The front was inaccessible to him. He wasn't going to be able to scale the gates or bluff his way through. He needed to see the back.

It took a while to figure out the topography. The compound was nestled into a cliff face, and to access a rear entrance, he needed to park on a fire road and make his way carefully down a rocky slope, several hundred yards away, past sage and shale. He stopped where the ground leveled off. The rest was rough guesswork and looking for tire tracks, however faint. He did a slow walk of the perimeter. No tracks, but the ground was hard-packed, so they might not show. He saw nothing on the first pass. He did the slow walk again and spotted a wash of sand and rock where the soil looked wrong. Like it had recently been disturbed. He followed that wash to where it connected back up with the base of the cliff, which was concealed by a rolling mass of desert brush. He pushed past the foliage. There, in the rock, he could just make out what looked like the faint outline of double doors, tall and wide enough to let a moving truck through. There was no keypad or door handle for access, but Argento was certain he was looking at the secondary exit for the compound. The place had once belonged to someone in Hollywood, Sumaya had said. Maybe they'd had it built to sneak out the back with their groupies. Argento didn't know how much money something like that would have cost, all the digging and excavating. They could have piggybacked on an existing tunnel. But Hollywood types had stupid money and spent it on stupid things. Dinosaur skulls and lion skin rugs. Why not a rear spy tunnel. And with the Hollywood star gone, the current occupant of the compound, Silver Hair, now claimed the clandestine back way out.

Argento looked up to a whirring sound overhead. A drone was passing. Maybe it was attached to the compound, a remote sentry looking for people doing exactly what he was doing. Maybe it was some high school kid's. Regardless, it was time to go. He hiked back up the stone wash, double-timing it, his breath catching hard in his throat when he reached his truck.

When he got back to the Baldwin, Argento called Andekker. "That car Kristin Reed rented ever get returned?"

"Some people believe conversations should start out with some kind of pleasantry."

"Not us, though."

Argento heard typing. "It did. Two days ago. Phoenix airport."

"Airport have video?"

"I'm sure they do. And I'm sure the Phoenix Police Airport Bureau would be overjoyed to work with you on that."

"Wondering if it was Kristin Reed who actually returned it."

"Well it probably wasn't the kid. You making trouble for Fenton PD?"

"They're not an actual PD. Not even close."

"What's that supposed to mean?"

"No idea," Argento said and hung up.

Tomorrow he'd return to Braylo. There were probably more places he needed to go in Fenton and more questions to ask, mostly centering around Silver Hair. Who was he? What was he doing? But he didn't know how to get the answers. The townspeople didn't seem to know, Sumaya wasn't going to tell him more, and he figured he'd gotten all he could out of a tipsy Redlinger. He had planned on asking Ruth, but the last few times he'd been by the front, she'd been gone and the reception desk was unattended. He could ask Silver Hair himself, but Fenton DPS seemed keen on keeping him behind the velvet ropes.

He rubbed Hudson's head. "What do you think, pal?"

Hudson yawned and pawed Argento's hand.

As he turned in for the night, Argento decided that in the morning, he'd take one last stab at getting some answers in Fenton. And to accomplish that, he would follow a simple mantra.

When you're not sure what to do, start trouble.

CHAPTER

13

efore he checked out of the Baldwin, Argento rose early for the sunrise, a majestic mix of crimson and burned orange that made him understand why some people traveled to the desert and never left.

"You come back and see us," Ruth said. She was at the front desk looking tired, her shirt creased, like it had been forgotten in the dryer. Hard being the only employee of a business, even a small one.

"Think my business in Fenton is done for good. But thanks for putting me up."

"Well, at least send me a picture of Hudson once in a while."

"You got it." Ruth hung his room key on the wall and checked his name off in the ledger.

"The room I stayed in, the remodel looks nice. Who did the work?"

Ruth smiled with a hint of pride. "I did. Not my specialty, but I can't afford to hire out for maintenance. You may have noticed we ain't exactly busting at the seams with guests."

"Hope the tourists find you."

She waved at him. "Safe travels."

Argento walked Hudson to the town's lone grocery store and got a pack of cigarettes and a single avocado. He paused at the impulse aisle and saw a display case of energy drinks in brightly colored cans, including one called Forward Front that he'd seen the Fenton DPS drinking. He bought the flavor Mango Fire Chili, which had ingredients on the side of the can with names like arginine and capsaicin. Maybe it would give him the soldiers' powers. He took a pull off the drink on the way out the store and immediately spat it out. It tasted like someone had stirred pepper spray into a glass of Sunny Delight. He'd stick with coffee and beer.

Outside, Hudson took a whizz on the southwest corner of the grocery store. It was his favorite place to pee, and he'd deposited so much uric acid there in the last few weeks that Argento was surprised the foundation was still standing.

While Hudson chased a fly around, Argento thought about how he'd only ever seen the silver-haired guy in the diner, as if he had no business elsewhere in town. Which was ironic because whatever was happening in Fenton, Argento figured Silver Hair was at the center of it.

He picked a spot diagonal from the diner, a rocking chair on the front porch of the hardware store, and waited. He was unemployed. He had nothing but time. Silver Hair didn't show for breakfast, so Argento lingered, watching the shadows retreat as the sun moved over the street. After a while, Olson came out of the store and brought out a bottle of water for Argento and a bowl for Hudson.

"Thanks."

"Stay out here as long as you'd like. You got that no-nonsense look about you that'll scare off the riffraff."

"Is there any riffraff in this town?"

"Actually," Olson said with a grin, "it might just be you."

Argento raised his bottle in salute. By 11:30, he'd burned through his water and a half pack of smokes and was about to call it a day and begin the drive back to Braylo when two Fenton DPS cars came around the bend. Tomlinson and Krebs got out of the first one. Redlinger and Cornejo got out of the second, accompanied by Silver

Hair and Agent Sumaya. The latter two walked toward the front door of the diner while the four Fenton DPS officers watched the street.

Argento palmed the avocado and then tossed it in a high arc toward Silver Hair. It was dark green, almost black. Like the shape and color of a grenade. Which was why he'd bought it. Some internal voice he didn't always understand had told him to stir the pot one more time before he left. It was a voice he often listened to.

The DPS response was immediate. "Incoming!" someone shouted. Sumaya knocked Silver Hair to the ground and dropped on top of him, covering his upper body. Cornejo followed suit, jumping on Silver Hair's lower torso, his pistol out. Redlinger threw himself on the missile and drew in his arms and legs. Tomlinson and Krebs took cover behind the engine blocks of their cars, weapons up looking for targets. A protective phalanx with no wasted movement.

Nothing blew up. Redlinger tentatively looked at the squished fruit underneath him. "It's nothing," he called out. "Fucking produce."

Argento stayed on the porch, Hudson beside him, his hands where the soldiers could see him. He was the only one visible in the area where the avocado had been thrown from so even if they hadn't seen him toss it, he would be the primary suspect. Krebs picked up the avocado in his good hand. Flung it aside in disgust and strode toward Argento, pointing his gun at him center mass with his good hand.

"You think you can fuck with us?"

"Krebs," Tomlinson said.

Hudson barked, short, urgent.

"It's just trash," Argento said. "Was aiming for the garbage can by the diner door."

Argento had guns pointed at him before but that didn't mean he liked it. He gave a hard pull on Hudson's leash and wrapped it tight around his hand so he could keep his dog behind him. Hudson barked again. More urgently.

Krebs kept coming, a wild light in his eyes. "Shut that dog up."

"Krebs," Tomlinson said again, more steel in his voice.

Krebs pushed the gun out at Argento like he was punching the air with it, spittle frothing his mouth. "Shut that fucking dog up or I will."

"Ssshh," Argento told Hudson, ruffled his head, and rose from the chair and started walking away from Krebs. Slow but steady. His inner voice had led him astray; the grenade stunt had been a tactical mistake, and he'd put Hud in the middle of it. Now he had to get him away from danger. He was banking on Krebs not shooting him in the back in broad daylight in front of witnesses. Hudson rotated his ears at Krebs but his barks subsided. "Good boy." Twenty feet away from Krebs now. Thirty.

Then Hudson turned back in the direction of the soldier and exploded with a torrent of growls, in full guard dog mode. Defending his owner. Protecting the pack.

Krebs, still on the move, sighted in one-handed, and put two bullets through Hudson's head.

Argento's dog went down without a sound and didn't move.

Now Krebs stopped. He lowered the gun and sniffed. "Fucking told you," he said, but the edge had gone out of his voice.

Something red bloomed behind Argento's eyes and he went for Krebs. No concern that the man had a gun. No technique. Just a full-on sprint powered by fury. He got one hand on Krebs's throat before someone Tased him. His muscles seized and he hit the ground hard. Then they were on him. They got zip ties around his hands. He snapped them off. They Tased him again and he tore the prongs out of his flesh as he bellowed and reached again for Krebs. Then Tomlinson came into his line of sight with a glistening needle that found Argento's flesh. Tomlinson's face took on a shimmering quality from where Argento thrashed on the ground, as if the lieutenant was made of liquid. Then Argento went liquid himself and flowed away.

CHAPTER
14

He came to in the back of a caged Fenton DPS car bumping over rocky ground heading straight into the desert, a howl trapped in his throat. Tomlinson was driving. Cornejo was the front passenger. They'd shot him up with a sedative. He'd seen medics do it plenty of times in the field on patients in the midst of psychosis. Versed or Haldol or something like it. But whatever they'd used worked faster than any sedative he'd seen. Sedatives took at least five to fifteen minutes to kick in and even when they did, they only calmed you, they didn't knock you out. What they'd given him had a component of anesthesia, something strong enough to work through an intramuscular injection, because he for damn sure hadn't been holding still enough for anyone to isolate a vein.

He tried to move but he was cuffed and shackled with a mesh spit protector covering his face. He felt sluggish but relatively uninjured. Taser pain was temporary and no one had stomped on his head. Probably worried about how it would look to the Fenton townsfolk.

Cornejo glanced at him in the back seat. He was chewing gum and he made a point to snap it. "Nice trick with the avo but you going against us? You're practice squad, bro. You ain't ready for game speed."

Tomlinson met his eyes in the rearview. "Your dog, that wasn't planned. Krebs had a bad run-in with a Haji mutt once. He doesn't do well with animals."

Argento didn't reply. Hudson. He'd seen the impact of the bullets. There was no chance of survival. Argento was trying to keep his seismic rage at bay because it wasn't useful right now. He needed to put the mask on, the same mask he'd donned when he was arresting child molesters so he wouldn't throttle them, the one he'd worn when seeing the man in court who'd shot his partner in the lungs grin at him and grab his own crotch during sentencing. The mask walled the feelings off so he could function. He would let the anger out later, at the right time, white-hot and cleansing.

They drove in silence, still heading straight out into the desert, off the road now, past a sign that said *Severe Dust Area 40 Miles*, past nothing into more nothing.

"You were patrol, right?" Cornejo said. "You weren't any kind of detective. You should have left it alone. Fucking Nancy Drew shit." He swept his hand across the window toward the empty expanse around them. "What do you think? I'd calculate your odds of survival out here at about point zero-zero-five percent."

"Seems high," Tomlinson said.

"Only because he could stumble on a film crew doing a documentary on Gila monsters."

"There are still some places in this world," Tomlinson said, "where there isn't anything for miles. No people, no shelter, no water. My men and I, we know these kinds of places. We've fought there. This is where you are now. This desert saw one inch of rain last year. That's half of what Death Valley got."

When they came to a halt, Cornejo snapped his gum again.

Another DPS car pulled up next to them and Redlinger, Krebs, and Silver Hair got out, the latter busying himself with his phone. Krebs opened the back passenger door and pulled out Sumaya, who was in handcuffs. He held a Sig Sauer against her ribs as she blinked into the sun.

"See that?" Cornejo asked. Snap went the gum.

Argento nodded.

"Insurance. You try anything and no more Sumaya. You kick, spit, even look at us funny, and she gets one in her pretty head. I know you wouldn't want that. You law enforcement types like to stick together."

Cornejo came around and opened Argento's door. He unshackled him first and then took off the spit mask. He left the cuffs on.

"Search him again," Tomlinson said.

Cornejo did a thorough check of Argento. He might not have had much police training but he'd searched prisoners of war in the field.

"You can keep your wallet," Cornejo said. "We ain't thieves. And they'll need it to identify you." He turned to Tomlinson. "He's clean. But who the fuck doesn't have a cell phone."

"Hobo Joe, that's who." Argento heard the voice from behind him. He turned. It was Belchert. He was standing next to a third DPS car by McBride, Henik, Chan, and Knox. The crew, all assembled.

As if reading Argento's thoughts, Tomlinson said, "I bring everyone for something like this. We work as a team. And anyone who has second thoughts later, they can't say they weren't there, didn't know, would have stopped it." Tomlinson was looking at Argento when he spoke but Argento had the passing feeling Tomlinson might be primarily addressing Redlinger. "What we're doing to you here is necessary, Kurt, but that doesn't mean I'm happy about it. You've made some bad choices with us. But you're still an American. We all gotta own that." He spoke slowly and methodically, like this was a speech he was accustomed to giving.

Argento looked over at Sumaya. She didn't meet his gaze. Her hair was disheveled and she was breathing hard.

"We're the good guys," Tomlinson continued. "We don't murder people. But this desert is different. It's like outer space. Everything out here wants to end you. If they ever find your body, they'll think you were a hiker who got lost or some shaman type who wandered out here for enlightenment and underestimated his water supply."

"Leaving me out here and putting a bullet in my head, same

thing," Argento said. He hadn't spoken since they'd put him in the back of the patrol car, and his voice came out in a low rasp.

There was a distant look on Tomlinson's face when he said "There's a difference to me. Maybe a small one, but the small things, they matter."

"If it was up to me," Krebs said, "I'd cut your eyelids off, bury you to the neck, and let the ants have you. You're getting off easy."

Cornejo worked his gum and said, "Forecast is a hundred and sunny for the next five days. You probably had some survival training. I know what you're thinking. Water from a cactus, right? Problem is, you need a knife to slice them open and then you still gotta know which ones you can drink from 'cause some of them are poisonous. Bet you didn't go over much of that in Detroit."

Silver Hair hadn't said a word. He glanced up from his phone, looking both reserved and haughty. Argento got the impression he didn't feel anything so far was worth commenting on. But he was wrong about that, because Silver Hair stepped forward and spoke.

"You need at minimum a gallon of water a day to survive in these conditions and that's only if you shelter in the day and travel at night. You don't have that gallon or that shelter. So here's what you can expect. In these temperatures, you'll start with heat exhaustion and finish with heat stroke. It's essentially a temperature-driven heart attack. It can happen in half a day, even if you're young and fit. These men," the man said, gesturing toward the Fenton officers, "would likely last a full day. A Bedouin could go maybe two." He got closer to Argento and Cornejo reflexively tightened his grip on Argento's arm. Argento noted that although his hair was silver, the man's forehead and the skin around his eyes were unlined. He put him no older than thirty-five. His voice was a high, grating monotone. He wore a handkerchief around his throat that only partially hid an elongated neck.

"The heat cramps will start in your arms, legs, and stomach followed by a piercing headache and full-body exhaustion. You'll lose your short-term memory, begin making tactically unsound decisions, wandering off course if you even had a course to begin with. Finally, you'll stop sweating and feel like your skin is on fire as your body tries to suck water out of anywhere it can find it—blood, fat, tissue. You'll know you're about to die when you begin involuntarily shuddering. Like you're on a roller coaster rattling up that first hill. I understand it's excruciating."

Silver Hair said this entirely without affect. Like he was reading from a pamphlet. Then he turned and walked back to the car. Argento saw something green stuck to the bottom of one of his shoes. It looked like a leaf. He would think about that later. Not a lot of green foliage in a desert town.

"Fucking cold-blooded," Cornejo said approvingly of Silver Hair's speech. He turned to Argento. "Any last words?"

"Yeah," Argento said. "I'm coming back to Fenton to kill you all." There was no bravado to it. Just a plain statement made in front of witnesses who deserved to know.

"Negative," Tomlinson said. "You're going to die bad in this desert. But if you knew what we were doing here, you'd not only stop fighting us, you'd join us."

"Look at him, though," Cornejo said. "All badass. He thinks he's gonna make it. Thinks he'll be his own hero."

Redlinger, who hadn't said a word since they'd arrived, took him by the arm. "I'll walk him out."

Argento went without a struggle. He had no other option. Krebs hadn't been wrong when he'd talked about the bond between law enforcement and any move Argento made would sacrifice Sumaya.

"Remember," Krebs called after them. Argento turned. The soldier still had the gun in his nonbroken hand pressed high and tight against Sumaya, a smile playing on his lips. "Tears waste water. So don't cry."

When Redlinger and Argento were a good fifty yards away, Redlinger spoke without looking at him. "They don't know I'm telling you this, but there's a rock formation that looks like a mushroom dead ahead the same way we're walking toward that break in the mountains. It's about twenty-five miles away. Follow the riverbed. If you can make it, there's water and supplies at the base. Don't ever come back to Fenton. Don't tell anyone about it. They'll kill us both."

Redlinger pulled a button off his uniform shirt and covertly handed it to Argento.

"Suck on this. It'll keep the saliva circulating. Buy you some time."

Redlinger took Argento's handcuffs off. Then he strode back briskly to the group. Argento saw Tomlinson uncuffing Sumaya and Krebs give her the gun he'd been training on her. She slid it in her holster. The hostage bit had been a lie just to get him into the desert without a fight. She looked up at Argento. Seemed like she was about to say something but didn't. Instead she just shook her head, like she was disappointed in him. Or herself. Or both.

Krebs waved at him and grinned.

They all got back in the DPS cars and drove off in a plume of dust, leaving him alone in the endless desert.

CHAPTER
15

The sun was out full force with azure sky stretching over the horizon. Argento had read somewhere that pilots called this weather "severe clear" but in his current circumstances, it might as well be called Fuck You. The calendar said early fall but it was summer heat beating down.

They could have stripped him, but they didn't want this to look like he was anything other than the stupidest hiker on earth. So he had his clothes, a T-shirt and jeans, and his shoes. His wallet, containing $300 in cash. They'd even left him his watch and sunglasses. Plus a shirt button to suck on. An embarrassment of riches.

Argento popped the button in his mouth and did another self-assessment now that he was upright and freed from the confines of the patrol car. He'd been worked over on the city street after Krebs killed his dog, but it was mostly the Taser's doing. He didn't feel seriously injured. No broken bones. No uncontrolled bleeding.

Now that the men were gone, he let the mask fall away as he thought of Hudson, his rage mixed with numbness. This was what life was. If you found something and you loved it, loved it so hard it hurt, it would only be taken from you. What would they do with Hud's body? Would they bury him? Argento was standing still but felt like he was in free fall. He knelt and picked up a jagged stone from the rocky ground and squeezed it in his palm as a low sound escaped his throat. He closed his eyes as the rock bit into his skin, trying to make his physical pain overwhelm the mental. When he went back to Fenton, he'd find Krebs.

Krebs would go ugly.

Argento opened his eyes. Snapped back to the present. His priorities were shelter and water, and with a mean sun over him, he'd need them soon.

Secondary concerns were animals. Rattlers, copperheads. Probably scorpions. He'd heard the small, translucent ones were the worst. Any carrion birds or coyotes wouldn't bother gnawing on him until he was already dead. Then there was the certainty of sunburn. His hair was short, but not so short that the top of his head would be scorched. He had olive skin from his father's Italian side of the family; that would help, but his face, the back of his neck, and his arms were going to toast. He squatted and rubbed dust and sand on his exposed skin to provide some nominal protection against the sun. It was going to be bad, but he didn't see it getting much past a shallow second-degree burn. If the burn progressed to deep second or third, hyperthermia would already have claimed him.

He'd need food at some point, but he could go a long stretch without it. Even if he had something to eat, digesting required a significant amount of water, which was hydration he couldn't spare. When he crawled out of this desert, he'd find a pancake restaurant and make up for lost time.

The main question, move or stay put, was easy. He needed shelter and there was nothing close by and he wasn't carrying anything to make a shelter with. Plus, if Redlinger was to be believed, there was a cache of water and supplies twenty-five miles ahead. Almost the distance of a marathon. If Argento could keep up a twenty-minute mile pace, he'd be there in a little over eight hours. He checked his watch. Eleven a.m. Sunset would be around 6:30, then an hour or so of twilight. He could make it before dark, if he pushed hard enough.

He walked straight in the direction Redlinger had indicated. Follow the riverbed, the man had said. Toward the break in the mountains. He could see the outlines of a current spread out along-side him. Usually, following it downstream led to civilization, but this one looked as if it had been dry for decades. Argento had to strain at times to see its contours, as the horizon was blurred by the sun's haze. There were rocks in that direction, but he couldn't tell if the mushroom-shaped formation Redlinger spoke of was among them. The landscape was all burned stone and red dirt, dotted by cacti. He didn't know if they were the drinking kind. He wasn't going to stop and find out. He figured any such efforts would get him far more dehydrated than replenished by any meager fluid he could squeeze out of one, especially without a cutting tool. He'd downed the bottle of water Olson had given him on the hardware store porch before Fenton DPS took him, which was a point in his favor.

Argento thought about Sumaya. He guessed she'd told him just enough truth in the diner to be credible. She was a good liar. Problem was, he didn't know exactly what she had lied about. Whatever it was revolved around Silver Hair, whom Fenton DPS was working so hard to protect. Their default response when Argento had tossed the faux grenade—throwing their bodies over his when they thought an explosion was imminent—wasn't a spur-of-the-moment reaction. It was something they'd specifically trained on. A presidential level of protection.

Argento mopped his brow with the back of his hand as he walked, using cacti and swaths of scrub brush as a frame of reference to help him maintain a straight path when the contours of the riverbed blurred into the landscape. Cornejo had been right; he didn't have much experience with the desert, but he was a hunter and a camper. He'd been on extended hikes with limited provisions and nowhere to reup on supplies. He was used to wilderness medicine, where the closest hospital could be hours away. But he had no idea if a twenty-five-mile hike under these conditions was possible. He knew a large part of survival was keeping a positive attitude. Not that this had helped his wife when esophageal cancer took her. Immune systems only fight off foreign invaders. Cancer cells aren't foreign. They're your own cells. He and Emily had learned that the hardest way possible.

Argento had been out in the sun around an hour. The button Redlinger had given him seemed to help but he already felt a deep thirst and the beginnings of a headache. The sun directly overhead was enough of a problem, but the ground temperatures would be worse. Argento figured the sand was 130 degrees and the rock would get close to 160 by midafternoon. If he keeled over on it, he'd need a skin graft. There were few signs of life. Just the faint sounds of some birds he couldn't see and the flash of the occasional gecko and the crunching underfoot as he walked over rocks and sand. He considered making an SOS out of rocks with an arrow pointing in the direction he was heading, but then considered the fluids he'd burn completing the task. Plus who would that SOS be for? No one was looking for him, and the odds of someone in a helicopter or private plane passing overhead and happening to look down at a random patch of desert to see the sign seemed remote.

He ran through some of his favorite Detroit athletes to pass the time. The Lions' Barry Sanders making his defender's legs wobbly. The Tigers' Cecil Fielder hammering the ball to deep center. Steve Yzerman, captain of the Red Wings, cutting and gliding to another hat trick. But Piston power forward Rick Mahorn was maybe his favorite. Not the biggest, not the fastest, couldn't even jump that high, but got by on strength, grit, and guile. When Argento heard Detroit had lost Mahorn to the expansion draft, he'd chucked a full beer at his living room wall.

He checked his watch. He'd been walking for two hours. Still few signs of life. No ATVs. No hiking expeditions. No food wrappers or discarded water bottles. The deep desert thinned out the tourists. He was in trouble, but people had beaten longer odds. Faith helped folks survive horrific situations. Argento believed in God's providence, but God had helped him plenty by getting him out of Whitehall alive, so Argento figured he might be on his own for this one. He ran his tongue inside his cheeks and readjusted his sunglasses. Without them, he figured his retinas would outright burn. He kept his gaze straight ahead at the rocks in the distance. It was hard to tell how far away they were. The desert probably played tricks on you, the lack of sufficient reference points making everything look closer than it was.

It was now midafternoon, but the temperature had only dipped slightly and his thirst had doubled. He sucked on the button and tried to think of what else was in his favor. The sun would go down. It always did. Then it would become a question of how far he could travel at night without veering off course from the riverbed and wandering in circles. For now, he kept on in the pressing heat. It hurt, but he knew discomfort. He was used to rivalries with other cops on SWAT about pain tolerance. One had taken a fistful of his own chest hair and ripped it out. Another held a lit cigarette lighter up to his palm until the flesh bubbled. Argento had won by pulling off the entire thumbnail of his nonshooting hand before a sergeant found out, called them numbskulls, and put a stop to it.

He moved ahead. The air felt heavy, like an extra layer soldered on his skin. He cycled through more Detroit sports favorites. Long-limbed John Salley and coltish Dennis Rodman from the Bad Boys. Catcher Lance Parrish, hard bat and even better arm, who used to be a bodyguard for Tina Turner, a fact Argento had learned on the back of Parrish's Topps baseball card. The 220-pound Joe Kocur, second on the Wings' all-time penalty list with nearly two thousand minutes in the box, who once cracked fellow tough guy Donald Brashear's helmet in a brawl and left him so sore he couldn't eat for days.

Argento was already bone-tired and dehydrated, his skull pounding with a savage headache. Even though he was wearing shoes, the bottoms of his feet felt swollen. He licked his lips and realized the button had fallen out of his mouth. He hadn't remembered that happening. He shifted to Detroit boxers. Joe Louis led the way, no question. Then middleweight Thomas "Hitman" Hearns and his '81 *Sports Illustrated* cover ("Better Pray, Sugar Ray"). The title holders and Olympic medalists—Breland, Biggs, Whitaker—who trained at the legendary Kronk gym before it fell into disrepair and the scrappers stole everything from the copper piping to the doorknobs. Detroit was not always kind even to its own sacred places.

Argento had lost track of time. He checked his watch. He'd been walking for hours. A blur of movement on the ground ahead redirected his focus, but it was over as quickly as it began. He couldn't tell what it was. Some kind of desert life. He thought about rattlesnakes. Couldn't remember if they always rattled just before striking or if that was just in the movies. He wasn't sure he'd mind a rattlesnake bite now. At least the venom would be additional fluid in his body. Whatever hydration he'd started the day with had already leached out. The ground around him was burned. His skin was burned. His lungs felt burned. He thought he'd experienced thirst before, at the end of a long run or after an intense training bout in the police mat room, but he now realized that had been nothing. This was true thirst, and with every step he took, he kept uncovering new dimensions to it. His situation was grim and getting worse by the minute. He thought of Krebs shooting his dog and then flashing him a game-show-host grin before he was marooned in the desert. He wanted to see that grin again. And then he wanted to pull it off Krebs and see how much of his face came with it.

Argento checked his arms. The skin was already red and forming blisters. His face and neck would be the same. He was officially on his way to second-degree burns. He kept walking. Everything around him looked dead or dying, the only nonearth color the green saguaro cacti rising some forty feet off the soil. He could feel the sun penetrating him from head to toe. People were not meant to live here. Early settlers would have steered around these lands. There was no relief from the heat. No cooling breeze. No water to drink, no trees to block the sun. Only the driving bright and a blanketing silence. He could look for which way the birds flew, because they were always in reach of water, but he didn't see any. He stopped to rub more dirt on his skin to ward off the sun, and the pause felt so good, so natural, that when he began walking again, his whole body groaned in protest.

His thoughts turned to his family. His father had been on the job for decades, a tough cut of meat who worked patrol his entire career. He was a remote man, prone to brooding, but the two of them had done things together. Fished, hunted, went to ball games in the city. His father had taught him how to shoot, drive, and fight before the police academy had even gotten its hooks into him. He'd had a stormy marriage with Argento's mother, who'd been ten years his senior, but she'd more than held her own. His mother was a history teacher and a classical musician and sometimes he'd see her sitting by the window, her fingers moving up and down as if still gliding over piano keys. She always looked so much younger than she was. Both were gone now, his father taken by a stroke, his mother by heart disease. He had an estranged sister he hadn't spoken to in years. And his wife, Emily. His Emily.

Twilight slid in but the relief from the heat was nominal. He walked. There was nothing else to do. The rock range was still straight ahead but he couldn't see the mushroom-shaped formation Redlinger had talked about or the riverbed, if he was still following it. It seemed nearly indistinguishable from its surroundings. Had he already wandered off course? He felt like his brain had been bleached out by the sun.

The light was fast fading when he saw something off to his left, maybe a hundred yards away. A spot of unusually bright red among the dull earth tones. He stopped. Then walked in that direction. It was a crimson shirt tied around the arm of a cactus. As he approached, he became increasingly aware that he was looking at something that shouldn't have been there. Not just the clothing, but what was underneath it. An unnatural lump on the ground. He drew closer, conscious of the way his feet sounded on the rocky terrain, until he found himself standing over the remains of a woman. And underneath her, the body of a boy. They were huddled next to a dying bush, as if its sparse branches could offer them any protection from the sun.

He remembered how the woman had looked so tired but resolute when she'd asked him for help.

He remembered how the boy's little fingers had curled around his on the front porch.

Argento had found the Reeds.

CHAPTER

16

Kristin's body was fully sheltering Ethan's. All Argento could see of the boy were the bottoms of his feet, blackened and dry. With what he guessed was over a week in the desert climate, Kristin Reed hadn't decomposed the way corpses usually do. There was no bloating or green discoloration, no skin slippage. She wore a T-shirt and shorts and the skin that showed was rigid and dark. Like a mummified husk. Insects and animals had made small divots in her face. Her head was positioned to the side, her features preserved in a grimace.

Argento turned her over gently so he could see Ethan. There were no obvious signs of weapon trauma to either body. He looked at the boy's face. He wanted to remember this, take a mental snapshot, use it as fuel for what came next. Then he turned Kristin back over, sat next to her and said a silent prayer. He tried to imagine their final hours. Kristin having to carry him, because no child could walk that far, and the extra weight weakening her further. Seeing him in agony. Knowing she couldn't stop it. Tying her brightly colored shirt around the cactus in the vain hopes of signaling anyone passing by in this wasteland.

The odds of coming across them in this desert had to be astronomically small, unless they had the same drop-off point he had and thought to follow the riverbed as well. Had Redlinger also told them there was water and supplies in this direction?

Argento must have been sitting by their bodies for longer than he'd thought because darkness had closed in. He looked up at the sliver of moon. Without sufficient illumination, he was sure to wander off course or stumble and hit his head on a rock, sealing his fate. If he remained here, he could rise at dawn, where the heat would be tolerable, and push forward. And remaining here would allow him to watch over the Reeds' bodies for the night. To bear witness. He felt he owed them that.

His headache still hammered away and he felt spent and nauseous, but his fatigue trumped all. He made a small arrow of stones pointing in the direction he needed to walk in case he got disoriented in the morning. The temperature had dropped significantly, a welcome coolness. He'd remembered a documentary he'd watched on the Sahara that said sand deserts could get below freezing because sand couldn't retain heat, but there was enough rock around him to hold in the day's residual warmth. He wasn't going to freeze to death. It was a small victory, but he'd take it. He fell asleep on the desert floor next to the dead Reeds.

He woke to an all-encompassing thirst and a striking sunrise. He ran a hand lightly over his face and neck. He had more blisters, and bigger than the day before, like they were engorging on themselves. He had to stand up in stages, fighting through dizziness and cramping. He was glad he'd made the stone arrow, because he was currently facing in the opposite direction and without a marker, he would have walked right back the way he'd come, away from Redlinger's water and provisions.

If there were water and provisions. That struck Argento as an increasingly big if.

The riverbed looked no more defined than it had yesterday and the rocks in the distance looked no closer. He shuffled toward them, working through his body's stiffness from sleeping on the hard ground. If the night air had been moist enough, he could look for dew on the surface of flowers and leaves. He didn't have anything to sponge it up with, but Argento figured he could just lick the droplets straight off their surface.

But there was nothing. Not a trace of moisture to be found on any desert foliage. Argento then remembered talking with Trapsi about the Arizona climate before his friend went on military leave, and Trapsi had said the rainy season ended in September. That was now.

His legs were balking at even a slow pace because the cramping hadn't gone anywhere. His clothes felt heavy. Even his watch felt like dead weight on his wrist. But there was no resting. If he stopped now and sat down, he knew he wouldn't get up. He wouldn't make it to another sundown, not without water. He had to stay on his feet or die.

He thought about the job. It had only been a year since he'd left. He'd been good at it. Won a medal once for carrying his gutshot partner a hundred yards to safety twisting through the cross fire of a gang shoot-out between the Seven Mile Bloods and the Cash Money Boyz. The captain who'd read out the description at the medal ceremony was some pretend cop from Personnel who'd butchered his name (Ar-GINT-Oh). You were supposed to get dressed up for medal presentations, but Argento had forgotten his suit so he'd gone to the random drawer at his station that was full of thrift store sport coats that cops could throw on for court and picked out one of the offerings, a gaudy velvet smoking jacket that was so notorious among the rank-and-file it was known as The Puma. Emily had come to the ceremony, and he thought she'd be mad at his outfit because he looked like a carnival barker, but instead she'd laughed and snapped a picture and told him how proud he'd made her.

He'd worked SWAT for a decent chunk of his career. The banner up at SWAT HQ said *Be Stronger Than Your Strongest Excuse.* He'd always liked that. The command staff had them put up a fancy *Ten Fundamentals of Policing* plaque with the usual offerings of Integrity and Community, and underneath someone from SWAT had written in Sharpie "Fundamental #11: Don't Be a Fucking Sally." He'd liked that too. While on a SWAT op, he'd once tossed a flash-bang into a run-down row house and the barricaded double murder suspect didn't come out but the rats did, tumbling over each other in their bid to escape. When they'd torn the door off its hinges and made entry, the suspect was naked and sitting in a lawn chair in his own kitchen looking defeated while holding a Löwenbräu, Argento's favorite beer.

Was that how it went? He might have been mixing that up with another day. Maybe there were two suspects. No beer. Cockroaches instead of rats. Argento's brain felt cloudy. He tried not to fixate on how good a drink would taste. He looked down at his arms. They had turned from red to dark crimson and were now lined with blisters, some of them two to three inches in diameter, hot and painful to touch. A few had popped and drained, leaving the skin underneath a glistening pink. He looked back up. Kept his gaze fixed on the rocks ahead. Was there a mushroom-shape in the distance? He thought so, but he couldn't tell if his mind was just showing him what he wanted to see. There was nothing to either side of him. Nothing behind him. Only the heat and the deep silence. He didn't know how far he'd walked. Maybe it had already been the twenty-five miles Redlinger had said separated him from the supplies. It felt like twice that. The pastor at Trinity Lutheran had once preached about the dangers the Israelites faced when making their long trek in the desert, through drought and darkness. If you went down with a sprained ankle under those conditions, your fate was sealed.

But for now, the mission was simple. One step in front of the other through the unyielding sameness until he reached the rock cluster. He squinted in the distance and something twisted in his gut. No. The cluster wasn't ahead of him anymore. Argento stopped in his tracks. Slowly turned. No rocks behind him. Just shimmering heat and brush. He knew he had to be hallucinating. A rock shelf couldn't disappear, and he couldn't have wandered that far off course. He shook his head to clear the visions, squeezed his eyes shut, and opened them again. The rock cluster had reemerged in front of him. Desert sorcery. At this rate, the next thing he saw was going to be a swimming pool under a palm tree. His stomach unclenched and he kept moving. The rocks still seemed impossibly far away. Maybe it didn't matter if Redlinger was telling the truth about the supplies. He wasn't going to make it that far. It was a blessing Hudson wasn't with him now. He couldn't stand to see him suffer in this broil. Hudson would have stayed with him until the end, even as his breath grew ragged and his paws baked on the ground. Hudson had a good life. His end had been quick. Argento tried to be thankful for that.

He checked his watch and found it was no longer on his wrist. He didn't remember taking it off. He began counting his steps. He got to a hundred and lost track. He tried again, got to seventy-nine, couldn't remember what number came next. What had Silver Hair said about heat stroke? How you'd stop sweating and feel like your skin was on fire? He was right about that. Smart guy. Too bad he was going to have to kill him.

Argento had suffered physical trauma in his life, both on the job and at Whitehall. He understood the difference between pain and agony. But he now also understood the difference between being thirsty and dying of thirst. Every breath he took entered his body through cracked lips down a bone-dry throat. He took his sunglasses off and dropped them. They were too heavy and were making him see things that weren't there. The only illusion he wanted to see was Emily. He had faith but not certainty and he didn't know if he would be with her again when he died. He hoped he would. But hoping didn't make it so.

The minutes bled by. He stumbled and caught himself. He knew he was locked in a death march. He took full steps for as long as he could and then he was down to half steps, but if he took two halves, that made a whole. It was a good sign he could do that math. His mind was still working. But when he slowed to a third of a step, he couldn't conjure how many thirds made a whole. He gritted his teeth and took a full step. A third step. A half step. Then a step backward. Backward, like he was desert drunk. He would have laughed but his throat was too parched. His skin felt like it was sizzling. He wanted to tear it off. He wasn't going to make it. Wasn't going to avenge anyone. In a hundred years, they'd find his skeleton in the desert and someone would wonder out loud what this asshole was doing in the middle of Hades.

No.

He wasn't going to die out here.

Not without squaring what they did to Hudson.

To him.

To the Reeds.

The reemergence of rage bought him a few more steps. He heard a sound, close. He stopped, thinking it was some sign of life nearby, but the sound came from him, from the rolling shudder working its way up his body from feet to neck. He wanted to keep walking but he was having trouble figuring out how his legs worked. They buckled and he went down. He clutched the crusted earth to steady himself, jerking his hands away just as quickly as the superheated rock and sand torched his skin. He tried to get back up but his whole being protested. If he couldn't walk, he'd crawl. He pressed forward on his elbows and knees. It burned, but the pain jolted him out of his mental fog. He cut his hand on something spiny. His leg dragged over a sharp rock and split open his pants below the thigh. He would do this, crawl until he couldn't crawl anymore. Then he would drag himself forward. Inch by inch. Until he couldn't move. And then he'd move some more. You could always go farther.

He moved in increments, face low to the ground and feeling the heat coming off it, his lips almost touching it, wondering if he should try to drink the pebbles and sand, just so there was something in his throat, anything, to replace the dry parch. His body was sending him every signal it was shutting down. Telling him that continuing like this was madness. That it was all over. He never thought he'd die like this. He always figured it would be gunfire on the job in some shitty alley in the dark and cold.

He stopped crawling. Started again. Closed his eyes. His whole world was heat, pain, and thirst. *Keep going you candy ass* came the voice in his head. *Why* said another. *Just stay here and rest.*

He was about to heed the second voice when his head hit something solid.

CHAPTER
17

rgento opened his eyes. He was staring at a wide span of rocks that stretched for twenty feet. He blinked and touched the stone that rose above him, unsure if it was real. It was red-hot and felt material enough. He tried to use an outcropping of rock to pull himself up, but his arms weren't listening to his brain, and he swayed and went to his knees. The movement made his head explode in pinwheels of agony. When he had his bearings, he crawled backward to get a better look at the formation.

The rock where Redlinger said he stored the water and supplies, what was it supposed to look like? Redlinger had told him but he couldn't remember. He blearily scanned the rock face. One part of the formation had a base that gave way to a narrow neck topped with a wide cylinder-shape. Some tiny spark in the back of his brain told him this was important. Argento dragged himself around to the back of it and searched the nearby ground as dark spots swam across his eyes. When he saw it, he couldn't process it at first. He assumed he was looking at another mirage. A green plastic rectangle was against the base of the cylinder-shape, nestled in the shade created by the rock canopy.

It looked like a jug of water.

Argento's trembling fingers tore at the jug's plastic screw-top.

It was all he could do to remove it. There was some kind of spout attached to the container but he flung it aside. He tried to raise the jug to his lips but his arms balked, the coordination this required too much for his current operating system so with a grunt, he knocked the jug on its side with his forearm. Pressed his mouth to the opening as water lapped out on his face, over his crusted lips, down his gullet. It was warm, verging on hot, but it didn't matter. After the initial deluge, he forced himself to sip, so he didn't throw it all back up.

He drank until he was satiated. Then he drank some more. The container was six gallons, according to the markings on the bottom. He pressed his forehead against the plastic. He didn't know how long the jug had been out there, but the water tasted fresh enough. There was sufficient shade under the rocks so he stripped off his shirt, wincing as the fabric moved over his blistering skin. His brain was beginning to sputter back to life, and the first responder training for treating heat stroke that he'd learned in the academy came back to him. He searched near where he'd found the water jug and located a backpack-size first aid kit. Inside were a half dozen ice packs, the kind that activated when you opened them. He popped all six, put one under each armpit and one each against his neck and groin, and held the remaining two on his forehead.

He closed his eyes and drew in the cool.

He lay like that for a long time. Then he drank some more water. He was feeling the rumblings of hunger, which he took as a good sign, because his body was able to send him a message about something other than dehydration.

It was plenty hot under the rock formation, but not too hot to sleep. He let exhaustion take him. When he woke, it was dusk. He used the remaining light to scour the rest of the ground around the mushroom-shaped rock. There was another pack next to the med kit, an Emergency Preparedness backpack like the kind you got from the Red Cross in case of fires. It held a flashlight with attached compass and extra batteries, a map, and some energy bars. He wolfed down two of the bars. They tasted like sweet chalk.

Redlinger had made good and then some. Argento wasn't sure how the man had found this rock formation, how he'd trucked this gear out there, or why he was helping him.

He'd have to ask when he got back to Fenton.

Argento returned to the water jug, which was marked *Desert Patrol*. He shook it. Still about half full. He checked the rest of the medical pack. Plenty in there he could use, including gauze dressings and adhesive tape, sunscreen, aspirin, and a snakebite kit, rounded out by a bottle of rubbing alcohol. He was glad he didn't find the rubbing alcohol before the jug of water because he knew he would have seen the clear liquid and guzzled it without a second thought.

Argento studied the map, which bore a red circle marking his current position. The most direct route back to civilization was some thirty miles northwest. It didn't look like he'd hit any towns, but he would get to the east–west interstate. Interstate meant cars and cars meant people and people meant help.

He used most of the dressings and medical tape to cover his blistering skin as a shield against infection from the dust and dirt around him. He rested some more. When night fell, he combined the contents of the medical kit and survival pack into one and hoisted it on his back. He figured one LED flashlight battery would get him around six hours but there was a replacement. The three gallons of water would buy him three more days. He'd travel at night and seek shelter during the worst of the daytime heat. The compass and light would guide him. Even if he veered off course somewhat, he couldn't miss the interstate carving a horizontal ribbon through the desert.

He set out into the blackness.

It was slow going at night. He had a flashlight, but he didn't want to tumble down an arroyo, so he moved with precision. The water jug was about thirty pounds and awkward to carry, but he took frequent rests. He didn't have to hurry now. Just keep a steady pace. The desert animal sounds—skittering, low-pitched whistles, distant howls—were more accentuated after sundown, the earthy smells more pronounced. He could hear crickets and even a frog now and again.

He walked into daybreak. Measured units of time by units of thirst. He wasn't sure how many miles he'd covered. Fifteen? Twenty? He kept going until he found a well-shaded spot under a canopy of mesquite trees and lay down against a boulder. He checked the compass. Still heading northwest. He figured he'd drank at least another half gallon of water during the night hike. He tried to doze off, but day sleeping, even with shade, was a tall order in this heat, so he rested more than slept. He finished off his last protein bar and fantasized about what he would eat when he made it out. A bacon cheeseburger and curly fries washed down with a jumbo chocolate milkshake. An Italian sausage and onion pizza Chicago-style flanked by garlic bread that oozed butter. He got up and moving again just before dusk, swapping out the flashlight battery for a fresh one.

The fourth day was a blur. Night walk. Day sleep under a cluster of palo verdes. A deep fatigue. A driving hunger. He was straining at capacity. He was no endurance athlete or ultra-marathoner. His body wasn't designed for this.

On the morning of the fifth day, he was out of water and staggering more than walking when he heard the faint sounds of music. As he drew near, he could make out the strains. Country. He wasn't a fan but he'd never been so glad to hear it. He went up a slight rise and there was the freeway spread out below. On the parallel feeder road, an SUV was parked blasting music while a guy in a cowboy hat changed one of its tires and two other guys threw a Frisbee nearby. He went down the embankment and stumbled, falling on his back. He tried to get up but couldn't. Tried to speak but his throat was too dry. He raised his head and saw the Frisbee guys' eyes on him. He imagined he looked like he felt.

"Holy shit," someone said.

CHAPTER
18

The man with the silver hair had now filled the wall leading to the lab with equations on both sides from top to bottom, as points of orientation for the final push. They would be largely meaningless to anyone but him.

Project A.

Project B.

He estimated A was 94 percent complete. B was 88 percent. He was in the refining stage now, shortening the incubation period, getting down to an error rate of zero. He was perhaps two weeks from completion. He'd recently had a classmate visit but the classmate had left. Now the man with the silver hair could fully concentrate on the work without distraction.

He looked at his monitors. One of the soldiers had been in his workspace to fix a minor electrical issue and had looked at his computer system and asked if it had enough RAM to play Tetris. The man with the silver hair resented the attempt at humor. It was a waste of his time. The thought of the Fenton soldiers venturing behind the monitors down the hallway and into the adjacent lab holding Project A and B made his stomach curdle. The equivalent of a beer-soaked tourist in flip-flops stumbling through the Vatican. Agent Sumaya represented only one small increment up from Fenton DPS. She too was a halfwit, but at least she occasionally wore a business suit.

As he rose for his daily swim, the soft chime sounded for the door. He checked the CCTV display. Sumaya. Think her name and she shall be conjured. He made sure she was alone, tugged up his shirt collar, and buzzed her through the steel doors. She entered briskly, her face tight.

"He's alive," she said.

"Not possible in that environment."

"The desert worked with the Reeds. He's not the Reeds. Had a feeling about him. So I put in a keyword search on police and fire scanners within a hundred-mile radius. This morning they sent an ambulance to the interstate for a report of a disoriented man walking near the freeway. Transported him to the closest hospital for dehydration and burns. I called them. He's registered under his actual name, condition serious but stable."

"He had help. There's no other explanation."

"I called local police to detain him. Tomlinson and I are driving out now. We'll be there in an hour."

"Then what?"

"I'll handle it," Sumaya said grimly. "Check the GPS activity on all of Fenton DPS for the last two weeks. Look for anything unusual. You'll know it when you see it." With that, she turned and exited.

The man with the silver hair took a moment to process these new data points. His fingers worked the keyboard. Sumaya had put GPS trackers the size of nickels on all of the Fenton soldiers' patrol and personal vehicles without their knowledge. If any of them had made a suspicious trip, he'd see it soon enough.

But there was nothing to see. The route history of each member he punched up all made sense. No one had driven anywhere that raised a red flag. They were supposed to stay within county limits at all times and they had complied. Company men, even though they didn't know which company they were working for.

The man with the silver hair switched over to his drone controls.

He had one of his own design hovering over Fenton at all times. When he'd been driven out to the Sonoran five days ago so they could rid themselves of the tourist, he'd had a drone accompany him from the top of the Fenton Public Safety building, using the autopilot function and making slight control adjustments with his phone. The unit's augmented solar-powered battery allowed for extended flight time, which meant it could easily make the distance into the desert and back. He'd had to launch it discreetly, of course, because Sumaya and the others wouldn't have wanted their actions memorialized. Bad form for the U.S. government to murder a citizen in the desert, especially when his only offense was accidentally getting too close to a national secret. But the man with the silver hair liked to have records of such things, especially if anyone got the notion to renege on a deal or shift an allegiance.

He called up the drone footage for that morning. It showed the DPS vehicles pulling up. Argento being led out in cuffs. A pause for conversation, then one of the soldiers, the increasingly melancholic one, took Argento out past the others and released him alone into the wild.

The man with the silver hair called up the profile photos of the Fenton soldiers on his monitor. Saw the name of the man in question. Redlinger. He replayed the sequence in his head.

Tomlinson had told Redlinger to walk Argento out, so Redlinger had.

No.

That wasn't right.

Redlinger had *volunteered* to walk out Argento. It hadn't struck the man with the silver hair as notable then but it did now. He backed the drone footage up. Zoomed in on Redlinger as he and Argento separated from the others. He could see Redlinger's lips moving as he spoke to Argento without looking at him. Then it looked like Redlinger handed Argento something, a small object that could fit in the palm of his hand, but it happened quickly and he couldn't be sure.

The man with the silver hair couldn't read lips. But he knew how to easily tap into an intelligence network that could. There was a private security conglomerate based in London that he used whenever he needed to outsource. They'd have access to forensic lip readers, both home and abroad. He took the enhanced footage of Redlinger speaking to Argento and sent it to them via encrypted message. Even the best lip readers could only pick up on 30 to 40 percent of what was being said, but he didn't need a legal transcript. Just a gist.

He got his reply within minutes. It was a breakdown word by word, with degrees of certainty (High/Medium/Low) affixed as well as other possible translations with ellipses where sounds were undistinguishable. As expected, it fell short of a transcript, but a few words and phrases deciphered with a High degree of certainty stood out:

> "rock formation."
> "twenty-five miles."
> "follow the ..."
> "water."
> "don't tell."

No matter how carefully vetted the operation, there was always a weak link.

He called Agent Sumaya. She picked up on the first ring. He could hear the rush of traffic in the background.

"It's Redlinger," he said. "Kill him."

CHAPTER
19

A rgento turned his head left. Turned it right. His neck worked. He moved his arms and legs up and down. They worked too. He was in a hospital bed with an IV in his arm. His body was roasted, like cannibals had gotten him on the spit. The burns hurt like hell, but he couldn't let them slow him down. There were places he needed to be.

When the nurse had peeled away his self-administered dressings, it had pulled the tops off some of his blisters, causing pain that made his eyes water. The doctor who'd examined him said he had partial thickness burns, the fancy term for second degree. They'd cleaned and redressed his wounds and were treating him with medical lotion, pain meds, and a constant IV, and waiting on blood and urine tests to see what kind of shape his kidneys were in after his intense bout of dehydration. His kidneys, the doctor guessed, were somewhere on the spectrum from banged up to acutely damaged, which in extreme cases could lead to renal failure and dialysis.

"Got no time for dialysis," Argento said.

"Well," the doctor said, "then let's hope the results of the kidney tests are favorable. But once your core body temperature reaches 107.6 degrees, it's fatal. My guess is you were close to that." She was a tall woman whose ID said her name was Fleming. She looked like the

WNBA's Candace Parker and sounded like she knew what she was talking about.

Argento thought back to how he'd stumbled out of the desert. The group of twentysomethings by the SUV along the interstate had given him a beer, which he'd downed in a few gulps and was the best-tasting thing he'd ever known. They'd also called him an ambulance, which had transported him to the closest hospital. Dr. Fleming had told him if his kidney tests passed muster, he'd be discharged with antibiotics and dressings.

It had been no small amount of luck that he'd beaten the desert. But prior to that, his luck had been bad. Now it had turned. Argento had the same amount of luck as anyone else. It evened out over time.

A businesslike woman from Admissions stopped by and asked him about health insurance. Argento told her he didn't have any. After he'd left the police force, he hadn't bothered with it.

"How do you intend to pay for this?"

Lady, Argento thought, *that is the least of my problems.* "Put me on the installment plan. But tell your receptionist I don't want anyone to know I'm here."

She gave him a quizzical look.

"Too many ex-wives."

"We give patients the option of having their names listed as Not for Publication," she said. "I'll put you down for that."

Argento didn't have any ex-wives, but it was an easy lie. Most of his coworkers on the Detroit police had been on their second or third wives. For Argento, there had only been Emily. He used to joke to her that he didn't fit in at work without at least one former spouse to complain about and she had chuckled, the chuckle that sometimes turned into a full-throated laugh, the one that had a hint of a rasp to it and ended in a sigh of contentment. It had been his favorite sound. It nourished him. His wife's laugh made him believe in God.

Argento checked his arm. His name was on his medical wristband. He hadn't volunteered it but they'd taken it off his Michigan driver's license from his wallet, which was currently in a bag along with the rest of his belongings under his bed. His name being in the system could be a problem. He wasn't sure how far Fenton's reach was, but paranoia had been his friend before and would be again. Sumaya would have feelers out. If there was a record of his stay here, she could find it. Then she'd come looking for him and she'd bring her friends. Her friends would not be Argento's friends.

He wondered if Dr. Fleming or anyone on the hospital staff would call the police about him. If it was clear he was a crime victim, like he'd been shot or stabbed, they were required to by law. In the absence of clear signs of assault, he wasn't sure. A man in rough shape limping out of the desert in the middle of nowhere was unusual, but was it a police matter? Maybe they'd want to question if he'd been with anyone else who might still need rescue. Or how he got there in the first place. Argento had no personal experience to draw from when he'd been on the job. Michigan didn't have a desert.

His question was answered when two uniformed deputies came through the door. It was an old-and-young combo. The older deputy looked businesslike. The younger one looked bored. Their uniform patch said *Maricopa County Sheriff's Department.*

The younger deputy took a small notebook out of his shirt pocket. He wasn't much for preamble. "So what happened?"

If he didn't say a crime occurred and claimed to have been alone in the desert, they'd lose interest. But they'd probably still generate a police report. So his name would be not only in the hospital database but in the law enforcement one too, presenting another conduit for Sumaya and her guns to find him.

"Hiking," Argento said. "Lost my way."

"You with anyone?"

"No." He'd tell law enforcement where they could find the Reeds. They deserved a proper burial. But the time wasn't right. For now, even though he was out of the desert, he was still in survival mode. He would address what happened to the Reeds, to Hudson, to him, but he'd do it his way. He didn't want police eyes on him when that happened.

"Okay, works for me." The younger deputy closed his notebook and headed for the door. The older one stayed right where he was. He had deep-set eyes and a brush mustache.

"No one hikes where they found you," he said. "Too flat. Too remote."

"I like my space."

"Like NASA." The younger deputy chuckled at his own line.

"You didn't bring enough water," the older deputy said. "Not even close. Doc says you had heat stroke. Second-degree burns. Like you'd been out there for days."

"Hard life in the desert," Argento said. "It's not for everyone."

"What trailhead you launch from?"

Argento didn't answer.

"Where's your car?"

Argento shook his head.

The radio squawked and the younger deputy answered it. "Free for a 10-21?" someone asked. *10-21.* Probably their department's code for a phone call. The younger deputy stepped out for a minute, and when he came back, something had changed. Argento could see it in his posture. His suspicion was confirmed when the younger deputy handcuffed him to the gurney.

"Sorry, dude. Someone needs to talk to you."

The older deputy gave the younger one a quizzical look and the latter shrugged and said, "I'll tell you in the hallway. It'll give him time to work on his frontier story."

"I'll talk to whoever wants to talk to me," Argento said, "but can I hit the bathroom first?"

"They got bedpans for that," the younger deputy said.

"Can you at least close the curtain?"

The younger deputy did so grudgingly, pulling it on its runners around the gurney, concealing Argento from outside view. Then the two deputies stepped outside and closed the door.

Argento took in his surroundings. A one-bed hospital room. No windows. Tiled ceiling. He had to assume that he was being detained because Sumaya had figured out he was still alive and sent a message to local PD to hold him until they could get there. But he felt reasonably sure they weren't going to try stranding him in the desert again. The law in Fenton wasn't operating with complete impunity; otherwise, they would have just gunned him down in the street alongside Hudson regardless of any witnesses, but he still represented a substantial threat to their mission. Which meant a bullet to the head in a discreet location was in his immediate future.

Argento didn't need to stick around for that.

The problem was the two deputies outside. He didn't want to hurt them. They didn't know his situation and were following orders that as far as they knew were legitimate. So he'd have to choose the best of some bad options.

But he was getting ahead of himself. He was handcuffed at the moment. He had to work that problem first.

There was a digital thermometer attached to a roll cart near the side of the bed. Argento hooked the cart with his foot and pulled it through the curtain where it opened in the back. Then he used his free hand to bring the thermometer's coiled cord to his wrist. The narrow tip of the thermometer neatly fit into the keyhole of the handcuff. Argento turned the tip around until he sprung the cuff link. He slipped the cuff off and stood. Some years ago, he'd been on hospital watch for a homicide suspect, a wiry guy with a history of escape. He'd seen the suspect successfully do the exact same thing with a roll cart thermometer before running for the door. Argento had thrown the man back on the bed like a lawn dart, cuffed both his hands to the gurney and added some leg shackles for good measure. But he'd been impressed by that maneuver and committed it to memory. He respected people with practical skills, whether they applied them for good or ill.

Argento got gauze and tape from the room's medical supply drawers, used the gauze to put pressure on his hand where he pulled the IV needle out and tied it down with the tape. He slipped out of his hospital gown back into his civilian clothing, wincing at the feeling of cloth on his raw skin. He took his wallet and backpack and tested his legs. They felt stable enough. Good, because he was about to run.

He opened the door and stepped into the hallway. The two

deputies were in the middle of a conversation. They looked at him, alarm registering on their faces. Both started toward him.

"Wait." Argento held up a hand. And just like that, they did. The power of suggestion. He was also two hundred pounds of blocky muscle with blistered skin. He looked like the kind of man you'd need to formulate an arrest plan for. A plan that preferably involved more than two deputies. A plan that ideally featured every single deputy working the shift and maybe a few that would be willing to drive in from home.

"I used to be police. You'll find out when you run my name. But the people who put my detainer in the system are coming to kill me. So I need you to let me go my way here. I haven't committed a crime. When I walk, it won't count as an escaped prisoner. I was never a prisoner to begin with. Detained only, not arrested. Besides, you can put it back on your department for issuing you faulty handcuffs. They shouldn't be so easy to get out of."

The older deputy actually took a step back. The younger took two steps forward. Drew his wooden baton.

Argento continued, now talking directly to the younger. "Pepper spray doesn't work on me. You hit me with that baton and I'll take it away from you. Don't try to stop me. I don't want to hurt a cop."

The speech he gave was mostly true. Pepper spray gave him some trouble, but he'd been trained to fight through it. But taking the baton away was far from a sure thing. Maybe he'd be fast enough to disarm the deputy. Or maybe the deputy was a stick-fighting champion who would give him the wood shampoo. No way to be sure until it happened.

But the deputies didn't know how much of it was bluster. What he said gave the older deputy a long moment of pause. The man looked to be on the wrong end of fifty. Not relishing an extended fight in a hospital hallway without plenty of backup. Argento could see it in his eyes.

But he saw the younger one's knuckles whiten on the handle of his baton.

"Screw that," the younger deputy said and came at Argento swinging.

CHAPTER
20

Redlinger was sitting by the fire pit with a beer in hand when they came for him. Krebs, Cornejo, Chan, and Belchert. He'd sent Gail and the girls to Gail's mother's house near Tucson. He was alone. That was what he wanted. Finally to just be alone.

"Where's Tomlinson?" Redlinger asked. "Too scared to show?"

Krebs said, "Him and Sumaya are driving out to the hospital to clean up the mess you left."

"So he's alive."

"Apparently."

Redlinger felt a stab of something. Hope, maybe. Or at least a small abeyance of guilt. "Good."

Cornejo spoke. "Desert was a sure kill. We know you helped him. Silver Hair figured it out."

There was no point in lying now. He had already lied for so long. "I stored some water and supplies at a rock formation a ways out. Told him how to get there."

"Why?"

"Supplies were supposed to be for any of us, in case we had to take that same desert walk we set the woman and kid on. But I told him where to find them. Dude didn't do anything to us. He just asked

121

some questions, threw fruit, and then we shot his dog and left him to die. All for what. Some fucking government project no one's even explained to us." Redlinger wasn't at all sure Argento would make it. He'd stored the gear at a landmark he didn't think anyone could miss and situated it not far from where they'd dropped off the Reeds, but although they'd dumped Argento along the same dry creek bed, it had been miles farther away from the provisions than he'd anticipated. But Argento had a way about him. Like he knew he was going to find a way to walk the fuck out of the desert. And then return and come for them all.

Chan asked, "How'd you stow that gear without getting picked up on GPS?" The GPS tags on their vehicles were an open secret among the soldiers. They assumed they'd be tracked. You didn't get assigned to a job like Fenton without accountability among team members.

"I got an ATV they don't know about. Store it off-site."

Belchert spat into the fire pit. "Any other covert shit you're doing?"

Redlinger ignored the question and asked his own. "You ever think about that mom and her kid we left out there?"

Belchert made a waving-off motion with his hand. But he flinched a little when he did it.

"They ain't our family," Cornejo said. "No more than the Hajis were."

"Ever think how they must have died?"

"Maybe they made it out," Krebs said. "Just like your boy Kurt."

"We're all going to answer for this. Before God."

"Settle down," Cornejo said. "Who else knew you helped him?"

"No one."

"Sumaya?"

"No one. They gonna move Silver Hair?"

"He doesn't want to move," Cornejo said. "Sumaya is trying to get him to, but Tomlinson said dude will quit if they make him."

"Be nice to know what the project is," Redlinger said. He wanted to laugh but not because it was funny.

No one responded.

"We did some bad things," Redlinger said. "Over there. Then we came here. Did worse." He ran his fingers through his hair. Looked at his palm covered in loose strands.

"We all saw shit we didn't want to see," Belchert said. "I don't remember needing anyone to hold my hand."

"Over there, Red," Cornejo said, "that was our reality. This is our reality now."

That was the problem. He didn't want this reality. The war and then the woman and child. The dog, the drifter. It was too much. He couldn't come back from it.

"So what if Argento shows back up here?"

"Green light," Belchert said. "We shoot him on sight."

"What we're used to anyway," Cornejo said.

"What does this mean for me?"

"We got some instructions," Krebs said and took out a handgun with a silencer already screwed on. Redlinger recognized the suppressor. It was one of the best in the world, generating a muffled pop inaudible past a hundred feet.

It was quiet around the fire pit. Redlinger was tired. And this wasn't wrong, what was about to happen to him. It would stop his moral rot from infecting his wife, Paige, Kelsey. If they kept him alive, they'd just treat him like a traitor. And he'd still have the nightmares. They might as well do it now. The secrets he had, he didn't want them anymore.

"Make sure Gail and the kids get my share."

"You know we will," Cornejo said.

"Don't leave my body where they can find it."

"Brother, ain't no one ever gonna find your body," Krebs said. Face flat. Eyes dead. Redlinger didn't know Krebs anymore. No more than himself.

Quiet again. This was the natural resolution to turning on his own. To breaking the code. The soldiers would forgive each other for just about anything, even mistakes under fire. But not betrayal. Of the men around the fire pit, no one seemed particularly bothered. No one was even breathing hard. Except Chan. Chan looked sick to his stomach. Couldn't meet his eyes.

Redlinger's time was up, but that didn't mean theirs had to be. He felt the need to warn them out of a sense of loyalty that he knew was surreal given the circumstances. "This guy Kurt, we had the wrong read on him. Don't take him lightly. He's dangerous. He's like us."

"Nobody's like us," Cornejo said.

Krebs took the beer bottle out of Redlinger's hand and guzzled the remains. Then he wiped his mouth on his shirt sleeve. "God damn it, Red."

Redlinger turned to Krebs. "Do it," he said. And Krebs raised the gun and pulled the trigger.

CHAPTER
21

When the younger deputy came at him with the baton, Argento met him head-on, moving in close to render the stick's reach ineffective. He took control of the deputy's weapon arm, gripped it by the shoulder and wrist, and propelled him through the hospital room door and up onto the bed. The maneuver took the deputy by surprise, and the breath whooshed out of him as he landed hard on his back on top of the sheets. His stick clattered to the floor.

The cuffs the younger deputy had put on Argento still dangled from the gurney. Argento secured the deputy's right hand to the rail. The younger man wasn't done. He punched Argento in the side of the face with his left, but he wasn't used to striking from a reclined position and it didn't have much force behind it. Argento shook off the blow and pivoted so he was leaning on the deputy's torso, pinning him against the bed. He didn't have to look far for the man's handcuff key. It was in a small basket-weave keeper near his belt buckle, the same place Argento had kept his own on the PD. The keeper held two keys: one long and sturdy that cops had to buy themselves from the police supply store; and another short and spindly, the discount kind the academy gave you for free when you graduated. He inserted the spindly one in the keyhole, and broke off the top with a sharp twist.

They'd need bolt cutters to remove the cuffs now. The younger deputy was out of the game.

He turned. The older deputy was against the far wall in his line of sight. He had his gun out and leveled at Argento's chest. Argento showed his hands so he'd know he was unarmed.

"Your partner's fine," he said. "He's taking a break."

"Get on the floor. On the floor or I'll fire."

"Then you'll have to back-shoot me because I'm walking out of here."

"On the fucking floor now," the deputy shouted.

Argento did what he said he'd do. He walked out of the room and down the hall. He glanced over his shoulder. The older deputy was still pointing his gun, but one-handed this time. The other hand was going to his radio. A 1985 court case called *Tennessee v. Garner* prohibited law enforcement from shooting fleeing felons unless they could articulate the suspect still presented an immediate deadly threat. It was a fairly high bar. The older deputy must not have felt Argento met it because no bullets went through his back. A nurse walking his way saw him, a burned-face man fleeing police, and she turned and hurried in the opposite direction. Argento didn't blame her. He made the corner.

And ran as fast as he could.

CHAPTER
22

The Regal Inn in Phoenix near the corner of East Mohave and South Seventh Street was thirty-nine dollars a night. Argento's room featured stained towels, carpets dotted with gum, and a softball-size hole in the wall that had been plugged with a glob of toilet paper. The moldy shower didn't work, which was fine by Argento, because he had no plans to be barefoot anywhere in that room; fifty-fifty the last guest had been a registered sex offender. The woman next door was a hooker with at least half-a-dozen separate guests over for fifteen to twenty minutes a pop, and Argento could hear them going at it through the sliver of a wall. The room's air conditioner was hit or miss, so he went outside for a cold drink. Someone had scratched the word "Dickbutt" on the lobby soda machine. A touch of class in the city.

The man at the reception desk hadn't asked him to show an ID when he'd checked in, so he told them his name was Pat Underwood, who was a lightly used utility player on the '83 Tigers, and paid cash for the room. The place would work. Cheap, anonymous, and in a neighborhood where people wouldn't ask why his face looked like a boiled ham.

He reclined on the bed, electing to stay on top of the blanket and sheets at all times, and held the soda to his bad knee, which was still twinging from his sprint through the hospital. He'd accomplished his goal of escaping while doing as little damage as possible to the local law but he still felt nauseous, a combination of his recent strenuous activity while still recovering from the desert and the sick feeling in his gut of having to tussle with the deputy, whom he counted as one of his own. He'd run into the parking lot where he'd encountered a guy in a beat-up sedan who looked ragged around the edges and paid him $100 to drive him the two hours to Phoenix. The man was heading there anyway and had been happy to oblige, no questions asked.

America, land of opportunity.

Argento mentally ticked off the crimes he'd committed at the hospital. Battery against a Law Officer for tossing the deputy on the hospital bed. False Imprisonment for handcuffing him. Obstructing for failing to heed the older deputy's orders. He didn't know if any of those crimes were felonies in Arizona. At least one of them would likely be. Which meant since they knew who he was, they could issue an arrest warrant that would be extraditable throughout Arizona and into neighboring states if not further. The Maricopa County Sheriff's Department had to be a decent-size agency, although that didn't necessarily mean they'd work faster than a smaller jurisdiction. His file could end up on the desk of some overworked investigator who had a dozen things to get to before he started on a case where two deputies had been seriously embarrassed but no one was hurt. Argento guessed he had anywhere between a few days to a couple of weeks until the warrant got entered into the system.

As a placeholder until then, Maricopa County would issue a crime alert identifying him as a wanted person with his name and description attached. He wasn't sure what the alert would have for a photo. Maybe his mug shot from Whitehall. He hadn't thought to check if the hospital had surveillance cameras, but he'd have to assume they did and the alert would include stills of what he'd last been wearing. He'd need a change of clothes. Whether Phoenix PD would pay much attention to crime alerts from the Maricopa County Sheriff remained to be seen. An offense against a fellow officer would catch their attention, but they probably had plenty of their own such alerts to deal with. When Argento was on the job, he got about twenty alerts a day in his email and those were just the local ones. He took to deleting most that came from neighboring jurisdictions; there was a burglary in Bloomfield Hills where someone stole a moose head from Tanner's Lodge? Who gave a shit.

But then there was the matter of Sumaya and Co. What would they do when they arrived at the hospital and found him gone? Argento being wanted by a different jurisdiction now could only complicate things for them. Would they try to brush Maricopa County SD aside and claim this whole thing fell under federal jurisdiction? That would mean questions and exposure they wouldn't welcome. No. They'd want to keep whatever they were doing in Fenton under wraps.

And whatever they were doing was something they thought well worth killing for.

Argento spent the day in his room after turning up his TV to drown out the amorous sounds next door. He ordered a pizza for delivery, a large sausage-and-onion Chicago style with buttery garlic bread, exactly what he'd hungered for in the desert. He wolfed down three quarters of it in one sitting, dozed off, woke, and ate the rest.

The next morning he paid for another day. He was still healing from the desert. He'd been able to remove his dressings because most of his blisters had scabbed over, and while his skin remained unnaturally shiny, it was returning to its natural hue. He hadn't stuck around for the results of his blood and urine tests, so he didn't know how his kidneys were looking; he figured if they went on the fritz, his body would send him a signal soon enough. But he couldn't just sit around and convalesce. He needed a plan for his reunion with Fenton DPS and Silver Hair. He ran a few scenarios through his head where he returned to Fenton, alone but heavily armed. He didn't win in any of them. It wasn't even close. He couldn't take on an entire Public Safety Department and storm Silver Hair's compound by himself.

He'd need friends, or at least backup. And that presented a problem. With his man Trapsi out of the country and the Detroit PD in his rearview, Argento didn't have any backup.

But before he could do much of anything, he needed money. After paying for the ride to Phoenix, two days at the esteemed Regal, and his large pizza and garlic bread, his initial three hundred was down to about eighty. And he didn't want to use his ATM card to get more in case Sumaya had some kind of electronic tip-off where she could track his location. He assumed such monitoring couldn't happen overnight and would require a warrant. Or maybe DHS did whatever the hell they wanted in the name of national security and got their results right away. Either way, he wasn't going to chance it.

Argento thought more about his lack of allies.

He did know one guy.

When Argento had helped Julie Wakefield escape the prison riot in Whitehall a year ago, her father, the Missouri governor, had been highly appreciative. As a token of his gratitude, he'd given Argento his personal cell, the one reserved for family and emergencies. A number he'd answer right away no matter where he was or what he was doing. Argento remembered the number and called it from his hotel room.

"Christopher Wakefield."

"It's Kurt Argento. I'm in Phoenix. I need five grand delivered to my hotel room, a change of street clothes, and a few hours with the best computer guy you can wrangle. I'll pay you back."

"You get right to the point, don't you?"

"You're a busy man."

"Consider it done. How's everything?"

"Still aboveground. Other than that, better if you don't know. How's Julie?"

"Good. She took the entrance exam for the St. Louis Police Department. Thinking you might have had something to do with that. She scored well. She has her physical agility test next week."

"They'll have to redesign that course to give her a challenge."

Wakefield didn't reply. Argento could almost hear him thinking.

Then he said, "Whatever you're involved in, are you on the right side of it?"

It was a fair question. It was one of many fair questions the governor could ask in this situation. "Trying to be," Argento said.

"I'll call you right back."

Twenty minutes later, Wakefield did. "A courier will be dropping the money and clothes off in the next few hours. I just need the address and your sizes. The computer tech is going to take a little longer. Tonight maybe. Can you wait there for him?"

"Sure. Just let them both know my face looks like I forgot it in a toaster. Don't want them to turn and run when I open the door."

"Will do."

"You have my vote, sir."

"You don't live anywhere near Missouri," the governor said. "How about you just be careful."

Argento gave Wakefield his clothing sizes, thanked him, and ended the call. He assumed the governor was handling this through an intermediary or two and would have plenty of layers of plausible deniability. But he was still taking a risk sending money for an unknown reason to a man whose past was getting increasingly questionable. Argento's actions inside Whitehall had earned him loyalty and goodwill in spades. He wasn't going to draw from that well too often. He could easily not talk with the governor for another twenty years.

Two hours later, there was a knock at his door and a young man in a suit handed him an envelope with the cash and a paper bag with two sets of clothing. T-shirts, light jackets, work pants, underwear, socks. Plus a plain blue baseball hat. Nothing that would stand out. Day laborer clothes.

"Just curious," Argento said. "Do you know who I am or why you're giving this to me?"

"No," the guy said. "I work for a private courier service. I pick up stuff. I deliver stuff. No weapons, no drugs, but just about anything else. Last week I brought some lady a disco ball and a tub of tapioca pudding. Three in the morning. I don't ask."

Argento let the man go to his next pudding drop-off. He changed clothes and tossed his old ones. He walked down the street to a chicken joint and brought some wings and biscuits back to his room and turned on the local news. There was nothing about a prisoner escape from a hospital. Maybe the deputies were trying to sit on it because prisoner escapes were embarrassing. Or maybe it wasn't newsworthy, not if there was a story about the rescue of a baby deer stuck in a storm drain they could cover instead. He lay back on the bed. Hudson should have been by his feet. He felt his dog's loss keenly. He didn't know what happened to dogs after they passed. Maybe their spirits lingered somehow. If any dog was worthy of an afterlife, it was Hud. He was a good boy. The best boy. He was glad Emily hadn't been around to see Hudson go. She would have taken it even harder than him.

Emily, Whitehall, Hudson, the desert. It had been a hard road of late.

Maybe God was testing him.

If that was the case, he didn't know if he was going to pass.

It was just before midnight when there was another knock on his door.

CHAPTER
23

rgento's visitor was not a computer guy, it was a computer gal and closer to a kid, eighteen to twenty tops and no more than a hundred pounds. She had short, cropped hair, a T-shirt with some kind of video game character on it, and jeans with scuffed knees. A backpack was slung over her shoulder.

"Computer help?"

Argento nodded and held the door open for her. She took a laptop and two cans of what looked like energy drinks from her backpack and set them down on the room's small table. The cans weren't the same swill that Fenton DPS drank. They had names that looked like they were written in Chinese.

"I know. Tech issue, send the Asian kid," she said. "But I'm good and I happened to be available tonight, so here I am."

She booted up her laptop. It had two stickers on it. One said *0 to 60 Eventually*. The other said *The More People I Meet the More I Love My Dog*. The laptop had no brand name he could see and sported a curved keyboard. Maybe she'd built it herself. She looked at him expectantly. She hadn't given her name or asked for his. He was good with that. He assumed whoever the governor had contacted to send this woman was reputable and vetted their clients, or she wouldn't be so blasé about being a petite female coming into a badly burned stranger's low-rent hotel room in a shitty neighborhood for an undefined "computer problem."

"Before we start," he said. "The people I'm going up against are dangerous. Cover your tracks. I don't want this to come back on you."

"That's quite an opener. Lay it on me. I'm a big girl."

"I need to find out about a Homeland Security agent named Marisol Sumaya. Filipina female, midthirties. Currently working in Fenton, Arizona, although I don't know if that's where she's based out of. I don't have a picture of her."

"Okay. You tried any of this yourself yet? I'm only asking because I charge two hundred an hour."

That seemed high to Argento. He didn't know the girl's name but he would think of her as 200. "I don't have a computer."

"You have a phone?"

Argento pointed to the hotel landline.

"Holy shit," 200 said. It was the second time in the last forty-eight-hours he'd gotten that reaction from a stranger. 200's fingers whirred over the keyboard. It was the only sound in the room. The hooker next door was blessedly quiet. It was Sunday and maybe she took Sundays off, with it being a day of reflection.

"Not much here. Someone with that name works for Homeland Security. These days they gotta post their salaries in a public forum. Transparency and all. But she's got no social media. No professional associations. No home address or school history. No listed relatives."

That struck Argento as odd. Law enforcement tended to keep a low profile online, but he didn't think anyone had zero web presence these days. Argento himself had paid for a police privacy service and signed a series of form letters to have his name removed from the most common online depositories. It worked reasonably well, but he had to start the whole thing from scratch after he'd refinanced his mortgage. Had he gotten the spelling of Sumaya's name wrong? No. He'd seen the name clearly on her ID and made a point to commit it to memory.

"How do you stay that quiet online?"

200 shrugged. "You gotta be diligent. It's a lifestyle choice, really. She'll use Protonmail, not Gmail, and register her phone in the name of some LLC in, like, Nebraska. She probably got on Optery. If she's smart, she'll stay off Tor because anyone who knows computers can monitor their exit nodes for traffic. I'd expect to see a ProtonVPN coupled with Algo."

"Algo."

"It's a free and open source VPN."

"VPN," Argento said.

"Virtual Private Network." 200 didn't sigh but sounded like she wanted to. She cracked an energy drink and took a long swig.

"What if she used to have info online but scrubbed it? Can you do an unscrub?"

"You can't erase your name from the internet, not really. Best you can do is muddy things. There are sites like Reputation.com that try to fool the search algorithms. Say you do something bad, like that drunk guy who took a crap in a drink cart on a United flight. You want people to forget that happened, but it's not like you can call up every news outlet and demand they take down their story. So you create new content that covers the old. Like a blog or a website. The way website algorithms work is by frontloading what's popular. A link to a *New York Times* article about you will make Google rank your page higher in search results than fifty links about you from smaller sites. If you want to take it a step further, you send out a name flood. That's how the pros cover their tracks. So if you're Special Agent Jen Smith, you make a bunch of pages about someone with the same name who is not Special Agent Jen Smith, but is, like, Boring Home Economics Teacher Jen Smith. It's just another way to game the system."

"So now what?"

"Anything she can hide, I can find."

"How?"

"I check the caches for all the main sites, use archiving tricks that scoop up the rest, and break out the Boolean search logic if I gotta. Plus I have a few other plays I keep close to the vest."

"All right. Can you"—Argento made a circling motion with his hand—"do all that?"

200 went to work. Argento tried to follow the screens she zipped through, but it wasn't long before he dozed off in his chair. When he woke, she had started in on her second energy drink.

"She cleaned up good. But here's a few things that might interest you. She's from a town called Shorliss, Nevada. Her brother died there a ways back. Heroin overdose. Local paper did a story and she was interviewed. Talked about how he wanted help but couldn't get the right kind."

"When was that?"

"September thirtieth. Ten years ago."

Argento nodded. The thirtieth was a week from now. He wasn't going to ask the girl about Silver Hair. He didn't have a name or occupation for him. But he did have a probable home base. The compound on the side of the cliff in Fenton.

"You mind?" he asked, motioning to her chair.

"Be my guest."

He sat, input *Fenton Arizona* in Google Maps, and searched until he had reached the outskirts of town and gotten to the back road that led up the hill to the compound. The map function ended there and he couldn't advance further.

"There's a house here higher up on the cliff face off a private road. I don't know the address. I'd like to know who lives there."

They swapped spots and 200 resumed her search. She whistled. "It's Trent Kilroy's old place. The action movie star."

Argento had seen a few of Trent Kilroy's movies, mostly when Emily was out of town and he'd been sufficiently bored. Kilroy was a musclebound martial arts guy who'd starred in movies with interchangeable three-word-titles like *Hunting for Justice* and *Blades of Dawn*.

200 was reading an article about Kilroy on her laptop. "Looks like

he was felled by ego, substance abuse, and alimony. Guess he had to unload the house after his movies started going straight to video."

"Unloaded it to who?"

"To whom."

"I'm not big on 'whom.' Not gonna start now."

"Fair enough. There's no individual owner listed. It comes back to a trust. There's a law firm attached to the trust that works out of Manhattan, if you're interested. Big outfit."

Argento could go to New York and dangle some high-priced lawyer out of an upper-story window until he coughed up what he knew, but it probably would be next to nothing. Some East Coast suit wasn't going to help him crack Fenton. "I'm not. Can you get the blueprints?"

"No. Already tried. And it wasn't publicly listed but I dug up some of the specs. It's 9,500 square feet, six bedrooms, four baths, with a home theater. Supposed to have great views."

"It say anything about why there's a guy on the roof with a rifle?"

"Nothing about rifle guy. Anything else you want me to run down?"

Argento's involvement in this case had started when he'd been asked to find Warren Reed. He knew next to nothing about the man. He hadn't found him in Fenton, so he hadn't thought about him much since, especially when Kristin and Ethan disappeared. But Warren was a thread to pull on. He gave 200 what he had. Warren Reed, married to Kristin Reed for fifteen years, son Ethan. Last seen in Fenton AZ. He didn't have the missing person flyers anymore— they were in his duffel bag in his truck, which was still in Fenton and now probably towed pending sale at auction, but he remembered Warren's birth date from them. He thought back to the kid's T-shirt from the diner. Denver Broncos. Argento wasn't a detective but he had a decent memory.

"Might have lived around Denver, or used to," he said.

200 typed away and then showed Argento a picture on a LinkedIn profile. "That him?"

Argento recognized the thick hair and glasses. He nodded. She went back to her keyboard.

"He's got a decent net presence. Facebook, Twitter, until recently. Serves on a board of directors or two. Went to MIT, no less. Works as an engineer, lives in Broomfield, Colorado."

"Any online activity this month?"

"No. But his social media postings were pretty irregular."

Argento was thinking of something Redlinger had said to him at the fire pit. Something Argento hadn't understood at the time. Redlinger was talking about how Fenton had two cemeteries and no hospitals. Then he'd mentioned school and how if you went to the wrong one, you could get killed. Argento had chalked it up to drunken ramblings. Maybe it wasn't.

"Where'd you say he went to college?"

"MIT. Massachusetts Institute of—"

"I know what it is," Argento said. "Was going to enroll there if the police academy didn't pan out."

200 snorted so hard a dribble of energy drink came out of her nose. "Your safety school," she said after she'd recovered.

"Can you get his college yearbooks online?"

200 nodded, her eyes bright, and punched them up. Argento started with Warren's freshman year. It didn't take long to find what he was looking for. The first-year pictures were organized by dormitories. Warren had lived in Baker House, a residence hall designed by famed Finnish architect Alvar Aalto, the yearbook boasted in a line at the bottom, the kind of fancy-pants detail that made Argento glad he hadn't gone to MIT.

Warren stood in the middle of the photo with a wide smile and that same thick shock of hair. He was surrounded by the dorm mates on his wing, most of whom were also grinning. Standing a few students away from Warren was a decidedly unsmiling kid who stood noticeably separate from the rest of the group, so much so that he was on the fringe of the picture. He had an unnaturally long neck, and although he was skinny, he wore clothing that still looked too small on him. He held one hand down and the other awkwardly clasped over it as if he didn't know where arms were supposed to go. The photo was pixelated but there was the distinctive neck plain as day, and the triangle of the face didn't change much over time. Argento was used to staring at faces. He'd spent decades at work carefully looking at folks to see if they were the same person whose mug shot was on the Wanted Person Board at his station. And the student Argento saw in the photo was someone he was certain he'd seen before.

In Fenton in the diner. Twice.

And later in the desert.

It was the man with the silver hair.

CHAPTER

24

His name was August Barrows and he'd attended MIT for just his freshman year.

"Let's see if he's anywhere else in the yearbook." 200 scanned through the digital pages. "He was in two clubs. Robotics and Botany. And, is that him? It isn't captioned."

Argento looked at the photo she pointed at, a shot of some students in a dining hall. It was a profile view and it was hard to be sure, but it did look like Barrows with a tray of food. Again, he was at the periphery of the picture. Argento studied the kid sitting next to Barrows. It looked like it could be Warren Reed again. Same smile. Same thick head of hair.

"I need everything you can find on this guy," Argento said. "Although I have a feeling it won't be much."

"You know anything else to help narrow the search?"

"He's maybe forty but he's already got silver hair. Like that news guy."

"News guy? You mean Anderson Cooper?"

"Yeah. He's probably ex- or current government. He lives and works in Fenton and has a whole police force on his payroll. Smart guy, talks funny."

"What do you mean funny?"

"In a high voice that says he's really smart and he's already bored with you."

200 went to work. Argento fell asleep again. He was still healing and didn't have any energy drinks to keep him up. It was daylight when he woke and she was still typing.

"You been working on this all night?"

"No. I mixed in some homework. But I didn't want to wake you."

"Where we at?"

"After MIT, he went dark. Before that, nothing. He may have changed his name."

"You did the cache and the archive thing you talked about?"

200 nodded. "Ran him through facial recognition as well, but that MIT picture is too pixelated and I couldn't find any other photos to plug in. And there's nothing tying him to Fenton, Arizona."

"So we don't think he's one of Sumaya's Homeland Security colleagues?"

"Not under that name. All I can tell you is he's an MIT dropout who used to wear floods."

Argento thought about how Barrows lived in the same small town where his old college classmate was last seen. A place few folks would have reason to visit. Hard to believe it was a coincidence. Maybe they were having a minireunion.

200 stood and put her laptop in her bag. She'd been up all night but she didn't look remotely tired. "I have class in an hour. If I come across anything else, I'll leave word for you here." She handed him a business card that had a number on it for a message service.

"Just remember, this is my problem. It's got nothing to do with you. Don't talk to anyone about it."

"I like to bounce my digital trail around in case anyone comes looking for me. It ends at an oil barge off the coast of Japan." She picked up her empty drink cans. Put one hand on his forearm and met his eyes. "I'm sorry about your dog."

"How'd you—"

"You said his name when you were sleeping. Hudson. You said he was a good boy." She gave his forearm a light squeeze and walked out, closing the door softly behind her.

Argento stood still for a moment. After Emily died, Hudson had let him concentrate on something other than himself. To lose him at any point would be an open wound. To lose him so soon after Emily...

He needed to focus. He needed breakfast and coffee and space to think. He washed up in the bathroom. He didn't want to stay in the same place for more than two nights, although he doubted he'd find another $39 hotel room.

To go out as a wanted man, he wouldn't need a fake mustache or an elaborate wig. His baseball cap and sunglasses would do just fine.

The hooker from next door was outside smoking meth out of a glass pipe when Argento went to check out of the room. She was a stringy Hispanic woman with her hair in a tight bun and a tattoo of a rose behind both ears. She looked tired and bored. She gave Argento a once-over.

"This hotel sucks, huh?" She smiled and made a half-hearted effort to hide the meth pipe. She had all her teeth but with the combination of her drug preference and chosen profession, it wouldn't stay that way for long.

"It could be worse."

"How?"

"Could be haunted."

She giggled. "Bet you got a story."

"It's not that interesting."

She got right to it. "I could do you this morning. Forty for everything."

She was a street prostitute who looked like Olive Oyl, but it didn't matter if she'd been a fitness model or the Princess of Monaco. If he slept with her then she'd be able to claim a piece of him. He wasn't willing to give that over. His wife still owned him, body and soul. Maybe she always would.

"Be careful out there," he said and stepped away.

She scowled and gave him the finger.

Argento walked under a low sun until the trash-lined streets, dismantled cars, and iron bars on the windows gave way to a neighborhood slightly more upscale. It felt foreign to be out in the world without Hudson, Argento's hand instinctively closing a few times as if holding an imaginary leash. Seeing the hooker smoke had ignited his own craving, so he bought a pack of Marlboros at a liquor store and smoked as he walked. He found a coffee shop called Ultimate Grounds that looked like it might serve a decent breakfast sandwich. A couple of teenagers in matching neon T-shirts stood outside the door with a sign.

One said, "I'm part of a student-led art and activist group and we're trying to—"

Argento held up a hand. "You lost me at art."

The kid gave him a sour face as he passed.

The coffee shop was playing a John Lee Hooker song, which was a point in its favor. It was populated by twentysomethings, moms with good tans, and a few guys in suits. A couple of elementary school kids were in one corner engrossed in a cell phone. When Argento had been that age, he'd played marbles. No one looked up when he entered. People operating in a comfortable cocoon, unaware of their surroundings. Argento had never lived that way. He wasn't sure he could if he wanted to. He ordered a large coffee and two fried egg sandwiches because one was never enough. He always thought better when he was eating. The guy behind the counter had green hair, a pierced nose, and a T-shirt that said, *I Love Pupusas*. There was a textbook on the counter behind him called *Philosophy of War* by an author with a complicated name.

Argento borrowed a pen and some notebook paper from Pierced Nose and found a seat in the corner where he could watch the door. He hadn't done especially well in high school, and he'd never gone to college. He'd been a decent enough linebacker that he probably could have started at a Division III school or rode the bench for a Division I, but he hadn't loved the game enough to pursue it. But while he lacked formal schooling, he had a sticky enough memory, even if he mostly used it for sports stats and car models. He knew weapons and fighting. How inner cities worked. How cancer blew apart your life. He wasn't sure he had the right brain to figure out what was happening in Fenton but he was going to take a shot at it, because he didn't have many other options. He had to go back there. He owed it to the Reeds, to Hudson. But before he did, he needed to understand what he was getting himself into.

He wrote down what he knew.

- August Barrows. Went to MIT where he'd been in the robot and flower club. Some kind of government brain working on secret shit in a movie star's compound. Liked to eat at the town's lone diner, which Olson from the hardware store said was recently propped up by a federal grant.
- Fenton DPS. Arrived about a year ago. Ex-soldiers pretending to be cops. Protecting Barrows. Would not outright murder civilians but were content enough leaving them for dead. Possibly also funded by a grant, according to Ruth and Dell, which meant the government had been exceedingly generous to the good people of Fenton of late.
- Agent Marisol Sumaya. Homeland Security. Lost a brother to an overdose. Running the show in Fenton, which she said was terrorism related, which was likely a lie from a liar.
- Warren Reed. Former MIT classmate of Barrows. Travels to Fenton for unknown reasons, stays at Baldwin, turns up missing after sending a text to his wife that something strange had happened.
- Kristin Reed. Goes to Fenton looking for Warren. Ends up dead herself in the desert along with her son.

Those were the basics but there was more. He had to rewind his brain to come up with it. The overwhelming show of force on the traffic stop of the seemingly harmless family in the Honda van with the Texas plates, when Chan and McBride had approached guns drawn and Cornejo had taken up a sniper position. How did that fit in? And if this project was so important, so secret, why was it being run out of Fenton, Arizona, at all? Fenton was remote but it wasn't surrounded by guard towers. It was an American town accessible to anyone who wanted to drive in. Why not have the whole thing headquartered in some DHS building completely closed to outsiders?

Whatever the Fenton operation involved, it was heavy-duty. Argento still wasn't sure who had the last word on decisions, Barrows or Sumaya. Maybe Barrows's power was only ceremonial. Like the Queen of England. Regardless, Argento thought the whole op had an off-the-books vibe to it. Or maybe it had started on the books but veered in another direction. Because Argento was pretty sure that even the Department of Homeland Security wasn't allowed to leave American citizens for dead in the desert just because they asked some questions about a missing family and lobbed an avocado at some guys.

Argento worked these things over in his head until lunchtime rolled around. He bought two more egg sandwiches.

Pierced Nose raised an eyebrow. "Pace yourself on the eggs. We don't have a chicken in back or anything."

"I'll probably have more for dinner."

"You gonna be here that long?"

"Nowhere else will have me," Argento said.

He sat back down with his lunch. He could call DHS, he supposed. He pictured how that would go. Dialing up Homeland Security headquarters and telling them his name was Kurt and he was a violent, unemployed transient who wanted to report that one of their agents, a Marisol Sumaya, who was guarding a top secret government project in Fenton, Arizona, had conspired to leave him for dead in the Sonoran Desert. This occurred in front of the Fenton Public Safety

Department, although none of them would corroborate this because they were all in on it too, and had shot his dog and also likely murdered an entire family called the Reeds, be great if someone could look into that. Plus while it was true he was currently wanted by the Maricopa County Sheriff's Department for assaulting a deputy, he had good reasons for what he did and would appreciate getting a break on those charges and by the way, this whole thing appeared to be spearheaded by some big brain with silver hair who spent a year at MIT in the Robotics club wearing dorky outfits. He figured halfway through his spiel, the call taker would transfer him to the agent with the least seniority to placate him with a "Sir, we'll certainly look into it," after which that agent would hang up and spend a minute or two telling whoever was next to him about this whack-a-doodle on the phone.

Argento stood and cracked his neck and back. He had to think this thing through not just forward and backward, but laterally. It wasn't his forte, but it was what the situation required. It would also require more caffeine. He went back to the counter. Pierced Nose was reading his *Philosophy of War* book. Argento bought two apple raisin muffins and another coffee.

Pierced Nose looked amused. "You can really put it away."

Argento nodded. "Won a rib-eating contest once against some firefighters. Book any good?"

Pierced Nose nodded.

"Since you're studying the topic, say I have an enemy. He's smarter than me. A lot smarter. And he's surrounded by guys with guns. And it's just me. How do I beat him?"

"Not much to go on."

"It's all I got."

"Let me think about that." Pierced Nose went back to his book and Argento went back to his table. He stared at his paper. Some contours were taking shape but there was still too much he didn't know. Like what could be in Barrows's compound that needed that level of protection. If the compound occupants were straight-up criminals,

Argento would assume it was something along the lines of guns, drugs, counterfeiting, or human trafficking. But a government-sanctioned project?

Then there was the town of Fenton itself. Were any of the people who lived there in on it? Someone had to have seen DPS shoot his dog in the street and haul Argento away in broad daylight. Argento wondered if they'd say anything. And who would they say it to?

And was the project a standing one or temporary? If it was temporary, when would Barrows likely finish it? Argento didn't know if the man was days or months away from completion. But if Barrows finished and left Fenton, Argento doubted he'd find him again. He'd disappear like he'd disappeared online. Like he never was.

There was a guy in a company shirt a few tables away on a work call talking about a shared vision and consolidating platforms. He was too loud and making it hard for Argento to concentrate. Argento looked at him with a flat expression on his burned face until the man noticed. He held Argento's stare for less than a second before he finished the call and busied himself with a memo pad on the table.

Argento reviewed everything he'd written down to see if there was something he'd missed. There was. The ShotSpotters all over Fenton. Like they were expecting a lot of gunplay, this in a town where the main offense, other than the ones Fenton DPS had committed against him and the Reeds, seemed to be the occasional double parker. He didn't know how the Fenton DPS had gotten the way they were. He'd had a Marine he worked with on DPD once tell him people who were good at being soldiers were too often bad at being people. That sounded strange to him. But he'd never been in the military.

His thoughts turned to the Reeds. Their final moments. Baking in the heat. The mother shielding her child. He thought of how their bodies had looked in the desert. He stood up again, as if the memory demanded it. Paced the room. He kept returning to August Barrows. Redlinger had called him a supergenius, although Redlinger had been sloshed at the time. Argento had read that the human brain could store something like 2.5 million gigabytes of data. He wasn't sure how they figured that out. You couldn't peel the brain open and see how many gigs spilled out. He didn't think his own brain had 2.5 million gigabytes of anything, unless some cholesterol from the egg sandwiches got up there.

He decided to change it up and have a few bagels with cream cheese for dinner plus another muffin. Pierced Nose was still on duty. Still reading his book when there weren't customers at the counter. A thirst for knowledge. Argento wished he still had the WWII novel he'd been reading at Trapsi's house. Then he thought about Trapsi's place. He'd been away from it for weeks. Mail was gathering. Plants were going unwatered. He was a shitty house sitter.

He came up with more questions and wrote them down on his paper. He'd filled three pages and most of a fourth. He went over them again. He had no new insights. He went outside and circled the block a few times. Trying to kick-start his brain. It was dark out, but the heat hadn't subsided much. Maybe he needed to go to sleep. Maybe answers would arrive in his dreams.

When he came back in, Pierced Nose looked up from his book. "We're closing." Argento checked the clock on the wall. It was nine o'clock at night. He'd been at the shop since morning. He dropped twenty dollars in the tip jar to account for holding the table all day. He headed toward the door.

"Hey," Pierced Nose said.

Argento turned.

"Two things. First, you're not going to beat him and his guns by yourself. You'll need help. Friends, or at least temporary allies. Second, you don't have to be smarter than him all the time. You just have to be smarter than him once. You just have to think of one thing he hasn't thought of."

First 200, now this. Argento was having success connecting with the young people. He looked at Pierced Nose for a moment and took in what he said. Then he gave him a thumbs-up and went out the door. He walked back a few blocks to where he'd seen a pay phone near a Circle K gas station. Still pay phones in the city if you looked long enough. He called the answering service from the card 200 had given him. The service told him he had a message.

"Found out one more thing about your Agent Sumaya from a guy in my network who got into the federal archives. She does work for Homeland Security. But that's not who she used to work for."

And then 200 told Argento where Sumaya used to work.

He listened to the message again. Then he hung up the phone. He tried to empty his mind so he could refill it with the addition of this new information. He turned the problem over in his head.

Then something clicked. Like the last mental tumbler he needed to spring a lock. And Argento had a pretty damn good idea what they were up to in Fenton, Arizona.

CHAPTER
25

I t had been a week since Argento staggered out of the desert. The blisters dotting his neck and arms were largely gone, and his kidneys seemed to be working all right. He had switched motels to one in the 1900 block of Van Buren that was $49 a night and had barred windows and a crumbling roof. The sign merely said *Motel*, but it had more amenities than the $39 Regal Inn, including bar soap and a shower curtain that wasn't stained brown. He could use a workout and would have asked if they had a fitness center on-site, but it was too early in the morning to be laughed at.

Argento was working on a plan but he needed three things to get it off the ground: a firearm, a car, and a map. Going to a gun store was out because his timetable didn't permit the federal ten-day waiting period, and he wasn't going to risk showing his license at the rental car desk at Budget in case Sumaya would get a warning ping. So his acquisitions would have to be extrajudicial. He'd assaulted a deputy at the hospital. Now he'd be stealing a gun and a car. It was a notable turn of events, but he'd had too much happen to him in the last month to feel anything but numb about it. He'd be selective about his victim. It would still be just as illegal, but it wouldn't be as bad.

He was in the kind of neighborhood where it didn't take long to find a target. He walked to the closest liquor store and sat across the street in the window bay of a by-the-slice pizza joint and drank a soda. There were two dealers posted on the corner and a decent stream of customers.

Argento was guessing the Phoenix PD wasn't doing a lot of narcotics enforcement on this particular block because the dealers were sloppy. They didn't even bother with a middleman. One guy kept a lazy lookout while the other pulled product out of his own sweatpants pocket and displayed direct to the buyers in his cupped hand without making much effort to hide it. Argento was too far away to tell what it was, but he assumed crack or meth. The customers were mostly broken-down homeless types who were pulling out, at most, five to ten dollars for a hit.

Not all street-level drug dealers were armed, but this one was. Argento could tell from the way he moved. His hands kept going to his rear waistband, where he'd do a series of pats, pulls, and tucks. They were subtle if you weren't looking for them. In police parlance they were called gun retention movements, the telltale, often unconscious signs of someone with a concealed handgun reminding himself his gun was there and secure. They didn't use holsters on the corner, and Argento had observed more than one gangbanger's gun slip down his pants leg to the ground.

Argento watched the dealer for close to an hour. He'd wait until he took a break and left the corner so Argento could follow him and get him alone. Then the guy made it easier for him by ambling across the street against the light, making traffic slow for him, and heading into the same pizza place Argento was. He walked past Argento toward the bathroom, which bore an *Out of Order* sign.

"It's closed," the cashier behind the counter said. "Lock's broken."

"Bitch open for me," the dealer said. He tried the door handle, which was unlocked, and went in. Argento waited a tick and went in after him. The dealer had just unzipped his fly but his pants were buckled which meant his gun was still secured in his rear waistband. He saw Argento.

"Get the fuck out. This a one-seater."

The dealer had a multicolored tattoo on the side of his neck that said *C.R.E.A.M.* If that meant the same thing in Phoenix that it did in Detroit, it stood for Cash Rules Everything Around Me. It was the tattoo of an asshole. Argento figured he was robbing the right person. Cream's hands were occupied at the toilet with the business of urinating, so Argento simply reached in and pulled the gun from the back of his pants. A Glock 19. The Honda Civic of handguns. It looked serviceable. Argento pulled the slide back. One in the chamber.

Most people haven't been tested in life-or-death situations and don't know how they'd react. Argento had known his fair share of peril. It never became old hat. He still felt the adrenaline spike, the tightness in his chest. But it was accompanied by a kind of laser focus. Cream was different. His reaction to a stranger disarming him in the restroom of a pizza joint was to twitch and say, "The hell?"

"Stay there and don't turn around."

Cream stayed put. It had been Argento's experience that if a dealer carried a weapon, it would just be the one. Most couldn't fight with their hands, so if you took their gun away, you took them away. They had no Plan B.

"I'm stealing your gun. Chose you because you sell drugs."

Cream was trying to come up with what to say, but it was a tall order to sound hard when another man just stripped you of your weapon while you were in a compromising situation. "You in a world of shit now," he sputtered.

That was true, Argento thought, but not because of this.

"You can keep your dope. Count to a hundred slow before you come out or I'll have to give you back one of your bullets."

Argento put the handgun in his rear beltline and pulled his shirt over it. The holsterless carry, just like the locals. He walked out of the pizza place and turned down an alley, breaking into a careful jog when he was out of sight of the drug corner. When he was several blocks away, he slowed to a walk as sweat from the Phoenix sun dripped down his chin, but kept pushing south and east toward the more civilized district of museums and state buildings downtown. Maybe the dealer had a car nearby, he and his buddy would jump in, and they'd go looking for him to reclaim their property. It was action Argento didn't need.

He took a bus across town and got off near the corner of Twenty-Seventh Avenue and West Indian School Road near a collection of head shops, thrift stores, and quick loans. He went in a place called Chinese Food and Donuts and bought a sweet roll so they'd let him use the bathroom. Inside the stall, he disassembled the Glock and checked the parts. Slide, frame, barrel, spring, mag. It looked to be in working order. It hadn't been oiled in a while, but Glocks would fire dirty. The magazine held fifteen rounds. He pointed it at the wall and dry-fired. He ate the sweet roll on the way out. It tasted like the place should just stick to Chinese food.

Argento walked a block and bought a screwdriver and a map of Phoenix inside a 7-Eleven. He was surprised, in the era of maps on phones, that they still had them, but convenience stores could surprise you. Argento had been in one in Texas that sold broadswords. He walked outside into the morning heat, feeling the sun's rays reawaken the still-healing burns on his face, and lingered near the store's parking lot and smoked a cigarette. Someone would come along. In this kind of neighborhood, they always did.

He'd been waiting for about thirty minutes when a tricked-out Escalade with a booming bass tore into the lot and parked halfway in a handicapped spot at the front of the convenience store. The driver got out and hitched up his sagging pants, which were the size of a rain-delay tarp, and sauntered into the store. He was midtwenties, of average build, wearing a hoodie that had some kind of marijuana theme.

Argento waited. Just because he played loud music and parked illegally didn't necessarily mean this man deserved to have his ride stolen. The car itself was a Platinum edition with glossy paint and chrome trim and gleamed from a recent waxing. Lifted suspension, customized gold rims, one of which probably cost more than Argento's wedding ring.

When the driver came out holding a few bags of chips and a tall-boy, he saw Argento looking at his car.

"You can't afford it," he said.

The store clerk, a harried-looking man with thinning hair, came out after him, breathing hard. "You must pay."

The driver wheeled and shoved the clerk backward with both hands. The clerk stumbled and hit the glass door with a thud, sliding to the ground. He started to rise.

"Stay down," the driver said. "You know you ain't gonna do nothing."

Argento had a winner. He scanned the driver for bulges in his pockets and waistline that would indicate a weapon. He saw none. He positioned himself in front of the front driver's-side door of the Escalade.

"What's your handicap?" Argento asked, nodding down at the blue wheelchair icon of the parking space.

Handicap set the chips and tallboy on the hood of the Cadillac as if to free his hands for a fight and started toward him. "The fuck you say?"

Argento showed him the Glock but angled it so the clerk couldn't see it. Handicap stopped in his tracks. Argento looked at the clerk, who'd gotten up and appeared uninjured.

"You all right?"

The clerk waved a weary, dismissive hand, like this was a daily occurrence. He scooped up the bags of chips and drink and went back into the store.

Argento glanced around. Coast was clear. It'd be awkward if a marked police car drove past right about now. He pushed Handicap against his own car door and patted him down one-handed. A set of keys but no weapons. He pocketed the keys and took the man's wallet, glancing at the Arizona ID before putting it back in Handicap's pocket. Damien Potter of nearby Mesa. He took a step back, giving himself a reactionary gap if Damien made a move. Argento held the gun at his side.

"Damien, I'm borrowing your car."

"The fuck you is."

"If you report it stolen, I'll know and you'll never see it again. I'll strip it for parts. Looks like you've put work into this ride. That would be a damn shame. Now if you let it be, I'll return it to this parking lot sometime in the next forty-eight hours, clean and gassed up with two hundred dollars in the center console for your trouble. That's the deal."

"You think I'm gonna let this be? I'll find you."

"You don't want to find me."

Damien's shoulders slumped. Resigned to his fate. "Weird fucking car theft," he muttered.

"It's my first," Argento said. "Probably not doing it right." He got in the Escalade and drove away as Damien shouted something after him that probably wasn't praise. When he'd gotten enough distance between himself and the 7-Eleven, Argento pulled into a vacant lot and checked the registration in the glove box. He wanted to make sure the car he stole wasn't already stolen. If the Cadillac was registered to Ingrid VanNostridge on Whispering Hills Drive in Paradise Valley, he'd return it to her and look for another ride. But the registration matched Damien's name and address from his ID.

Argento knew cars reasonably well and there had been no shortage of Escalades in Detroit. Recent models came standard with OnStar GPS tracking. He got out, opened the trunk, lifted the liner, and set aside the spare tire. Then he unscrewed the trunk plate with his 7-Eleven screwdriver and peeled back the shell. The OnStar module was conveniently marked with its logo. It had three wires. He unplugged all three. OnStar wasn't the only tracking game in town. SiriusXM radio also offered location service, but even if Damien had signed up for it, they only covered certain models that didn't include Caddys. He'd be running dark now, unless Damien had installed some aftermarket GPS he didn't know about.

Argento wasn't sure if Damien would report the car stolen. Maybe his offer to return the Cadillac in better shape than he found it was just strange enough to be convincing. And guys like Damien often had arrest warrants and wanted to avoid police contact. They got their brothers or girlfriends to say they were driving the car last so they could report it stolen. So it might still get entered into the system as hot. To guard against a cop running his plate and trying to pull him over at gunpoint, he could swipe a plate off another Cadillac to disguise the auto theft. But he was reluctant to do so unless he could establish the owner of the plate was an asshole the caliber of Damien or Cream. Argento was committing crimes, but he was trying to avoid a crime wave.

He checked his map. There looked to be a family farm on 172nd Avenue on the west side of town. He drove straight there and ran the Escalade just off-road along the perimeter, splashing through a swath of mud from the field's recent irrigation. The Arizona soil was part sand and part sticky clay, and the spatter covered just enough of his rear license plate to make it unreadable, but not so much that it looked like someone trying to deliberately conceal a stolen ride. He didn't have to worry about a front plate. Cars in Arizona weren't required to have them.

He settled in the driver's seat. Turned the car seat massage function to High. It felt good on his lower back. It was about 260 miles to Shorliss, Nevada.

Time to reunite with an old friend.

CHAPTER
26

rgento sat in the back of Marisol Sumaya's car watching her stand in front of her brother's grave. She remained there for a good twenty minutes. Then she laid a flower on the headstone and walked back to her car, which she'd left unlocked. Even federal law enforcement got complacent in rural cemeteries.

When she got in the front seat, he said, "Agent Sumaya."

She gasped and twisted around to look at him. He'd noticed she was right-handed from watching her eat at the diner and which side of her body Krebs had returned the firearm to in the desert, so he patted down her right side and found no sidearm. Maybe she didn't think a gun was necessary while she was off duty visiting a dead sibling's grave. When he'd been on the job, Argento had worn his gun everywhere. Even to church. In Detroit, it had been a needed accessory. Like a hat or a watch.

"I've got a gun on you," he said. "Look straight ahead."

She did, her breath quickening. "How'd you find me?"

"It's the anniversary of your brother's death. Figured you'd come here. Been waiting since dawn. You should lock your car."

"Are you going to shoot me? I'm a government agent." Sumaya's breathing was ragged but her voice was steady.

"You're not much of one."

"Answer the question."

"We'll see," Argento said, "if you tell me the truth."

"I've read up on you. You're no murderer."

"But that was before you dropped me in the desert, Marisol. It changes a man, being left to die. So I'm good with leaving you the same way."

Sumaya said nothing. Her left hand was on the steering wheel and she was gripping it so tightly Argento could see the veins below her knuckles.

"We'll start with a test. Tell me Silver Hair's name. Trick is, I already know it. So if you lie, I'll shoot you in the back through this seat. Then I'll keep asking questions and you'll still have to answer, but it will be harder because you'll have a bullet in your spine."

"Okay," Sumaya said. Sat utterly still. Her breathing had slowed. "His name is Michael Dav—"

"No," Argento interrupted. He pressed the barrel hard against the seat so she could feel it. "Welcome to wheelchair life."

"Fuck!" The word came out in a hiss. "Wait!"

Argento did. He was good at waiting. Plus he didn't want her to call his bluff. He had come to the cemetery in a stolen car and was holding a stolen gun, but he wasn't going to shoot her, not like this. There were still rules.

But she didn't know that.

Sumaya shook her head. "You don't know who he is. How could you?"

"Been looking into things. His first name is a month of the year. Give me his last so I know you're operating in good faith."

"You have no concept of what he . . . what this is . . ." Her voice trailed off. She met his gaze in the rearview. He held it.

"When I'm done shooting, you won't have any feeling from the chest down. But you'll always have parking right in front."

She stiffened. Closed her eyes. Argento waited. "Barrows," she said after a time. "August Barrows."

"That's the one. So how smart is he?"

"Mind like his comes along once in a generation. He's the franchise."

"The tale you told about working on terrorism. That's not what you two are doing."

"So what are we doing?"

"You're DHS, but that's just a cover. You used to be DEA. I'm betting you still are."

"So what."

"So what's Barrows working on in the compound with the blessing of the DEA?"

"I won't answer that. Go ahead and shoot me."

"How about I tell you my theory," Argento said. And did. When he was finished, he watched her face in the mirror.

She opened her mouth as if to speak. Closed it. He could almost see the light change in her eyes. She didn't have to say anything.

He knew he was right.

CHAPTER
27

When she'd collected herself, Sumaya said, "Thought you weren't an investigator."

The drug problem, Argento understood from hands-on field experience, was a three-legged stool made up of users, dealers, and supply. If the DEA wanted to win the drug war and had the smartest man in the world on their side, they'd task him with eliminating one of the legs of that stool. Argento had figured out which leg.

"Turns out if I spend enough time in a coffee shop that has muffins, I can puzzle things out. What's the name of the project?"

"It doesn't have one."

"Every big government project has a name. Enduring Freedom. Clean Sweep."

"It's just called The Project."

"Okay. Who's running it. You or him?"

She took in a deep breath. Blew it out. "Joint control. At least it was. They just took me off the job. After you escaped. Waiting to hear where they're gonna ship me."

"Sorry to screw up your career by not dying," Argento said. "Who's taking your place?"

"No one. My partner's still there."

"Who's that?"

"No," Sumaya said. "Gun or not, you don't get everything."

"He's gonna finish this thing?"

"Shouldn't be long now. Barrows says he's close to the end."

"If you care about what happens to your partner, get him out. Get all your people out. Your secretary. Your IT guy. Because I'm going back to Fenton. Let your watchers in DC know. Use government language they'll understand. Tell them to anticipate an adverse outcome."

Sumaya shook her head. "Fenton DPS would kill you the minute you cross the county line. And even if they didn't, there's no way for you to get in the compound. You can't sneak up on the place because there are ground sensors you won't see that alert to any weight over forty pounds. And even if you reach the front doors, they're fireproof and bullet-resistant, and beyond that, there's more security inside you don't even know about, guys who shoot first and ask no questions."

"And a helicopter on the roof to take Barrows away at the first sign of trouble."

"And that."

"The easy fights aren't any fun."

"You're not a cop anymore. You're a wanted fugitive for assaulting a deputy at the hospital. What are you gonna do, try to put Barrows and Fenton DPS under citizen's arrest? Even if a world existed where you could, every single one of their names is already tucked away on a list for a preemptive presidential pardon. You got no move here."

"Speaking of the hospital, what were you going to do if I was still there when you arrived?"

Sumaya didn't say anything for a moment. She looked away from the rearview. Her face was strained. Almost like she was trying to hold in a cough. "I don't know. There's no playbook for this anymore."

The cemetery was empty. Serene, well-tended. A backdrop of evergreens, the grass as emerald as they could get it in south Nevada. It was a fitting resting place. Emily was buried at Mount Olivet Cemetery in north Detroit. Argento had gone there once a week, alone.

He would sit against her headstone because her name was on it, and his back touching her name made him feel close to her.

Argento asked, "Your people tracking me?"

"You use your ATM, try to rent a car, get on a plane, they'll know."

"A judge sign off on that?"

"We have broad discretion. And a lot of resources."

"How'd you get your soldier police department?"

"Broad discretion," Sumaya said. "Lots of resources." It didn't come across as sarcastic to Argento. She just sounded weary.

"They need much convincing?"

"We sold them on the project being critical to the nation's interests, which it is. And we're paying them the kind of money that changes the way you think."

"They were happy to maroon me in the sticks with no water."

"You should see the résumés of these boys. The kind of fights they've been in, the friends they lost, all for a grunt salary. They came back from overseas different. And now they're making two million each tax-free for working this project. They aren't going to leave that kind of money on the table. They don't care anymore what they have to do for it."

Argento was about to say *Redlinger might care* but stopped himself. Redlinger had helped him at great risk to himself. Argento wanted to keep his name out of it.

"What happened to Warren Reed?"

"I wasn't there," Sumaya said.

"Doesn't mean you don't know."

"I can't—"

"You're going to tell me," Argento said. "Because I still have a gun to your back. Because I'm still the guy you left to die in the Sonoran and whose dog your people killed. And I spent two decades on the job. Saw some shit myself. Lost some friends, just like your Fenton boys. Didn't turn me into piss stains like them. And during that time, I got lied to plenty, which means I know when I'm getting played. So get it right."

"Warren and Barrows, they knew each other," Sumaya began.

"They went to MIT together. They lived on the same floor of the dorm. Then what?"

"Barrows...called him. Invited him to Fenton. Told him to keep it quiet."

"Why?"

"They had stayed in touch over the years. I think Barrows considered him a friend. I think Warren might have been his only friend."

"And?"

"Warren actually showed up. They had dinner at the diner. I didn't approve it. I didn't even know until it was already happening."

Argento waited for the rest to unspool.

"Barrows told him what he was working on. Not in so many words, but enough so Warren could figure it out. I think he was trying to impress Warren. Barrows doesn't...interact with people a lot. I think he let the conversation get away from him."

Argento wasn't going to stop Sumaya from talking but he could already see where this was headed.

"I had Fenton DPS follow Warren back to the Baldwin. To find out for sure what Barrows had said. They made contact with him in his room where he was on the phone. DPS believed he was about to reveal sensitive information about his meeting with Barrows. I'm told there was a struggle."

"A struggle with lots of blood," Argento said. "The room's all redone. New carpeting, drywall. To cover up the damage."

"It was regrettable."

"That's all you got? Regrettable?"

"Yes," Sumaya snapped. "It was awful collateral damage for a project that is going to change the world. Not just a city, not just a country. The world. Do you understand that?"

"I understand Warren Reed was murdered because he felt sorry for a weird classmate and made the mistake of eating with him. How'd you get that one past Ruth at the Baldwin?"

"She was on vacation," Sumaya said. "We told her it was bikers who did the damage. She believed us."

"Warren was an engineer, not a reporter. Who would he tip off?"

Sumaya had already started shaking her head midway through Argento's question. "He'd already texted his wife, said something strange had happened to him. And because he's credible. Anyone he tells is the wrong person because then we've lost control of the information and it's out in the public domain. No. For a project of this magnitude, you don't take that chance."

"Any consequences for Barrows for leaking?"

Sumaya dropped her chin to her chest and then looked back up. "We penalize him, we delay the project. We just tried to keep him on a shorter leash."

"Fenton's a town open to anyone. Why not have this project deep in some fed building in DC?"

"Barrows wanted to stay in the movie star's place. And the climate's good for his allergies."

"Got to cater to the MVP."

"If he's not happy, he stops working. Same rules that apply to us don't apply to him. You know they bring in a team of doctors to the compound every month to do a full health screening on him? He travels with a cooler of his own blood in case he needs a transfusion. He's contracted with the United States government for over a decade. He's been behind breakthroughs in everything from AI to vaccines. He's irreplaceable."

"This thing can't last. I figured it out in less than a month and I was lucky to graduate high school. You already have three missing people, a shot dog in the street, and me. You can't just drop everyone in the desert. People talk."

Sumaya rubbed her forehead like she was trying to ward off a headache. "It was never intended to be long term in Fenton. We gave him a year after which we'd move to a more secure location. He's got three weeks left and then we're packing up shop whether he wants to or not. I've watched him work. I believe he can do this. Not everyone in my office does. There's a division. Some think it's a fool's errand. But I have to believe he can."

"You do, don't you? Because of the Reeds."

He let her feel the full weight of his stare in the mirror.

"In the diner, when I asked about the Reeds, you said you couldn't let anything happen to a mother and her child because you were a mother yourself. Was that true?"

"No," Sumaya said. "I'm not a mother."

"I found their bodies. Kristin and Ethan. Along the riverbed. Was she asking too many questions?"

Sumaya didn't say anything.

"Kristin died trying to shield her son from the heat. Her body was on top of his. It was one of the worst things I've ever seen."

Sumaya made a sound in her throat. Put both hands on the wheel. Stared straight ahead.

The pain and acute stress of the last week boiled over. "Fucking talk to me," Argento growled and jabbed the gun so hard into the seat Sumaya let out a grunt.

"She didn't think you were going to show for your meeting. So she parked her car blocking the gate of the compound." Sumaya's words came out fast but controlled. "She wouldn't leave. She was talking about how she knew a reporter from the *Post* who was going to help her find out what was going on in Fenton."

"So she had to take the desert walk. Her and her boy."

"That was Barrows's call." Sumaya tried to say it matter-of-factly, but her voice betrayed her and the words came out thin, almost as a question.

"Joint operational control, remember. Your call too."

"It was a horrible thing we did. To the Reeds. You think I don't know that? But it was part of an awful price that we are willing to pay. You have to...look at the long view."

"I'm not a long-view guy. I see a dead mom and kid in the sand, someone tries to off me and kills my dog, I'm going to do something about it."

Sumaya turned and stared right at him. Reclaiming her voice. "You want to die over a woman and kid you spent ten minutes with, be my guest. This is a zero-fail mission. So if you go back there, there's a guy on the compound roof with a machine gun who'll make you wish you hadn't. You want to be a crusader, crusade somewhere else, because this operation falls under the Patriot Act. That means do what you have to and don't file any reports when shit goes sideways because they don't want to know. It's a results business. Nobody cares if you tried hard."

"Just because the overlords say you can doesn't make it right."

"Truman dropped two nukes to end a war," Sumaya said, her voice rising. "Murdered two hundred thousand people, most of them civilians. His name is on high schools and battleships. The world thanked him for what he did. They'll thank us for this."

"This isn't a war."

"The hell it isn't. You were a cop in Detroit, for God's sake. You've seen the ODs. The screaming kid left alone in a crib with bugs in his hair because Mom is out getting her fix. Dealers shot up over turf wars and the bystanders who caught one in the head because wrong place wrong time."

"This operation, you think it's worth the lives of two adults and a child, and my dog, none of whom did a damn thing to deserve it except wrong place wrong time?"

Sumaya nodded. "It is worth more. Worth my life, worth yours."

"Don't see you volunteering yours like you volunteered mine."

"Given the chance I would."

"I don't think it's worth any of that. Think I'll take a blowtorch to it."

Sumaya stayed quiet, a look on her face he couldn't read.

"We ain't both right," Argento said.

"You got any more questions? This gun-in-my-back shit is getting old."

"If Fenton Public Safety calls for backup, who shows?"

"A DEA Special Response Team from Phoenix. But they don't know about the project. They'd be going in blind."

"No call to Braylo?"

HARD TOWN

"We don't want them in the loop. Federal problem, we stick with federal cops."

Argento thought of Andekker, the Braylo deputy. He was glad they wouldn't get the call. He didn't want to be in a position where he'd have to go head-to-head with him. "Who does know about this?"

"Me. My partner. Tomlinson. DEA command staff. And a few folks in the U.S. government, the kind of people who can get same-day meetings with the president. No one else. For their protection. And to avoid leaks."

Argento let that sink in. The wind was moving through the evergreens. Wind sounded different in a cemetery. He couldn't put his finger on why. "How'd you get to be such a true believer. Him?" Argento gestured in the direction of the headstone of Sumaya's brother.

She looked where he was pointing. When she looked back, her eyes were wet. "His name was David Sumaya. His girlfriend introduced him to heroin at a party. Got addicted from the jump, overdosed a year later at nineteen in the bathroom stall of a nightclub. You know what David told me a few days before he died? That he felt like he was put on this earth just to do heroin. That was his only purpose. He had a full scholarship to Stanford. He volunteered at an after-school program for at-risk kids. And he died alone on some shitty bathroom floor. It's happening everywhere, variations on the same story, and we just accept it because that's the way it's been. It's a problem that can't be solved. Well, this is the solution."

"How exactly does it work?"

"If I could fully describe that, we wouldn't need Barrows."

Neither of them said anything for a time. Sumaya rubbed her eyes and then cast a backward glance at Argento, as if to see if the gun was still there. Argento pushed the muzzle forward against her seat to remind her it was.

"If this operation is so scaled up, why just two agents?"

"DEA brass wanted a small footprint. We're right near the border. If the cartels sniff around and find out, they'll roll in heavy."

"That's why the Hispanics in the Honda minivan got the full court

167

press," Argento said. "Your boys were jumpy as hell. You thought it might be a scout."

"Turns out it was just a family of four passing through."

A station wagon approached down the winding drive from the main gate. The back was full of flowers. Argento watched it pass. The driver was a woman of about eighty. She wore a colorful hat with a band around it. The kind no one wore anymore.

"I'm sorry about your dog. I am."

"What happened to his body?"

Sumaya didn't answer for a moment. She looked like she was gathering herself. Then she said, "They burned it in Redlinger's fire pit."

"'Him,'" Argento said. "Not 'it.'"

The woman with the hat got out of her car down the road. She took some flowers out of the back seat and walked among the headstones with a cautious gait. She had a curious smile on her face. Maybe remembering something about her friend or relative that had given her pleasure.

"So what happens to me?" Sumaya asked.

"You stood by while a woman and child were killed. A few hours of community service should do it. Roadside trash pickup or something."

"You're a funny guy, Kurt."

"I think it's funny that I'm going to let you live. Maybe it's because when I get back to Fenton, I'm going to be doing some things I'll probably feel bad about later. I don't want to start feeling bad now."

"What I've told you isn't going to change anything. If you go to the cops, local or state, they'll arrest you for assaulting those deputies. Then you'll be that loud prisoner in the cell insisting it was all a setup. The one nobody listens to. You're all alone on this." Sumaya turned fully in her seat and stared at Argento. Her voice was an octave lower when she said, "You think this whole thing boils down to Big Guy versus Little Guy, don't you? And you want to fight for the Little Guy. You're wrong. Naïve."

"You want to do this project, get another Barrows. Start over. Do it right."

"There is no other Barrows. There's no . . ." Sumaya narrowed her eyes and focused in on him. "If you go back there and somehow make it through because you're the luckiest man ever born, salvage everything you can from The Project. All of Barrows's ongoing research is deposited into an electronic reservoir. When he's completed it, he's going to forward the project's final abstract to HQ via a secure link so we can access the entire collection. Then we can understand it and replicate it. He can send it from his phone if he has to. Make sure he does. Don't do it for my brother or for me. Do it because you know it's the goddamn right thing."

Argento stayed silent.

"So do I need to worry you'll change your mind about killing me? Worry one day I'll hear a knock on my door and it'll be you?"

Argento put his gun back in his waistband. "Won't be any knock," he said.

CHAPTER
28

A state trooper fell in behind Argento on the way back to Phoenix from the cemetery. Time to put the field mud to the test. Maybe the trooper would pull him over for an obstructed plate anyway. If he failed to yield, he didn't know if the trooper would chase him. Pursuit policies varied significantly by jurisdiction. Some agencies could only pursue for violent felonies. Others, until the wheels came off. Argento guessed highway patrol was more the latter. But the trooper didn't bite. He paralleled Argento briefly, giving him a once-over. Then he drove by.

When he got back to town, Argento ran the Escalade through a self-serve car wash, gassed it up, and put two hundred in the console like he'd promised. It was dusk and the heat had faded for the day when he returned Damien's Cadillac to the same 7-Eleven parking lot he'd borrowed it from. Damien was a turd, but he wasn't doing it for Damien. He was doing it because he said he would.

As he walked from the lot, Argento thought about how Sumaya was right; if Argento went back to Fenton alone and tried to breach the compound, Fenton DPS would reduce him to a wet smear. Pierced Nose from the coffee shop had echoed the same sentiment. He needed help. On the drive home from the cemetery, he'd come up with the rough outline of a strategy that, when he thought about it, sounded like the ramblings of a madman. But he was looking at formidable obstacles and limited options, so he figured it was either a batshit-crazy plan or no plan at all.

Argento picked a new motel about half a mile from his old one, a place equally run-down with plenty of vacancies and a night clerk who openly watched anime porn at the desk. Argento wanted to stay on the move. Thinking like a crook was tiring. But he'd picked up a car and a gun and then used that gun to force a confession out of a federal agent, so maybe he was getting good at it.

He lay on the bed fully clothed because it still wasn't the kind of hotel where you'd get under the sheets. Mulled over his preposterous idea. There might have been other options but he could think of only one.

Recruiting a drug cartel.

The cartel was ideally suited for what Argento needed. They'd be well equipped. Highly motivated. Have no problem with extreme use of force.

No one else would do.

Argento had worked Street Crimes for years, which meant plenty of time chasing dope dealers. He'd also run some joint operations with the DEA, mostly providing additional muscle on search warrants, where the feds always wore balaclavas both during the raids and after when they were booking the suspects, to maintain anonymity as a guard against reprisals from the dealer's shooters. So he knew the basic structure of drug organizations. On the lowest rung of the ladder was the street-level dealer slinging small hits. The street dealer's connect would be a second guy who didn't need to stand on the corner because he was doing his own runs selling a few ounces to known clients. The second guy would be linked in to a third who sold by the pound and used couriers to keep an appreciable distance from the transaction, selling direct to a buyer only if he knew them well.

The third guy would know how and when drugs were getting over the border. Would be in on money drops and coordinating dope runs to a city like Phoenix. The third guy would have a contact in Mexico who'd be an established member of the cartel. Argento knew Phoenix was a distribution hub for the Sinaloa cartel, so you'd have to go one or two more people up the Sinaloa ladder until you got to a decision-maker. Someone who had the ear of the big boss.

It was the third guy who would ultimately take Argento where he needed to go. There was no realistic plan to address what was happening in Fenton without the cartel. He'd look to form a temporary truce to take on a mutual enemy. But to get to the third guy, he'd need to deal with the first and the second guys. He couldn't skip a step. There was an order to these things.

He slept badly that night, dreaming of the desert and Hudson and the dead Reeds, all of them under the hot sun, Ethan's skin red and flayed, the boy muttering words he couldn't understand. When he woke, he took a moment to shake off the vision. He could hear a couple next door in a loud, age-old argument about who drank the last beer. The bugle in the morning.

He walked to a bus stop, passing a busker playing the saxophone enthusiastically but not especially well. Argento still put a five in the man's open case. He liked people who worked for a living. He took the bus to a military surplus store on the east end of town that opened early and bought a holster for his Glock, handcuffs and key, a backpack, a pair of binoculars, some medical supplies, and a $30 TracFone with a hundred minutes, paid in cash.

The guy behind the counter was wiry and smelled of cigarettes. He wore a camouflage bandana and had a holstered revolver at his side. Arizona was an open carry state. Argento had no problem with that. The kinds of people who worked in military surplus stores tended to be the kinds of folks you wanted armed if things kicked off.

"I like it," the man said when he rang up Argento's phone purchase. "Don't want the government tracking you."

"No I don't," Argento agreed. He looked around. He was the only customer at the moment. "Got anything off-menu?"

The counter guy cocked his head. "Meaning..."

"Could use a Taser. For self-defense."

"Of course."

"Not the contact stun kind. The prong kind. With as long of a burst as you got."

"If your intention is for a lawful purpose, like self-defense, I might have one in back. Pulse series. Fifteen-foot range. Guaranteed muscle lock-up for thirty seconds. Comes fully charged. It'll set you back $550, which is more than you'd pay online, but I ain't checking no IDs or running no background check."

Argento put $550 of the governor's money on the counter. The guy took it, and five minutes later Argento had an electronic control weapon to complement his Glock. A block down from the surplus store, he bought the best breakfast burrito he'd ever had at a food truck called El Norteno. It was the freshness of the tortilla and the tang of the salsa, he figured, that put it over the top. Plus the liberal inclusion of bacon. It was so good, he bought another and ate it on the way to the bus stop.

Back at his hotel, Argento charged the phone. He had a general idea of the Phoenix neighborhoods just from the short time he'd spent there, but it would be helpful to get an insider's view from a subject matter expert. So he called the front desk of the Central City precinct and asked to speak to the shift lieutenant. He was put through. It had been Argento's experience that you could usually get a police lieutenant on the phone for a cold call even on a larger department. If he'd asked to speak to the captain, they would have taken a message.

"Central City precinct, Lieutenant Foltz."

When Argento spoke, he took some of the gravel out of his voice to sound like a suburban guy who wore pleated shorts and played pickleball. "Hello sir. My name is Kevin Mannion and my family and I are thinking of relocating to Phoenix for my work but have some concerns about crime. We don't want to move in next door to a drug house for instance. What are your recommendations?"

Argento was fortunate. He'd gotten the lieutenant on a good day. The man was chatty. Argento guessed he was near the end of his shift, or maybe closing in on a vacation.

"Well, Mr. Mannion, the worst area at the moment is Alahambra. Got your rolling gun fights, carjackings, street rips. Rough boundaries are south of Northern Avenue, west of Seventh Street, east of, say, Forty-Third Avenue, and north of Grand. Steer clear."

"What are the worst streets within Alahambra?"

Foltz paused. "The paper did a story on Pacheco Boulevard a few months back. Called it 'Three Blocks of Hell.' Post Office won't deliver mail there anymore because there have been too many attacks on carriers. They interviewed a resident who said there's no God on Pacheco. That seemed a bit much to me, but only by a little. When we have the staffing, we try to hit it. Street cops, SWAT. But we're down a few hundred officers citywide and they ain't being replaced. They gutted Narcotics to try and plug the gap. Problem is, a lot of the Pacheco violence is drug-related. Kinda need Narcotics for that."

"That's too bad," Argento offered.

The lieutenant was just getting warmed up. Argento heard papers rustling in the background. "The morons in charge forget what the street is like. Their answer to everything is inventing more fucking forms to fill out."

Argento didn't say anything. The lieutenant wasn't really talking to him anyway.

"We pulled detail at a block party last week, some lady who heads up an inner-city center spent twenty grand of taxpayer money to have candy shot out of a glitter cannon for a dozen kids. Twenty grand, but I'm wearing an expired ballistic vest because there's no budget for new ones."

Argento was getting a different vibe off Foltz now. Not a close-to-vacation feel. More like a close-to-retirement one.

"How much longer you got?"

"Pulling the pin in three months," Foltz said, some cheer restored to his voice. "Be the happiest day of my life."

"Thank you, sir," Argento said. "Hang in there. And I appreciate the info on Pacheco Boulevard. I'll be sure to stay away from that region." He hung up, slid his Glock into his holster, and covered it with his shirt. Then he checked his map, walked out of the hotel room, and took a bus to Pacheco Boulevard.

CHAPTER
29

The newspaper had been spot-on about Pachecho. *Hellish* was a fair description: three blocks strewn with trash and discarded syringes, populated by gaunt, hollow-eyed addicts stumbling down the block and transients sleeping near spatters of their own vomit. A small corner park with a padlocked gate featured a play structure that someone had set on fire, leaving the plastic climbing wall blackened and curled upward. Argento saw a paper-thin hooker on her knees servicing a john in the alley, the only nod to discretion being a grimy bedsheet tossed over her shoulder that only half-covered her efforts. The dealers were out in force looking for their next sale, enduring the searing heat. A kid in a diaper wandered into the street unattended and Argento started toward him before a mother in a long, dirty T-shirt with one breast hanging out scooped the kid up with a loud "Fuck, Jose" and took him back in the house.

Argento had spent years policing streets like this. The anchor business would be either a liquor store or a quick loan. A lone social service agency on the block would try gamely to keep up with the overwhelming demand; a handful of those agencies were headed by directors siphoning off tax dollars to fund private vacations and shopping trips. These neighborhoods were rarely dull. Once in a while they were funny; he still remembered being part of a police Thanksgiving turkey giveaway in the projects when he handed a ten-pound bird to a woman and then watched her circle the block and come back in a different outfit to try for a second one. But mostly they were dirty and depressing, populated by the broken and the lost, punctuated by periodic explosions of violence, some of it random, some of it focused against a rival, a perceived insult, or a case of mistaken identity that left some unlucky soul twisted and bleeding in the street.

He leaned against the wall of a dingy hotel with an awning that advertised Color TV and smoked. His time in the sun had darkened his already Mediterranean skin. Maybe that would help. He could pass for a local.

The dealers were more careful than Cream had been. They wore backpacks likely containing a change of clothes to throw the police off if they had to flee, and they hid their hand-to-hand exchanges with their backs to public view or stepped around the corner into an alley. But they still didn't seem used to law enforcement scrutiny. Didn't look up to see if any cops with binoculars were surveilling them from a window across the street. It didn't take long for Argento to notice that they pulled their product from a nearby drainpipe. From the looks of the discarded corner-cut baggies on the sidewalk around him, the drug of choice was crack.

Argento had been in a police training once where some bow tie from the DA's office talked about how three things had to be present for crime to occur. The first was a motivated offender. The second, a suitable target. The third, the absence of capable guardians. When those three elements converged, crime flourished. Pacheco Boulevard was a good example of this. Argento would have liked to see the bow tie come to Pacheco and observe it in person, but he doubted the guy would have gotten out of the car. He wouldn't have wanted to soil his wingtips.

After about twenty minutes of Argento smoking on the corner, the dealers sent out a scout to see about the auslander. The inquiring party was a Hispanic kid of about thirteen wearing a baggy Phoenix

Suns jersey with a player's name on the back Argento didn't recognize. He'd stopped following the NBA after the Pistons' last dynasty had ended, but by then the game had already changed and players celebrated garbage-time dunks by thumping their chests like they'd just survived Bunker Hill, showoffy children in adults' bodies.

"Who you is," the kid asked. It was too hot to be wearing a jersey, and there was a sheen of sweat on his upper lip.

"A capable guardian."

"Huh?"

"No one special. No school today?"

"Half day."

"It's ten thirty in the morning."

"Half a half day," the kid said. "You a cop?"

"Can't be. I don't have a radio."

"They got them little ones now."

"Yeah, but they at least need an earpiece."

The kid looked at Argento's ears. Seemed satisfied. "You still on the wrong corner."

"How do you know which corner is right for me?"

"It's them saying that. They think you trouble." The kid gestured across the street where two dealers watched them. Both were late twenties, maybe Mexican or Honduran, Argento guessed, by their dark skin tone and their current proximity to the border. One was tall and broad with long hair in a ponytail, a T-shirt with a rapper on it, and sweatpants with elaborate designs on the legs. The other was similarly sized but more conservatively dressed in a polo shirt and jeans. One would be the brains. One would be the muscle. But their style of dress didn't necessarily tell him who was which.

"I'm not trouble," Argento said. He'd told Cornejo and Belchert he wanted to follow them like an embedded journalist. Figured he'd stick with that. "I'm a writer. The paper did a story on this block, saying it was a tough corner. I'm just doing follow-up."

"You don't look like no writer."

"What do writers look like?"

"Wear glasses and shit. Got mustaches."

Argento shrugged.

"You gotta go to school for a long time to be a writer?"

"Need some school."

"Think I could do that?"

"Sure," Argento said. It seemed appropriate for the corner that he was doling out career advice to a drug lookout regarding a job Argento didn't actually have. He regarded the kid. He was painfully skinny, all ribs and attitude. This block on Pacheco was maybe all he knew. If Argento had to guess, he'd say the kid's dad was in jail and his mother worked two jobs or not at all. People in his life had probably let him down a lot.

The kid sauntered across the street to report his findings to Sweatpants and Polo Shirt. Polo Shirt seemed to be doing most of the conversing. Then the kid came back.

"They says to fuck off. Say they didn't like the first story. Don't want no attention brought to the block."

"They can't come over here and tell me themselves? They gotta have a kid do it?"

"You don't want Enrique over," the kid said, jerking his head across the street. "Enrique get mad, hurts people."

Argento was guessing Enrique was Sweatpants. While he didn't particularly care for being told to go screw himself by a couple of corner boys, he didn't need a fight here and now. So he walked. He went down the street and around the block but came back up through the alley, avoiding the clumps of human feces and stepping over two transients, one of whom was furiously masturbating. All grist for his follow-up article on Pacheco. The hotel that advertised color TV had a side entrance off the alley out of line of sight of the dealers. He went in and paid forty dollars for a room on the top floor overlooking the boulevard. The clerk, a wizened Asian woman, asked for ID. He gave her an extra twenty, and she quit asking.

His room had a mattress that'd recently been urinated on, the efforts to clean it half-hearted. Someone had scrawled "RIP Munchy" on the wall in permanent marker. But there was a chair that still had three of its four legs so he sat on it, parted the curtains and watched the street with his binoculars.

The kid in the Suns jersey was still out working the sidewalk. He was a lookout and a runner, a jack-of-all-trades. Argento had seen a thousand boys like him. Maybe they were all doomed, maybe some would claw their way out. But they were tough and alert and had the art of self-reliance already down; there were no connections they could call on to get them out of trouble. No rich uncle to sign them out of juvie or bail them out of jail. And that was the problem. They didn't have enough responsible adults in their lives telling them that being the eyes for a street dealer was a bad idea and they should heed the quaint advice to be in school instead or learn a lawful trade.

Sweatpants and Polo Shirt didn't stray far from the block. Argento's suspicions about Sweatpants being Enrique were confirmed easily enough when he zoomed in on the man's face with the binoculars and saw the word *Enrique* tattooed on his neck in flowing script. So Enrique was the heavy. That likely made Polo Shirt in charge. Enrique went across the street to get a soda, and Polo Shirt moved closer to the drainpipe where they kept their stash. Polo Shirt didn't eat or drink anything other than the bottle of water he kept with him. No rest for the machine. They brought a third guy into the rotation briefly in the early afternoon, a heavy guy with a shaved head, but he didn't stay long.

Business was brisk. It had been several hours and during that time, Argento had only seen one squad car pass, and they weren't even moving at patrol speed. "Rollers," someone from the corner called out and the street activity abated just for a moment until the car drove by.

Eventually it was quitting time. Most dealers weren't on the corner all day and night, especially when it was hot. At some point they punched out. Some had kids. Some cared for elderly parents. They were people too. Shitty people but people all the same. Polo Shirt drifted away from his place of business around four. Still time to beat the worst of traffic. Argento hadn't seen Enrique give Polo Shirt a stack of cash representing the day's proceeds or any leftover product, but it would make sense that he did. Of the two of them, Polo Shirt would be the one carrying the money and dope because he'd be less likely to get pulled over on the way home. He'd probably had a valid driver's license. It'd be hard for the cops to get in the car if he wasn't on probation or parole, had a clean license and no warrants. When Polo Shirt left his spot, Argento waited with the binoculars trained on the street. A few minutes later, a white Nissan Altima came around the corner. No tricked-out rims, no loud muffler, no booming bass from the after-market stereo. The windows weren't tinted, and Argento could see with his binoculars that Polo Shirt was at the wheel. He had a paint-stained hardhat on the seat next to him. Nice touch. *As you can see, Officer, I'm just a clean-cut regular working man driving a regular car doing regular things.* Polo Shirt turned off Pacheco, and Argento committed the plate to memory.

It was time for Argento to pack it in as well, but he'd been cooped up in the room all day and needed to hit the head before he left. His room didn't come with its own toilet because forty dollars only got you so far on Pacheco—management probably blew all their money on the color TV—but he'd seen a community bathroom down the hall when he entered.

A chubby bearded guy holding a motorcycle helmet was leaning against the bathroom door. Argento nodded at the door to indicate it was his destination. The guy didn't move.

"You gotta pay the toll," he said. The languid quality to his voice and his bloodshot eyes told Argento he'd had four too many drinks. He wore an orange Maricopa County Jail ID bracelet on his wrist with his picture on it. Some cons would keep them on for weeks even after they were released. Some were proud of them.

"Bathroom toll? That's not how America works."

"Then turn around and go back where you came." The guy belched loudly. It had been Argento's experience that typically only drunks, people with weapons, or fools messed with him. He didn't look like a soft target.

Argento pointed to the man's wrist. "What were you in for?"

"Fucked up some fag in the club. I don't like 'em. But I can tell you ain't one."

"Real loss to the gay community that you're straight," Argento said. "I'm going to be using that bathroom. But I don't need to be one of your problems."

The man pushed off the door with his foot, wobbled a little, and put his meaty palm on Argento's chest. Gave a moderate shove. Argento didn't budge but felt the familiar, hot blast of anger that so often led to bad decisions. He pushed it down. Easy. He took a few steps back and looked at the guy's head. It was smaller than the rest of him and about the same size as Argento's own. He motioned with his chin to the man's helmet. "Motorcycle come with that?"

"Yep," the guy said proudly. "Brand-new Harley. Parked right outside."

Argento nodded. "I'd love to see it."

CHAPTER
30

For the next several days, Argento used his new Harley to follow Polo Shirt at the end of his shift. To do a tail right, he'd need things he didn't have, like a couple more drivers, a switch car to throw Polo Shirt off, and a few differently colored bike helmets, but Polo Shirt wasn't overly vigilant and didn't seem to notice the motorcycle several cars behind him. Polo went straight home the first two days. Decently maintained cottage in a working-class neighborhood. Kids' toys in the front yard. Elementary-age daughter greeting him at the door.

On the third day he went where Argento was hoping he'd lead him. He went to the stash house.

The address was in Alahambra, 2215 Gaines Street, a single-family A-frame with gang graffiti on the exterior and a torn eviction notice on the front door, which was secured by an iron gate. Polo went in with a duffel. There was no youngster to greet him at the door and no toys in the front yard, only beer bottles and chip wrappers. He came out empty-handed twenty minutes later. Argento watched from an appreciable distance on the motorcycle. Then he took off, staying under the speed limit, watching for police, although he'd run the bike along the same mud track as the Escalade to obscure the stolen bike's plate. He'd never owned a motorcycle before but had driven enough friends' bikes over the years that he felt comfortable on them.

Argento rested up at the hotel. When it was time, he dressed in a black windbreaker and dark cargo pants. He put his backpack on, kept the Taser in his beltline and the Glock in a holster. He only had one magazine for the gun. But if he needed more than one mag, in a stash house, by himself, he figured he was already dead.

He drove the short distance to Gaines Street. It was two in the morning. Up with the bartenders, the convenience store clerks, and the paramedics. If his plan worked, 2215 Gaines would need a few of those medics. He made a pass by the front of the house. All looked quiet. He parked the Harley a half block down in an alley and walked to the back.

Argento figured that a midlevel dealer could have anywhere between five and fifty thousand in cash on-site, along with whatever dope was in reserve. It'd be tucked away somewhere, in toolboxes or an air compressor tank, the bottom of a box of laundry detergent or behind a heating grate. Argento had seen all of these hiding places while executing search warrants.

The house would be fortified, front and back, to give the occupants time to arm themselves against intruders and/or flush the dope if the police came calling. Maybe a backyard pit bull, sometimes with its vocal cords cut so it could launch a surprise attack on any interlopers. Or lines of low-hanging fishing hooks to scalp cops. There'd be at least two guys with guns inside. Maybe more. That's how they got down in Detroit. Argento didn't think Phoenix would be much different.

The back gate to the yard was locked but it rose only seven feet, making it easy enough to scale. Argento hoisted himself up and peered over the fence. The yard looked like a rummage sale gone to seed; odds and ends ranging from rusting camping gear to car parts were all laid out in a bed of trash. A sagging wooden picnic table took up the yard's middle, covered by clothing laid out to dry. No movement. He climbed the fence and swung himself over to the other side.

It wasn't a pit bull in the backyard. It was a Rottweiler, a brawny one missing half an ear, the kind of dog they called "ghetto elk" in

Detroit. The Rott emerged from a dark corner and surged toward Argento, but he already had the Taser out in his left hand and fired, burying the two prongs in the dog's skin. He held the trigger to deliver the shock and the Rott seized up. He hated doing it, because he loved dogs and this one was just doing his job, but while the Taser smarted like a son of a bitch, it did no lasting damage. He kept the current flowing as he scanned the backyard. He had thirty seconds until the shock ended. It took him fifteen to find the leash. One end was staked to the ground. Argento looped the other end around the picnic table to cut it down to a third of its length. He hooked it on the Rott's collar and let go of the Taser's trigger, moving quickly away. Once the voltage stopped, the Rottweiler popped back up, like nothing had happened, and lunged at him but the chain held.

"I'm sorry, pal," Argento whispered.

The Rottweiler wasn't done yet. He barked continuously, straining at the leash. Argento took up a position just behind the porch under a tarp. Waited for the back door to open. The sentry in this case was a man in his underwear, his gut hanging over the front band and a tattoo of the Virgin Mary covering his back. He held a sawed-off shotgun loose in one hand. He had no phone. No keys.

Shitty watchman.

"Que pasa, Rufus," he said in a sleep-slurred voice. Then he saw the new configuration of the leash around the picnic table and wheeled, but it was too late. Argento violently jerked one of the man's legs skyward from the bottom of the porch, causing him to flip up and fall heavily on his back. He lost his grip on the shotgun. Argento took it from him and vaulted onto the porch. He kicked Shotgun down the remaining few steps, went through the unlocked back door, and secured it behind him.

Argento found himself in a kitchen. The interior smelled like body odor tinged with the charred rubber chemical associated with crack. He unloaded the shotgun, pocketed the shells, and set the weapon down behind the refrigerator. He had no interest in relying on a firearm he hadn't personally inspected. He stayed where he was.

Listened. He wasn't going anywhere, not yet. He was banking that the remaining occupants would come to him. Because outside, Rufus was only barking louder.

Footsteps upstairs. Cursing. Then the creak of someone descending the stairs. Argento flattened himself against the wall. He'd see them before they saw him. The man that entered the kitchen had more clothes on than the first guy. He wore a pair of boxer shorts and a sleeveless T. He approached the rear door cautiously. Saw that it was locked. He undid the bolts. Opened the door a crack.

"Pablo," the man called out. Argento checked the second man's hands. In his right, a .38. But no visible phone. No keys. And his boxers didn't have pockets to store them. Send one watchman out to check on a noise, he doesn't return, send another after him the same way with no plan. Just bad ideas compounded over time. Argento stepped out into the room and shoved Sleeveless T headfirst into the door. He trapped the gun hand against the outside of his thigh and twisted out the .38. Then he hit Sleeveless T in the face with it, making a wet, cracking sound. He opened the door and pushed him down the steps after Pablo. Secured the door and dropped the .38 in his pocket.

Two down. Not necessarily down for the count, but they couldn't get back in the house without a ram, and they didn't have weapons or phones.

Rufus had stopped barking. Argento wasn't sure why. Maybe he was checking on the condition of his masters. He probably hadn't seen them tossed on their asses before and was processing this new information with his dog brain.

Argento leveled the Glock and moved toward the stairs. People tended to store valuables on the upper floor, away from points of entry. He was aware there could still be a third guy. And a fourth and a fifth. But Argento was betting there wasn't a third, because the second guy would have woken the third guy and they would have come down together to check on the first man.

Argento moved up the staircase with his back to the far wall so he could see as much of the upper hallway as possible, walking up the outer edge of the stairs, which was less likely to creak than the middle. He reached the top. Closed bedroom doors on either end of the hall. Bathroom in the middle, which was clear. Argento checked the first bedroom, which consisted of a bare mattress on the floor, soiled sheets, and mounds of unwashed clothing dotted with bugs.

But he'd been wrong about no third guy. In the second bedroom, a man slept on the carpeted floor. He was snoring, the empty bottle of Hennessey next to him likely contributing to his deep sleep. Argento didn't see any weapons around him, so he let him be and started his search. He was on borrowed time.

It took him six minutes. The money stash was inside a fresh pair of Nikes in a bedroom closet. Both shoes were stuffed with rolls of bills in denominations from hundreds to fives. It was thousands of dollars. Maybe tens of thousands. The Nikes weren't even in a box. The laziest of hiding places. Lt. Foltz had said on the phone that Phoenix PD had recently gutted Narcotics. The easy-to-find cash was the natural result of this. People weren't used to being raided so they let their guard down.

Argento put the money in his backpack. He listened. Heard nothing but the snores of Hennessey in the next room. No shouting outside. No sirens. He didn't expect the latter because of a complaint from Pablo or Sleeveless T. There'd be no *Officer, a stranger came in our house and took away our weapons and drug money.*

Argento descended the stairs, Glock out. He had every intention of leaving the same way he came in. He preferred the known threats to the unknown. If Pablo and Sleeveless T were in any condition to tussle, he'd oblige them. When he reached the kitchen, he heard a whimpering sound close by. He went dead quiet. Heard it again. It was coming from the downstairs bedroom. He approached the door and checked it. Locked. The whimpering grew louder. A female voice. On the younger side.

He didn't have time for this.

Argento had his TracFone. He could get safely away and call it in. An anonymous 911 report of a girl possibly being held against her will in a dope house. But there was no guarantee that would resolve anything, not in time. And he was right there. In a position to resolve things.

He reared back and kicked in the door.

When the door came back on the rebound, he pushed it away and saw it opened into a small room. Argento checked the corners. Clear. The carpet was bunched and stained, and the room smelled of spoiled food and sweat. There was no furniture in the bedroom, save for a thin mattress and bedframe.

On the mattress was a girl. She was handcuffed to the frame, naked, her face bloodied and puffy. She looked about seventeen. Someone had scrawled "Ho" on her stomach in permanent marker. She was awake, but stared numbly ahead and did not look at Argento when he entered the room. There were two crack pipes on the bed next to her, blackened on one end and stuffed with copper wire.

Argento did a quick scan for injuries. Nothing looked life-threatening. No open wounds or broken bones. She was most likely dehydrated and in shock. She'd live. Argento had to move fast now. Even without phones or weapons, Pablo and Sleeveless T could be arming themselves with the help of a friendly in the neighborhood and calling for backup. But Argento didn't want to carry the girl out of the house naked and he didn't see any clothing in the bedroom.

"I'm going to get you out of here," he said in a low voice. "I'll be right back." She gave no acknowledgment. He left the room, sprinting up the stairs two at a time. He ducked into the closest bedroom and grabbed a shirt off the clothing pile. It was a Buffalo Bills throwback jersey with *Simpson* on the back. He returned, and the girl flinched as he got close to her. It was fortunate he'd brought the handcuff key. On TV, people would shoot the handcuffs off, but in reality, all that might do was twist the metal, not magically pop the lock, and likely create a nasty ricochet. He used the key to undo her cuffs and pulled the baggy jersey over her. It hung past her knees.

"Can you walk?"

The girl nodded slowly. Argento helped her to her feet and she swayed toward the floor as if she had just gotten on stilts. Argento caught her before she fell and lifted her over his shoulder. She weighed less than a hundred pounds. He made for the rear door, and just as he unbolted it, she snarled and bit him in the neck just above the collarbone. Her teeth sunk deep. The pain was exquisite.

"Pablo!" she screamed. She wanted help, but not from Argento. She wanted it from the man with the shotgun Argento had thrown down the stairs. Which meant Argento had badly misread the terrain.

She didn't want to be rescued.

This was where her drugs were.

This was home.

And she was being taken away from it by a stranger.

Argento pivoted and flipped the girl onto the kitchen table. She grunted and flailed her arms. Then he went out the back door, fast and low. Sleeveless T was motionless at the foot of the stairs. Argento had hit him hard with the .38. Maybe too hard, but it felt right to swing away. Pablo was gone. So much for the girl's knight in armor. Rufus was still tied around the picnic table. He barked but there wasn't as much enthusiasm behind it. He didn't want to be Tased again.

"I'm sorry, pal," Argento told Rufus because it bore repeating. He sprinted to his motorcycle. He saw a curtain move in the window of a house down the alley, but no one challenged him and no one came outside. The neighbors were probably used to odd sights and sounds from 2215 Gaines.

He drove off on his stolen bike with thousands of dollars in drug money secured in his backpack and an appropriated .38 in his windbreaker pocket, blood streaming down his neck from a human bite.

Saturday night in the city.

CHAPTER
31

Back at his hotel, Argento washed out his neck wound and covered it with antiseptic cream and gauze. Then he counted the money. It was just shy of thirty grand.

At dawn, he returned to Pacheco Boulevard and went to Polo and Enrique's corner. It was between shifts, no one was selling, and few people were out in the relative cool of the morning. A pair of slack-faced junkies loitered in the alley behind where Polo and Enrique posted up, one sitting so far forward it looked like he was trying to inspect the bottoms of his own shoes, the other standing but teetering, the dope fiend lean. Neither took note of him, so Argento put half the money in a plastic bag and hid it under a milk crate, then covered it with trash. He kept the other half in his backpack. Then he crossed the street and waited. He didn't see the kid in the Suns jersey. When Polo and Enrique showed on the corner around eight, he walked up to them with his backpack on. He'd left his Glock and Sleeveless T's .38 at the hotel. If what he had planned worked out, he'd be getting patted down and they'd take his guns from him anyway.

Both men stared at him impassively.

"I'm the guy who robbed your stash house last night. Took thirty grand. Here's half of it." Argento unslung the backpack and dropped it at their feet. "I'll return the other half on one condition."

Polo looked at Enrique. Enrique looked at Polo. Then Enrique picked up the bag, which contained the $15,000 Argento said it did. He grunted and showed it to Polo.

"Sure, I'll play along," Polo said. His voice had only a faint trace of a Spanish accent. "What's the condition?"

"You get me a meet with your boss."

Argento watched Enrique. It was as if he could see the exact moment his brain turned on and told him to do something. "I can smoke this fool right now," Enrique said, pulling up his shirt to reveal a silver .45 in his waistband.

"But then you'd still be out the other fifteen. You tell your boss you got took?"

Polo and Enrique shared another glance that Argento took to mean they hadn't—they were sitting on the information until they had decided how to deliver the message. Argento figured getting your stash house robbed was not highly regarded in the drug business. It was the kind of thing that could lead to turnover in an organization.

Enrique said, "Where the rest of the money at?"

"Close."

Polo said, "You stole from us. Now you think you can just hand it back, no harm done, if we get you up with our guy?"

"No, there's harm done. I hit one of your boys in the face with his own gun. But I also showed you your security weaknesses, so now you can shore them up. It all balances out."

"This dude crazy," Enrique said, tapping his fingers on the handle of the .45. "Let me do him."

Polo ignored his partner. "What you want to talk to him about?"

"Personal."

"Li'l man said you was a journalist."

"Thinking about getting into that. Kid okay?"

"What you care?"

"He shouldn't be out here."

"He out sick. You gonna ask about the guy you pistol-whipped?"

"Don't care how he is," Argento said. "Unless he was your cousin or something. Then I'm sort of sorry."

"He ain't my cousin," Polo said. "He a fucking moron."

An older man shuffled up to the three of them. His beady eyes and rail-thin frame made Argento think of a goblin.

"Lemme get some of that hard," he said, holding a ten protectively close to his chest.

"Fuck off, prospector. We talking," Polo snapped. The old man looked like he was about to burst into tears. He plodded away down the sidewalk.

"Limited time offer for both of us. I got places to be. You're losing business. Make a decision."

"Give me the other half and we'll see."

Argento found that too stupid to respond to.

Polo looked deep in thought. Enrique spat on the ground.

"Fuck," Polo said, and made the call.

In half an hour, an older-model gray Mercedes drove up and parked midway down the alley. Enrique followed Argento to the car and patted him down. Then he opened the rear passenger door and Argento got in. Enrique made to get in the rear driver's-side door, but the driver stopped him.

"Wait outside," he said. Enrique did as he was told.

The driver turned in the seat and looked at Argento. His hair was wet and slicked back, his eyes bright. He looked like an animated squirrel. He spoke over the sound of the car's AC, which was running at full throttle.

"Who are you and what do you want?"

"I'll keep my name out of it. I want to meet your boss."

"Why?"

"Personal."

The driver thought about that for a moment. "What's in it for us?"

"I'll do you a favor."

"Like what?"

"Who do you have trouble with out here?"

"Trouble?"

"Anyone trying to make a run for your block?"

"We got shit locked down tight here."

"There's always someone who wants what you have."

Squirrel's phone rang. He checked it. Texted something and put it away. Stared at Argento.

"What makes you special? You keep bad company?"

"Don't keep any company," Argento said.

"You for real?"

"People seem to think so."

"You got guns?"

Argento nodded.

"Got any experience with fighting?"

Argento thought back to his time in Whitehall where he'd had to battle convicts floor by floor, including one man he'd dropped down an elevator shaft.

"Some," he said.

Squirrel turned the air-conditioning down a tick, as if he needed less noise to help him think. Then he got out of the car and walked down the alley with his phone to his ear. Calling his boss, most likely. When in doubt, make it someone else's decision. He returned in a few minutes, sat in the car, and put his arm over the seat. "So we don't know if you legit or you crazy, but we about to find out. There a rip crew on Lathrop making some noise about coming over to Pacheco. Something happen to them, my boss will meet you."

"What do they call themselves?"

"Lathrop Street Mob."

"They got colors?"

"This ain't the Bloods and the Crips," Squirrel said. "They wear whatever the fuck they want."

"I'll call you when it's done," Argento said. Squirrel gave him a number and he put it in his phone. He got out of the car and Squirrel drove off down the alley.

When Argento turned, Enrique was right in front of him. "Where the rest of our money?"

"Your partner is sitting on it."

Enrique turned to where Polo was resting on the milk crate. Polo stood and swept the trash aside to reveal the plastic bag of cash. "Damn," he offered.

"One more thing," Argento said. "There's a girl in the house on Gaines who was cuffed to a bedframe. She's in bad shape. Get her to a hospital and send me a picture that shows you did."

Enrique snorted. "That shorty our side piece. Fuck you and fuck your picture."

Argento hated drug dealers. They were a cancer. He'd once burned a dealer's stack of cash in front of him while the guy had watched in disbelief. You could do that back then, before body cameras. He'd needed to be patient so far, but he'd done the calculations and maybe he didn't have to be patient with Enrique anymore. He was past Enrique's level now, having made contact with #2 and with a bead on #3.

"She goes to the hospital," Argento said. "Or I'll come back here and beat you silly with your own gun."

"Motherfucka," Enrique said, lifting his shirt again, "you better—" The move was entirely predictable but Enrique was too dumb to know it. Like a dog chasing a bird he thought he was actually going to catch. Argento was faster. He often was. Plus he had the advantage that guys like Enrique often coasted on their size and meanness. They weren't used to people challenging them. It made them sluggish to react to threats. So he reached in and snapped the pistol from Enrique's waist before the man got a finger on it. He held it at his side.

"It'll start like that," Argento said.

Enrique took two steps back. His eyes cut away. If Argento had made a mistake here by disarming him, it'd be worth it. He turned to Polo.

"Make it happen."

"You'll get your picture," Polo said. He seemed relatively unruffled by what happened to Enrique. He was a more experienced operator than his coworker. You spend enough time on the corner, things stopped surprising you.

Argento held up the .45. "I'm not big on getting backshot. Gonna turn this over to the nearest constable." He got on his motorcycle and rode away. Somewhere there was an actual city of Phoenix where people lived healthy lives and worked real jobs and went to school to better themselves, but that true city was far from Pacheco Boulevard and Gaines Street, and would likely be even farther from where Argento was driving next. He was in the hinterlands. It was a place he knew. A place that sometimes even felt like home.

CHAPTER
32

On his way to Lathrop Street, Argento received a picture on his phone. It was a shot of the girl from the stash house in the back of an ambulance. She was still in the Bills jersey he'd given her. He didn't know how she'd gotten to the house in the first place or the extent of what had been done to her there, but at the hospital, a social worker could get involved. A drug counselor. A parent. Maybe that was how you came back. You healed your body first and hoped that your spirit would follow.

The Lathrop crew wasn't hard to track down. They were rolling eight deep on the unit block that bore their name standing around an SUV that was playing shuddering bass, which Argento imagined was rattling the glass in the adjacent houses. It was noon, but Argento was guessing that wasn't a problem for the Lathrop lads because if you didn't have a job, you didn't have to go to it.

He watched them from the doorway of a convenience store down the block. He guessed at least half were carrying. There'd likely be another gun in the SUV. He checked their backstop to see where incoming rounds would go. They were in front of a long, spray-painted brick wall that fronted a vacant lot. More than suitable. Earlier he'd parked his motorcycle at the back end of that lot at the mouth of a narrow alley. He checked the likely flight path of outgoing rounds. He figured a line of parked cars would absorb most of them, but bullets that went high would be a problem because there were seven homes on the block. Three were clearly vacant with boarded-up fronts. That left four to contend with.

You use your ATM, try to rent a car, get on a plane, they'll know, Sumaya had said. Argento went inside the convenience store. Swiped his debit card to buy a water and a granola bar. Sumaya told Argento a DEA Special Response Team out of Phoenix would respond if there was trouble in Fenton. He was counting on them responding here too for him. If no one showed, he'd call Phoenix PD. Tell them he was a wanted man and wished to turn himself in for the assault at the hospital. But DEA would be better. They'd be deployed with more personnel and bigger guns than the local PD.

Which was exactly what Argento wanted.

The cashier at the convenience store was a balding Black man in his late fifties. He eyed Argento and then looked outside the window at the Lathrop boys.

"Gets worse every day out here." His voice was a tired baritone. "I grew up hard like they did. Not far from here. But I didn't sell drugs, didn't rob people. There were consequences back then. Mostly from my father. There was right and there was wrong."

Argento nodded.

"You take dope out of the picture, maybe these kids are playing ball or going to the pool or something. World be a better place."

Argento stayed quiet. There was a small club of people who always knew the right thing to say. He'd never been in that club. He took his water and snack and went back outside to wait. After twenty minutes, two of the eight members of the Lathrop crew broke off. The rest remained on the street. Drinking and smoking in the eighty-degree heat. Catcalling any women passing by, old or young. Argento knocked on the four doors of the homes on his side of the street. He got an answer at three. He gave them all the same message.

"Might be some shooting on this block soon. Leave if you can. If you stay, keep away from windows."

He repeated the warning in rough Spanish for two of the families; Emily had been fluent and he'd picked up some along the way. The recipients of the message seemed both alarmed and confused by his words. The third door was answered by a man of about seventy with one filmy eye who wore cut-off sweatpants and no shirt.

"Ain't nothing new," he said. "There's always shooting." He shut the door in Argento's face.

Half an hour later, a nondescript white van with tinted side windows rolled down the street and parked within line of sight of the convenience store. No one got out. When he'd worked with them on the job, DEA street teams favored plain vans, sometimes with work logos on the side instead of the ubiquitous government Suburban. Argento trained his binoculars on the front windshield. Helmets. Green Battle Dress Uniforms. Exterior heavy vests. DEA SRT. They wouldn't rush in. They'd sweep the area first, and if they got eyes on him, they'd formulate an arrest plan and get their personnel in place. As far as the DEA was concerned, he was a high-value target to be considered armed and extremely dangerous. They would have likely done his Threat Matrix, where he'd be scored in different categories including access to and proficiency with weapons, his criminal history, and the magnitude of the offense he was currently wanted for. Argento figured he probably scored pretty well on that Matrix, especially after the carnage at Whitehall. Top tenth percentile at least. He'd be disappointed with anything less.

He ignored the van and walked up to the crew intending on doing something Emily had always said was one of his special gifts.

Bugging the shit out of people.

He couldn't understand much of the lyrics to the music rumbling from the car speakers, but the refrain seemed to be anti–law enforcement and pro–popping caps in snitches. The two men closest to him turned and squared up to him. One had four gold-plated front teeth and a notch carved in one of his eyebrows. The other had long locs and a forehead tattoo that said *Try Me, Bitch.*

"Would you fellas mind turning your music down?"

Gold Teeth made a low sound in the back of his throat. "You know where you is?"

"How much those teeth set you back?"

"Stack and a half. Why? You want to get you some?"

"What's the maintenance like?"

"You gotta use a special paste. It's like jewelry cleaner and shit."

"Cool," Argento said. "What you all doing drinking and joking during work hours? Or maybe your shift at the plant doesn't start until later."

Locs cut in. "What's up, white belly? You out here trying to make your first Black friend?"

"I'm here to see the man running the Lathrop Street Mob." Argento turned to Locs. "Or lady."

A collective "Ooohh" rose from the rest of the crew. Argento watched Locs's hand instinctively drop to his waist, and he could see the outline of a handgun at his beltline under his baggy T-shirt.

"Gonna stop you right there," Gold Teeth said. "And I'm gonna assume that you walking up here talking noise a sign you got mental problems. This Lathrop Street in Phoenix. This a hard town. You a guest and you ain't being polite."

"I won't be long. When I leave, you all can go back to whatever you usually do." He looked at one of the Lathrop crew who was wearing a sideways ball cap that said *Hood Hu$tle* in urban cursive. "Which appears to be wearing stupid hats."

"Ohmygod," Hood Hu$tle said. "Dude don't want to live long."

"Let me guess," Argento said, "you've all got guns."

"Enough for you," Locs said.

"Few bullets," Hood Hu$tle said, "might fix his mental problems."

The hostility was already simmering. Time to bring it to a boil.

"Neighborhood I'm from," Argento said, turning and taking in all six members of Lathrop, "soft guys like you put on lipstick, try to pick up construction workers at the bar."

Locs moved forward, his gun already out. A Beretta with an extended mag. Gold Teeth put his hand up to stop him. Stared at Argento with a look that Argento took to be one part anger and two parts curiosity.

"I don't know what this is," Gold Teeth said measuredly. "And I suppose I could let it be. But that ain't how it go on Lathrop. Just remember. Your bitch ass came to us. You wanted this. Don't know why. But that on you."

Then he put his hand down.

And the Lathrop crew was on him.

It began as a flurry of punches and kicks. Argento saw the flash of a second handgun coming out just before he covered up. He dropped to the ground and rolled under the SUV.

"Come on out, trick!" someone hollered, and hands grabbed at his feet.

When he'd been delivering his schoolyard insults to the Lathrop crew, Argento hadn't bothered to look back at the DEA van to see how they were positioned. He didn't want to tip off Lathrop that the law was close by. But he knew the feds had eyes on him and would be waiting for a signal from the agent in charge for when to move in. He'd just accelerated their timetable by being feloniously assaulted by multiple armed suspects. They'd have to roll now. No choice. At least he hoped so. Because if he was wrong, he was about to be dragged out from under the SUV and beaten to death. He'd fought multiple opponents before. But six at once would get stupid fast.

But Argento wasn't wrong. He heard someone shout, "DEA Police, put your hands in the air." A second or two of dead silence. Then a lone outgoing gunshot from the SUV followed closely by an incoming DEA barrage of rapid fire. Argento scrambled to the other side of the SUV just as one of its tires blew out. The body of a Lathrop crew dropped to his left. He'd been shredded by bullets and his upper body looked like pulled pork. Argento looked to the right. Hood Hu$tle was emptying his magazine in the direction of the white van before he jerked like a marionette and crumpled. Argento cleared the underside of the SUV and bear-walked to the other side of the street before he got up and ran. He climbed the brick wall and sprinted through the vacant lot behind it as fast as his tender knee would allow. His motorcycle was where he left it. He jumped on, bathed in sweat, not bothering with his helmet. If the DEA agents were smart, they'd have a chase car in position, but they wouldn't be able to fit through the narrow cuts between homes where his motorcycle could.

Behind him, the gunfire had slowed to sporadic bursts. He didn't look back. He started up the motorcycle, his heart rate still spiking, blew down the narrow alley, and was gone.

At the hotel, he did a self-check. His injuries amounted to nothing more than soreness and a split lip. Lathrop had gotten a few kicks in, but they had sneakers on, not steel-toed boots, and he'd managed to roll under the car before they'd done much damage.

He turned off the lights, sat in the room's lone chair, and closed his eyes. He was spent, the wash of adrenaline replaced by fatigue. He awoke in the chair with a start and checked his watch. He'd been sleeping for hours. He turned on the television and found a local news station and watched until it showed the breaking story out of the Valley of the Sun. Shoot-out in Alahambra between suspects and federal agents. Five shot, four dead with one critical. None of the dead or wounded were from the federal agency, which was not named. Press conference from authorities to follow.

Argento picked up his phone. He called the number. "It's done," he said to the voice on the other end. "Send me the time and place for the meet." He hung up. Sat in the chair for a time. Then he got up and walked to the closest liquor store and bought a pint of midgrade whiskey. He returned to his room and took a long drink straight from the bottle. He felt sick, but it wasn't because of the alcohol burning in his stomach. He thought back to when his most serious offense was threatening Agent Sumaya with a firearm. The bottom had dropped out since then. Setting up the Lathrop crew for a gun fight with the feds wasn't the only choice he could have made. But it was the only choice he could think of. He was used to bouncing ideas and tactics off other cops who knew as much or more than him. But there was no one he could call now, no one he could explain this to. He had only his own counsel to fall back on. And his mind wasn't clear. Maybe the desert had burned it beyond repair.

He raised the bottle to his lips for another drink and then let it fall to the carpet. Booze wouldn't help. It was sober work in front of him now. He laced his fingers behind his head and closed his eyes again. None of the good guys got hurt. That meant something. And it was on Lathrop for not noticing the van. If they were gonna run the block, they needed better lookouts. He laughed, but not because it was funny. It hadn't been close to an even bout. The DEA team had body armor, assault rifles, and training. Lathrop might have had one or two real shooters, but there would also be at least one guy who'd probably blow off a testicle drawing his piece. Argento had heard the first shot come from the Lathrop side. That had sealed their fates because the DEA had returned fire with superior weapons, numbers, and cover.

He'd put those agents in harm's way. He ran his fingers over his scalp. *But that's their job, isn't it?* He knew how he'd like it if someone pulled the same trick on him. Be like a football cut-block five seconds after the whistle. No honor in it. His plan was spiraling away from him. Maybe he didn't care. Maybe the desert had fried his soul too.

He would pay for his choices, one way or the other.

Argento knew he needed to stop second-guessing himself. He needed to sleep. He didn't do either. He turned on the television where a late-night pitchman was prattling on about some kind of miracle cure. In his darker moments, Argento wasn't sure there were miracles. There was only hard work and some good fortune and any help you could get from others. You wanted a miracle, maybe you had to engineer it yourself. He slumped in the chair. He wanted Hudson to be with him. Hear his even breathing, his nails clicking on the floor. And Emily. She could have pulled him out of the pit he was in. She would have known what to do. She always did.

When Argento finally did sleep, he first dreamed of Whitehall, trying vainly to save people as his useless arms faded from his body. Then he was standing at a beach. He could hear faceless shrieking and when the waves broke toward him, they were tinged with blood, a new nightmare on top of the old.

CHAPTER

33

Squirrel came through. Argento sat in Squirrel's Mercedes with him and #3 in the parking lot of a Thai restaurant in a decent neighborhood in Chandler. Polo and Enrique were nowhere to be seen. Argento guessed they hadn't been invited.

"You guys want anything?" Squirrel asked. #3 took a pass. Argento asked for chicken curry and mango with sticky rice, and Squirrel placed the order on his phone. Argento didn't know how this meeting would go. If it jumped bad, at least he'd have food he liked.

"You look like shit," Squirrel said.

Argento didn't respond, but Squirrel wasn't wrong. He had woken early to twisted sheets and a sheen of sweat, and the Lathrop kicks had left a half-dollar-size bruise under his right eye to add to the split lip.

"What you pulled off with Lathrop," #3 said, "how'd you swing it?"

"Magic," Argento replied. He made it sound casual, but he felt pressure tightening across his chest. Like the four dead from the Lathrop crew had been piled on top of him. Like someone wanted him to feel their collective mass.

#3 hadn't offered his name and Argento hadn't asked. He was comfortably middle-aged and a little soft around the middle, a man of about forty with gelled hair and a smooth complexion. He wore a college ring and had a nice watch. Probably didn't fly commercial.

"I'm serious," #3 said.

Argento didn't answer.

When #3 realized he wasn't going to, he shrugged. "Okay, so what do you want?"

"A meet with a shot caller from the Sinaloa cartel."

"A what?"

"You heard me."

#3 eyed Squirrel. Squirrel put his hands up as if to say *Don't ask me.*

"What makes you think I can set that up?"

"Because you're two big steps up from the street. You'll know a guy who has cartel contacts. That guy can get me up with a decision-maker."

"What's this all about?"

"I have information they need to hear."

"Tell me first. I'll decide if they need to hear it."

"Can't. It's just for the top."

"Then it's not happening."

"So after the shit I know goes down, I'll find them on my own. Then I'll have to tell Sinaloa I wanted to warn them but you wouldn't let me."

"You trying to talk tough?"

"Just being practical."

"So you want a meeting, do you? You wanted a meeting with him," #3 said, nodding to Squirrel, "a meeting with me. You're big on meetings, aren't you?"

"I am right now."

"I put you in a room with Sinaloa and you're just fucking around, that'll come back on me."

"I took care of your Lathrop problem in about three minutes. I am not fucking around."

"You got some stones, you know that?"

Argento thought about that. Real stones would be asking for #3's boss and doing him a favor to get an audience with #4 and so on until he was having a champagne brunch with the head of the whole Sinaloa cartel himself, but he was running out of time and every favor he granted would make it more likely he or some innocent would get killed. This was where it stopped.

"We got some more guys like Lathrop," Squirrel said, "you could inconvenience for us. We'd pay you this time."

"That trick only works once."

The three of them sat in silence. Squirrel went in the restaurant and brought the food. Argento ate while both men looked at their phones.

"Give me your ID," #3 said. Argento handed it over. He knew he'd have to. Sinaloa would want to know who they were dealing with before they agreed to be in the same room as him.

#3 took out a small light and shone it on Argento's Michigan driver's license. A black light, like doormen at clubs used to ferret out fakes. He handed it back, satisfied. "You sure you want to be talking to these guys? They murder cops. Judges. Hell, the Mexican Army is scared of them."

"I'm sure. But it will have to be stateside. I'll get flagged at the border, maybe not going over but for sure coming back. Got some folks after me."

"You talking about those feds that shot up Lathrop?"

"Those are the ones."

"So you're just a one-man band here, huh?"

"I'll be waiting on your call." Argento had already finished his curry and sticky rice. The latter had just the right amount of mango and the rice wasn't too sweet. He was used to eating fast. Habit of being on the job where hot calls frequently interrupted your meal. He thought about the one-man-band comment. No one else had shown up to play.

Argento didn't get a call that day or the next. He spent his hours jogging in the early morning before the heat set in, with a drugstore brace to cushion his knee, and working out in his room, a collection of exercises he'd picked up during his academy days—push-ups, sit-ups, mountain climbers and shadow-boxing. Tried to clear his thoughts of Lathrop and the girl on Gaines Street. No DEA contact team pounded on his front door. Phoenix was a big city. Lots of nooks and crannies to hide in, and they hadn't found his yet. At noon of the third day, his phone buzzed. He picked up. #3 told him where and when the meet would be.

Argento packed what few things he had. He had to keep his mind right. He was about to walk into a room with Sinaloa. Known for hanging headless corpses off freeways to warn their rivals. He figured they'd feel the same way about killing him as they would hitting a chipmunk with their car.

His margin of error in that room would be zero.

CHAPTER
34

rgento parked his motorcycle in the pressing heat, and two big
uglies checked his ID and patted him down. They led him past a
hardscrabble dirt yard through the front door and into the living
room of a single-story adobe house with blacked-out windows and
peeling paint on the shutters. One of the men stayed behind him.
The other reposted at the door. The address was on the outskirts of
a small Arizona border town called Agua Mora. The town seemed
to consist of a gas station, a dollar store, and a sprinkling of shabby
homes like the one he was in.

The first thing Argento noticed was the living room's sparse
décor. The second was the floor, completely covered in plastic, good
for keeping bloodstains off the hardwood. The cartel welcome. It was
cool in the room, almost chilled. Maybe the temperature at which
this kind of business was conducted.

Three men rose from their chairs. One was in a white suit, short
and slight with glasses. He looked like an accountant save for the
thick slab of scar tissue on the side of his face. Argento had gone to a
police training on the cartels where'd he'd learned that certain cartel
members wore suits with ballistic paneling sewn right in to combine

fashion and protection. Some slept under bullet-resistant blankets. It was a life where it paid to be watchful.

The two other men were twins. Late thirties, early forties, brawny, both with gold Desert Eagles in shoulder holsters. One wore a tank top. His entire left arm was an uninterrupted tattoo, some kind of sun god/skull design. His right arm was sprayed with puckered bullet marks. Argento noted two more men standing by swinging doors that led to a kitchen in the back of the house. Both carried short-barreled rifles.

No one extended their hands. It wasn't that kind of meeting.

Argento knew this house contained the men Sumaya was most scared of. The men whom the DEA was trying so hard to keep their secret from. There were other facets of organized crime who'd have skin in the dope game, everyone from the local drug crews like Lathrop to the Italian mob—but in terms of reach, resources, and savagery, the cartels were unmatched. They were far and away the primary threat. Everyone else was just a spoke on their wheel.

Argento was conscious of where he was standing in relation to the men. At some point, when entering a room of those who might wish you harm, you would invariably have to turn your back to at least one of them. So you get a sense of where people were and what they were doing there. But there were too many shooters in this space. It didn't matter what his positioning was. He was unarmed in a house full of killers. If Sinaloa wanted him dead here, he'd die.

The short man spoke first. "My name is Uriel. I represent the interests of the Sinaloa cartel. I am told you have something to tell us." His voice was smooth, almost melodious. He reminded Argento of a CEO or lawyer, like Sinaloa had their own in-house legal counsel.

Argento gestured at the plastic covering. Looked at Uriel.

"We have driven a considerable distance," Uriel said. "If we decide you are wasting our time, we will make use of the plastic."

"That move work on this side of the border?"

"People in Sinaloa," Uriel continued, with a quality to his voice as if he was explaining something he'd gone over many times before, "they come to us for food, medicine, new soccer goals. So we have their loyalty. This kind of relationship extends to Agua Mora. The local police know we use this home from time to time. They will not come here without our express permission. I could have you killed right now and they would ask me if I wished to bill your family for cleaning the spinal fluid off the walls."

"Club soda would get most of that out," Argento said. "No need for a big bill." It was an absurd thing to say. But he was in an absurd situation. Standing on plastic in a cartel house preparing to negotiate with some of the worst people in the world about a town of trained killers and a cloak-and-dagger government project.

The twin closest to Argento with the sun god tattoo scratched his jaw and almost looked amused. "Club soda." Second Twin remained stone-faced. He had small dark eyes that had stayed on Argento since he broke the plane of the doorway.

Uriel said nothing. Just sat and extended his palm toward Argento. *Talk.*

So Argento did. He told them everything he knew about Fenton, what he'd been told by Sumaya, and what he suspected the project was. He talked about ex-soldiers pretending to be cops, the fortress compound with reinforced doors, bullet-resistant windows, and an array of sensors, Barrows, Hudson shot in the street, being stranded in the desert, escaping the hospital, luring the DEA team into a fire-fight with Lathrop. About Barrows's research going into an electronic reservoir. He'd had three days of prep to practice this narrative when he'd been alone in his motel room. He knew he needed to get their attention fast and hold it.

When he was done, Uriel said, "So you came to us."

"You have a vested interest. Plus I looked at the compound. You'd need a rocket launcher to get in there. So I thought I'd see about some guys who had one."

"It's quite a tale. Why should we believe you?"

"You have my ID. You already did a threat assessment. You know I used to be Detroit SWAT. You saw I have a warrant for assaulting a police officer. Probably a high-risk want from the DEA. I'm not some clown off the street."

"That's all you bring to this room?" First Twin said.

"No. There's also your knowledge of human nature. I try to cross you, someone drops me in a vat of acid. Or puts me in a rolling tire and lights it. Human nature not to want that."

"Not just someone," First Twin said. "Me."

Argento nodded. Gestured toward First Twin's shoulder rig that held the gold Desert Eagle. "Nice gun."

"It solves my problems."

Outside, silence. No sounds of birds or children playing. No traffic. No vigilant neighbors to notice that a stranger on a motorcycle went in the house but didn't come out. Or to report the sounds of screaming. Gunshots. Power tools.

"Your story," Uriel said. "Tell it to me again."

Argento did. Maybe Uriel wanted to see if any of the details changed. Like a detective doing statement analysis. Then Uriel asked questions and Argento answered them. Uriel sat back in his chair and propped one knee over the other. Stared at Argento across the room.

"Other than your previous status as law enforcement and a current wanted fugitive, which we did confirm, you have no evidence of what you say. No videos, photographs, witnesses. You're just a former American policeman asking us to believe you want to help the Sinaloa cartel."

"I don't want to help you. I want you to help me. And you could send people to Fenton to see for yourself. But you're running out of time. The information I got was that this project will wrap up in weeks, if not days. Or they might stash Barrows in some other cliff fortress that will take you a while to find. Either way, we're on the clock."

"How convenient for you that the timeline is restricted in such a way that it would be difficult to verify your claims."

Argento looked around the room of cartel gunmen. "I'm wanted by the same kind of people I used to work for and in a house looking at plastic that's laid out for my corpse. Nothing about this is

210

convenient for me. I could call up the DEA Special Response Team to come here and help confirm it in person. But I figured you may not want to break bread with those guys."

Second Twin said something in low, guttural Spanish and pointed to the floor. Argento only caught a few words. One of them was "madre." He looked at First Twin for explanation.

"Ramon says the DEA put an informant in with us a few years back," First Twin said. "He tried to trick us like Ramon says you're tricking us. This is where he died, on this floor, calling for his mother."

Second Twin, Ramon, added something else in low Spanish.

"He didn't like having his vertebrae crushed one at a time," First Twin translated. "Ramon says you won't like it either."

Uriel steepled his hands. "This man, Barrows. Even if he is eliminated, what is to stop someone from using his notes in this electronic reservoir you referred to and just continue his work?"

"The DEA agent I spoke with said he only trusts himself. He's been holding on to the recipe for the project until it's fully complete and ready for launch. Reach him before then and the information is still just confined to his head."

"And if we do nothing?"

"Get a new business model because Barrows is going to change your old one to where you don't recognize it anymore. And you'll need to find something else to sell. Umbrellas or birthday cards."

Uriel drummed his fingers on the arm of his chair. "I understand our interest in this. I don't fully understand yours."

"Someone has to answer for what happened to the Reed family. And they tried to kill me. I didn't much care for that."

"No," Uriel said, rising from his chair. "It would have to be more for you to come to us, to risk your life for strangers. And this government project you speak of, it is impossible we wouldn't already know about it. We are Sinaloa. We hear everything. People talk to us. Even if they have to whisper."

Argento heard a click. He half turned. The man at the front door had locked it.

Uriel tilted his head, as if reassessing Argento. "You thought you could walk in here with this story? I've decided you have wasted our time. Do you care, Senor Argento, if you live or die?"

Argento stood. If he was going to go out, it'd be on his feet. "Not as much as I used to."

"Ramon," Uriel said. Second Twin didn't go for his holster. He pulled out a long knife from his belt instead. It was just smaller than a machete and it wasn't for opening boxes. Argento's pulse barely jumped. Maybe because he'd already faced death multiple times over the last week. His baseline was off. Knife or not, he'd handle Ramon. The rest would get him. But he'd send Ramon to Hell.

Ramon started toward him. "Hermano," First Twin said, and Ramon stopped short. First Twin looked at Uriel.

"You said it would have to be more for American law to come here for the cartel's help."

"Yes," Uriel said.

"They killed his dog."

Uriel was silent. Ramon stood still, knife in hand, eyes locked on Argento, breathing hard. Like a bull waiting for the gate to open.

First Twin whistled and the swinging doors from the kitchen parted. A hulking black mastiff trotted over and stopped at his side. First Twin scratched him behind his ears. The dog had the traditional droopy mastiff face and probably weighed nearly as much as Argento. He didn't bark at the sight of a stranger. Just regarded Argento calmly with his big brown eyes, like he was scanning it for emotion. Then he yawned and looked away.

"What's his name?" Argento asked.

"Manco. He came from Iraq. He responds to twenty different commands. He's seen some times, haven't you, Mancito?" First Twin pressed his lips to the top of the mastiff's head. Then took in Argento. "What was your dog's name?"

"Hudson. They shot him in front of me."

First Twin nodded. "Now I understand why you're here." He turned back to Uriel. "Call him. Let him decide."

If Uriel was bothered by this sudden change in the room's power dynamics, he did a good job of not showing it. He simply nodded. But Argento could hear Ramon's breathing get heavier. Ramon preferred the original plan.

"Step outside," First Twin said to Argento. "If you run, Ramon would like that. Ramon is fast."

Argento did as instructed and walked out to the dirt front yard, the immediate uptick in temperature making sweat collect at his temple. Both door guards followed him and settled into a stand-and-stare posture. Argento wanted a cigarette but he had run out. He didn't say anything to the guards and they didn't say anything to him. They probably didn't have a lot in common to talk about. Uriel said he had the local U.S. police in his pocket. Argento wasn't so sure about that. He'd heard of such things, but he'd like to think if the cartel approached the local sheriff to enlist his services, he'd tell them to fuck right off. Not every department was Fenton DPS. Most were righteous.

Call him, First Twin had said. He wondered if the "him" might be the head of the Sinaloa cartel, who for the past decade had been a man named Tomás Canchola-Ibanez. Known to his men as Las Cruces, or The Crosses, a name representing the grave markers of all the men he'd killed himself or had killed. Argento had learned that in his police cartel training. Las Cruces was one of the premier faces of the drug war. It was a war Argento had fought hard and lost in Detroit. It hadn't even been close. There were twice as many drug dealers as drug treatment beds; you arrested a dealer, another took his place within the day, sometimes one more violent and unpredictable than the first. Destroy one cocaine lab, the locals could construct a replacement before the smoke had cleared.

An hour passed before First Twin came to the door and motioned for the men to return. Argento would know soon enough what came next. Ramon's body language would tell him. It would either be the beginning or the end.

When he passed the threshold back into the cool of the room, Ramon was seated and using his knife to trim his fingernails. He didn't look up. It was a strong signal that the phone call to Las Cruces was favorable to Argento.

"The local police," Uriel began, "you said there were nine of them."

"That's right."

"If we were to accompany you to Fenton, they would be your responsibility alone, for your country takes the killing of policemen far more seriously than ours. So how would you accomplish this? One man against nine trained American soldiers?"

Maybe Uriel thought he was putting Argento on the spot with the question. But Argento had been ruminating on it since he'd escaped the desert. He told Uriel his plan. Not all the details. Just the broad outline. Uriel looked at him unblinkingly. Argento couldn't tell if he was impressed or he was about to laugh. Argento turned to First Twin, who was just as impassive. Ramon stood again. The knife came out. As if Argento's words had created an opening for the original plan of carving him up on the plastic. First Twin narrowed his eyes and shook his head. Ramon sat back down.

"In sports," Argento said, now looking alternately at First Twin and Uriel, "sometimes a slow team plays a fast team."

First Twin and Uriel remained blank-faced. Waiting.

"If you're the slow team and you want to beat the fast guys, you get them to play on your terms. You don't try to match their speed. You make them match yours."

Uriel looked at First Twin, but First Twin didn't take his eyes off Argento.

"And, not for nothing, I blew through your street operation in less than a week so I could stand in this room."

"As soon as you engage the Fenton police," Uriel said, "they'll call in more men."

"They won't. Two reasons. The first is professional pride. These guys are used to doing their own mop-ups. Second, they don't want any local law enforcement getting a glimpse of their operation. That's why their closest backup is a DEA team out of Phoenix. It'll take them time to get there. By then, we'll be a memory."

Uriel gave a slight nod. "You have answers for our questions. But we'll see how you do in the field. My men will go with you to Fenton." He nodded toward First Twin. "He will lead them. If the nine policemen are handled, we will breach the compound and take Barrows. Then our business together will be finished."

Argento didn't say anything. There didn't seem to be an opening to negotiate.

"I find you," Uriel said, "to be in somewhat of a unique position. You have no family we may influence. Our research suggests you have but one friend, the man whose house you are staying in, but he is overseas and currently out of reach. So we are left with you. If you lied, if you hid something, if you try to double-cross my men, Ramon will find you. He will look deep down at the person you are underneath. He will accomplish this by removing all of your skin while you are still alive."

Hearing his name, Ramon looked up. Blinked with his small eyes. Then went back to his knife and his fingernails. There was something low-simmering, almost feral about him.

"Wait by your phone," Uriel said.

Argento walked up to First Twin. When he was close, he caught a faint whiff of something coming off the man's skin. Argento couldn't quite place it but it smelled medicinal.

"What's your name?"

"Manco," First Twin said.

"Just like your dog."

Manco stroked the mastiff's head. The dog made a low sound in the back of his throat. "We are one."

CHAPTER
35

When Argento was gone, Manco walked over to pacify Ramon, who was pacing on the plastic, hands clenched.

"I know you are disappointed," Manco said. "But it is what El Jefe wanted."

"I would have left enough of him to feed to Mancito." Ramon held out his hand and the mastiff came over and licked it.

"Manco," Uriel said and pointed at the rear door. The two men cracked beers from the fridge and walked into the backyard, which was made up of the same scrubby dirt as the front and was barren save for a rusted swing set. They were facing south, toward Mexico. Toward home.

"What did he say?" Manco asked. It felt good to speak in Spanish again. Manco had made himself proficient in English because it was the language of money, but the words never felt right.

"He said there's been rumors of such a project for years but they've intensified of late. Said there may be merit to the American's claims. Says the American has all the right enemies. It is a gamble but one we must take."

Manco had been born into Sinaloa. His father was a soldier before him. He'd worked his way to the upper echelons and was now trusted by

Las Cruces for all vital assignments. Sinaloa used hydraulic presses to brick kilos and Manco routinely dealt with shipments as high as twenty thousand pounds of cocaine with a street value exceeding $250 million. Cocaine was still king in Sinaloa, although heroin ran a close second and meth was approaching fast. Then there was the promise held by a relatively new drug to Sinaloa, fentanyl, which Manco was still learning about, but which he believed had the potential to outsell them all. It hadn't always been that way. Las Cruces didn't use to bother with meth. Considered it a crude product not worthy to carry the Sinaloa brand. But the business adapted and you had to adapt with it.

"You were right to have me call him," Uriel said without meeting Manco's eyes. Of course Manco was right. If he hadn't intervened, Ramon would have spilled the American's guts on the floor and Las Cruces would have been furious. He'd use this information against Uriel later, when the time was right. Because he wanted Uriel's job. He had watched him for years and knew he could do it. Wear a suit, talk instead of fight, be in rooms where high-level business decisions were discussed. He couldn't be a soldier forever. He was forty, but already his reflexes had slowed. His eyesight had lost some sharpness. His knees hurt from the constant pounding of moving fast with heavy gear on, although he had a Sinaloa doctor make him a special cream that he smeared over his kneecaps every morning. The cream made him smell like a hospital but it helped. He had nothing left to prove as a gunman. He had killed everyone Las Cruces had asked him to. He had both learned and taught blood lessons during two decades in the field.

"The question is," Uriel said, "whether the American can handle those soldiers on his own to clear a path to the compound."

"I think he might."

"We'll need proof of death. Fit him with a camera that live-streams Like the surfers use. We won't go to the compound until he's already gotten his hands bloody."

"He won't wear one of those. He used to be police. He's not going to record himself taking lives."

"Pictures then," Uriel said.

"Pictures," Manco agreed.

"Why do you think he can do this?"

Manco didn't answer right away. He was trying to figure it out himself. He sensed something in Argento. Something he didn't see in many men. He'd shown no fear in the house, even when death was coming for him in the form of Ramon with a blade. Manco respected that. He understood it. He'd researched Argento, including what he'd done at the prison in Missouri. It had been well covered in the news. The American was a man used to violence. And if he was telling the truth about how he was stranded in the desert, he had made it out like God's favorite. The police officers Manco was used to dealing with were stupid, greedy, and weak. Argento seemed different.

"I think he's like me," Manco said.

Uriel finished his beer and tossed the bottle into the yard. Manco did the same.

"Will Ramon be coming with me?"

"No," Uriel said. "Las Cruces thinks Ramon is too volatile to be in an American town. Besides, he has need of him back home."

"And when it's finished, what of the American?" With Sinaloa, there were typically only two answers to this question. Kill him slowly or kill him quickly.

"Make it fast," Uriel said. "Leave no trace."

Manco nodded. Thought of Argento's scorched features. His dull affect even in the face of certain death in a room with sheeting to keep him from leaking onto the floor. "He looks," Manco said, "half-dead already."

CHAPTER
36

rgento knew that the cartel tasking him to handle all of the Fenton DPS by himself was also an easy way to get rid of him. But even if he survived, when Manco and his men got what they wanted in Fenton and their interests no longer aligned, they'd execute him. Of that, Argento had no doubt. They'd want to sever their connection to him, to Fenton, to Barrows. It was the easy choice.

So he'd plan for that.

He was in a new motel in Phoenix, one step up from where he'd been staying, mostly because he wanted a room with consistent hot water where he could sleep underneath the sheets. *Soft*, Argento thought. Getting soft. At this rate, his next place would be a suite with a sunken tub and free robe. He'd disassembled the .38 he'd taken off Sleeveless T and the .45 from Enrique and dropped the pieces in a nearby mailbox. He wasn't going to use either weapon but he didn't want the wrong person to get hold of them. The United States Postal Service could take it from here. They always knew what to do.

Argento looked at the list of supplies he needed for his return trip to Fenton. If you want to start the revolution, you got to get organized. Some of the items he could find at the military surplus store. But for one of them, he'd have to go elsewhere, because he couldn't just stride into Fenton blasting off rounds. If he trigged the ShotSpotter, he had a strong suspicion Fenton would go on lockdown and DPS would whisk Barrows away via the helipad or the back exit. It would be standard procedure when protecting an asset like Barrows. There'd be a time for shooting. But it would have to be after the cartel contingent breached the compound gates.

Elite Archery was near the corner of East Cholla and Thirty-Second Street. Two men were behind the counter, both fleshy with biker beards and parchment skin from a lifetime spent in the sun.

"Help you?" one of them asked.

"Looking for the best hunting crossbow you got."

"That's an easy one," the first guy said. He went to a back storeroom and emerged with a long-scoped weapon, the front of which branched out in the traditional crossbow design. "This is the Sentry II. Fastest bow you can get commercially. Shoots a carbon fiber bolt around five hundred feet per second with two-hundred-foot pounds of kinetic energy. It's got a safety and a removable stock. And the option to add a five-arrow mag if you want."

The man handed it to him. Argento felt the weight. Sighted it across the store.

"What's the range?"

"If you don't care about hitting your target, about five hundred yards. Everyone else is better off less than a hundred. But even a beginner can be accurate at thirty."

"Lethality?"

"Fifty yards," the second man said. "But twenty to thirty is your kill zone because gravity starts dropping the arrow after that. The weapon's accurate, it has good penetration, and if you use a hunting broadhead, it'll cause enough tissue damage to down your target even if it misses a vital organ."

"How loud is it?"

"Standard crossbow comes in between eighty and ninety decibels, but this one is higher quality, which means less vibration. It's about half that."

"I'll let you test-fire it," the first man said. "You'll hear it sing." Argento followed him to the back storeroom where they had a mini archery range set up with a traditional bull's-eye target. The first man showed him the weapon's operating system and how to cock it from the bottom after each shot. Argento put a bolt through the outer ring of the bull's-eye. Reloaded and did it again. It was a smooth shot. No recoil. Reasonably quiet.

The first man said, "You're a natural."

Argento was betting he said that to all the customers to grease the sale, but the man wasn't wrong. Weapons had always come easy to Argento. They made sense. He would have preferred a bow and arrow, because that was what he'd used during Michigan Septembers hunting deer, but he needed something he could fire with one hand if it came to it. Cops used to do that on a regular basis decades ago. He'd seen black-and-white photos from shooting ranges where officers would have the gun extended in one hand and the other hand deep in their pocket.

"Will it put a bolt through a windshield?"

"You expect to encounter a deer driving a car there, fella?"

"We live in uncertain times."

"Yeah," the second man chimed in. "It'll go through glass. I tested it on my ex-wife's Kia Sorento."

"Seriously, Earl?" the first man said.

Earl shrugged. "She weren't in the car at the time."

"I'll take it." Argento was given a choice of colors, including jungle camouflage. He chose matte black, which would make the weapon harder to detect at night. He paid with Governor Wakefield's money, which was dwindling.

Earl cocked his head at Argento. "What are you hunting, friend?"

Argento thought about how Krebs shot his dog. About how the Fenton soldiers left him and a woman and her child outside to slowly roast to death in a wasteland.

"Animals," he said.

Argento found a shuttered auto junkyard a few blocks from the archery store and scaled the fence. He waited a tick to see if any guard dogs would bolt toward him but none appeared, so he moved through the yard until he found a mangled mideighties Buick with no tires. Earl said he'd successfully shot a crossbow bolt through his ex-wife's car, but Argento needed to see for himself. He lined up the shot on the Buick's driver's side from twenty feet away and let fly. The arrow pierced the windshield and buried itself halfway into the seat. Satisfied, Argento climbed back over the fence.

Then it was back to his hotel for another waiting game, like there'd been when he was arranging with Squirrel to meet with the cartel. It gave him time to think. Maybe too much time. He had gone to a police ethics training once where the instructor talked about the just world theory, about how, in the end, righteous people are rewarded and evil people are punished. Some OG from the back of the class had said, "I've seen that happen like twice." Argento didn't know how much weight to assign to the just world theory, but if evil was to be punished, you couldn't just wait around for someone else to do it.

He jogged in place. Shadow-boxed in the corner. Practiced movements with the Sentry II, using all the space of the small hotel room, coming around a corner, getting eyes on target, both one-handed and two. He could hear his old partner Trapsi's voice in his head. *Gotta sharpen the saw, bro.*

When evening fell, he had broken his record for most consecutive nights alive, no small feat given how his week had gone.

When his phone buzzed, he picked it up on the first ring. It was Manco. They were a go. Tomorrow midnight. There were some details to coordinate. Responsibilities to parcel out. Then Manco hung up.

Argento went to bed early to prep for the heavy day. He hoped he wouldn't dream. *Manage your sleep like you manage your money,* one of his SWAT instructors had told him. With four hours of sleep you were at only 70 percent of your cognitive ability. Rest was overnight therapy for both body and mind. When Argento woke, it would be time to take Fenton over, for the better. The civilizing conquest, like the Spanish thought they were doing with the Aztecs.

Argento knew there were good people in the world.

But none of them were patrolling the streets of Fenton, Arizona.

CHAPTER

37

The cartel rendezvous point was a few miles outside of Fenton at the end of an old mining road. Argento got there first and smoked a cigarette. He figured he'd get one good last one in.

A rumble in the distance announced their approach. As the sound grew closer, he saw it originated from four black Humvees. They stopped in a line, and Manco got out of the passenger side of the second vehicle. His gear lacked for nothing. A ballistic helmet with night vision goggles, an exterior heavy vest that looked to be rated against rifle rounds, and an automatic shotgun. Argento could see the other occupants of the Humvees were similarly outfitted. Good. They were going to get plenty of trigger time. He doubted they had to field questions about their weapons at the border. Probably had their own checkpoint express lane where the Mexican authorities wished them the best and waved them through.

There were no greetings exchanged or wasted words. Argento detected the medicinal smell coming from Manco again, the same one he'd picked up at the house in Agua Mora, but stronger this time. Argento spoke first, his crossbow at his side. "I'll handle any sentries on the perimeter. Then I'll torch the police station. The fire will draw in any DPS stragglers. I'll post up and hit them outside. Then I'll give you the call to move on the compound."

"As discussed, you will send me a picture of every man you kill. We'll be in our cars waiting until your targets are down and the station is on fire," said Manco.

"Thought we could just use the honor system."

"When you get your hands dirty first, it shows your commitment to the mission."

"You'll get your pictures."

Manco nodded at the Sentry II. "Running quiet, I see."

"For as long as I can."

"I'm leading Team One. When we receive your call, we'll breach the front of the compound and eliminate the helipad. Then we enter and take Barrows. Team Two will block the rear exit to choke off their escape. Meet us at the compound if you're still alive. Afterward, rally point is at the diner."

"You've got encrypted radios?"

"Of course."

"You gonna use one of those Humvees to block the rear exit? If they have enough of a runway they could still punch through."

"We have a different vehicle for the back. It's waiting for us on the other side of town. It'll hold." Manco reached into a cargo pants pocket and came out with what looked like a slim digital watch. "Put this on. Pulse monitor. I can track it with my phone. If you die before we get to the compound, we'll readjust our plan."

"Should I have one of those for you?"

"You asking that," Manco said, "makes me think you wonder if you called the right people."

"I called the right people. But the soldiers in Fenton have put in some field work. They're the right people too."

Manco pointed to his right arm where Argento had seen the bullet scars back in the house in Agua Mora. "Six times I've been shot. Stabbed twice. All in worse places than here. This town won't kill me. I decide when I die."

"When this is over," Argento said, "I'll miss our conversations."

Manco smiled faintly. He was still smiling when he said, "If this turns out not to be what you say, or you try and fuck us, we'll find you. We always do. Then you'll be the body in a trunk they can't identify because it's got no face, no hands."

"I'll do my part. You do yours. We'll get along fine. I'll take a stroll past your guys so they recognize me and don't light me up when I'm at the compound."

Manco extended an inviting hand toward the Humvees. Argento made the walk past the four vehicles, which looked to have military-grade armor and bullet-resistant windows similar to the Bearcat they'd used on SWAT for officer rescue and active shooters. The one Manco had ridden in had one occupant. The other three each contained four men. A total of fourteen shooters. At least half of them wore crucifixes around their necks, as if their comings and goings were sanctioned by Christ himself. If they were anything like the dealers back home, some of them would have $2 bills in their wallets for luck in case the crucifix wasn't enough. They looked at him without expression. None of them seemed rattled. None of them spoke. Argento wondered how many times they'd done wet ops like this before.

He walked back to Manco, who took a slow look around, like a final inventory of what was to come. Manco was facing away from Argento when he said, "Ramon is my shadow. If something happens to me, he will hunt you. He'll never stop." Then he got back in the passenger side of the Humvee. The caravan rolled out toward town, thick tires crunching over gravel. Argento straddled his motorcycle. The night wasn't overbearingly hot. The stars were out, high and clear. Decent conditions for an incursion.

Pierced Nose from the coffee shop had said two things he'd liked. The first was that to accomplish his mission, he'd need friends. The second was that he only had to outthink his opponent once. The first time Argento had come to Fenton, he'd been run out of town and almost died. He'd lost. So he'd changed the rules. Now he was returning with a crossbow and a small army of cartel shooters.

He was betting Sumaya and Barrows hadn't thought of that.

CHAPTER
38

Argento looked over Fenton from the top of an arroyo tucked behind the mining road, letting his eyes adjust to the darkness. There were few lights on in town this late. Fenton wasn't much for nightlife. It looked peaceful. Inviting. The kind of down-home place with clean streets where you could still get a nickel shave. But Argento knew better. Gold Teeth had said Phoenix was a hard town. Argento would say the same for Fenton. It was a place that had not been kind to him. A place where the town security force had, according to Sumaya, orders to shoot him on sight.

Argento would give himself the same orders for them.

His motorcycle was quick and mobile and he could shoot the crossbow one-handed from it if he needed to. Fire and go. The archer's drive-by. But the sound of the bike engine this late at night would draw attention. Make it harder to sneak up on people. He needed to be fast and silent.

He'd go the rest of the way on foot.

As he made his way down the arroyo's side, he knew there was a chance he was too late. Maybe Barrows had already finished the project. Turned it over to his superiors. Hopped in the helicopter on the roof of the compound and disappeared as a folk hero genius.

Argento would know soon enough.

His primary weapon was the Sentry II. He had his Glock in a holster. He wore a standard ballistic vest good against handguns, a loan from the cartel. Its trauma plate would defeat a shotgun slug but not a rifle round. He was okay with that. Anything heavier would weigh him down. He removed some coins from his pants pocket and dropped them on the ground. No jingling. The goal was no noise at all.

He wore the same backpack he'd taken to 2215 Gaines, filled with the supplies he'd gotten at the military surplus store, including a couple of tourniquets, plus a few other things he'd picked up along the way. One was a rolled-up copy of the *Arizona Republic* newspaper. Another was a Sharpie, which he took out and with it wrote the Fenton DPS roster along the length of his forearm. He didn't have any trouble remembering their names.

Chan
Cornejo
McBride
Henik
Knox
Belchert
Tomlinson
Krebs

He left Redlinger's name off for now. He still wasn't sure what he was going to do about Redlinger.

He was about to enter combat with an elite team of ex-soldiers. Argento shared some of their tradecraft but they were guaranteed to have been in more gunfights than him. Argento was an excellent shot when compared to the average street cop, proficient enough to make his department's tactical team, but he'd been second-tier among his SWAT coworkers. He probably wasn't going to outshoot anyone in Fenton. Krebs had illustrated that when he'd shot Hudson with his nondominant hand when both shooter and target were moving.

And if DPS zeroed in on his location on the ground, he'd be shredded. He had to keep the ratio of contact low. One-on-one was ideal. No higher than one-on-two. And whenever he could, go close quarters. He'd be able to absorb more punishment than they could. To hit harder. He was a fighter, so it made sense he was headed to where the best fight could be found. Where he could take measure of himself.

He had an idea Manco was like that as well.

Argento had one more advantage. While Fenton DPS knew he was alive because Sumaya would have told them he'd escaped the hospital, they didn't know he was coming back. And even if they did, enough time had passed since they'd dropped him in the Sonoran that they'd likely have trouble maintaining the necessary vigilance. Bunch of warriors sitting around waiting for a war. In short, they'd be bored stiff. It would have started whenever they arrived in Fenton for the first time and began patrol operations. The initial month or so would have been a welcome change from the combat missions they'd known. Maybe the second month too. Then complacency would set in. They had a nice police headquarters with a fully stocked gym and probably got fed well up in the compound and at the diner. But other than having to deal with Argento and the lone traffic stop of the Honda minivan with Texas plates, they'd had no stimulation. No danger. Negligible calls for service. They didn't even write parking tickets. It was hard to maintain an appreciable level of watchfulness under those conditions.

Argento knew from personal experience. He'd been lethal cover on several homes during standoffs and even if the target was a murder suspect, after an hour or two, you tended to lose focus. Sag a bit off your rifle stock, your thoughts wandering to dinner and what the weekend might bring. People were only built to be watchmen in short cycles.

None of that meant his mission had a high probability of success. His death was a probable outcome. But he wasn't scared of dying. He had lost too many things. His job, Hudson, Emily. Now he was only scared of dying without squaring things. Dying for nothing.

Hudson. After Emily, Hud had been the lone constant in his life. His dog was never far from him because Hudson knew Argento needed him. He curled at his feet while he read. Slept beside him. Watched him with his doleful eyes. Argento loved him unconditionally. He'd been family. His dog's life was worth the same to Argento as any man, woman, or child in Fenton.

His thoughts turned to what he was about to do. This was no rescue mission. It was retribution, nothing more, and the kicker was that if Barrows's project was successful, stopping it would actually cause net harm. And the men he was going after had put on a uniform and fought for their country. That counted. But that was just where they started, not where they ended up. Now they had no center. They had done things you weren't allowed to do.

Salvage everything you can from The Project, Sumaya had told him. Could he do both? Save Barrows's research while still making him and his soldiers answer for what happened to Hudson and the Reeds? Sumaya had spoken of a secure link Barrows was to send to DEA headquarters, a final summary of The Project that would let the DEA implement it in the field. Argento predicted Manco and his men might have some mild objections to that link being sent.

Argento took a tube of black face paint from his pack and darkened his face, neck, and hands. He was put on this earth to pursue the wicked. So had his father on the job before him, who was rumored to have thrown a recidivist child rapist off the top of a seven-story building and claimed he'd jumped. His father had never admitted to it. Just muttered *Those were different times* into his beer. Argento rolled the kinks out of his back. Stretched out his hamstrings. If he was moving fast under fire, he didn't want a pulled muscle slowing him down. Fenton DPS had murdered an entire family. Shot Hudson down. Left him to die. And no one was going to do anything about that. If he didn't act, nothing would happen to them. Even if he could bring it to light, there would be multiple layers of deniability leading to a murky chain of command about who ordered what when. Some spokesperson brought in for cleanup would say they didn't have a good explanation for what happened but the interests of national security forbade them from saying more.

That was unacceptable.

He did another gear check. His head was swimming, and some part of him was trying to postpone what was coming next. He couldn't help the nagging feeling that he needed to talk to someone first before he went operational. To get their counsel. In Agua Mora, Uriel had remarked on how Argento had no family. But there was one person. His pastor in Detroit at Trinity Lutheran Church. A hardy woman of fifty whose sermons contained wisdom about both Scripture and living in society. He'd sought her out after Emily's death and she'd done what she could to help keep him afloat. She'd once told him it wasn't enough to be a good person in a kind of soft, generic way. The good had to be tangible. *The world*, she said over coffee one morning in her study, *should be specifically better for us in it*. He dialed her home number from memory. Even if he didn't give her any specifics, she'd know him well enough to tell him that whatever he was planning, he should reconsider. And maybe he would. But no one picked up. He hung up without leaving a message. It was a long shot. The hour was already late in Arizona, and Michigan was two hours ahead. She'd have been asleep for hours.

He tried to pray but the words wouldn't come. He checked his watch. It was time. After all his reflection, he knew two things.

The first was that what he was about to do was likely the wrong decision.

The second was that he was going to do it anyway.

Regret would only serve as a distraction now. He'd wring his hands when it was over. He'd told them in the desert that he would come back and kill them all. Argento decided to keep his word.

CHAPTER
39

ornejo went first.

Argento found him on the outskirts of town in uniform smoking a cigarette, his squad car nowhere in sight, a pair of night vision goggles propped up on his head where they didn't do much good. Argento's first thought was solo foot patrol, maybe because Tomlinson wanted to cover more of the town's perimeter or because Cornejo was just overconfident. But Fenton DPS wouldn't be doing much as solo units. Cornejo was probably heading home to get some rest after his shift. Some first responders wore their uniform to the house and maybe Cornejo lived with someone who didn't want him smoking there, so he had to smoke here and now. It was lazy, regardless. Argento would probably have missed him if he hadn't seen the cigarette ember. Cornejo had let his guard down. Visualizing the cold drink waiting for him in the fridge.

Argento inhaled deeply. Slowly blew the breath out through his nose. And moved toward the burning ember. It would make the most sense to go after Tomlinson from the jump. Find the leader, cut the herd. But he'd have to take them as they came. He walked slowly. Cutting through the silence like water. Felt his way with the toe of his boot. He imagined himself with sensors on his body. Sonar. Like a submarine in the pitch-black. His head, which had been cloudy, felt clearer now. He made no sound. He could walk all day and into the next. The desert had taught him that. He imagined the distance between Cornejo and him as an ever-shortening rope. Argento remembered how Fenton DPS talked to each other louder than they needed to. Cornejo might have trouble hearing him even on his best day. Tinnitus from planes overhead and machine-gun fire with earplugs proving next to worthless. Some of Argento's SWAT coworkers, especially the ones that doubled as bomb techs, had the same ringing in their ears and would buy box fans just to drown out the sound so they could sleep.

A hundred yards. Ninety. There were a few scrub trees nearby he could use as cover. After that, it was just open air.

Cornejo turned halfway toward him. Stubbed out his cigarette and lit another. And turned back away. Cornejo, he of the shirtless pull-ups at the police station, the long facial scar, and the wings tattooed on his back. The one who'd asked for Argento's last words in the desert, said Argento was practice squad, that he wasn't ready for game speed.

This is game speed, Argento thought, as he drew closer, still cloaked in darkness, moving so quietly he imagined he could hear the faint sound of sand and rock falling from his shoe treads with every step.

Eighty yards. Seventy. Argento a dark mass traveling through space. Now treating each movement as an end to itself to slow his speed. Toe down first to check the ground for anything that would make noise, the crunch of stone, the snap of a twig. Then ease the heel down. Closing in on the man before him.

Sixty yards. Fifty. No more trees to conceal him. A tingling ran down his neck.

Forty, thirty. Argento made no sound. Not a whisper, not a rustle. It was so quiet he thought he could hear Cornejo breathe.

At twenty yards, he leveled the crossbow, sighted in, and put a bolt through the back of Cornejo's neck. Cornejo's cigarette drooped from his mouth and he spun in an awkward half circle, one hand weakly pawing at the arrow in his throat. Argento quickened his pace, put another arrow through Cornejo's head at ten yards and a third at five. Cornejo went down. Argento stood over him. Cornejo wasn't moving. Argento watched the light fade from his eyes. Picked up his radio, undid the earpiece, and turned it off before putting the unit in his pocket. Then he picked up Cornejo's still-lit cigarette and took a long drag with a hand that had a faint tremor to it. He felt something buzzing in his head. He took a photo of Cornejo's corpse and sent it to Manco. A transactional record of snuffing out a life. His phone vibrated. He checked the number. It was his pastor from Detroit. Too late, Reverend. He couldn't answer now. He had crossed the bridge and was committed. To an assignment with a low survivability rate. But it reminded him of what one of his weathered SWAT lieutenants used to say when you didn't have a snowball's chance in hell.

Get out there and roll a bigger snowball.

He took the Sharpie from his pocket and crossed Cornejo's name off his arm.

CHAPTER

40

rgento heard Belchert and McBride talking before he saw them, although he was far enough away that their conversation was just a murmur. He moved to the sound, staying off streets and sidewalks when he could. When he reached a corner building that had a direct view of the diner, he got low and took a peek. Belchert and McBride were leaning against the hood of their patrol car outside the diner drinking coffee from disposable cups. Each held the coffee in his off hand. The soldier's gun hand was to remain eternally free. Cops were the same way.

The diner sign was lit up, the only neon in Fenton. Argento didn't look at it. He didn't want to lose his night vision.

The door jingled, and Cassidy and a pair of cooks came out. Cassidy locked the door behind her.

"Until tomorrow, boys," she said.

"Make an honest man out of me, sweetheart," Belchert offered. Cassidy snorted good-naturedly and got in her car. Soon it was just Belchert and McBride, Belchert the ropey man with the thin French beard who'd called him Hobo Joe, McBride the 250-pound flatnose with wrestler's ears and meaty forearms.

Argento stayed down and watched. He'd wait to move until they were in their car. McBride said something Argento couldn't hear.

"It's a fucking soup sandwich is what it is," Belchert replied. He tossed his coffee cup at a nearby trash can, missed badly, and didn't bother to pick up the litter.

"Amateur," McBride rumbled. He walked over and scooped up Belchert's cup and deposited both it and his own in the garbage. The two men got in the patrol car: Belchert in the driver's seat, McBride filling up the passenger side with little room to spare.

But it wasn't a car. It was a death box with two sedentary targets who, if they took fire, would need time to duck, go for their weapons, and try to escape out the door.

It was time they didn't have.

Argento moved out of the shadows straight at the front of the squad car. Neither man could hide the shock on their features, not just of seeing Argento, but that he was walking right toward them with a painted face carrying a medieval weapon. The first arrow was for Belchert, exploding through the windshield into his cheek. Argento cocked the crossbow and shot McBride the same way. Then he alternated, Belchert, McBride, Belchert, until both men looked like life-size voodoo dolls bristling with pins. At his size, McBride required a few more arrows. Like how the old gladiators in the arena had been, beefy men whose increased mass let them suffer severe wounds without immediately dying.

Argento moved closer. McBride was still in the passenger seat, his head lolled to the side. Belchert's shoulders were twitching, his face contorted in an open question. In a town that felt like it harkened back to the old west, it seemed right that there were arrows in people.

"It's Hobo Joe," Argento said. "Back from the boxcar."

He took out the Sharpie. Showed his forearm to Belchert as he crossed out his name and McBride's. Belchert was mouthing something. Maybe he was trying to say sorry. The penitent man. Argento leaned closer to hear.

"Fucking crossbow," Belchert murmured, looking at him almost in wonderment. Then he coughed wetly as a shiver went through his body. He closed his eyes and didn't say anything else.

Argento took a picture of McBride and Belchert and sent it to Manco. His hands were steady but the buzzing had returned to his head. He tried to blink it away. He had to move fast now or the rest of Fenton DPS would realize people were missing or dead. He popped the trunk and found an expandable tarp in back that was used to tent crime scenes. He unfolded the tarp over the top of the squad car to conceal the broken windshield and the dead men inside. Keep any prying eyes at bay for a time.

Then he headed for the police station.

CHAPTER
41

There was only one squad car parked outside Fenton DPS head-quarters. Argento wasn't about to storm the main door. Anyone at the front counter would have more than adequate cover while they delivered rounds to unwanted guests. He'd need a ruse to draw them out. But it couldn't be overly dramatic. If he shot up a patrol car or even broke a window, he'd get too many of them at once and they'd come out ready to fire. Something more subtle was called for. Something odd but not sinister that would likely just draw out one. He reached in his pack and got out the copy of the *Arizona Republic*. He'd never had his own paper route growing up in Michigan, but he'd subbed for a few kids. He tossed the rolled-up paper at the front doors of HQ. His aim was true and bounced off the door glass with a soft thump. Then he took up a position behind the engine block of the squad car.

A minute later, Chan came out the front door and stared down at this odd after-hours delivery, then looked around for the source. His sidearm was still holstered. Argento aimed his crossbow for the throat and was prepping to fire when Chan's practiced soldier eye spotted him, his face twisting in alarm.

There was a three-second rule in combat shooting. That was

how long it took the average gunman to acquire a target, zone in, and deliver a round. Chan was faster than that. He drew his sidearm and already had his arms locked out to deliver rounds when Argento fired, sending the arrow through the man's right biceps which were now positioned as a shield for his neck. Chan grunted and dropped his gun, then staggered back through the station doors. Argento fired again and the arrow broke through the door glass, but he couldn't tell if it hit its mark. No time to waste. He sprinted inside after Chan, taking Cornejo's radio out of his pocket and pressing the Transmit button to block out Chan's traffic if the latter tried to call for the cavalry. The soldier had dropped his gun, but there'd likely be a secondary firearm close by, either underneath the front counter or close to it. The desk sergeant at Argento's old precinct had favored a Beretta shotgun.

But when Argento entered the station, Chan was well past the counter standing in front of a corridor door futilely trying to transmit on his collar mike while cycling through a set of keys. Argento's broadhead was jutting out of his arm, and a second arrow hung loosely from the front of his uniform: The arrow that Argento had fired through the door had likely hit the trauma plate of Chan's vest and failed to penetrate before getting caught up in his shirt. Argento fired again just as Chan opened the door, but the bolt caromed off the door's metal. Argento let go of the Transmit button, surged forward, and caught the handle just before Chan could close it. There was a brief tug-of-war for control of the door, but Chan was wounded and Argento was stronger—he flung it open just as Chan swung the butt of a Colt Commando assault rifle at him that smashed into the crossbow and knocked it to the floor.

"Gotta kill you," Chan said, his breath coming hard. Something strange about the way he said it. Almost like an apology. He had been able to rearm himself quickly with the Colt because the two men were currently standing in the station's armory, surrounded by racks of assault rifles, submachine guns, and shotguns. Argento was lucky it was standard practice not to store weapons hot in the rifle racks, or Chan would have turned his head into pink mist instead of being forced to use the Colt as a club.

Argento had the Glock but he wasn't going to use it. He didn't want to set off the town's ShotSpotters and alert the rest of Fenton DPS to his presence before he had to. He wasn't sure if the sensors would be sensitive enough to register an indoor gunshot—the automated gunfire systems in Detroit wouldn't always register the sound of bullets that were partially muffled from being fired inside cars—but he wasn't going to chance it. The federal government had the budget for fancier sensors than Motown.

But first things first. Chan had a deadly weapon he was about to load. It was a workable problem that didn't surprise Argento; everything had been going much too smoothly until now anyway. With the crossbow down, Argento didn't have a weapon he could fire. What he did have were fast hands. He hit Chan in the stomach with his best Sunday punch, which buckled the soldier's knees and sent out pressure waves through Chan's body that his vest could only partially absorb. Argento balled his left fist, placed it in his right, and delivered an elbow shot to Chan's mouth that blasted out his front teeth and twisted his head like a bottle cap. He didn't see where the teeth went, but Chan staggered backward against the armory wall and went down on his side wheezing and clutching his throat. Argento had seen that before and surmised that Chan's teeth had become lodged in his lungs. The Fenton soldier raised one hand palm up, as if trying to surrender now that he'd lost. Trying to make peace when peace was never an option.

Argento stepped out of the armory and picked the crossbow back up. It bore a long scratch from the rifle blow but looked undamaged. He pointed it at Chan's head.

"Where's Redlinger?"

Chan was still wheezing. "We . . . killed him," he managed between breaths.

"Why?"

"Because he—" Chan coughed "—helped you." His voice sounded like it was being fed through a meat saw.

Even if Chan was telling the truth, there was no name to cross off on Argento's arm. He hadn't put Redlinger on in the first place. Redlinger's fate didn't surprise or sadden him. He had no feelings about it at all. He had no room for them.

"God takes it from here. You good with God?"

"No." Chan's voice was so low it was just above a whisper. The soldier stared at him. No challenge in his expression. Only acceptance. Like he'd expected this. For just a moment, Argento hesitated. Then his mind flashed to the day when Kristin had left him with her son on his porch while she used the restroom. Ethan had reached out and captured one of Argento's fingers and held it. Argento could almost feel it now. Warmth from a child's hand. He never had kids but he'd been raised to protect them like his own. Now Ethan was a blackened corpse underneath his dead mother, who had insects burrowing in her skin. Chan had been there for that. And for Hudson's last moments. And when Argento was marooned in the Sonoran.

Argento pulled the trigger of the Sentry, and Chan didn't say anything else. Argento wiped blood off his neck that wasn't his. He crossed Chan's name off his arm, but his hand shook again when he did it. The buzzing in his head that had started after he'd killed Cornejo had intensified. He felt like he was seeing the world through a red shroud. He used to be a cop. He was something else entirely now, born out of necessity. Like he had new skin that was on too tight.

He took the picture of Chan for Manco and pressed Send.

Argento turned his attention to the rest of the police station. Chan wouldn't have been alone. Foolish to staff even a small HQ with a single cop, especially at this late hour. There'd be at least one more. The door to the gym down the hall was closed, but Argento could hear loud death metal music coming from inside. It was loud enough that he should have picked up on it as soon as he'd entered the station, but his fight with Chan had created the kind of auditory exclusion typical of high-stress incidents that Argento was in no way immune from.

Argento looked through the gym window. There was one occupant and he was in gym clothes doing dips on a Nautilus machine. Argento checked nearby for a gun belt but didn't see one. A hand-held radio absent the collar mike was on a weight bench within arm's reach. Argento could only see the back of the man's head. But he knew him. Argento had burned his visage deep into his memory banks. He would recognize him out of context, in civilian clothes, with a shaved head, a fake beard, a surgically reconstructed face. He would know him by his voice, his walk, his affect. It was the man who'd crumpled up his missing person flyer of the Reeds. The man who welcomed him to Fenton by punching him in the bar. Who'd put two in Hudson's skull. Who'd told him not to cry when he was let out in the desert and waved goodbye to him with a game show grin.

Argento let the crossbow fall to the floor. It'd be too good for Krebs.

CHAPTER
42

rgento stepped into the gym and closed the door behind him. In three long strides, he reached the bench holding Krebs's radio and tossed it in the corner. Krebs saw Argento's reflection in the wall mirrors and jerked up off the dip stand and spun toward him. He was wearing a loose cut-off T-shirt that showcased his tribal tattoo. The front of the shirt read *I Fight Where I'm Told. I Win Where I Fight.* The music was deafening. Sloppy, for a special operator. Argento had just murdered Chan down the hall using a newspaper and an arrow while Krebs was working his triceps and listening to Pantera.

Krebs faced Argento and moved backward to the line of free weights against the rear wall. Turned off the music on a portable speaker and picked up a twenty-pound barbell with his unbroken hand. It was a good choice. Heavy enough to do damage but not so dense to be unwieldy.

"Where's Chan?"

"No longer with us."

A shadow passed over Krebs's face. "Guess we're killing you twice." His voice was steady, the words of a man who knew he was in a bad spot but who'd been in bad spots before. "Just you?"

"I brought some guys."

"Friends of yours?"

"Not really. But no friends of yours either." Argento showed him the forearm that bore the Fenton DPS roster. Then he took out the Sharpie and drew a line through Krebs's name. He wanted him to see it. His hand didn't shake like when he crossed out Chan's. The red shroud was gone. He saw Krebs with a piercing clarity. There were two men in a room. Each wanted to end the other's life. It was something that still made sense to him.

"You can turn the music back on," Argento said, "if you don't want to hear yourself dying."

Argento gave Krebs credit. He had only one working hand and no firearm. But he didn't try to run. Didn't try to negotiate. He squared to him. "Giving up," Krebs said, his voice low and clear. "It ain't my thing."

He surged forward, swinging the barbell at Argento's face, moving faster than he had in the bar when he'd broken his hand on Argento's skull. It was human nature to backpedal when someone was trying to brain you with a blunt object, but when you backpedaled, two things happened. The first was you created a substantial risk of tripping on whatever obstacles were behind you. The second was you made too much runway for your opponent to keep swinging. Better to move in. Clinch. Buy time. If you controlled distance, you controlled damage.

Argento met Krebs full force, using his barrel chest to jam up the hand holding the free weight. Krebs tried a course correction by launching a headbutt but his timing was off, and Argento pivoted as it glanced off his shoulder. Argento took hold of Krebs's loose T-shirt underneath his arm and pulled it over his head hockey-style. Crude but effective. Krebs's arms went up, trying to claw the shirt off, and Argento jerked the free weight out of Krebs's hand. He crouched and swung it at Krebs, putting his full two hundred pounds behind a concentrated blow that exploded into Krebs's face, making it clear to the soldier that although the fight had just begun, he'd already lost. Krebs staggered and toppled over a weight bench, his back on the

243

floor, his legs resting against the side of the bench with his feet sticking straight up. He tried to rise and Argento hit him in the face a second time. And a third. And again. Krebs's eyes went leaden. Argento regarded the twenty-pound weight in his hand. Then set it down in favor of something heavier.

A ninety-pound kettlebell.

Krebs was still on his back, legs in the air, eyes half-closed. Argento stood over him. Hudson had been a child of heaven. He didn't know what Krebs was. He raised the kettlebell over Krebs's head with both hands. All the fury of the last several weeks building, waiting for release. He lost himself in it.

He wondered if God ever closed his eyes.

Argento brought the kettlebell down. Again. And again. Trauma doctors used the Injury Severity Scale to assess a patient's wounds. An ISS score was between zero and seventy-five. The higher the number, the worse off you were. They'd have to create a new scale for what he'd just done to Krebs. Seventy-five wouldn't begin to do it justice.

It was a bad death.

But Krebs didn't deserve a better one.

When he was finished, Argento put his hand against the wall to catch his breath. He caught a glance of himself in the mirror. Sweat and blood glistened on his painted face. He sent a picture of Krebs to Manco. Then he went back to the armory. Chan's handheld radio was squawking.

"Chan, you up?" The traffic was digitized, which made it hard for Argento to tell who the voice was on the other end, but he guessed Tomlinson.

Chan was not up, Argento thought. Neither was Krebs. Or Belchert, McBride, Cornejo.

"All units," the voice came again. "Just heard some dead air. Give me a status check."

The dead air stemmed from Argento running into HQ holding the Transmit button to keep Chan from sending out an SOS. Argento pressed the Transmit button on Cornejo's radio and spoke, simulating a patchy transmission: "I'm up...but...smoke in our station... electrical...put it out." He was banking on the digital radio traffic distorting his voice enough where he could pass for Chan. He hadn't intended on doing this. He had the broad outlines of his plan down, but as far as the rest, he was building this plane while it was still in the air.

"En route," the voice said. "Henik and Knox are coming from home."

Good, Argento thought. He went back in the armory. Picked up the key ring Chan had been holding as well as a can of gun-cleaning solvent. He took a Remington 700 from the rack, the same one Cornejo had used on the roof to sight in the family in the Honda minivan. With the Remington, there was no assembly required. He left the weapon's heavy attachable tripod behind. At the distance he'd be shooting, he could just use the built-in bipod on the fore end of the rifle. He selected an H&K MP5 from the adjoining gun rack with a thirty-round mag, the same weapon Detroit SWAT used on high-risk ops. He loaded the MP5, pocketed three extra mags, and slung both rifles, then left the armory and went to the wall by the station's front counter. The fire systems panel was similar to the one at his police station in Detroit. He hit the Silence Alarm button. Then he flipped through Chan's key ring until he saw one labeled Utilities. The utility room was marked as such and he found it down the hallway across from the gym. He opened the door. The room contained the controls for the sprinkler system. The individual water pipes weren't marked but they featured large blue gate valves, so Argento turned them all off to be sure. When he returned to the front counter, he squirted lines of the highly flammable gun solvent on the carpet and lit them with a torch from his pack. The carpet started a slow smolder—Argento was familiar enough with home renovation to know modern carpets were often made with varying degrees of fire-resistant material, so he doused some stacks of printer paper and a plastic trash can with the solvent and lit them too. Fenton DPS had night vision goggles—here was a heat signature that would register. He tossed the crossbow onto the growing pyre so he didn't have to worry about prints and DNA. He didn't need to be an archer anymore. He'd silenced the alarm and turned off the valves to avoid the shrill ring of the gong that sounded whenever water passed through pipes to feed sprinklers. He didn't want to wake the neighbors. Didn't want them anywhere near what was coming next.

Argento took a picture of the growing blaze and sent it to Manco. On his way out the door, he called him.

"I've been tracking your progress," Manco said. "Your heart rate's high. You on track to finish this?"

The watch monitoring his vitals. Argento had almost forgotten about it.

"Six of nine are down. The rest are on their way to HQ. I'll be on the roof waiting for them."

"You've only sent me five photos."

The sixth man. Redlinger. "They did some internal housecleaning. Sixth man is off the board."

"You can stop taking pictures. We're about to move on the compound."

"Execute," Argento said.

CHAPTER
43

arrows lay at the bottom of his endless pool, hands clasped behind his neck. He drank in the quiet. When he couldn't hold his breath any longer, he surfaced and drew in oxygen intoxicant. The feeling of euphoria he'd been riding had diminished only slightly. After working so diligently for so long, after breaking down the perception of what was humanely possible, after being doubted and rushed, he had earned this respite.

He scrubbed himself dry and donned his khakis and white button-down but added a suit coat. Today he'd wear something different because an hour and thirteen minutes ago, he'd completed Project A and Project B. He hadn't yet told Sumaya's replacement. He was still reveling in the moment. His instructions were to send The Project in final summary to HQ via a secure link, a link he knew to be ironclad because he'd personally designed the encryption software. The link would grant the DEA access to every scrap of research he'd done along the way, a step-by-step user's guide for The Project so even a slobbering field agent could implement it. But he wasn't ready to share, not yet. He first wanted to tell Sumaya's replacement in person, and for that, he'd need to pick the precisely right words to deliver news of this magnitude, so they'd remember not just what he'd accomplished but how he'd announced it.

He would have preferred if Warren Reed could have seen his triumph. Warren had been the only one at MIT all those years ago who he'd ever connected with. And Warren had been an engineer in his own right, allowing him to have fully appreciated how truly difficult Barrows's own feat of engineering had been. But no matter. Warren was gone, through no fault of Barrows's own. And Barrows remained.

He found himself thinking again of Cassidy, the red-haired waitress. Felt blood rushing to his groin. With the project now complete, he would force them to bring Cassidy as his reward. And he would show her things she didn't wish to know. Would break her just like the teenager from Phoenix. Being a witness to mayhem and death didn't bother Barrows. Such things never had. As a boy, he'd seen a woman hit by a fast-moving train. Bystanders screamed, or held their hands to their faces, but he hadn't looked away or even cringed. He watched with studious interest as he worked out the math in his head, the speeds, weights, and angles, gauging them in part by how the woman's head had landed over here but her arms had landed over there.

Barrows lit a cigarette and smoked one right after the other, vestiges from The Project running like tracer fire through his brain. DNA using the letters A, C, G, and T, RNA using A, C, G, and U (the T subbed in for U and vice versa). He'd been methodical with The Project. Run every conceivable variable. And to think his handlers had suggested peer review. They had strayed outside their field of expertise. Epistemic trespassers.

He hadn't bothered to erase the equations he'd drawn on the wall, for they were just guideposts; the precise recipe for The Project was still predominately in his head. He'd keep it there for now. Even after he sent the secure link to the DEA, this wouldn't signify he had merely handed over the keys to the kingdom. Although The Project worked as it was designed to, there would still be a need for ongoing refinements, including accounting for fluctuations in soil and weather patterns. He would issue directives on these matters. Like royal edicts. They didn't have to make sense to others. They just had to be obeyed.

He went to the lab, entered the twenty-character code on a keypad, then handprint and retinal scan, and the doors opened. The side rooms contained dedicated equipment for The Project tasks: the first for microscopy, including a scanning electron microscope, the second a cleanroom with PacBio DNA sequencers, and the third a condensed BSL4 biosecure growth chamber. Most genome editing on this scale would require a space the size of an industrial agricultural plant. He required but a single floor of a home.

Project A and Project B were contained in the main control room in small adjoining greenhouses that ran to the back wall. Barrows peered into the greenhouse for Project A to see the object of his efforts for the last year. *Erythroxylum coca* with its straight branches, thin leaves tapered at the end, and small flowers on short stalks. He looked into B, *Papaver somniferum*, a toothed silver-green plant, the white flowers forming a disk over a capsule of seeds. Both plants were withering. He had enjoyed his time with them. He valued living things that he didn't have to talk to.

So what now? He would give himself permission to down-cycle, but that never lasted. There was always the next project. He knew what his handlers would want. They were entirely predictable. Something in the realm of counterterrorism. Safeguarding nuclear controls or guarding against bioweapons. Insipid tasks, nothing that would truly test him.

He would have to come up with his own challenge.

The door chime sounded. He exited the lab, making sure the exit sealed behind him, and checked the CCTV display. It was the Black one, the supervisor. Tompkins or Thompson. Barrows confirmed he was alone. He pressed the intercom.

"What is it?"

"We got a report of smoke in the police station and there's a few guys that aren't checking in on the radio. We're heading out to get eyes on the ground. Your in-house security team is in place, but stand by. This could be a full evac."

"Fine," Barrows said and turned away from the CCTV monitor. The Black one seemed marginally more intelligent than the men he supervised, although that said distressingly little.

He stood in the center of his workspace. Smoke in the police station. Men not checking in on the radio. They were the problems of the rabble and they did not concern him.

CHAPTER
44

The office building across the street from the police station had a fire escape that gave Argento access to the third-story roof. He placed the MP5 down, set up the Remington near the ledge, and watched the progress of the blaze below. The smell of smoke was strong, and with the fire alarm silenced, the crackle of flames was the only sound in the early-morning stillness. Fenton DPS had no buildings abutting it and there wasn't much wind to speak of, which was good, because Argento had no intention of burning down all of Fenton. The townspeople didn't need to suffer on account of their ringer police department. But police headquarters was his. He wanted to send them a message from the Reeds.

He waited with the Remington. On SWAT, due to budget reasons, he'd shared his sniper rifle with another officer, who'd taken the liberty of etching the words *You're Fucked* into the weapon's stock. Argento favored the 700. He'd trained extensively on it. There were more high-tech weapons on the market, but the Remington was more than adequate. And when it counted, the best gun was the one you knew.

As a cop, Argento had always prepared for what was happening in the moment and for what might happen in two minutes. What if the suspect took a hostage? Or the barricaded gunman drove his car right out through the garage doors? He was currently showing Fenton DPS how little prepared they were for him. Because if you had a decent tactical plan, the element of surprise, and the right weapon, you could turn an elite combat platoon into little more than a beer club. The endings of Cornejo, Belchert, McBride, Chan, and Krebs were proof of that. Men who had been promised two million tax-free dollars for protecting The Project. The tax-free part struck him. It was a solid indicator they were doing something no one wanted a record of. Because if it was a legitimate enterprise that could withstand scrutiny, the feds wanted your tax money.

He heard the siren before he saw the engine, the sound carrying in the quiet. He waited until it stopped. Give them a few moments to gear up; he remembered how Chan checked the rooflines the first time he saw him in Fenton. Then he took a quick peek over the ledge. Tomlinson, Henik, and Knox were in full turnouts next to a Fenton Fire Department rig and were probably wondering why none of their buddies had shown up to help fight the fire. Argento didn't know more than the next guy about fire operations, but he'd never seen fewer than ten firefighters show up to a working blaze. Everyone had a job, whether it was attacking the fire source, water supply, or search and rescue. But Fenton was going to have to make do with these three because everyone else was indisposed. Tomlinson, with the same kind of MP5 slung that Argento had taken from the armory, went to the side of the building, presumably to the electricity and gas shutoffs. Henik and Knox hooked up to a fire hydrant and directed water straight through the open doors of the police station.

When Tomlinson returned, Argento ducked below the edge of the building before the lieutenant could see him. When Argento looked back over the edge, Tomlinson had repositioned himself on the other side of the rig. Argento had no shot on the lieutenant, but the lieutenant had no line of sight on him either, and Henik and Knox had their hands full with the fire. When the flames had subsided, both men went inside while the lieutenant stayed out on watch.

Argento waited until the fire looked to be out. He was trying to bleed as much time as he could to let Manco and his men get into position on the compound. When Henik and Knox emerged from the front doors, they were still in their firefighter gear, but now both were armed with MP5s, which meant they'd found Chan in the armory and Krebs in the gym. Tomlinson was still behind the rig. Argento used the edge of the building as a shooting platform and prepped the Remington to fire. He'd done it a thousand times, although he'd never had to deliver sniper rounds at another human being. The weapon had a safety, but no one on SWAT used it. He put Henik in his sights. The Remington was single-action, the trigger pull no more than four pounds. His .308 bullet would crater Henik's head. Maybe shear it from his neck. The time for quick and quiet was over. He slid his finger over the trigger.

Hesitated.

Something about the way Chan had looked when he'd died. Like he was searching for divine intervention. But there was no saint for the godless. Maybe that applied to Argento now too. He'd ambushed the man. And he hadn't played the drums to announce his advance on Cornejo and the others, but he'd either been directly face-to-face or at least in harm's way himself. He'd gotten dirt under his nails. This was different. He was hidden on a roof with a rifle. Death from above. It felt cowardly, even though he had no doubt if he dropped his weapon and announced his surrender, they'd light him up just like Sumaya said they would. He'd never spoken to Henik or Knox, but they'd both been there in the desert dropping him off—they'd already tried to kill him once. They didn't deserve a fighting chance.

Then why wasn't he shooting? And why, after he'd killed Krebs, had the rage drained out of him so quickly and been replaced by a deep hollow? Argento felt bile rising in his throat. He looked skyward and blinked the sweat out of his eyes. Looked down at the Remington.

Henik was sweeping the street with the MP5. He was a rangy man with a shaved head and a slight pigeon-toe to his gait, like Ron Cey. Knox, half-a-head taller, his face expressionless, was on the radio, likely trying to raise his coworkers or get through to the compound. Tomlinson was nowhere to be seen. Argento made a decision. A kind of violent compromise. He dropped the sights, waited until Henik went stationary, and delivered a round at his left hand. Detroit's SWAT sniper minimum standard was being able to place multiple shots within a two-inch diameter circle at a hundred yards. He would have liked to confirm his zero first with this particular rifle, but seventy yards was a layup. Argento was at close range, there was no wind, and he was armed with a scoped weapon he knew. The round went where he'd wanted, and Henik's fist blew into ragged chunks. Argento worked the action, ears ringing from the rifle's report, and fired again, the second round carving a fissure through one of Knox's feet.

Maim instead of kill.

Civilized.

"Contact roof!" Henik shouted, already moving as he grabbed hold of Knox with his good arm and dragged him to the other side of the fire rig. The two of them still had three working arms between them to apply tourniquets to their injuries, but Argento hoped he'd put them both out of the fight. He scanned for Tomlinson but didn't see him, and his inner SWAT voice told him he'd exposed himself too long and it was time to get the hell down—just as the lieutenant's MP5 spat and Tomlinson fired off half a mag at the rooftop where Argento's head had been a half second before. A shard of wood from the railing embedded itself in Argento's brow. He got as low as he could and felt his face. It was still attached to his neck. He pulled the shrapnel out. Shallow wound, not much blood. Tomlinson had avoided getting caught up in the frenzy and rushing to the side of his downed men. He'd taken a moment to survey the scene and transitioned from defense to offense.

And now Argento was behind in the count.

There was no more need to be on the roof. He wouldn't put it past Tomlinson to have access to an explosive to direct at his position and send him tumbling to the street in flames. But just walking down the fire escape wasn't going to play. Tomlinson could have already relocated to a spot where he could stitch him with bullets as he descended.

He needed something to occupy the lieutenant. He took a knee. Looked left. Looked right. From the beginning, Argento knew that to pull this operation off, he was going to have to be more intuitive and creative than he'd ever been. He was still in that realm of elevated thinking. It was a matter of survival. He raised the Remington and aimed for the utility pole that fed into the police station. Shooting at power lines—the same thing idiots in Michigan used to do for fun.

Live power lines represented a deadly hazard to touch or drive over. If you got within a few feet of them, they could wind their way toward you like a sentient snake. If they landed on your vehicle, you were safe as long as you stayed inside, but step out and raise a foot off the ground and the voltage would blow that limb clean off. Your only option was to shuffle or do an undignified hop away with your feet together until you were at least fifty feet clear.

Argento aimed for the conductor where the line dead-ended. It was about an eight-inch diameter plate made of porcelain with what looked like ribs coming out of it. It took two rounds to crack it before one line came dislodged and fell, taking another with it. The first line draped into the street on concrete, not a good conductor, but the second landed over the fire engine, which was. It made a noise like the chattering of a water faucet. Tomlinson would have to get himself and his men out of harm's way. Argento had bought himself some time. He slung the Remington and MP5 tight on his back, took the stairs to the fire escape two at a time and hit the pavement running just as an explosion came from the fire engine; the steel rim of a tire popped as north of ten thousand volts tried to find its way back to the earth. He jogged toward the edge of town where his motorcycle was stashed, ignoring the warm pings popping under his kneecap, as his leg let him know it registered the extra bulk of the two rifles.

Behind him, machine-gun fire came from up on the hill. The compound. Manco and his men were making entry. It sounded like the finale of a war movie. Argento imagined the display screen for the compound's ground sensors and ShotSpotters melting from all the alerts.

His bike was where he left it behind a grove of trees. He fired it up and drove toward the compound. Toward August Barrows, Manco, and the cartel shooters.

To the endgame.

CHAPTER
45

Argento sped up the path of the cliff face past the sign that said *Private Road Do Not Enter* until he reached the gates leading to the compound, the thick barrier that rose fifteen feet and spanned the width of the road.

The kind of barrier you'd need a rocket launcher to get through.

The gates were pushed wide open and blackened on the edges. It looked like a giant flaming hand had just slapped them aside. He had needed the cartel to force entry to the compound, take out the helicopter, engage the occupants inside, and seal the back. They had performed the first task as advertised. Argento gunned the cycle and went up the drive. The helicopter on the roof was a smoking husk. Second task complete. With the chopper down, if Manco's people had managed to block off the back exit, that meant there was a good chance Barrows was still inside.

All four cartel Humvees were parked in the driveway at staggered angles. Three of the four had swaths of bullet holes punched through their windshields. When Argento had talked to Sumaya in her car at the cemetery, he'd told her any staff remaining in the compound were fair game, but that was just to light a fire under her to evacuate as many civilians as possible. He didn't want to hurt them and he didn't want the cartel to hurt them either.

This was why he hadn't told Manco about the roof gunner.

The man Argento had seen the first day he'd approached the compound.

A man guarding one of the most important scientific developments in the last hundred years. A man who most certainly had been told, *When in doubt, fire at will*. Which meant it would be open season on the cartel invaders. That was okay with Argento. He had brought a mini-army with him but it wasn't his army and he didn't care what happened to them. If a dozen cartel enforcers died in a gunfight, no one would be releasing any doves.

Argento no longer saw a shooter on the roof, but when he looked inside the passenger compartment of the lead vehicle, his handiwork was obvious. All four occupants were corpses; the passenger was missing half his head, the driver's mouth gaped in protest at what bullets did. Whatever the roof shooter had been firing, it was belt-fed and delivered hundreds of rounds a minute. Like something used on the tops of armored vehicles. You blanketed an area with enough firepower and you were both sword and shield. Argento checked the rest of the Humvees. Each contained the carnage of at least one dead cartel shooter, most unrecognizable. None of them were Manco. Argento added them up. Ten of the fourteen down. Four remaining.

The front doors to the compound were torn wide open. Sumaya had said they were fireproof and bullet-resistant, but they hadn't been resistant to whatever the cartel had used to blow off their hinges. Two more cartel members lay still in front of the doorway. One had three holes in his chest. The other had about forty. The two corpses side by side illustrated the difference between getting shot and getting shot to pieces. Argento had never met anyone who held up particularly well to rifle fire. Down to two cartel shooters. There was additional security inside, Sumaya had said. Guys he didn't know about. That had to be true because someone other than the roof gunner had smoked the cartel in the doorway and it wasn't any of Fenton DPS, because they were either dead or still navigating live electrical wires. Argento was about to find out how deep of a bench this project had.

He kept the Remington slung and led with the MP5 as he approached the threshold into the hive. Action movie star Trent Kilroy's old place. Now a fortress for August Barrows. They'd made Barrows a hard asset to reach. But six months ago, a man with a hatchet had scaled the fence to the White House, sprinted across the lawn and gotten through the front doors and halfway up the staircase that the president was at the top of before he was intercepted by the Secret Service. No security was foolproof, not even for the most powerful man on earth.

There was an excellent chance that the MP5 in Argento's hands, a weapon he was familiar with, worked the way it was supposed to. But given where Argento currently found himself, he wanted 100 percent certainty. From the doorway, he test-fired the MP5 into the corner on single shot and auto. Felt the smooth recoil, heard the sharp report, magnified indoors. He pocketed the used magazine and replaced it with a full one. Good to go.

If Manco and his crew had cut the power, the backup generators were filling in nicely. The entryway was fully illuminated, all ornate stone columns, desert hues, and walls of tinted floor-to-ceiling glazing. He could hear gunfire above him. The house had three floors. It sounded like it was coming from the top.

Time to push his luck. He moved past the entryway. He'd gone into homes before expecting to take a bullet and this was no exception, but he made it to one of the stone columns without incident. He called Manco.

"Third floor," Manco said. "What were the shots down there?"

"Making sure my gun worked. On my way. Any resistance between here and there?"

Manco hung up like Argento hadn't asked a question.

Argento went looking for the stairs. He moved past an open kitchen that looked like a movie star had meals prepped for him there: polished cabinetry, a huge fridge-freezer, and a breakfast bar.

The ceiling had a wave design to it, a mix of orange stucco and rich brown mahogany setting off recessed lighting, like a gaudy knockoff of a Cheesecake Factory.

Ahead and to his left, Argento spotted a blood trail going into the bathroom. He followed it. The bathroom was something straight out of a Vegas dream. A stone sunken tub set against a marble wall that ran with what looked like fingers of molten lava. His-and-hers sinks. It looked to be a room designed for heavy cocaine use.

The trail of blood ended near the bathroom closet. Argento listened. He could hear breathing behind it. He raised the MP5 and opened the door. A woman was crouched in the back, her hands up to guard her face. She was about thirty and wore a T-shirt and jeans. There was a toilet brush at her feet. Argento lowered his weapon.

"What are you doing here?"

"I clean the house," she said, not meeting Argento's gaze. Argento knew there was no guarantee Sumaya would listen to him when he told her to get all the staff out, but he silently cursed all the same.

"What's your name?"

"Gabriella," she said softly.

"Are you hurt?"

Gabriella looked at the blood trail in front of her. "It's not mine."

"All right, Gabriella. I might look like a bad guy but I'm not."

"Okay," she said, as if in a trance.

"Are there any other cleaners in the house? Any other staff?"

Gabriella shook her head, still not making eye contact.

"I'm going to get you out of here."

"Okay."

"All you have to do is follow me."

Argento walked out of the bathroom. Gabriella stayed close behind. As they approached the front doors, a cartel shooter in full body armor appeared and filled the doorway. He had already been through the wringer—his left arm was bound with a field dressing, the skin scorched at the edges. He had a rifle, some variation of the

AK-47, but held it in sagging arms. Long guns didn't do much good if you couldn't keep them upright.

"No," the man said in accented English, looking Gabriella up and down. "She comes with us." He reached for her with one hand and lifted the AK with the other.

There was no time to negotiate, so Argento shot him in the forehead with the MP5 without breaking stride. He wouldn't be snapping a picture of this. Taking anyone other than Barrows wasn't the plan, and the only reason for the cartel to grab Gabriella was as a hostage or so they could pass her around later. It wasn't a fair shooting, but his truce with Manco and his men had always been temporary. He kept his head on a swivel coming out of the doors. Where there was one shooter, there was usually two. You had to look for the second guy. Maybe Manco hadn't brought all the gunmen to the rendezvous point. Maybe he had some floaters.

But when Argento broke the plane of the doorway, the driveway looked clear.

Gabriella was rooted to the spot, her hands over her ears in reaction to the loud crack of the MP5. Argento took his Glock out of the holster and handed it barrel down to her. It was a risk. Maybe she'd just shoot him in a panic. But he didn't want to send her past any more cartel shooters without protection. And like Sumaya had said in the cemetery, there was no playbook for this anymore. "Do you know how to shoot this?"

She nodded, and took it with a quivering hand.

"Might be more like him out there. But run, then hide, then fight."

She stood motionless, the gun pointed down.

"That first part is run," he said. And she did, legs churning right over the cartel body, moving more like a confident varsity athlete now than timid house cleaner.

Argento went back into the house, picked up the dead cartel shooter by the feet, and dragged him behind a couch. He had to hope Gabriella was right and there weren't more civilian staff to contend with, like a parking valet or whoever had treated Krebs's arm when he'd broke it on Argento's head.

The stairs going up were wide and regal, like they were built for a duchess. Argento ascended, his feet sinking into plush carpet, the MP5 out on point. The second floor was quiet. He moved to the third. The stairway opened up into a home theater with five rows of reclining seats, the walls papered with movie posters from Kilroy's career. The room had a built-in trophy case on the side. Argento didn't see any Oscars, but there was a Blockbuster Entertainment Award for the film *Hurricane of Fire*, which Argento recalled as being loud and shitty.

Argento went right, staying a few feet from the walls because errant bullets liked to skip off them. He didn't need to push himself any harder. He was already at maximum velocity. He forced himself to concentrate on his breathing and metered the corner.

Manco was alone standing by a set of double doors. His face was smudged with what looked like soot. He had slung his shotgun and held what looked like a Kinetic Breaching Tool in both hands that resembled a cross between a rifle and a square shovel head, half again as large as the type Argento had used in the field. Manco gave no indication the weight of the heavy tool bothered him. He acknowledged Argento with the slightest of head nods.

"Just heard another shot downstairs," he said.

"Thought I saw something."

Manco locked eyes with Argento. Cut his eyes down to Argento's empty holster where the Glock had been. A good few seconds passed before he looked away and gestured toward the doors. "He's in there."

"Armed?"

"We'll find out."

"There still security in the house?"

"One in back. Two on the roof. All down."

"Your people?"

"One out front, more in back. Rest are dead." Manco reported this information without affect, as if he was talking about the victims of some remote natural disaster, not men he worked with.

The double doors were of the automatic variety with no handle or knob. Manco put the breeching tool up to the top of the door closest to him. He pressed the trigger at all four corners and then down the seams, the KBT making a pneumatic sound as the door gave way. Manco pushed it down with his boot, and the metal clanged on the floor. Argento would have preferred a ballistic shield under the circumstances, but Manco merely dropped the KBT, unslung his shotgun, and stepped into the room. Argento followed behind. Manco would serve as his ballistic shield.

The room was one giant workstation. Three computer monitors towered above a desk; the middle one rivaled the size of the screen in the compound's home theater. Three keyboards and a swivel chair. There was nothing on the walls. No filing cabinets, no other furniture. No coffee cups or knickknacks. It looked barren and space-age and smelled like cleaning agents.

August Barrows stood in front of the monitors, as if trying to protect them. His silver hair looked longer than Argento remembered. He wore a navy suit coat over khakis. Without a handkerchief or shirt collar to conceal it, his unnaturally long neck looked precarious, as if at any moment his head would tumble off it. No need to primp if you were the world's smartest man. He didn't look that different from the freshman year photo Argento had seen where he was wearing ill-fitting pants and didn't know how to smile.

There was a cell phone on the counter behind Barrows. The encrypted summary link for The Project could be sent from his phone, Sumaya had said. Argento took a mental snapshot of it for later.

Manco moved to Barrows, who hunched in on himself as Manco did a rough search of him that turned up no weapons. Barrows looked from Argento to Manco, then stayed on Manco.

"Who are you?" His voice was the same high monotone Argento remembered from the desert.

"Manco."

"They were supposed to evacuate me."

263

"They can't now," Argento said. "I killed them."

"You made it out of the desert."

"It was unpleasant."

Barrows sniffed and gazed at the floor. "You're not allowed to hurt me."

Manco almost looked amused. "Who says this?"

"The United States government."

"That is not a problem for me," Manco said. "I do not live here."

"Please," Barrows said. "I have children." Up close, Argento could see the veins near his eyes. He took another look around the work-space. He didn't see any photos, bad crayon drawings, or handwritten *Have a Great Day Daddy* notes. He looked back at Barrows. This was a man who had never in his adult life sat next to some jelly-faced kid and watched a cartoon or put a bandage on a skinned knee.

"You don't have children," he said. "And when we take you out of this lab, you're not going to have anything at all."

CHAPTER
46

Manco slung the shotgun and took out a knife from a sheath on his vest. A long, wicked blade, like the one Ramon had brandished in Agua Mora. Maybe they'd bought them together. A way for twins to bond.

"No," Barrows said. "No no no."

"Take me in your lab," Manco said. "Or I'll put this in your stomach and pull it out your back."

Barrows offered no resistance. He walked almost gingerly toward a hallway that ran off the back of the workspace. He was an invaluable talent who hadn't thought to arm himself at the sound of shots fired outside. Argento wondered if he'd ever picked up a gun in his life. Maybe the DEA didn't trust him with one. Feared he'd be the smart but clumsy type who, when armed, would only pose a threat to himself.

The three men walked past a long room of servers and computer towers. Argento could feel the heat emanating through the door. They passed walls filled with scribbled math, like the chalkboard problem the kid janitor had solved in the movie where Mork had a beard. At the end of the hallway, Barrows stopped at a door with a keypad and screen next to it. He began punching in the code, but his hand shook and he had to start over.

Manco said, "I am not patient."

Barrows smiled, but it was all nerves and looked like a smear. Argento noticed that his lips had a bluish tinge. A sign of stress, not cold, because under stress, blood pooled from the extremities to the heart. Barrows held one hand with the other to steady it and pressed a series of digits followed by a handprint and a retinal scan. The door opened.

Time to look behind the curtain.

Argento was in a sizable lab with three side rooms leading off of it. One side room's door was open, and he could see a microscope that looked fancier than the one he'd used in high school biology. In the main space, there were cabinets, exhaust fans, and an autoclave, but most of the room was taken up by two mini greenhouses next to each other that ran the length of the space to the back wall. One greenhouse contained what he recognized as the coca leaf. The other was the poppy. The source of cocaine and heroin. Both plants were blackened and dying. Which, Argento knew, was the point of The Project. To eliminate supply. He'd never seen heroin or cocaine cultivated indoors before. It was so easy to get the finished product in the city, maybe nobody even thought to grow their own.

"Does it work?" Manco asked.

"I just finished," Barrows said, unable to hide the pride in his voice.

"How?"

Barrows opened his mouth to speak and stopped.

"If you talk, you extend your life."

"It's . . . classified."

"I am not against torture. My knife makes people—"

"Torture doesn't work," Barrows cut in. He spoke like he was reading from a book report. "The subject of the torture merely says whatever they have to in order to get the pain to stop. It didn't work in Latin America, in Vietnam. It won't work here."

Manco tapped Barrows's cheek with the flat side of the knife. "I'll show you it works."

"I've created a microbe," Barrows said hurriedly. He paused, as if remembering who he was talking to. "Microbes are microorganisms, especially bacterium that cause disease."

"And?"

"It binds to the coca leaf and poppy and destroys them."

"What's the delivery system?"

"Liquid, solid, or gas. It could take the form of seeds or a spray from an airplane."

Manco looked from greenhouse to greenhouse. "How is this different from the defoliants they've tried before?"

"The crop dusters flying over the Colombian coca fields didn't work because the farmers would just start over and replant, plus the planes couldn't reach the smaller farms. There were too many and they were too remote. And aside from Colombia, there was still Bolivia's and Peru's production, so it was an inefficient process." Barrows's hands had stopped shaking. He was back in his element. Holding court over the slack-jawed masses. "But I've designed the microbe to not just wipe out the current plants but to drop toxins deep in the soil to prevent future growth for decades. They won't be able to replant. Plus the microbe easily becomes wind-borne, so seeds dropped in one field can also reach adjacent fields, including those remote farms. It generates a comprehensive target area. I estimate that with sufficient resources, we could wipe out both crops in nine months." Barrows looked at them expectantly, like he was waiting for someone to applaud the individual effort.

Manco put his hand on the outside of the greenhouse housing the coca plants and ran it along the glass. "If you developed a virus this strong, why aren't you wearing a biohazard suit?"

"No need. I built the microbe as a targeted strike that doesn't affect other vegetation, people, or water systems." He turned his attention to Argento, who he probably saw as more reasonable than Manco because he had not yet held a knife to him. "You killed my men."

"You could run an ad," Argento said. "Get some more."

"I don't...what do you intend to do with me?"

"That's his department," Argento said, pointing at Manco.

Barrows straightened himself. Buoyed by his explanation of his scientific breakthrough. "You should think twice about crossing me. I have powerful friends." The fact that he thought he could gain ground referencing his powerful friends while in front of his powerful enemies was a sign to Argento that Barrows wasn't as smart as they said. He gestured at Barrows's waist.

"You missed a belt loop."

Barrows looked down and his face flushed. He pulled his belt out and corrected the problem, his hair tumbling in his eyes.

Manco had examined the contents of both greenhouses to his satisfaction. He walked over to Barrows. "Impressive. But I will be shutting this project down."

"On whose authority?"

Manco punched Barrows so hard in the face the blow made a liquid sound. Barrows staggered and stayed on his feet but was no longer tracking with his eyes. Manco's way of answering, "On the authority of the Sinaloa cartel." Then Manco handcuffed Barrows and pushed him toward the lab's exit doors.

Argento had never been in a secret government lab before. He wouldn't put it past the DEA to have the whole place rigged to blow if the lab was compromised. Maybe the government people were sore losers. But nothing exploded as the men left. Barrows was stumbling, spittle dripping from his chin.

"We'll leave out back," Manco said. He reached inside his pack and removed a cannister the size of a can of soup and tossed it through the lab doors before they closed. He tossed another into the room of computer servers and dropped a third on the floor by the monitors. Some kind of time-delayed incendiary. Argento took the Remington off his back and slid it over to the monitors near the third disk. The rifle felt unwieldy on his back, and the explosion to come would remove his trace evidence from the trigger and stock. Sumaya had told Argento about how Barrows would send them the completed project summary via an encrypted link, but Argento hadn't told the cartel that. They weren't making any efforts for data retention, other than taking Barrows, but even if they wanted to save something from the lab, Argento didn't know how that would go. A 128-gig thumb drive from the pharmacy wouldn't quite cut it. It would take a semi full of thumb drives to even make a dent in the room full of servers. Maybe this was why Manco was opting for the clean sweep.

Barrows saw what Manco was doing. He looked like he was going to say something, to protest, but his face was still slack and he moved with difficulty. If you've never been hit hard in the face before, it takes you a while to readjust to society.

Manco spoke in Spanish into his collar mike. Something along the lines of "Package secure. We're coming out."

Barrows turned to Argento. There was blood running from his nose and his eyes looked glazed. "Help me," he said, a warble to his high monotone.

"No," Argento said. But when Manco's attention was on his radio, he took Barrows's cell phone off the counter and slipped it in his pocket.

CHAPTER
47

Argento was on board with exiting the rear of the compound because he hadn't had much time to hide the cartel gunner he'd head-shot near the front doors; the body would prompt questions from Manco he didn't want to answer. Manco led the way with Barrows at his side. Argento brought up the rear. The back stairs led to a corridor with rock walls, a space that'd been tunneled out of the cliff so Trent Kilroy could avoid scrutiny and truck in his hookers and blow. There were lights embedded in the walls and a musty odor that followed them to the corridor's end, where a huge metallic exit door to the desert outside was open.

And blocked by a silver cylinder truck.

It was the kind used for long-hauling chemicals, the rear bearing a large red decal that said *Stay Back: Not Responsible for Road Debris.* At the rendezvous point on the mining road, Argento had questioned the use of a Humvee to seal off the back and Manco had said he had a different vehicle in mind.

That was accurate.

There was a dead man pinned against the doorway by the truck's back doors. Thirties, with a military haircut, in street clothes. Part of the compound's in-house security. His right hand was open, and a handgun lay on the floor by his feet. Argento wasn't sure if he'd been caught unaware by the truck barreling toward him or if he'd been frozen at the last second before physics took over and the high-speed metal pulverized his organs. Argento hoped the end was quick. He didn't know this man, who hadn't wronged him. He wasn't Fenton DPS, but maybe he'd been in on the murder of the Reeds. Or maybe he knew nothing about it and was a decent human being just guarding where he'd been ordered to guard. Argento had told Sumaya to get them all out. He'd told her and she hadn't. She'd contributed to this man's death. But he'd brought the cartel to the party. Argento gripped his MP5 so tightly one of his knuckles cracked. This operation was never going to be clean. If he ever thought so, he'd deceived himself.

Manco got back on the radio and barked a command. The truck lurched forward. The man's body stayed in place, as if now a permanent part of the doorway. Then Manco assumed an outward firing position, and his automatic shotgun boomed. Ears ringing, Argento saw what Manco saw. It was Henik, his MP5 in his remaining workable hand approaching the rear exit from behind the cylinder truck. The soldier was so close, Manco's shotgun blast unraveled him. Manco furiously backpedaled as a barrage of gunfire followed from outside, chipping off wood and slivers of stone from the doorway. Argento caught a glimpse of a stationary Fenton DPS SUV some twenty yards from the exit. Tomlinson was in the driver's seat. Knox was firing from the passenger side, still in the fight with just one usable foot. A tough kid who wanted his untaxed two million. Argento could have ended the soldier with one shot from the Remington when he was up on the roof but had elected to try and incapacitate him instead. He was already paying for his restraint.

"Cease fire, pendejos!" Manco shouted. "We got your fucking scientist."

The gunfire stopped as quickly as it started.

"Cover the rear," Manco snapped as they double-timed back down the corridor. Argento heard another exchange of gunfire. He presumed it was the driver of the truck versus Tomlinson and Knox. Argento was betting on the latter in that dustup. Suppressive fire went directly against Argento's training because as a cop, you didn't fire unless you had a specific target. But if Tomlinson and Knox caught up to them in the compound, it was over, so he laid down rounds as they retreated until the MP5 went dry. He slapped in another mag and charged the weapon on the run.

The three of them were moving too fast toward the front doors for Manco to see the cartel body behind the couch. Manco barked something in Spanish which Argento roughly translated to "Coming out . . . burn it." He opened the back door to a Humvee that looked less shot up than the rest, and pushed Barrows inside.

"Get next to him," he told Argento. Argento did as he was told. Manco reached in and secured the chain of Barrows's handcuffs to a metal ring extending from the back seat. A custom-made addition to the Humvee for when you belonged to a major drug syndicate and had to extract a scientist who threatened your way of business.

"You still have guys on the ground here?"

Manco's expression didn't change. "They should have been faster." He started up the Humvee and went down the drive. A minute after they cleared the compound's front gate, a deafening boom behind them rattled Argento's teeth. Even with its weighty undercarriage, the Humvee shook. Argento looked back. Thick smoke and flames pluming up from where the compound had been. Argento had never been on the bomb squad, but given the force of the blast, the catalyst had to be more than the cannister explosives Manco had dropped on the third floor.

Manco was still looking straight ahead when he said, "You pull out the gas lines to the stove, dryer, water heater. Leave flares on the way out. They burn long enough to let the gas fill up the house before they ignite."

When in doubt, blow up the castle. Trent Kilroy's place was no more, at the market cost of a few flares, around twelve dollars. If Tomlinson and Knox had pursued them through the house instead of driving around the long way, they'd have been reduced to cinders.

Barrows twisted to look back. "It doesn't matter," he sputtered. "I still have it all in my head."

"That's why we're bringing your head with us," Manco said. "You'll show us how you did it and how to stop it."

The Humvee clattered down the road to Fenton. The rally point was the diner. For the team breakfast. But Argento wasn't sure who they'd be rallying with. The assault on the compound had thinned out Manco's men. Maybe the cartel had a dozen more members at the diner waiting to dispose of him now that he'd served his purpose.

There was a car behind them. Not Fenton DPS. A second Humvee. Likely containing the men Manco had said were posted out back. Argento had figured Tomlinson and Knox would have already killed them. But there was also the cylinder truck driver to contend with. Maybe Tomlinson and Knox hadn't killed him either. Argento was starting to lose track of who was where. But he was certain that Manco was going to put a bullet in his head. There was no upside to keeping him around. Even if Sinaloa was impressed with his performance against the Fenton soldiers, they weren't going to offer him a spot on their roster.

Argento put his seat belt on. He reached over and put on Barrows's. They'd both need to be buckled in for what he'd planned next. If Manco noticed, he didn't show it. They were fast approaching the center of Fenton. When Manco turned the corner toward the diner, Argento reached up to the front seat, twisted the steering wheel and aimed right for Fenton's lone stoplight. Argento had been to his share of traffic collisions and knew they now engineered traffic lights so if they were struck by a vehicle, they would break away instead of cutting your car in half. He hoped Fenton's signal was in line with the times. Manco cursed and slammed on the brakes, but he was too late. The front of the Humvee smacked into the light pole. Argento waited for the gunshot sound and spray of white powder that accompanied the deployment of the front airbags, which needed a collision of eight miles per hour to activate, waited for the large inflatable pillow to pop off in Manco's face, disorient him, make it nearly impossible for him to draw a weapon, and give Argento the time and space to make a hard move.

But there was no sound. No spray of powder.

Argento had just learned, in real time, that Humvees didn't have airbags.

Manco reached for Argento's MP5. The two men fought for control of it. Argento was strong but Manco was matching him, twisting the stock of the weapon one way while Argento strained to twist it the other. Barrows made a keening sound in the back seat and closed his eyes. With the second Humvee behind him, Argento was in a bad spot that was getting worse by the second. He was battling to retain his primary weapon. He had given his secondary weapon, the Glock, to the maid. Manco and the two shooters in the Humvee behind him had firepower, positioning, and murder on their mind.

All Argento could do was make them work for it.

CHAPTER
48

A rgento's reprieve came in the form of the Fenton DPS SUV that barreled toward them off a side street with Tomlinson at the wheel and Knox in the passenger seat firing at the second Humvee on full auto with a long gun through a shattered front windshield.

Saved by the police.

Manco and Argento each instinctively let go of the contested MP5 in the front seat, as they bailed out of their respective sides of the lead car, leaving Barrows alone in the back still handcuffed. Argento got down just as the Fenton SUV T-boned the second Humvee at about forty-five, flipping it twice with the shriek of rending metal as it landed on its roof fifty feet away with no side impact airbags to cushion the tumble.

Argento wasn't sure how heavy Humvees were. Somewhere in the range of ten thousand pounds. Maybe their armor made them prone to rollovers. If that were true, it'd be the kind of thing someone like Tomlinson would know to take advantage of.

The striking vehicle on a T-collision always fared far better than the vehicle struck. All the Fenton SUV had to show for the impact was a smashed grille and a partially crinkled hood. But no airbags went off. There was no way the Fenton fleet weren't equipped with them.

It must have a retrofit on-off switch that Tomlinson or Knox had hit before impact to avoid being slowed down. It worked because Tomlinson was already out of the driver's side of the SUV, fast and fluid. Knox, he of the blown-out foot, stayed in the vehicle and covered down on the lead Humvee Barrows was in, which prevented Argento from trying to retrieve the MP5 from the front seat. Tomlinson pointed the barrel of his own MP5 at the driver's-side window of the upside-down Humvee, where there was no ballistic paneling. He shot off a volley that left chunks of the occupants' bone and skin plastered against the rear windshield. Two more cartel out of the picture.

Argento stayed so low his face was on the pavement, using the engine block of the Humvee as cover. He had nowhere else to go. If he ran from the Humvee, Manco, Tomlinson, or Knox would tattoo him with bullets. His only advantage was Tomlinson wouldn't fire blindly at his position for fear of hitting Barrows. He sensed motion to his left. Argento could only see his feet from his position on the ground, but he knew Manco was firing his shotgun at Knox from the other side of the Humvee. If the two of them canceled each other out, he'd just have Tomlinson to deal with.

Manco's shotgun stopped booming. He'd gone dry. Then Argento saw the cartel gunman's hand reach around blindly in the front of the Humvee until his fingers closed on the stock of the MP5. He pulled it out and down. The rifle went rapid-fire toward Knox's position, maybe half a mag dump. Argento couldn't hear Knox laying down any more rounds. Someone had already won the gunfight or was out of ammo.

Argento could undo Barrows's cuffs and use him as a human shield against Manco's and DPS's bullets while he moved to a better tactical position. It was a viable option, but he knew that even if his brain sent his hands the signal, they wouldn't respond. It wasn't just a matter of morality. It was physiology; under intense pressure, the body resorted to its most basic level of training, and Argento had never drilled on taking a hostage.

He couldn't see what happened next because his view was blocked by the passenger side of the Humvee, but he could hear it. More MP5 rounds from Manco directed at Tomlinson. Then the steady report of a handgun from Manco, which meant he'd fired the rifle dry and had transitioned to his sidearm, his last gun. Another handgun return-ing fire from Tomlinson's position, which meant the lieutenant was in the same boat with his MP5. Then nothing. Argento took a quick peek toward the wrecked Humvee. On one side, Knox was no more, his seated torso a mass of bullet holes, his head drooping forward and tucked toward his legs like he was about to attempt a macabre som-ersault. Tomlinson was down on the other side of the vehicle, arms flung out to the side. The lieutenant's reluctance to subject Barrows to friendly fire had hampered him in the exchange of rounds with Manco. Manco had no such restrictions. It was likely why he won.

The Humvee had about sixteen inches of ground clearance. Argento was out of guns and bullets, but he wasn't out of hands. He slid underneath the frame, grabbed one of Manco's feet, and jerked skyward, a maneuver he had field-tested with Pablo on the back porch of the dope house on Gaines Street. Manco toppled onto his back. Argento slid out from under the vehicle and was on him, fighting for control of his gun hand, which held a Smith & Wesson .40. Manco fought back, trying to jab his thumb through Argento's left eye. Then Argento saw that the slide to Manco's S&W was locked back, so he twisted away and got to his feet. Ground fighting wasn't his specialty, and odds were Manco was better at it than him. The knife Manco had menaced Barrows with was in a sheath on the front of his exterior vest, as were his extra S&W mags. It was a shitty place for them. Argento had seen cops make the same mistake on the job, and he'd always told them to relocate their gear where a suspect couldn't so easily grab it. Argento proved this point by getting in close to Manco like a boxer's clinch, pulling his blade and magazines out of their holders and tossing them onto the roof of the diner. He didn't try to keep the knife; he was practiced at defending against knife attacks, but not with launching them. Metro police departments didn't teach you to stab people.

Just the two of them now. A face-off with no weapons, just handwork. Manco removed his ballistic helmet and dropped it. Wiped sweat off his forehead with his palm. He'd been wearing his seat belt when Argento had steered into the traffic light. Otherwise, he'd be wiping off blood. Argento dried his own perspiring hands on his pants. His T-shirt under his vest felt like a wet napkin. He blinked the sweat out of his eyes.

"You should have told us about the roof gunner."

"If I had, maybe you wouldn't have gone."

They were in the middle of the street in the business district of Fenton, but some folks must have lived above their shops because Argento saw a few lights turned on and a face or two in nearby windows. The fire at the police station, the car crashes, the gunfire. Argento imagined the calls to Fenton PD were coming in thick and fast with no one to answer them. That didn't mean the DEA response team wasn't in transit from Phoenix. Someone would have contacted them the moment the compound was breeched. Argento didn't want to be around for that. He'd have to make this quick.

It wasn't Argento's first hand-to-hand fight to the death. It wouldn't be Manco's either. Argento didn't believe this was a man living the high life in the cartel mansion. He'd put in field work. The guy they sent in with a photograph and some piano wire. Adrenaline sluiced through Argento's body, lending his arms and legs a welcome jolt. It was a familiar sensation. He was designed for this, the kind of street fight where it didn't matter how you looked or what your name was. There were no judges and no rules, which made it the ultimate meritocracy. The best man always won.

"Ramon can take care of your dog," Argento said, "when you cross to the other side."

Manco spat on the ground and shed his outer vest carrier. It was a smart move. It would only serve to slow his movements and create grip points for Argento. The cartel leader moved toward him and did some kind of quick reset with his feet that momentarily took Argento's eyes off Manco's hands. A cheap parlor trick, something Argento would never have tried himself and never thought he'd fall for. But he was wrong because Manco's left arm shot out in a backhand punch that exploded into Argento's cheek and sent up a spray of sweat. The right that immediately followed landed underneath his eye. It was a fast, brutal punch, about as hard as Argento could throw himself, and his vision blurred and he lost his moorings for a moment. And then Manco was behind him, his arms around Argento's neck from the back.

There was a violent science to attacking the neck. It was a complex, powerfully built structure that took a lot to injure. To break someone's neck, their shoulders had to be stable and still and the maneuver required time and overwhelming force. Manco was applying the latter like he had done this before.

Argento didn't panic. He never did. He centered himself, turned his head to the side and buried his chin in his shoulder so Manco couldn't get a solid hold. He caught the same smell coming off Manco that he'd detected in the house in Agua Mora and on the mining road before the assault on Denton. The chemical smell. Now he could place it. It was a cream for joint pain. The kind of thing Argento had used himself after a heavy SWAT operation. The odor was originating lower on his body. Closer to his legs.

Manco had bad knees.

With a grunt, Manco tried to rip Argento's head back the way he wanted it. It was a mistake. Manco's technique wasn't working but instead of changing it up, he just doubled down. Argento went with the momentum and used it to twist out of his grip, the move lubricated by Argento's sweat-soaked hair and skin. Then he kicked Manco in the side of the leg at knee level as hard as he could, like he was trying to blow the kneecap out of his flesh and across the street. Manco took one step forward and went wobbly, his left hand going to the ground for balance. His stable fighting platform had just turned spindly.

When he rose, Argento met him with a straight right to the throat. It was an aimed strike. A surgical strike. Intended for the larynx and hyoid, the small horseshoe-shaped bone at the front of the neck and below the jaw, instrumental in swallowing. The only bone in the human body not attached to another bone. Over the years, Argento had discussed with his fellow SWAT team members where they would punch someone if they only had one shot and their life depended on it. This was Argento's answer to that question. He wouldn't have tried it on a twenty-year-old, but Manco was pushing forty and his bones would have lost some of their rigidity. Argento's fist found its mark.

And took Manco's air away.

The cartel shooter staggered back, like a fighter who couldn't find his own corner. Both hands went to his throat, and Argento moved in and punched him in the kidneys. Manco's tongue was already protruding and his face was crimson. The vein in his neck pulsated as his throat collapsed in on itself. He coughed wetly and fell on his ass. Opened his mouth as if to say something, a curse, a concession speech, but could only produce a rasp that turned into a swollen-throat rattle as he suffocated, clawing at his face and neck. His features went slack. He'd decided to die.

The fight hadn't been pretty, but Argento had been good enough to grind out a win. All the adrenaline had leaked out of him and his breath came in hard puffs. Manco had landed solid blows, and now the pain flowed in. But it was manageable, centered to his face, where his right eye was swelling into a slit and his cheek felt spongy. He'd dislocated a finger so he popped it back in. As he turned away from Manco's body, he saw light bursts out of the corner of an eye that looked like rain, a residual image from the blow to the head.

The voice he heard next was clear and commanding. A female voice.

"Get down on your knees."

Argento slowly turned and found himself looking straight at Ruth, the manager of the Baldwin Hotel. The woman who'd favored the Arizona Cardinals and appreciated his dog.

She was wearing a DEA badge around her neck and pointing the laser sight of an AR-15 at his chest.

CHAPTER
49

It made sense when Argento thought about it.

Sumaya said she had a fellow DEA agent in town as backup. He'd asked her what his name was and she'd played along by saying he kept a low profile. But Sumaya's partner was a woman. Argento had always underestimated women, partly because he'd never had a female partner—there were no women on Detroit SWAT. He remembered when he was in the police academy going through a computerized use-of-force simulation involving responding to a tavern brawl. A leggy female sitting at the bar that he'd initially thought was the victim had produced a small handgun and lit him up. Afterward, the use-of-force instructor had walked over to Argento and grinned. "You know what chivalry will get you in this town?" He'd tapped his own skull. "Head-shot."

Working at a hotel would be good DEA cover. You'd see everyone who was coming into town to stay for a while. See if they were the prying type, like Argento. What was more, the proprietor of the Baldwin would have needed to be in on the cover-up of the Warren Reed shooting in room eleven. Make sure the blood was washed away and the bullet holes were patched. He wondered why they didn't take room eleven permanently out of service after his murder. Maybe they thought that would look even more suspicious than just fixing it. Regardless, it had been there for him to see and he'd missed it. Because he was a SWAT cop, not a detective. Maybe he'd expended all his brain power figuring out the nature of Barrows's project in the compound.

Ruth's pants were streaked with dirt and she had a smear of blood on her forehead like she'd already had close contact with Manco's men. "Get down on your knees," she said again, with more edge to her voice.

"I prefer to stand."

She kept the AR pointed straight at him with no sign of strain. She didn't get those forearms from hauling paint cans. They came from toting heavy weapons and gear. "I could shoot you right now."

"I don't think so."

"Why?"

"Character," Argento said. "Maybe you have some. Were you there?"

"Where?"

"When they left Kristin and Ethan Reed to die in the desert. Did you walk them out? Tell the kid everything was going to be okay?"

Ruth tried to keep her face neutral, but her body language suggested otherwise. Her shoulders drooped almost imperceptibly.

"You try to stop it?"

"I'm not answering your questions. On your knees."

"I get it. You're a true American on a noble cause. Makes me want to listen to the national anthem."

"You," Ruth said, her jaw hard-set, the laser sight of her rifle still trained directly on Argento's chest, "just got in bed with the worst criminals on earth to undo a righteous cause that will help millions because of three dead people, one of whom you never met, and a dead dog. Fuck you."

"Barrows told me he just finished The Project. Sumaya said he was supposed to send it to HQ on an encrypted file. He do that?"

Ruth didn't respond. But Argento thought he saw the answer in the crease of her brow. No. Barrows hadn't sent anything. Argento's mind cycled back to his own current situation. Being unarmed and charging at a fed with an assault rifle was a fool's errand. Even if there was an opening, Argento wasn't going to take it. He didn't want to hurt Ruth, even if she'd made decisions that damned her. He was tired of killing. He'd been in the fight, but now an agent had the drop on him with a rifle. So he'd lost. He'd started out with a dead dog and worked-over kidneys, so the best he could have hoped for was breaking even. But he wasn't going to turn himself in. Wasn't going to get buried in some remote federal prison for his assault on Fenton's soldiers. He'd been in lockdown before, at Whitehall. It hadn't worked out.

"Last warning. Comply or I'll shoot."

"After what I've done tonight," Argento said, "maybe you should. But I'm not cuffing up. I'll give you Barrows's phone. You can make him send the file. I'm not staying for what's next." He walked away from Ruth toward the Humvee with Barrows in the rear seat. For at least the second time since he first arrived in Fenton, he waited for a bullet in the back. But it was one thing to issue a shoot-on-sight directive. It was another to carry it out. Maybe Ruth wasn't a murderer. Not everyone was. He'd know soon enough. He took out Barrows's phone from his pocket and placed it on the roof of the vehicle.

Something he couldn't name told him to look back her way. It wasn't anything he saw or heard. More like a ripple in the air that something wasn't right. He'd gotten the same feeling before. Sailors had a similar attribute called dead reckoning—the ability to navigate a vessel without instruments, letting instinct and experience be their guide.

When he turned, he saw two things. The first was Ruth with her AR at a low ready position, which meant she hadn't yet made the decision to fire.

The second was Tomlinson walking toward them.

Manco hadn't quite killed him.

The lieutenant was in bad shape. He walked like he was just learning how, a kind of herky-jerky forward stumble as if he were trying to shake off insects crawling up his legs. He sported an angry red welt on his forehead, and part of his skull had been sheared off by gunfire. More of a reanimated corpse than a man, a corpse with a sidearm in his hand he was struggling to aim.

Argento knew people reacted to injuries differently, just like animals. A deer could run a hundred yards with its heart shot out by a .30-06. You could kill a man with a freak punch that caused a subdural hematoma but a window washer could fall fifty stories and live to tell the tale. Every trauma was unique. And bullet wounds yielded their own strange results. Argento had seen GSW victims with half their heads blown off still maintain a steady heartbeat. His partner had been shot on the job by a .38 that had simply caromed off his jaw, leaving him shaken but merely bruised.

Ruth saw where Argento was looking. She pivoted so she could still keep Argento in her peripheral vision and looked toward the Fenton lieutenant, visibly starting at his ghoulish appearance.

"Tomlinson. It's me. Ruth. A friendly."

Tomlinson didn't acknowledge her. He kept up his slow stagger. Whatever part of his brain that still worked wasn't recognizing her.

"I'll call you an ambulance," she began, her words trailing off as she no doubt realized that with Fenton DPS cross-trained as firefighters, Tomlinson already represented the only ambulance.

The lieutenant made a low sound that didn't seem human. Then he began to fire, wildly with no target acquisition. The first round went into the dirt in front of Tomlinson's own feet. The second broke the side-view mirror of Barrows's Humvee. Argento didn't see where the third bullet went because he was already on the move. Over the years, he'd become adept at preplanning when it came to a gunfight. It was one of the reasons he was still alive; if someone started shooting, he'd already have an idea where to go for cover. Mailboxes were crap unless you were facing a slingshot. A dumpster would stop some handgun rounds. Block walls provided an excellent shield if they were filled with concrete. You worked your way up from good to better to best.

The primary option, the engine block of the Humvee, was too far away. But behind him was a concrete curb, eight to ten inches high. He made it there and got low just in time for the fourth and fifth gunshots. Then Tomlinson's slide locked back. The lieutenant's hand automatically went to his belt and grabbed a fresh mag, but he was dazed and tried to jam it in backward. Argento stood up from behind the curb. Tomlinson was fifteen yards away. Argento ran at him, closing the distance in two heartbeats, channeling his linebacker days as he smashed into Tomlinson's chest. The force lifted the lieutenant off his feet and sent him tumbling through the ether. The gun and magazine skittered across the pavement, and the back of Tomlinson's head slapped hard against the street.

Argento checked for his secondary threat. Ruth. Maybe she'd changed her mind about not shooting him. But she was prone on the ground, still and bleeding, the AR next to her. Argento moved closer, scanned her for injuries, and checked for a pulse. Nothing. She was wearing a vest, but it looked like at least one of Tomlinson's errant rounds had penetrated the unprotected portion of her side between shoulder and upper arm.

Argento went back to Tomlinson. The lieutenant was straining to get up, his head wound so massive it revealed a triangular section of brain. Then he gave up standing and crawled in a loose circle. Not toward Argento. Not away from him. Just moving for the sake of motion, desperately invoking one last use of his muscles and tendons and will to prolong his life for another few seconds. In SWAT training, it was called an extinction burst. Argento watched him until he stopped crawling. Stopped breathing.

If Argento had shot Tomlinson from the rooftop, Ruth would likely still be alive. He wasn't sure what to do with that. Wasn't sure what to do with most of what had happened in the last two hours. It was time to leave Fenton, Arizona, for good. He had worn out his welcome. He took one last look at Tomlinson's body. It was still Manco's bullets that killed him. It had just taken a while because the man had grit. The deer could run a hundred yards with its heart blown out.

But not a hundred and one.

CHAPTER
50

One of the lights Argento had seen on above the Fenton shops before he tangled with Manco was from Olson's hardware store. Now the man himself was walking toward him, with his ever-present ball cap on. Argento surveyed the rest of the street. No one else had come out. It was just the two of them. Argento looked at Olson's hands to see if he was armed. Argento was still in fight mode and if Ruth was a fed, who the hell knew what Olson was. But he held no weapon and there was nothing in the man's bearing that suggested a threat. When he spoke, it was with quiet caution.

"I'm sorry about your dog. Heard the shots outside my store that day."

Argento didn't reply.

"I have his collar. It came off in the street when they moved him, so I picked it up." He held it out to Argento, the plain brown band with Hudson's name on a metal tag. "I washed the blood off. Figured you wouldn't want to remember him that way."

Argento took it. Felt his throat tighten. He gripped the collar tightly for a moment, feeling the leather bite into his skin, and then put it in his pocket. Nodded at Olson. He looked around at the Fenton DPS bodies in the street. "You probably got some serious questions about all this."

"I seen Ruth's badge around her neck. Didn't know she was the law. But I saw from my window how the other uniformed fella shot her, not you. I don't have no questions about the rest of them boys. Anyone kill someone's dog like that, they're gonna be wrong about other things."

"It was more than my dog. They murdered the man I was looking for. Murdered his wife and boy too."

Olson looked at Argento square. "Then they're where they're supposed to be." He adjusted the ball cap on his head and raised his head to gesture at a spot behind Argento. "Where you fixing to take him?"

Argento looked where Olson was looking. The Humvee. Barrows was slumped down, but his head was still visible in the back seat

"Where he's supposed to be," Argento said. He took Barrows's phone off the Humvee, got in, and put it in reverse, then pulled away from the damaged traffic pole. The Humvee sounded clunky but still ran. He pulled up next to Olson. "You calling this in?"

Olson's face didn't change expression when he said, "Not sure who I'd call it in to."

Barrows craned his long neck from side to side as he looked at Olson and then strained to see past him. Looking for Tomlinson and Ruth. "What will you do with me?" His voice sounded tiny and strained.

"It's time," Argento said, "to leave the palace."

Dawn was breaking as he drove Barrows into the desert, doing a rough retrace of the route he remembered from before, past the cacti, gulches, and red rock. He scanned the sky like it would tell him something. A rust-colored hawk flew overhead. The sunrise was God's splendor, like a promise made real. It was beautiful country that Argento would be leaving behind.

"So you're supposed to be something."

"I am the smartest man who has ever lived," Barrows said.

"You on that list of people they'll freeze and thaw out later?"

"Liquid nitrogen cannot preserve the complex workings of the human brain."

"You're fun to talk to."

They drove in silence for a spell.

"They should have pulled you out of Fenton," Argento said. "Soon as they learned I'd survived the desert."

"They wanted to. I wouldn't leave. I was too close to finishing."

"How'd you create your potion to knock out cocaine and heroin?"

"You wouldn't understand."

"We got some time. Use words regular people use."

Barrows took him up on the invitation. Maybe he was eager to share his story. He spoke of how he'd developed his plant virus using an advanced version of tech known as "Cas9," which was essentially a biological find-and-replace for DNA. How a polymerase chain reaction was the key step in the process of DNA sequencing accomplished through a thermocycler. About erythroxylaceae, alkaloids, and transfection.

After a few minutes, Argento cut in. "You're right. I don't understand. Were you going to ask other countries if it was okay to unleash that stuff on their fields?"

"We could have a team of international lawyers go through the jurisdictional issues. But we're the United States of America. We aren't going to ask for permission. We're just going to do it."

"Lot of bodies behind this project."

"For every million they spent constructing the Golden Gate Bridge, the life of one worker was lost," Barrows said blankly. "Anything of this magnitude requires sacrifice."

"Not yours, though," Argento said. "Just other people's."

"How did you find out my name?"

"College yearbook. You were standing next to Warren Reed wearing pants that didn't fit."

"Warren was my friend."

"But you weren't his, were you, August? Friends don't have friends shot in hotel rooms."

"I'm not culpable. Not my decision."

"It's nobody's fault. It never is."

Argento scanned the landscape as he drove. He wasn't going to find the exact spot Fenton DPS dumped him off. There weren't enough landmarks. But he'd get close enough.

Barrows was looking at the landscape as well. A bead of sweat trickled down his forehead. "Why did you come to Fenton?"

"Because a woman asked me for help. Because doing nothing doesn't work."

"You were a police officer. You should want cocaine and heroin eradicated."

"I do. And you're going to help me. We'll get to that."

Argento was talking more than he was used to. The adrenaline coursing through his system had subsided, loosening something inside him. And he was in a car with the self-proclaimed smartest man in the world, so he might as well get some conversational laps in with him while he could.

Barrows kept scanning from side to side. As if trying to commit the path they were taking to memory. Then he said, "You intuited what I was doing in my lab."

Argento thought back to the three legs of the drug stool. Users, dealers, and supply. He knew you could never stop drug use; the desire for a chemical fix was eternal. The toothless addicts in Detroit and Phoenix were proof enough of that. And you could arrest the dealers but they'd be replaced. Cream, the man Argento had taken the gun from in the pizza restaurant—there was another one waiting in the wings. There was another Polo Shirt, a fill-in Enrique. And sometimes the new blood was more violent and unpredictable than the dealers they subbed for. That left the supply. The smartest man in the world would target the supply. Argento thought back to when Barrows and Fenton DPS had left him in the desert.

"When you dropped me off here, you had a green leaf attached to your shoe. Probably from your lab. Got me thinking about you in the botany club at MIT. So you were probably good at plants. Add to that the DEA involvement and a big project guarded by men with guns, and what do you have? A smart plant guy would go right to the source and figure out how to kill off the worst dope that comes in leaf form. That's cocaine and heroin. And how do you kill plants? You make a virus."

Barrows took that in. Then he said, "It wasn't my idea to leave you in the desert."

"I don't recall," Argento said, "you being too against it."

When he was far enough out from civilization, Argento stopped the Humvee. Got out and undid Barrows's cuffs with the key he'd bought at the military surplus store in Phoenix. He checked Barrows for any GPS tags, including in his shoes. Barrows looked down at the red lines on his wrists from the metal. Nodded to himself.

"I'm going to cut you a deal, August." Argento showed Barrows his own cell phone. "Sumaya said you could send your finished project to DEA headquarters on this phone. You told me you finished. So send it like you're supposed to, and I won't kill you. I'll leave and you can call for help. Your people are probably on their way here anyway. Probably got your phone all GPSed up."

"I don't believe you."

"You got a lot to lose if you're wrong."

"No," Barrows said. "You want revenge for your dog, for the desert. You wouldn't let me go."

"You're right. I do want revenge. And at first I didn't think your project deserved to make it. Not on the backs of the Reeds and my Hudson. But I'm trying to keep some perspective. Sumaya called this project critical to the nation's interests. Okay. I'll go with that. So send it. For the nation's interests. It's what you're supposed to do anyway. Send it and you'll live. Which is in your interests."

"And if I don't?"

"Then I'll smash your phone and let you off another twenty miles out into the desert. But I made it. And you're smarter than me. Bet your brain looks like the console in one of those nuclear control rooms. So this should be easy. But there's no rain in the forecast. And there will come a point where you're going to try to drink the sand."

Barrows looked around unblinkingly with his bird neck. Like a commuter that just got off at an unfamiliar train stop and needed to get his bearings.

"You know all about the heat cramps, the memory loss, the feeling your skin is on fire. The way you shake right before you die. You explained it to me before."

"I know," Barrows said.

Argento pulled a button off his shirt and handed it to him. "Redlinger gave me one of these. It helps, for a little—"

"I'll do it."

Argento gave Barrows the phone and watched as he typed in some kind of code. Then he typed some more. Argento couldn't keep up with all the keystrokes but Barrows ended the barrage by pressing Send.

"It's done," he said.

Argento studied Barrows for a moment. Then he got in his car and drove back the way he'd come. Behind him, Barrows stood still, a hand up to block out the sun.

As the Humvee jostled over the uneven terrain, Argento tried to clear his head. He looked at his arm, which bore the names of the Fenton DPS soldiers. Knox's, Tomlinson's, and Henik's names weren't crossed off yet, although they'd all met the same end. He took out the Sharpie, laid his arm against the steering wheel, and blackened the arm from wrist to elbow, rendering the names unreadable. If he got stopped by the law with an arm covered in the crossed-out but still legible names of recently murdered men in the employment of the federal government, things wouldn't go his way.

He'd only made it a few miles when he hit the brakes. An old Reagan quote was rattling around in his head. *Trust but verify.* He took out his phone and deleted the pictures of the dead Fenton soldiers. Then he called Sumaya's office from memory. Despite her pending transfer, she still picked up her old number on the second ring.

"I told you to get your people out."

He heard a sharp intake of breath on the other end of the line. Sumaya didn't need to ask who it was.

"What did you do?"

"You'll know soon enough. Barrows said he just sent your office the completed project. That true?"

He waited for a minute, two, five. Then she got back on the line. "No. He didn't send it." Her breathing was unnaturally loud, like she'd just been sprinting. "He . . . deleted it. The link is gone." Her voice rose. "The reservoir is scrubbed. We don't have anything. We don't have—"

Just as Argento hung up, he thought he heard Sumaya begin to scream.

He set his phone under one of the Humvee's tires and ran it over. He got out, scooped up the pieces and kept them in his hand, scattering them in the desert as he drove back to Barrows.

CHAPTER
51

August Barrows waited until his captor's Humvee disappeared from view. He was stranded in the desert with no water, shelter, or transportation. Other than his periodic swimming, he was not a particularly fit man and did not endure physical hardship well. But Barrows didn't mind bad news. It simply meant a problem for him to solve. And in this case, it hardly rose to the level of problem at all. He had his phone to call for help. And even if he didn't, August Barrows was an irreplaceable asset to the United States government and because of that, he was equipped with a GPS microchip. It wasn't in his pockets or his shoes, which his captor had searched. It was embedded in his skin between his shoulder blades. The unit required a once-a-week wireless charge from a terminal in his office, but he'd been dutiful about it, which meant, phone or no phone, the DEA response team would be en route to pick him up shortly. He'd hardly be in the Sonoran long enough to experience even mild thirst.

He'd planned for this contingency. For twelve other contingencies. What he hadn't planned for was the statistical anomaly of someone like his captor, a man too stubborn and stupid to know when to quit. But he would get past this. His soldiers were dead, but they were mere commodities he'd acquired. There would be more. People would always be assigned to work for a man like him. His compound was burned to the ground, but they would buy or build him another. He would have his captor killed in the most painful way he could think of. He'd have to go with a private contractor because the DEA could be squeamish about such things, but he'd pay handsomely to have it done right. Something antiquated and merciless. With spikes. Mutilation. Rats. Barrows would use his imagination.

And he had a vivid imagination.

Then there was the matter of locating the hacker or hackers who'd helped his captor learn his real name, because there was no chance a simpleton ex-cop had tracked him alone. No matter how well they hid or where they bounced their signal, he would find them, and whatever he did to the cop, he'd have the same thing done to them. Then he'd move on to everyone who supplied him with weapons and equipment. When he hurt them, their screams would signal they were sorry they'd strayed into his world, a place they'd never belong.

And Cassidy. She'd never felt the same way about him that he'd felt about her, no doubt because she was deficient in the social bonding hormone oxytocin. He now understood that he'd only ever been a faceless customer to her, a source of residual income from his generous gratuities. She'd suffer the same fate as the others.

She would scream until her throat bled.

When his captor had handed Barrows his own phone back to him and told him to send the project link to headquarters, it was all Barrows could do not to chuckle. This man trying to give him orders. Barrows had done the opposite. He'd deleted the link, including the electronic reservoir containing the entirety of his work on The Project. It would remain in his head, for now. The DEA couldn't have it, not yet. Because they hadn't handled him in the way a titan like him should have been handled. When they built him a new lab, when they surrounded him with men who could actually protect him, he would re-create The Project. Not before. He would be in control from here.

And it would be full control, not the vacuous joint command he'd suffered through with Sumaya.

When he deleted the link, Barrows had shown the DEA the consequences of treating him lightly. He'd shown them what full control looked like.

Noise behind him. Wheels on rock. He turned. The Humvee returning. Coming straight for him. Fast and not slowing.

The head-on collision knocked Barrows out of his shoes, and he went airborne before collapsing in a heap on the warm ground. He processed what followed in short bursts, understanding, at some detached level, what was happening to him. He had sustained a significant head and torso injury and was bleeding profusely. Hypovolemic shock would soon settle in.

He heard a car door close. His captor was now standing over him. Saying something. Barrows couldn't make it out. He heard the individual words but they didn't form a whole. No matter. He would rebuild himself. He tried to say it out loud, the part about rebuilding, but he couldn't quite form the words. That meant the collision had impacted the Broca's area of his frontal cortex, the hominid track linked to speech production. A fixable problem. He would simply shift the responsibility of the Broca to another region. Through sheer intellectual brawn, he would physically remodel his own brain to compensate for the injury. Because he was the smartest man who had ever lived. His name was Augun Billows and he would kulp out of this sitsun. He would risl.

No. Risl, no word. He wuld techilan?

Whetz.

Bilkkss.

CHAPTER
52

Argento got out of the Humvee and followed the trail of blood and skin to where August Barrows lay mangled on the ground, his head resting on a jagged section of rock that had split his skull. The impact of the collision had launched Barrows some fifteen feet off the ground in a kind of helicopter spin, and his right femur was protruding from his thigh. He looked like he was trying to say something but Argento couldn't make it out.

He figured Barrows deserved an explanation. Man hits you with his car at fifty on purpose, he should say why. "You broke your part of the deal. That deal was the only thing keeping you breathing."

Barrows twitched and said something that sounded like "Risl."

"Agent Sumaya said something to me when I was in her car with a gun to her back. She said everyone in Fenton working on this project, you, her, Fenton DPS, was already on a list for a preemptive presidential pardon. Which means after you get out of the Sonoran, you'll skate on everything you did. And I can't have that. Because you're not just my enemy, you're Warren and Kristin Reed's enemy. They died because of you. Their boy died because of you. Kristin had to watch it."

Barrows twitched again. "Techilan," he said. It sounded like a question. The substantial front bumper of the Humvee had blunted his linguistic ability.

"She doesn't forgive you. Thing is, she's got no one left to speak for her but me. And maybe God won't forgive me either for doing this. But I'll take that chance."

Barrows said "Whetz."

"This also covers all the bad shit you've done I don't know about. And everything you were planning on doing."

"Bilkkss," Barrows said.

"Got mixed feelings about bringing the cartel here. Don't have any mixed feelings about this." Argento gestured down to where Barrows lay. Barrows didn't say anything. His eyes were wide open and staring at the void. On to the next life.

Argento felt like he had to add something, even though Barrows couldn't hear him. "I'm not always this way," he said. He rubbed his face, fatigue running in a tight cord behind his eyes. Then he got in the Humvee and drove in the opposite direction of Fenton. He'd have to ditch the car soon. Too much front-end damage, from hitting the traffic pole and then Barrows. It would draw attention he didn't want, attention that soon would be magnified, because in Fenton, a storm was about to hit land. He imagined the team lead of the DEA SRT arriving on scene, seeing the carnage, and then getting on the air. Saying something like *Send me another team. Send me everyone.* as he realized there wasn't enough ink in his pen to properly document this. Then the mass of county, state, and federal law enforcement that would descend, unmarked cars, command vans, guys in goggles and jumpsuits with rifles, the coroner wagons, the news crews. Reporters who spent a lot of time on their teeth and hair would report that the whole town was one massive crime scene.

There'd be plenty of repair work for Olson from the hardware store.

Part of Argento told him to return to Fenton to pick up his truck, which was still parked in front of the Baldwin. More than that, to scoop out the ashes from Redlinger's fire pit where Hudson's body had been burned, in the hopes that his dog's remains were still there. He knew he couldn't risk doing either. He hadn't been able to clean the blood off Hudson. Hold him and say goodbye. He had a picture of his dog in his wallet alongside a photo of his wife. That would have to carry him.

He couldn't go home to Detroit. The feds would have people looking for him. But that wasn't all. He'd teamed up with the cartel and now one of their top shooters and his team were strewn all over town. Manco had said if something happened to him in Fenton, Ramon would never stop looking for Argento. Argento believed that. He'd met Ramon.

So where to? He recalled the line in a country song that went something like *too stupid for New York, too ugly for Los Angeles*. That sounded about right for him too. But wherever he was headed, he had one more stop to make before he got there.

CHAPTER
53

The State of Arizona's Superior Court website had only one match for a Wayne Ellerbee. His first case was civil—a divorce proceeding from a Krystal Ellerbee. The second two cases were criminal, one a drunk driving and the other a sexual assault conviction where he'd been sentenced to six years, which he'd already served. He was listed as a part-time employee of Trident Investigations. His Phoenix address was also listed in the court records. The magic of open records. Argento drove to his house and parked across the street. It was a battered bungalow in a run-down neighborhood. When a loutish-looking man in tight jeans and cowboy boots emerged from the front door and walked down the driveway toward his mailbox, Argento intercepted him curbside.

"Wayne Ellerbee?"

The man wiped his mouth with the back of his hand. He was wide-shouldered with a hard belly and an asshole mustache. "Sure."

"Kristin Reed talked to you about finding her husband. You tried to get romantic and grabbed her. Broke her arm. Happened in front of her son, boy named Ethan."

Ellerbee took this accusation in stride, as if it wasn't unusual. "Bitches lie."

Argento nodded at Ellerbee's face. "She stabbed you with a fork. Lines up pretty well with those tine marks I can still see on your cheek."

Ellerbee processed this information. He didn't give off the impression of being a deep thinker. "Didn't grab no one," he said, but with more caution in his voice than bravado. "Don't need to. Got women lining up for me."

"You don't have to worry about Kristin. She can't testify against you. She's dead. Her son is too."

"So what the fuck we even talking for?"

"Because you still have to answer for the broken arm. It's like an unpaid bill."

"Screw off." Ellerbee checked his mailbox, which was empty, then turned and walked back toward his front door. Argento followed. In any given situation, he tried to think what Joe Frazier would have done.

"How about a fight?" he said to Ellerbee's back.

Ellerbee spun around. "Man, you don't know when to quit."

"First punch is yours." Argento put his hands at his sides.

Ellerbee didn't need convincing. He let fly with a roundhouse to Argento's face. It was a solid hit. Argento felt his nose give way and cant to the right. It was what he'd been after. He was a wanted man now and he needed to be more difficult to catch. A badly broken nose that he'd allow to heal crooked would help. Even if it didn't change the symmetry of his features enough to throw off the facial recognition software that 200 had been talking about in the hotel room, it would make him harder for some cop to identify from a wanted person flyer.

The second benefit of eating the punch was it gave him a split-second window to trap Ellerbee's extended right arm against Argento's body. He hooked Ellerbee's fist under the crook of his right arm and used his left hand to violently torque against the straightened limb at the elbow. He heard the loud crack as Ellerbee's forearm bones fissured.

Ellerbee cried out as his face went bone-white. Argento did the left arm. Same hand positioning and overwhelming force applied. Same sharp crack of the forearm bones, but this time, Ellerbee's biceps became detached and rolled up like a ball of yarn under the skin. Ellerbee slumped to the pavement, his eyes searching for release from the pain. It would be months before he could dress himself.

Argento left Ellerbee writhing in his own driveway and drove north. He'd preplanned his visit by buying ice and ibuprofen, assuming Ellerbee would be agreeable to punching him in the face. He swallowed three of the pills and held the cool pack to his nose as he went. It still hurt, but Argento didn't mind some measure of pain. Pain meant God was paying attention to him and knew who he was.

He looked at his face in the bathroom of a roadside diner. Manco's punch had left an impression too. The cornea to Argento's right eye looked like it had been dipped in red paint. He washed up as best he could and then found a table in the back. It felt right to be in a diner. Everything had started in one when Kristin Reed had approached his table at Powell's in Braylo. It had taken shape in the Bronze Dollar in Fenton. It was ending here.

Argento thought about what was next for him. He needed to pay the governor back for the money he owed. But that meant accessing his pension funds, which the DEA would probably be tracking. He'd need to leave a message for Trapsi about his house being vacant again. Another message for Andekker telling him where the bodies of the Reeds could be found.

The waitress came with his order. Argento ate in silence. Thought about what his life would look like now. He'd have to get used to not saying his own name or where he was from or what he did for a living. He'd accomplished what he'd set out to do in Fenton, avenging the lives of three murder victims the government had tried to cover up. But while he'd done right by the Reeds, he hadn't for society at large. He'd tried to save The Project. Tried to give Barrows's phone to Ruth, but Tomlinson shot her. Gave Barrows a chance to send it to DEA HQ, but Barrows had run a game on him. So unless the feds had someone smarter than Barrows on the payroll who could retrieve what he deleted, cocaine and heroin would still be in play. Nothing would change for the thirteen-year-old lookout in the Suns jersey on Pacheco or the bloody addict he'd tried to drag out of the house on Gaines or for overdose victims like Agent Sumaya's brother David. Not for them or any of the scores of people like them. Argento knew drugs were like a balloon. You push in one point and it just pushes out somewhere else. If it wasn't cocaine and heroin, it was meth and pills. Synthetics. The DEA would never be out of business. People would always use, even if they knew it would wreck their lives. But it was cold comfort. Argento still felt empty and frayed. He'd made too many trade-offs.

When the waitress brought him the check, her gaze lingered on his burned face. Red eye. Misshapen nose. "You win the fight?"

Argento gave a faint smile but didn't answer because he didn't know.

He got back on the road. He had no map but it didn't matter. For him, each destination would be about the same as the next. But he wanted to have a goal in front of him. It would help him cope with what he'd lost. So he decided to go north. Away from the border and Ramon and Sinaloa. He took Hudson's collar from his pocket, wrapped it around his fingers, and rested them on the steering wheel.

He was glad he had it. He would keep it close.

The sky was a torn sheet of red. When night fell, he kept driving as he watched the headlights of the anonymous cars coming south. Fenton, Arizona, had turned him into someone else. He'd need time and space to find out how to turn back. He drove until there were no more buildings, no traffic, just the dark road unfolding before him and the silent desert on both sides, everything set down on the same clear axis, as if someone knew where he was headed and wanted to show him the way.

ACKNOWLEDGMENTS

I used feedback from a number of talented professionals in writing this novel. Many thanks to the following:

Tom McElroy, desert survival expert, who helped me shape the chapters where Argento is abandoned in the Sonoran.

Dr. Greg Hess, Pima County medical examiner, for answering my questions on the effects of the Arizona desert climate on the bodies of the dead.

Sgt. Tim Neves, SFPD specialist sniper, for his breakdown of the Remington 700 rifle.

Dr. Christopher D. Tyrrell, curator of the Milwaukee Public Museum's Herbarium, for his counsel on everything from DNA sequencing to plant viruses to the nomenclature of lab equipment.

My pal Dr. Albert Won for his assistance with hospital procedures.

Dr. Paul Chestovich, trauma and burn surgeon, for answering my many questions on burns and burn treatment.

My man on the ground in AZ, Anthony Williams, for his breakdown of Phoenix neighborhoods. I have been to that fair city many times, but he gave me the insider's scoop.

ACKNOWLEDGMENTS

Nick Selby, cybersecurity expert, for his insights into computers and hacking, and just generally acting as my life coach.

DEA Agent Abigayle Moyer for her vital perspective on the drug trade.

Mark DeWeese, Contra Costa, CA, firefighter, for his firefighting wisdom.

SFPD Sgt. Jeff Smethurst, former electrical linesman, for his guidance on power lines.

Marina Kirk, the facilities coordinator for my police station, for her practical take on fire alarms and sprinkler systems.

Ofc. Tommy Smith, SFPD bomb squad, for his knowledge of explosives.

My old street crimes partner Sgt. Anthony Scafani and now-retired Sgt. Darren Nocetti of SFPD Narcotics for fielding drug questions I couldn't answer myself. It's worth noting that at the time of this writing, fentanyl is king and has changed the drug game throughout the country. It hasn't yet achieved that position in my fictional world, which I've always imagined to take place five to ten years in the past.

I have taken some liberties with the information the good people above provided in order to suit the purposes of this novel. All mistakes are my own.

Much gratitude for my early readers Andy Tantillo, Brent Ewig, Jason Allison, and my brother Nate Plantinga, all of whom had sharp feedback that made this book better. You guys always bring it.

As for my super agent, Caitlin Blasdell, I salute you.

Many thanks to my talented editor, Kirsiah Depp, for schlepping me along for another novel.

A tip of the hat to production editor Bob Castillo, who sees all things with his practiced eye.

Another hat tip to copyeditor Mark Steven Long, whose saves would make an NHL goalie proud.

A shout-out to Albert Tang, who designed the striking cover of this book. When I first saw it, I thought, *I hope my book is good enough to justify this cool cover.*

Finally, I am aware of the unwritten rule in fiction that you never kill a dog. I don't take this lightly; I am a dog owner and dog lover. But the death of Hudson is the inciting incident that propels Argento through this book. The lower deep that Emerson talks about in the epigraph. And it's my goal to take chances in my writing, to craft a story where things aren't always tidy or predictable and no one is safe. There's another rule in fiction that the only thing that matters is whether something works on the page. Only the reader can answer that question.

ABOUT THE AUTHOR

Adam Plantinga is a patrol sergeant with the San Francisco Police Department whose first two nonfiction books—*400 Things Cops Know* and *Police Craft*—have become his calling cards to the world of thrillers. *400 Things* was nominated for an Agatha, a Macavity, and was deemed "the new Bible for crime writers" by the *Wall Street Journal*. Adam's fiction debut, *The Ascent*, was published in 2024 and became a *USA Today* bestseller.